FORT WORTH PUBLIC LIBRARY

S0-BDO-103

"Thanks for your help, Norris." She flashed her beguiling smile. "If you need anything else, don't hesitate to call."

Sensing a hidden meaning in her statement, Norris met her gaze and approached. "The same applies to you," he said.

Dahlia trailed her finger down the buttons of his shirt. She sighed. "I keep trying to tell myself if nobody knows about our relationship, it doesn't make me terrible." Her head dropped. "I should know better. My grandma taught me better." She looked deeply into his eyes. "Why don't I feel ashamed?"

Norris's heart pounded. Was Dahlia asking him or herself that question? Could she feel the change their relationship had taken? It wasn't just feel-good sex. It was so much more. He saw something in her eyes. Something that made him want to open up about feelings he had never wanted to feel.

"Dahlia, I . . ."

BLINDSIDED

TAMMY WILLIAMS

Genesis Press, Inc.

INDIGO LOVE SPECTRUM

An imprint of Genesis Press, Inc.
Publishing Company

Genesis Press, Inc.
P.O. Box 101
Columbus, MS 39703

All rights reserved. Except for use in any review, the reproduction or utilization of this work in whole or in part in any form by any electronic, mechanical, or other means, not known or hereafter invented, including xerography, photocopying, and recording, or in any information storage or retrieval system, is forbidden without written permission of the publisher, Genesis Press, Inc. For information write Genesis Press, Inc., P.O. Box 101, Columbus, MS 39703.

All characters in this book have no existence outside the imagination of the author and have no relation whatsoever to anyone bearing the same name or names. They are not even distantly inspired by any individual known or unknown to the author and all incidents are pure invention.

Copyright © 2009 by Tammy Williams

ISBN: 13 DIGIT : 978-1-58571-342-4
ISBN: 10 DIGIT : 1-58571-342-2
Manufactured in the United States of America

First Edition

Visit us at www.genesis-press.com
or call at 1-888-Indigo-1-4-0

DEDICATION

To my family, friends, and all you readers.

ACKNOWLEDGMENTS

I thank God. I thank Him for making it possible for me to write a single word. I thank Him for giving me the gift of knowledge, and the desire to share with the world stories I hope offer entertainment and reflection. I thank all my family for supporting me and giving me the encouragement I need. Your unwavering love sustains me. I must take a moment to thank a dear cousin who helped me tremendously with the "One more question" I always had as I wrote this story. DCH, your help has been a tremendous asset. And last, but not least, I thank the readers. Readers who have supported me from my growth in fan fiction, to those who discovered me when they purchased *Choices* —you helped to make *Blindsided* a reality.

It is my wish you find Norris, Dahlia, and their story as compelling as I did.

Thank you one and all!

CHAPTER 1

"You don't have to worry, Lara, I won't take advantage of your friend." Norris Converse smiled brightly at the friend in question. Had he not met the gorgeous Dahlia Sinclair on his own two months earlier, he'd be giving his best friend's wife big thanks for sending Dahlia and her business his way. "I'll see you and Ryan later. Bye."

Norris hung up the phone and approached his lovely companion. "Lara's afraid I'm going to disturb your fragile sensibilities." He laughed. "Little does she know."

"Thanks for not saying anything to her." Dahlia smoothed out her skirt, which was slightly wrinkled from their torrid encounter on his desk. "I don't think she'll understand our arrangement," she said, combing her fingers through her short, perfectly coiffed dark hair.

"Our arrangement?" He pulled her close to him. Her curvy body fit perfectly against his, and at a couple inches shy of his six feet of height, she was a woman he didn't have to strain his neck to kiss. It was like she was made for him. "You mean hot, guilt-free, no strings sex? What's not to understand? It's my prescription for a full and happy life."

A hint of rouge toasted Dahlia's rich brown cheeks. Norris smiled. He enjoyed teasing her about their arrangement. He enjoyed everything about Dahlia the dazzling divorcée, a fact he found exciting and unsettling. He didn't get this excited about women. They generally came and went. But not Dahlia. And as much as it scared him, he rather liked it.

Agnes, his trusted assistant and self-proclaimed mother in Denburg, South Carolina, had announced Dahlia and shown her in more than half an hour before. Less than two minutes later, Dahlia lay atop his desk with her glorious long legs wrapped about his waist, moaning her pleasure.

A very proud and notorious playboy, Norris had never allowed his extra-curricular activities to cross into his business life. To indulge a woman in his workplace was a staunch no-no. At least it used to be. Thinking of what he and Dahlia had just shared aroused him all over again. He pressed up against her. A deep groan rumbled in his throat.

"Uh, uh, uh." Dahlia took a step back. "We need to move on to other things, Norris. This meeting is about my audit."

"You saying we need to get down to business?" He grinned.

"Yes, real business." She walked over to the leather couch and picked up the portfolio she had set down on her way in. "I think I have everything you need."

Norris stared at her as she rifled through the papers. *If only she knew.* He remembered the night they met. Valentine's evening, a holiday along with Thanksgiving and Christmas that comprised his no-women days. Those holidays gave women the wrong impressions, and he wasn't trying to dole out false hope.

That night, he and Dahlia had both reached for the last copy of *Shrek* in the video rental store. After some silly bantering over who should get the rental, and realizing they knew some of the same people, they wound up watching together at her place. And before the movie ended they were in each other's arms.

He hadn't been with another woman since then, and had no desire to be. Dahlia's beautiful heart-shaped face, brown eyes, and full lips kept him transfixed, and her impressive business mind was an aphrodisiac in itself. Thoughts of her filled his days and nights, drawing him dangerously close to a line he never wanted to cross.

Norris shook his head. The singing birds and blossoming flowers of springtime must have gone to his head. He didn't do relationships and Dahlia didn't do them anymore. That's how they both wanted it, and that's why they worked so well.

He buttoned his shirt and moved behind his desk. "I know audit is a scary word, but from what you told me, you kept pretty accurate records for the day spas you sold, and I'm sure the same is the case for the salon you still own, so this should be a breeze."

"I hope so. The last couple of years have been a bit trying. Which might explain this audit." She sighed, handing over the portfolio.

"Try not to worry. More often than not it's minor calculation errors. And this is just an audit of the year before last. I'll take a look at all this, see where we stand, and go from there."

3

"Thanks for your help, Norris." She flashed her beguiling smile. "If you need anything else, don't hesitate to call."

Sensing a hidden meaning in her statement, Norris met her gaze and approached. "The same applies to you," he said.

Dahlia trailed her finger down the buttons of his shirt. "I keep trying to tell myself if nobody knows about our arrangement, it doesn't make me a skank." Her head dropped. "I should know better. My grandma taught me better." She looked deeply into his eyes. "Why don't I feel ashamed?"

Norris's heart pounded. Was Dahlia asking him or herself that question? Could she feel the change their relationship had taken? It wasn't just feel-good sex. It was so much more. He saw something in her eyes. Something that made him want to open up about feelings he never wanted to feel. "Dahlia, I . . ."

A feathery soft finger touched his lips, silencing him. His breath lodged in his throat. Her touch was his undoing.

"I know what it is," she said. "It's the sexy waves in your jet-black hair, and the devilish twinkle in those sparkling gray eyes that render women helpless. Tall, dark . . . Well, at least as dark as your Greek-Anglo ancestry will allow." She laughed. "And handsome." Her fingers brushed his cheek. "You're irresistible, Norris Converse."

"You're irresistible." Norris softly kissed her lips, all too aware he was heading down a slippery slope with no way of stopping himself. "I'll call you."

As Norris opened the door, he stepped into all-business mode for Agnes, who expertly pretended not to be paying attention. The full-figured older woman with flaming red hair and an accent that rivaled Scarlett O'Hara's thought she'd mastered the technique, but Norris had known her too long to fall for it. He suspected she'd probably had her ear to the door a time or two, grinning like a nosy preteen.

"Thank you for coming in, Ms. Sinclair," Norris said, escorting Dahlia to the elevator.

"Thanks for your time, Mr. Converse."

He smiled. "My pleasure."

"You have a good day, Ms. Sinclair," Agnes called out to Dahlia as the elevator doors opened.

Dahlia smiled. "You, too. Good-bye."

Norris approached the circular reception desk when the elevator doors closed. "Any calls for me, Agnes?"

The woman grinned at him. "That was a long meeting."

"She's a friend of Lara's and being audited."

"What's that red stuff on your lips?"

Norris brushed his fingers against his mouth.

"Gotcha!" said Agnes, her green eyes dancing with joy.

Norris grunted, annoyed at falling for her trick. Dahlia didn't wear lipstick that smeared.

"Why do you have to be so secretive? That one's really got your nose open."

"She does not have my nose open," he said a little too quickly. "Norris Converse's nose is open to no one."

Agnes laughed. "If you say so." She handed him a pink message sheet. "You had a call from a Dr. Gail Elders."

"Gail Elders?" He hadn't heard that name in seventeen years, but it was one he'd never forget. She was the beautiful older woman who'd had a hand in creating his legendary persona. Norris smiled as he scanned the message. She wanted him to meet her at the hospital. He could do that. "My calendar is clear for the rest of the day, so I'm going to head out a little early."

"I don't think your Ms. Sinclair will like you meeting up with another woman."

Norris considered those words. *If only.* A part of him wished she would care. He frowned at Agnes. "Don't you have some papers to file or something?"

"In fact, I do."

"Then you do that. I'll see you on Monday."

Norris spent the short drive back to his condo trying not to think about Dahlia and the way she made him feel. Ryan had given up preaching the merits of monogamy as a much-appreciated birthday present. Now, three months into his thirty-seventh year, monogamy had become a constant daydream he wouldn't mind making a reality. Even the idea of a little Norris or two running around excited him. Norris grunted. Ryan's domestic heaven was killing him.

Norris moved through his living room, shedding his clothes as he made his way to the shower. The steamy spray pelted his tense muscles. How could he feel so incredibly good physically after spending quality moments with Dahlia, yet feel like his life was the pits?

He shouldn't be miserable. He had more money than he'd ever be able to spend, he was good looking, and women fell at his feet. For years, those things had been enough. Now he wanted more, and he wanted it with Dahlia.

Norris stuck his head under the forceful spray. *C'mon, man. Get it together.* He slapped his face. Great sex didn't equal great relationship; it just meant great sex. And with Dahlia, he had someone who was willing and available whenever he was. It was a charmed life. Then, there was Gail Elders, beautiful Dr. Gail, asking to see him. He turned off the shower and wrapped a fluffy white towel around his waist. What the hell was he complaining about?

"I'm sorry I'm so late, Reese," Dahlia said to her client when she finally made it to her salon. "Where's Diana?" Reese and her best friend were never far apart.

"She's babysitting for the Andrews tonight, and had to take care of a few things beforehand," Reese said, sliding the book she'd been reading into the backpack settled between her ankles.

Dahlia smiled. Diana's cousin Lara, and her husband, Ryan, had dinner plans with Norris. *Norris.* Dahlia willed her heart to stop pounding from memories of their salacious encounter. Five fast minutes in a hot shower had washed away his intoxicating masculine scent, but no amount of soap or water could wash away the indelible mark Norris had made on her.

She could still feel the warmth of his skin against hers, the feel of him as he moved inside her, and the tickle of his breath when he dusted her neck with kisses. Dahlia's face grew warm. Her heart raced faster.

"Dahlia, are you sick?"

Dahlia blinked, shaken from her wanton thoughts. "What?"

"You're flushed. If you're under the weather, I can always re-reschedule," Reese said in a strained voice.

Dahlia laughed at the well-meaning teen. "Fear not, Reese, you won't have to reschedule. I'm not sick." Lovesick maybe, but she didn't want to think about that. "I'm a little preoccupied, but up to the challenge of making you more beautiful than you already are."

Dahlia smiled at her young customer. A very sweet girl, though the slightest bit vain, Reese had flawless golden brown skin, light eyes, and flowing curls of coal black hair, which made her as striking as she was pleasant. Most of Dahlia's clients would give their eyeteeth to have the 'good hair' Reese had, but Reese was chomping at the bit to get it cut.

The two had met a year earlier when Dahlia participated in Career Day at the high school. When Reese learned Dahlia had graduated from Columbia University, a school she had aspirations to attend, they developed a friendly mentor/mentee relationship. A friendship made stronger when Dahlia realized her former Sunday school teacher was Reese's mother.

"C'mon, let's go back to my chair."

Dahlia ushered Reese to the first booth in a row of seven. She had loved styling hair from the time she was six, spending hours in the flowing manes of her baby dolls. Through the vocational program at her high school, she studied cosmetology and received her license, which she put to work when she started Columbia. A few hours after class and weekends at Sadie's House of Beauty had generated a hefty savings toward the purchase of her first salon. Now she lived her dream, making women look and feel beautiful, while listening to them talk about everything or nothing. She loved it.

Her parents had had conniptions when she'd disclosed her plan to open a beauty salon. *"Why waste a Columbia MBA in a beauty shop? Dahlia, this is madness!"* her father shrieked. But he said scant little when DBS, Dahlia's Beauty Salon, pulled in six figures after three years in operation. And at age thirty-two, with her original hair and nail salon in Denburg and four flourishing full-service day spas across South Carolina, Dahlia had made her first million. Her studies in entrepreneurship didn't go to waste. Unlike her twelve years as a wife.

The devastating end of her marriage prompted the sale of her day spas and forced Dahlia to face single life at thirty-four. The abrupt change in her world led to a year-long sabbatical in St. Thomas—her time in paradise a journey of self-rediscovery. She returned to Denburg a brand new Dahlia, and jumped back into the work she loved in the salon that had started it all. Fourteen months later, things were going well.

"Dahlia, I didn't realize you were back." Marci Jackson, the newest, youngest, and most religious of the shop ladies, exited the shampoo room with a client and directed her to the booth next to Dahlia's. "You had a call earlier," she said. "The message is on your desk."

"Do you know who it was?" Dahlia asked.

"She said her name was Leslie."

In what seemed to be a choreographed move, the necks of the five other stylists in the shop snapped to the right, fixing questioning eyes on Dahlia.

"You reckon that's your sister, Dahlia?" asked Ms. Flo, the eldest of the group and the busiest busybody of the bunch. She was a direct contrast to Marci, who read her Bible and tried new coloring techniques on her mannequin in lieu of dishing the dirt on what got done to who and why. "You haven't heard from her in what? Two years?"

"Yes, Ms. Flo, it's been about that long."

"She still in Atlanta?"

"I wouldn't know." Dahlia draped Reese and escorted her to the shampoo room, leaving Ms. Flo and the four remaining shop ladies, who fell comfortably between gossip hound and bible hugger, murmuring in her wake about the call and its ramifications.

"Are you okay?" asked Reese. "You seem a bit flustered."

She had been flustered after being with Norris. Heck, just being around him made her feel flustered in a way she'd never thought she would again. A feeling she was in no rush to claim. Right now she wasn't flustered.

Surprised and a bit steamed, but not flustered. "I'm good, Reese," she said.

"I don't know. I've never seen you anything but together, but today you seem a bit distracted. Is it just this Leslie person or is it someone else? Someone with a Y chromosome?"

Dahlia's cheeks grew warm. Was she that obvious?

"Uh-huh. It is a man." Reese giggled.

"All right, Miss Smarty Pants, enough of that," Dahlia playfully chided. "Lie back."

Reese settled her neck into the rest. "Is he nice?"

"I never said there was a he." Dahlia wet Reese's hair. "Too hot?"

"It's perfect," Reese answered. "You didn't have to say it, your expression said it all. He must be nice. He couldn't make you this giddy if he wasn't."

Dahlia blinked. Was she acting giddy? "Was that a romance novel you were reading when I came in?" she asked. "Your mind seems to be on one track right now."

"*The Great Gatsby*. Required reading."

"A classic." Dahlia squeezed some shampoo into her palm. "You enjoying it?"

"Eh." Reese's hand motioned so-so. "Is Leslie your sister?"

Dahlia laughed as she scrubbed Reese's scalp. "I thought business was your thing. You suddenly want to be a reporter?"

"I'm sorry, am I prying?"

"You don't know the answer to that?" Dahlia quipped.

Reese made a hissing sound. "Sorry."

"Don't sweat it. Lucky for you I like you." Dahlia shampooed and rinsed and repeated the action for the next several quiet minutes. "Leslie is my younger sister," she finally confessed as she turned off the water and squeezed the excess from Reese's hair.

"You're not close?"

"Not anymore." She saturated the damp hair with conditioner and slapped on a styling cap. "Let's sit you under the dryer for a few minutes."

As Reese deep-conditioned, Dahlia slipped into her office. What in the world did her sister want?

Norris ignored the smiling women he passed on his way into Denburg Memorial Hospital. Never short of female admirers, he knew one look in their direction would send them flocking over, and he wasn't interested in fighting off advances.

An attractive blonde at the reception desk pointed him in the direction of Gail's office. A couple of months ago, that honey would have been his lunch. She clearly had a serious hankering for him. The way she smiled and licked her lips as if she'd just finished a serving of her favorite dessert said it all. He thanked the receptionist for her help and headed down the curving corridor to Office 110. He knocked on the door.

"Come in," said a voice that took him spiraling back over seventeen years.

Norris cracked the door. The soft scent of jasmine erased the pungent smell of hospital antiseptic. Gail loved jasmine. He remembered she always had the scented candles burning at her home. Norris peeked around the door to find the lady behind her desk looking as beautiful as ever. "Dr. Gail."

"Norris." She approached him with open arms.

He returned her warm embrace. "It's been a long time."

"Too long." Gail took a step back. "Look at you. Just as handsome as ever."

"And you're just as stunning. More." Her flawless dark skin was as supple as ever, and her warm brown eyes still sparkled like two bright diamonds. "You never did share directions to the fountain of youth."

"No directions, just a fact of nature. Good black don't crack." She laughed, returning to her chair.

Norris chuckled with her. She used to always say that. "My first taste of forbidden fruit." He took the seat in front of her desk. "That's what you called yourself."

"I was, wasn't I?"

"Depends on what you call forbidden. I'm aware and have always appreciated the many beautiful hues of the world, but your race didn't make you forbidden. The fact that you were thirty-five and I was twenty is a different story."

"The old lady and the stud."

"You weren't old, and I wasn't a stud. At least not until you got finished with me." He smiled. "I had some great times with you. I was a little hurt when you disappeared."

"I thought it was for the best."

"Maybe." He brushed his hands against his thighs. "It's been nearly seventeen years. What prompted the call?"

She tucked a wisp of straight black hair behind her ear. "I think that can wait a few minutes. I want to hear about you. I know you're an accountant."

"I have my own firm downtown, but you already know that. How long have you been back in South Carolina?"

"Just over a year. I missed it here."

"Where did you go?"

"New York. Long Island. I wanted to spend some time with my parents. They were up in age, and both very sick. They died a few months after I moved back."

"I'm sorry to hear that, Gail."

"Thank you. It was very tough for a while. I was their miracle baby. They were from big families and wanted a big family, but had a hard time conceiving. There weren't a lot of options back then, but when all hope was lost, along came me. Mom was forty-three." She expelled a breath. "How did we get on me? I was asking about you. What's new in your life?"

Norris smiled. *What was new? Dahlia, Dahlia, and more Dahlia.* "You know me," he said.

"I do. That's why I'm wondering. You got tired of it yet?"

"It?"

"That playboy lifestyle. Back in the day, I could tell you had a lot of living inside of you dying to be lived. But

I also knew that need wouldn't last forever." She clasped her hands together and perched them on her desk. "Your blonde, blue-eyed friend. Your shadow, uhm . . ." She snapped her fingers.

"Ryan?"

"Yes. Ryan. How is he?"

"Wonderful." Norris laughed, pulling out his wallet and a snapshot of his best friend with his family. "Expecting twins."

Gail gazed wide-eyed at the photo. "His wife's black."

Norris gasped. "She is?" He laughed as Gail rolled her eyes. "Ryan lost his first wife eight years ago, but after three years of mourning, he and Justin found Lara, and she's fantastic. They've been happily married over four years."

"What a beautiful little girl they have."

"Sweet Angelica." Norris smiled with thoughts of his precious goddaughter. "She's incredible. A little heart-breaker." He returned the photo to his wallet. "I feel like a proud grandparent pulling out this picture. I don't know what's happening to me."

"It's endearing, Norris. You've changed so much. A good change. Not that you were a bad person before. You've just . . ."

"Grown up?" He shrugged. "It was bound to happen."

"I guess so. You have snaps of your own little ones?"

"Can't take photos of what you don't have. No wife or kids."

"You don't want children?"

"Well . . ." He tilted his head from side to side. "A thought has passed through my mind a time or two. What about you? You ever find the right guy and have kids?"

"Yes and no."

"Sounds like a story."

"It is quite a story. And somewhat involved."

Norris crossed his legs and settled into the chair. "Let's hear it. I'm not going anywhere."

Gail sighed. "Hmm. I honestly don't know where to start."

"The beginning is always good."

She nodded. "All right, the beginning. When you walked into the E.R. with your severely sprained wrist, I was at a crossroads in my life. You were young and flirtatious, and I took advantage of you, and I'm sorry."

"You didn't take advantage. I was a willing participant."

"I know, and that's how I took advantage. I wanted something from you, Norris, and when I got it, I left. No good-bye, and no explanation."

"We weren't in a relationship. Not a real one. You didn't take anything I didn't give. It was six great weeks. I would have liked a goodbye, but I don't have any regrets. Is that why you called me over? To apologize?"

"No. I'm—I'm not sorry about what we shared. That time with you gave me the biggest thrill of my life."

Norris laughed. "I fancy myself a thrill-giver, so I'm glad to have your joy confirmed. But, honestly, Gail, any thrill I gave you was equaled by the one you gave me. That was an incredible time for me."

"Me, too. And you did give me joy, Norris, so much joy, and that's what I need to tell you about." Gail closed her eyes for a long moment, drawing a deep breath.

Norris watched her closely, curiously. Though it had been years, he couldn't recall ever seeing her at a loss for words. It made him nervous. "Gail, what do you need to tell me?"

She lowered her hands and met his gaze. "I think it might be easier to show you."

Gail turned the picture frame on her desk in his direction. A beautiful, smiling young woman with flowing curls of dark hair and the golden skin promised by tanning lotion companies stared back at him. Norris held the picture closer. The girl had light eyes. Gray eyes. His heart leapt to his throat. "Gail?"

"I was an only child, Norris. Before I left Denburg, I thought long and hard about how it would feel to be all alone, and I didn't like it. I had my cousins, but it wasn't the same. I wanted my own family, and when you walked into my E.R., I saw a way to get it with no ties. You didn't see my seduction coming, but by the time I was done, I had what I wanted. I had your baby, Norris. You have a sixteen-year-old daughter."

CHAPTER 2

Dahlia picked up the phone a couple of times, but after five minutes of start and stop, she finally stopped. She hadn't spoken to her sister in two years, but with that Atlanta area code staring her in the face, calling Leslie would remain impossible. Once inseparable, now more than miles kept the sisters apart.

Dahlia folded the message in half and placed it in back of her desk drawer. She needed potato chips. Grabbing three quarters from the mug on her desk, she checked in on Reese at the dryer and then high-tailed it to the vending machine.

Halfway through the bag of ripple chips, her comfort food, Dahlia closed the package. Potato chips had always been her weakness, but eating in itself was the true culprit. Unlike her parents, Leslie, and her older brother, Quentin, she had always struggled with her weight. *'You're big-boned like your granddaddy,'* Flora, her maternal grandmother, who was of slight build like Dahlia's mother, used to always say. Her grandfather died before she was born, but Dahlia found comfort in her grandmother's words. Only after she'd lost the weight during her sabbatical did she realize the fat on the bones and not the bones themselves had made her big.

That truth didn't come easily. Grade school through high school had been a nightmare. Fat, smart Dahlia. *You're such a pretty girl, why don't you lose a few pounds?* Dahlia tossed the bag into the trashcan next to the vending machine. She still cringed when she thought of that line from 'well meaning' family members and friends. Older people seemed to feel reminding someone of his or her physical imperfections was a God-given right.

Thanks to the chips, she'd have to spend at least thirty extra minutes on the treadmill tonight. Losing eighty pounds wasn't easy. In fact, aside from accepting that her lie of a marriage had come to an end, it was the hardest thing she'd ever done.

Dahlia smiled at her reflection in the glass of the vending machine. Having gone from a round size twenty to a curvy ten, she looked good and felt even better. Norris constantly showered her with compliments. He had a way of making her feel like the most beautiful woman in the world. In fact, Norris had a way of making her feel a lot of things, many of which she didn't want to feel.

Intelligent, funny, wealthy, gorgeous, and an incredible lover who wanted no ties, Norris personified a dream walking. The fact that the no ties line had become a bit skewed for her didn't mean she couldn't clear it up, because a relationship was the last thing she wanted. Relationships were hard and painful. What she had with Norris worked because neither wanted that monkey on their back. They were about making each other feel good, and mixing emotions into that would break the magic and make things tense. And she wanted her life free of tension.

Dahlia made her way back to Reese. She'd been under the dryer ten minutes, enough to thoroughly condition her thick mane of curls. She gave the girl's shoulder a pat and lifted the dryer hood. "Time to rinse."

"I think you should cut my hair," Reese said when she was settled at the sink. "Preferably like yours, classy and cute."

Dahlia started rinsing. "I'm not cutting your hair."

"Aw."

"Reese, as grown up as you think you are, you're only sixteen. I'm not going to cut your hair unless your mother says so." Dahlia finished rinsing, wrapped a towel around Reese's damp hair, and ushered her back to the booth. "How is Gail doing? With her wedding two weeks away, I bet she's excited."

"She is. Excited and anxious. Ben's the same way."

"I hope their excitement turns into a lifetime of happiness." Unlike her dozen years with a lying cheat.

"They'll be very happy," Reese said. "And who knows, maybe you and your guy can keep the trend going." She smiled in the mirror at Dahlia.

Dahlia wagged an admonishing finger, a warning she could use on herself. Because try as she might, she couldn't help thinking about Norris and having a happy future with him.

"I . . . I don't understand," Norris stammered, his eyes never leaving the picture. "How did . . ."

"I think you know."

"But we used protection."

"No birth control is infallible. Plus, I provided the condoms, making sure some of your swimmers had extra freedom."

Norris saw so much of himself in the young woman's picture. He couldn't deny she was his if he wanted to. His gaze met Gail's. "Why didn't you tell me?"

"I didn't want you to know."

"And now?"

"And now I realize keeping Reese from you was wrong. It was unfair to you and her."

"Reese? That's her name?"

"Yes. I wanted to name her after you. I decided to use the last half of your first name and came up with Reese."

"You should have told me."

"No, I shouldn't have, not then. What I did was wrong, but I did it for the right reasons. You were twenty years old, Norris. I didn't want nor expect you to have a hand in raising her. I wanted Reese for me, and I didn't want to share her."

Norris glanced from the photo to Gail. He'd been a father for sixteen years and never had a clue, because she'd thought it was best. He clutched the armrests, trying to settle the anger threatening to erupt in him. "How could you keep her from me?"

"You're upset."

"At a bare minimum!" Norris said in a clipped voice. He sucked in a breath. "She's my daughter."

"Yes, she is, and that's why I called you. It may be sixteen years late, but I want you to know her now."

Norris watched her closely. Her words were sincere, he knew that, and it calmed him a degree, but there was something else. Something she wasn't telling him. "There's a reason you're doing this now," he said. "What is it?"

Gail's nervous chuckle broke the tense silence as he waited for her response. "You still read me well," she said.

"You taught me how." It was a gift he'd been able to use with a lot of women, and not just in the bedroom. "Why are you telling me about Reese now?"

"Like I said, I want you to know her."

"I get that. *Why now?*" he repeated.

"I'm getting married in a couple of weeks."

"And?"

"I've been fortunate to have career and financial success, good health, a beautiful daughter, and now a wonderful man in my life. I have a lot to be thankful for, but there are so many people in this world who don't have basic human needs. People in Uganda. My fiancé, Ben, is a doctor, and he and I want to help those people. To provide them with things we take for granted."

"That's very admirable, Gail, but I still—"

"In providing this help, I need your help," she broke in.

"You want a donation?"

"Yes, but of your time. Ben and I want to leave for Uganda right after the wedding, and while I'm away I want you to get to know Reese."

"Get to know her?" Norris leaned closer to her desk. "What are you asking?"

"This is your time, Norris. I want you to be Reese's dad."

"You want me to take over raising an almost-adult child I have yet to even meet," he rephrased. "You must be kidding."

"I think you know the answer to that. I've thought a lot about this, Norris, and I think it's for the best."

"Whose best? Mine? Our daughter's?"

"Both of you, and for me, too."

"Does she even know about me?"

"Not specifically."

Norris grunted. "I'll take that to mean no."

"I wasn't ready to talk about you when she asked. She knows you and I had a brief relationship and then parted ways."

"How much does your trip to Uganda have to do with your sudden need for me to know Reese?"

"A little and a lot. Norris, I'm not leaving Reese to go to Uganda; I'm going to Uganda to accept leaving her with you. Not telling you about her wasn't my best move, but like I said . . ."

"You wanted a baby for yourself and I was just a means to an end." Norris groaned and walked to the office window. Two young children traded swipes with each other while a man and woman followed behind mouthing what appeared to be demands they stop fighting. They were probably a family. Parents and children. He'd been a parent for sixteen years and had never known it.

"What are you thinking?" Gail asked.

Norris turned to her. "So many things."

Gail leaned back in her chair and crossed her arms. "Give me your worst, Norris. I want to know what you're feeling."

"What I'm feeling? Okay. I feel angry to have missed sixteen years of my child's life. I feel proud and I'm in awe of her. Reese is a beautiful girl, and to see some of myself in her . . . It's a joy I can't put into words."

"She's a wonderful young woman, and you can get to know her. I'll be honest, Norris. The reason I feel the need to leave while you're getting to know Reese is because I have been selfish when it comes to her. To see her bonding with you, and loving you—I don't know if I'll be able to take it, but I understand it needs to happen. The time I'm away will give you both the time you need to form these bonds, and give me time to accept it's happening and also help those in need."

"You make it sound like it will be so easy."

Gail shook her head. "Oh, no, I don't believe for one second it will be easy for any of us, but I have faith we can make it happen. You and Reese need to know each other."

"She's going to be living with me?"

"If you both agree. If not, I have someone in mind to be her guardian. Regardless, Reese will be available whenever you want. She is your daughter."

Norris expelled a long breath. "My daughter."

"I gather you don't question it, but if you want to have a DNA test done, I can arrange it."

"That's not necessary, Gail. I have all the proof I need. I just . . . Everything else is so . . . I need time to think."

"I understand." Gail extended a business card with all her numbers. "Just remember I'm leaving in two weeks."

Norris moved over to the desk and took the card. "Right, two weeks." He picked up the picture. Reese. His daughter. And he thought he had issues dealing with his unexpected feelings for Dahlia. "You'll be hearing from me."

Norris drove aimlessly about the city, trying to come to terms with the changes that had occurred in his life. Dealing with the idea of falling in love was one thing, but to learn he had an almost adult daughter . . . His body shivered. A daughter.

Two hours into his mindless travel, Norris remembered his dinner plans with Ryan and Lara and shot off to the Oceanside Grille. He arrived at the restaurant just as drink orders were being placed.

"Scotch on the rocks," Norris said to the waiter, sliding into the empty seat across from his friends and breathing in the smell of fresh seafood and charbroiled steaks.

The man scribbled the order and went about his way.

"Scotch?" said Ryan. "You don't drink anything stronger than dry wine."

"It's been a long day, and I need a stiff drink." Norris smiled at Lara. He had a lot on his mind, but his best friend's wife glowing with the beauty of impending motherhood was a sight to behold. "How's the gorgeous mama feeling tonight?"

"Like I'm carrying two little ones who seem intent on using my womb as a kick ball," Lara said, looking down at her tummy. "But it's just to remind me they are happy and thriving, and that's what matters." She smiled, rubbing her distended abdomen. "Ten more weeks."

Ryan's hand joined Lara's on her belly. "They're so glad to be around their Uncle Norris again they can't stay still," he said, looking at Norris. "It's been forever since we've spent quality time together."

"We still see each other all the time," Norris said. "We had dinner the other night."

"Yeah. But all you do is eat and leave."

"Tax season," Norris said, which wasn't a complete lie. Between work and Dahlia he had time for little else, but managed to squeeze time in for Ryan and his family. "April fifteenth was yesterday, but folks are still scrambling. It's a busy time of year."

"Is it just work?" Ryan asked. "You seem distracted right now, and I know something's been on your mind for a while."

The waiter returned to the table with the drink orders, rescuing Norris from his friend's questioning blue eyes. He drained the iced dark liquid in one swallow. The potent whiskey burned a fiery pathway from his throat to his belly, reminding him why he didn't drink scotch.

"Another?" asked the waiter, placing glasses of orange juice in front of Ryan and Lara.

Norris shook his head. "No, thank you," he croaked, reaching for his water glass and taking several big gulps.

"Are you ready to order?" the waiter asked.

"We'll need a few more minutes," Lara said.

The man nodded and left.

"You gonna tell us what's on your mind?" Ryan asked. "And don't say it's nothing."

"Okay, it's something." Norris closed his eyes, thinking of Gail's bombshell. "It's really something, but I can't talk about it right now. I will soon. I promise."

"You sure, Norris?" said Lara. "You seem a bit scattered."

"I'm good, Lara." He gave her hand a reassuring pat. "Really, don't worry." He drank more water.

"So, how did things go with Dahlia today?" Lara drank some juice. "This audit has her on edge. Did you calm her at all?"

Norris smiled. Did he ever. Dahlia had an amazingly calming effect on him, too. He lowered the glass.

"Uh-oh," said Ryan. "There's the look."

Lara's brown eyes narrowed with suspicion. "What's with the grin on your face, Norris?" she asked.

"Grin?" Norris pressed his hand to his chest. "Me?"

"Yes, you. Dahlia's a beautiful woman. You're not sizing her up for the kill, are you?"

Norris clicked his tongue in mock outrage. "Lara, I'm shocked. Norris isn't a predator."

"Is that a no?"

"Yes, that's a no." He was sizing Dahlia up for a lot more than the kill. The more he thought about it, the more the idea of longevity appealed to him, especially after hearing he had a daughter. "Dahlia has nothing to fear from me."

"Good, because she's still getting over a painful divorce. She's only been back in Denburg a little over a year, and my hair will not be happy with her being gone again. The last thing she needs is the Norris Converse treatment."

"The Norris Converse treatment?"

"I don't have to explain it to you."

Norris nodded. "You're right, you don't." 'Love 'em and leave 'em' had been his mantra for a long time, but now he was ready for a new tag line. "Your friend is safe, Lara." He checked his watch. Seven-fifteen. Dahlia was probably home now, and he really needed to see her. "I hate to cut out, but there's something I have to take care of."

"Something to take care of?" said Ryan. "Norris, you just got here."

"I know, but this can't wait, and you two never get any time alone." Norris stood, smiling as he gazed at Lara's belly. "Well, you manage to find some time, but you know what I mean." He laughed. "Order whatever you want, it's on me."

"I know something's troubling you, Norris," Lara said. "I can make myself scarce if you need to talk to Ryan."

"No, Lara, you don't have to do that. There is something, but I'm not ready to talk about it. When I am ready, I want you to be there."

"Think you'll be ready to talk soon? Maybe tomorrow?"

Norris moved around the table and kissed Lara's cheek. "Yes, inquisitive one, I do. Shh," he said, stopping Lara's next question at the moment her mouth opened. "I'm not saying anything else until then. You two enjoy your dinner." He gave Ryan's shoulder a jocular pat. "I'll see you tomorrow."

"You sure?" Ryan asked. "I don't think my wife can wait much longer than that for an opportunity to grill you."

Norris chuckled. "I'm sure."

The couple's curious mumblings followed Norris as he walked toward the exit of the restaurant. Maybe he should have told them about Reese tonight, but something stronger demanded he tell Dahlia first. The same force that had him dreaming of having someone to whisper things to and fall asleep with every night, an incredible force that had opened his heart to love.

CHAPTER 3

The soft hum of the treadmill grew louder as Dahlia prepared for her final cardio workout: a five-minute, six-mile-per-hour run. She had already completed the first half, an hour of three to six-mile intervals that ranged from an incline of two to fifteen. When she first started this method of training, Dahlia thought it would kill her, but a year later, she loved the challenge of going a step further. And after the chips she'd indulged in earlier, she had all the incentive she needed. Not that she really needed one.

Thoughts of Norris filled her head, and she needed a distraction from those smoky gray eyes and devilish smile. That incredible touch, his laugh, his voice, his scent . . .

She shook her head. *Stop it, Dahlia! You don't think about a bed buddy like that.* She didn't know how one should think of a bed buddy, as Norris was her first, but no ties definitely didn't mean endless dreams, both awake and asleep, of a man you were just supposed to be having sex with.

The belt speed picked up and Dahlia hopped back on. Three minutes into her run, with sweat trailing down her forehead and her heart pounding in a quick, rhythmic beat, the doorbell rang.

She grunted. Who was interrupting her workout?

Dahlia grabbed a towel from the handle of her stationary bike and made her way to the door. She looked through the peephole to see Norris looking a bit out of sorts.

She pulled the door open. "Hey, this is a surprise."

"I'm sorry, you were working out. I knew that, but . . ."

"No, it's okay, I was about done. Besides, you being here means I can have another kind of workout."

Norris managed a weak smile, nothing like the all-out body press she usually received when offering up the goods. Something troubled him. She stepped aside to let him in. "You okay?"

"I don't know," he said, making his way around her and into the living room. He rested his head against the back of the couch. His hands covered his eyes. He sighed deeply.

"What happened to your dinner plans with Ryan and Lara?"

Norris lowered his hands. "I left early. I thought they could use some alone time, and I was a little distracted."

Dahlia said nothing, but she agreed. She had never seen him so pensive.

"I want to tell you something," he said, "but it's quite a story. And if I'm going to unload on you, I think you should be comfortable. It could take a while."

"You saying I'm stinky?" she quipped, getting the laugh from him she was hoping for.

"Never. I just don't want you to catch cold in those sweaty clothes."

"All right, I'll only be gone a few minutes."

Roughly ten minutes later, she returned to the living room to find Norris eating her box of baked cheese crackers. The bite-size snacks had become a favorite of his. She couldn't believe a man who grew up in Wisconsin had never had a cheese cracker before she introduced them to him. Then, again, Norris didn't strike her as the conventional Wisconsin guy.

Norris shook the empty box. "I'm sorry, I got a little hungry. I'll buy you some more."

"Don't sweat it. All you had was crackers?"

"No, I also had an apple and finished up the pasta salad and your milk. I didn't realize how hungry I was. I hadn't had a bite since lunch, and I worked that off when you came by my office this afternoon."

Dahlia's whole body flamed under Norris's intense perusal. He could sell the look in his eyes as a newfangled blowtorch. Suddenly her pink tank shirt and matching full-length cotton bottoms felt like a cellophane bikini. Not since Jonah had a man had such a physical effect on her. It unsettled her.

Dahlia motioned her thumb in the direction of the kitchen. "Have you had enough to eat? I can whip up something if you're still hungry."

"No, I'm good." He gave her a once-over and smiled. "I've never seen you in pajamas before."

"PJs don't exactly fit in the arrangement we have."

He nodded. "Right."

Dahlia joined him on the couch. "What's got you so unsettled tonight?"

"I honestly don't know how or where to start. Not a lot surprises me, but this is something I never expected." He blew out a long breath. "Not in a million years."

Norris's hedging put Dahlia on edge. Whatever he wanted to tell her was something emotional, and if his emotions were anything like hers . . . She couldn't hear it. Feeling what she felt for Norris and keeping it to herself was one thing, but to hear he was feeling the same was a validation she didn't want to contend with. Such a confession from him would cross them into the relationship world, and she didn't want to have another relationship. She didn't want that battering ram called love slamming into her heart again. She couldn't handle it.

"Norris, maybe you should talk to Ryan about this."

"I will, but I wanted to talk to you first."

"But Ryan's your best friend."

"We're not friends?"

"We're lovers."

"Is that all?"

Dahlia pulled her top lip into her mouth, a nervous habit she acquired from a desire to lie but an inability to do so. She didn't know what to say. Why was he doing this?

"I found out something today," Norris said, rescuing her from her struggle, but making her guts clench in anticipation and dread of what he might say. "Dahlia, I have a daughter."

Dahlia blinked. Norris had started his sentence the way she thought he would, but the finish . . . "You have a daughter?"

Norris nodded. "I didn't want to blurt it out like that, but it felt necessary." He closed his hands around hers. "You're the first person I've told. Saying the words out loud makes it seem more real, but it's still so unbelievable. I've only seen a picture of her, but she's a beautiful girl." He smiled. "She kinda looks like me."

"Wow. You're a daddy." Dahlia gave his hand a little shake. "How are you feeling?"

"Stunned, proud, angry. Reese is sixteen years old, and I just learned about her today."

Dahlia blinked. "Reese?" she said.

"That's my daughter's name," Norris explained. "She's named after me. Sorta."

"It's a lovely name." *Maybe this was just a coincidence. The name Reese wasn't very common, but . . .* "You say she's sixteen?"

"Yeah. Her mother, Gail, and I met the summer of my senior year at college. I was on the baseball team and I took a nasty shot to the wrist from a wild pitch. The next morning it hurt like hell, so Ryan drove me to the E.R., and that's where I met Gail. She was my doctor, and a beautiful older woman I was immediately attracted to. We had some good times together."

Dahlia couldn't believe it. Norris's daughter and her mother were people she knew. And he was right. Reese did look like him. She'd never noticed before. *Norris and Gail?* That blew her mind. "You and an older woman?"

"Older, yes, but not *old*. Gail was thirty-five, and I was a twenty-year-old punk kid who thought he was Mr. Smooth. We had six weeks together. As quickly as she came into my life, she was gone. And now I learn we had a daughter."

"Why didn't she tell you?"

"She didn't want me to know. She told me she wanted to have a baby, and I was her way of getting it. For sixteen years I've had a daughter, and for the last year and a half she's been right here in Denburg. I could have passed her on the street a million times."

Dahlia nodded. Reese was the best friend of Lara's young cousin, Diana Monroe. Norris and Diana's parents were friends. There were all these connections at work, and no one was the wiser. No one but her.

"If finding out I have a daughter wasn't enough of a surprise, Gail informs me she's getting married in two weeks and then leaving the country to do relief work in Uganda for six months."

Uganda! Gail hadn't mentioned that to her, either. "Uganda?" Dahlia said.

"Yes. She has a need to help," he said. "While she's away, she wants me to get to know Reese. Have her live with me."

"How do you feel about that?"

"Worried. I'm her father and we're strangers. What if Reese doesn't agree to this?" He sighed. "What if she does?"

"Either way the answer is the same. You get to know her. She's your daughter, and that matters."

"She's biracial. Did I tell you that?"

I already knew. "No, you didn't," Dahlia said.

"Gail is African-American." Norris dragged his hands over his face, sighing heavily. "When I think of my parents' reaction to meeting Lara, I shudder. They treated her like she wasn't there, and said some of the most ridiculous things after she and Ryan left. And the thoughts they put in poor Justin's head. Oh, man."

"Justin?"

"He heard them talking about Ryan and Lara burning in hell for being together. Justin was five and took it literally. Scared the poor guy to death."

Dahlia shook her head. She hadn't heard about that.

"This happened years ago, and it was the last time I saw them, but it's a memory I will never forget. How am I going to subject my daughter to that kind of treatment?"

"You can't be responsible for your parents, but you can be responsible for yourself. Do you want to get to know Reese?"

"I do, but with what she has to look forward to, I wonder why she'd ever want to get to know me."

Reese pushed away her half-empty plate. "I'm done now," she said, staring at her mother, who sat across from her at the dinner table. "Are you going to tell me what's wrong?"

"You didn't finish your meatloaf," Gail said.

"Mom?"

"Why does something have to be wrong for a mother to make a nice meal for her one and only child?"

"Because I know you didn't cook my favorite foods and buy a chocolate chip cheesecake, my favorite dessert, just to do something nice for me. You do nice things for me all the time, but this feels different."

Gail nodded. "You're right. I want us to talk tonight."

"We always talk."

"Not about this." Gail drank some lemonade. "You used to always ask about your father."

"Yeah, and you never said much. More like nothing. Which is why I stopped asking."

"That's going to change. I want to tell you about him."

"Why?" Reese asked, her mother's desire to discuss her father worrying her all the more. Horrible thoughts filled her head. Was her mom sick? Reese tugged at a curly lock. "Why talk about him now?"

"He's your father."

"He's been that for sixteen years, but it never warranted discussion from you."

"Things have changed. You remind me a lot of him."

"Is that why you didn't like to talk about him? Because you saw him when you looked at me?"

"No, I kept quiet because I was selfish. I wanted to be your only parent, so I robbed you of knowledge of your father and the opportunity to know him, and I'm sorry."

"I always wanted to know him, but I don't feel like I missed out on anything. You were everything I needed, Mom."

"I did the best I could, but I was still wrong. I want to tell you about him now."

"We don't have to do this." Reese motioned her head toward the kitchen. "I'll get the cheesecake."

Gail grabbed Reese's hand. "We should finish talking first," she said. "You're old enough to know the truth."

"What truth? Some things are obvious. He was a white guy. You told him you were pregnant and he ditched you. Is that it?"

"No, that is not it, and I don't like your tone." Gail released Reese's hand and took another swallow of her lemonade. "I don't want you to have animosity toward him. He did nothing wrong. If you want to be angry at someone, be angry at me."

"I don't want to be angry with you. I don't want to talk about this. Why are we talking about this now?"

"Because it's necessary."

"Why? Is something wrong? Is he trying to take custody of me or something?"

"No, he's not trying to do that, but since you mentioned custody, you should know we have made contact, and I want you to spend some time with him."

Reese gasped. "Whose idea was that?"

"Mine."

Unease settled in Reese's stomach, killing her appetite. Something had to be wrong with her mother. She couldn't listen to any more of this conversation. "May I be excused?"

"No. We're not done."

"I am."

"Baby, I've been thinking about this for a long time, and it's time you get to know your father. You're getting older, and you need to have a strong male figure in your life."

"Hello. Ben?"

"Ben is wonderful, but he's not your father."

"My father hasn't been my father. He's never been in my life. How can he be a strong male figure?"

"His not being in your life isn't his fault, Reese, it's mine. I never told him about you."

Like some errant arrow, the words went through Reese's ears and straight to her heart, stinging her soul with disbelief and hurt. *I never told him about you.* Did her mother really say that? "Why not?" she asked.

"Because getting pregnant was my idea. I wanted it to be you and me."

"And now you want it to be you, me, and him."

"No, I want it to be you and him. I want you to know your father, Reese. I think it's time you met him."

CHAPTER 4

Norris slid off the couch and onto the floor, clutching a throw pillow to his chest. He loved the comfort of Dahlia's place. It wasn't overloaded with furniture and a lot of stuff; it was homey and wide-open, an interesting contrast to the Italian leather furniture and African art that made his condo look more like a spread from an interior-decorating magazine than a bachelor pad. But he loved his place. It suited him. Like Dahlia's place suited her. Different personalities converging. Much like they did that first night.

Dahlia joined him on the floor. "What are you thinking?"

"At this very moment? My first time here." He smiled brightly with the memory of their bodies twined together on the cool surface of her hardwood floor. "Wasn't exactly conventional, huh?"

She chuckled. "No, it wasn't. I usually don't bring home men I meet while renting a movie, but learning we knew some of the same people and the fact you were renting *Shrek* had me convinced you weren't a madman."

"Just one with questionable taste in movies."

"You're in touch with your fun side, there's nothing wrong with that. It will only help in getting to know your daughter."

"My daughter."

"I'm sure she'll warm up to you just like that." Dahlia snapped her fingers.

"I wonder. I'm telling you, my parents are something else. You never wondered how Ryan and I became friends?"

"Lara said you guys met in second grade. Schoolmates."

"Yes, we were, but I'm heir to a multi-million dollar fortune and I grew up in Wisconsin. That doesn't seem strange to you?"

"Now that I think about it . . . How did that happen?"

"My folks. My father, Harold, grew up in Wisconsin and believed in hard work and doing it yourself. My mother, on the other hand, was from an old Greek family as wealthy as my dad's was poor. They met in New York, where Dad was trying to make his mark in the financial world. After meeting the daughter of Constantine Katsoros, he didn't have to worry about doing it himself. He let mom's unlimited money do it for him."

"If they met in New York, how did you end up in Wisconsin? You spent some time in Greece, too, right?"

"Yeah. Dad loved Mom's money, but he didn't want to raise children who didn't value a dollar. We lived in Greece until I was seven, at which time they decided it best that a caring staff in Wisconsin raise my brother, sister, and me. You know, be around regular people and establish ourselves without the aid of the Katsoros millions. We didn't want for anything material, and we took some nice trips during the summer, but Wisconsin became home. We attended public school and grew up like," he made quotes with his fingers, " 'regular' kids."

"And what were your parents doing while the caring staff took care of you and your siblings?"

"Genevieve and Harold? What else? Traveling the world, spending money, and partying with the crème de la crème of society. Julia, Lane, and I got to see them for a couple of hours on Thanksgiving and Christmas Eve, but that was about it. Now, every other year at Thanksgiving, my parents alternate spending the holiday with each of us. Won't be my turn again for a couple more years."

Dahlia shook her head, sighing. Norris could tell what she was thinking without her saying a word. The sad pity in her eyes said a mouthful.

"You can say it," he said.

"I don't know what I want to say."

"I do. Poor little rich boy, grew up with so much but had so little. You're right. The strange part is that to this day I crave my parents' approval. Lane's the oldest, and Julia's the youngest and the only girl, not that the distinction helps them, but I'm just an extra. I want to make them proud. I want them to be happy for me and in the choices I make. I wonder if I can ever make that happen."

Dahlia grunted. "Why would you want to?" she mumbled.

"I heard that, you know."

"Good. You mentioned their reaction to meeting Lara, and she was your best friend's girlfriend. How do you think they'll react to your daughter?"

"I don't know. I hope fine. She's my daughter."

"You think that'll make a difference?"

"I don't want to believe my parents are racist."

"They don't have to be racist to have a problem with you presenting them with a biracial grandchild. Reese isn't a baby, and she's going to feel that tension."

"I think it will be different this time."

"But you don't know. Because of my weight, I've been the person who stuck out in a crowd. It's even more painful when a family member puts emphasis on your difference, and it's not a good feeling, Norris. I've lost the weight, but I'll always be that fat kid. That pain never really goes away. You don't want to subject Reese to unnecessary scrutiny from her own family."

Norris brushed his finger against Dahlia's cheek. She had talked about being overweight, but he could never equate it to the curvaceous stunner before him. Now, it was becoming real. As real as the feeling he'd developed for her.

"I'm sorry for what you've gone through, Dahlia. I think you're beautiful, and I would think so even with the weight."

"Really?" She opened the end table drawer and pulled out a photo. "What do you think?" She handed him the snapshot.

Norris studied the picture of full-figured Dahlia, finding the same smile and bright eyes that drew him in from the moment they met. He smiled. "I think St. Thomas was good for you. You've gone through quite a dramatic physical transformation, but you're just as beautiful in this photo as you are now."

"Come on. You wouldn't have noticed that Dahlia."

"You're wrong." Norris glanced from the photo to Dahlia. "You're more than just a body to me."

Their eyes met and held for a long moment, the quiet saying more than any words ever could. Remaining a step ahead of commitment and relationship as they nipped at his heels had been hard, but Norris had grown tired, and hoped and prayed that when his legs gave out Dahlia would be there to catch him. Worry that she wouldn't have kept him running, but at moments like this he couldn't help but think . . . He leaned in for a kiss.

"What are you going to do about your daughter?"

Norris blinked. "What?"

"I asked what you're going to do about your daughter," Dahlia said, returning the photo to the drawer and settling into the nearest corner of the couch. "How do you plan to deal with your parents?"

"I don't know. I love them because they're my parents, but I've learned to live without them. Servants raised me. That's what makes it hard to know what to do about Reese. I want to know her, but I don't know how to be a father when mine was always more a visitor in my life. I don't want to fail her."

"Like your parents did you?"

"They did, but I've always known who they were. I'm a stranger to Reese. Is it fair I disrupt her life to say, 'Hi, I'm your daddy. Let's make nice?' What if she's not interested?"

"You don't know she's not. What will you do if she is?"

"I'll buy parenting books, get tips from Ryan and Lara, and pray I don't ruin her life. I don't want her to hate me."

Dahlia patted the cushion beside her. "Join me."

Norris moved to the couch, feeling immediate calm when his hand settled in hers.

"You're afraid, aren't you?" she asked.

"Am I really supposed to answer that? A man's not supposed to own up to fear, especially about a sixteen-year-old."

"Don't worry, I won't tell anyone."

Norris smiled. "Thanks for saying so."

Her fingers brushed his hair. "What are you thinking?"

I think I love you. "I think she'll resent me," he said. "Gail and I didn't exactly have an ideal relationship. Hell, I've never had a relationship with any woman, it's just been—"

"Arrangements?" Dahlia offered.

"That works," Norris said. "I've missed out on so much with Reese. Her first smile, her first steps, and her first day of school. Sixteen birthdays, sixteen Christmases, and sixteen years of sweet goodnight kisses. And all Reese knows is I wasn't there for her and her mother. Not exactly a good beginning for a relationship."

"Would you be happier if Gail had never said anything?"

Norris watched Dahlia closely as he considered her words. He could extend the same question to her about the change he thought their relationship had taken, but from the time he'd spent with her, he knew such a question would blow up in his face. Her reaction before he mentioned Reese said as much.

"I would have been happier knowing about Reese from the beginning, but I wasn't given that option. I know about a teenager, and Gail wants to leave her alone with me. She couldn't have made this any harder."

"Let's talk about your fear, Norris."

"I'm afraid of losing Reese before I get the chance to know her. She's not a baby, Dahlia. I can't cuddle her and rock her and bribe her with a stuffed toy. I have to stumble my way through this, and build a father/daughter relationship that should have been established sixteen years ago. Gail should have told me about her. She should have told me."

"I was thinking the same thing when I learned my husband was cheating on me. He should have told me."

Norris's eyes narrowed. "You think this is the same?"

"No, but I'm trying to make a point. You're afraid of the unknown. How you'll handle being a father and how your daughter will respond to you. Well, when I was going through my divorce, I was wondering how I was going to make it on my own. Jonah had been a part of my life for sixteen years, the same amount of time you've been without Reese. So I know fear."

Dahlia hugged a throw pillow to her chest. Her dark eyes took on a faraway quality. Norris waited for her to say more. They'd discussed her cheating ex, the less than amicable divorce that ended twelve years of marriage, and her vow to stay clear of relationships many times before, but tonight felt different. It seemed Dahlia wanted to say a little more. Pushing her would likely cause her to clam up, so he just waited quietly.

"Fear. I could write a book about fear. Finding my husband in bed with another woman, in my house . . ." She closed her eyes, blotting glistening tears with long lashes. "Trying to figure out how to go on from there, that's fear. Aside from hair and how to run a business, Jonah was all I knew. We met as freshmen in college and got married before grad school. He had been a part of my entire adult life, and I had to find a way to live my life without him."

Norris brushed away the tears rolling down her cheeks. He'd seen her cry before, but not like this. Happy tears that streamed from laughing until her stomach cramped from his silly stories, and bittersweet tears that flowed ever so slowly at the conclusion of a sad movie, but not sorrowful tears from a place deep in her heart where a stabbing ache still resided.

Dahlia had always put up a tough-girl façade, a veneer that said, 'I'm on top of things. I do what I want, when I want, and how I want,' but he'd suspected it was just a disguise, and tonight made it clear. He had enjoyed the game she played. It had enchanted him. But this hurt was real, personal, and she was sharing it with him. They were sharing. He liked it.

She moved away from his caressing thumb. "I don't know what's going on with me." Dahlia wiped away the remnants of tears. "We were talking about you."

"That's okay. I like hearing more about you. Your husband was a fool."

"My husband was a man. A very attractive man with some coin and a line." A humorless chuckle erased the brief silence that followed her words. "A couple of lines. One to lure me, and another to reel me in. A big, foolish fish."

"Dahlia . . ."

"No, it's okay. Three good things came out of my marriage ending: I lost a loser of husband before I lost more of myself, I shed eighty pounds that had been weighing me down for years, and I got in touch with a Dahlia that had been silent for too long. It wasn't easy, but after finding my way through a pile of empty potato chip bags, I found a good place."

"Potato chip bags?" Norris said curiously.

"Some people fall into hard times and lose themselves in a bottle of booze. I lose myself in ripple chips. 'My name is Dahlia, and I'm a chipoholic.' It's my cross to bear, but admitting a problem is the first step to getting help, right?"

Norris laughed. "It's good you can find humor in this."

"After a while, you can always find a way to laugh about things that once brought you pain."

"Thanks for sharing this with me."

"I wanted you to see that as difficult as this situation seems, you can get through it and find a good place with your daughter."

"Maybe we can," he said. "I can't deny I'm still a bit mortified about this fatherhood thing, but there's a good anxiousness in the mix, too."

Dahlia eyes sparkled as she smiled. "That's good to hear."

Norris wanted her to say more, to talk about that Dahlia she'd mentioned who'd been quiet for too long, but he knew he'd have to keep wondering because Dahlia's time for sharing had come to an end. From what he'd come to know of the inner workings of Ms. Sinclair, sparkly eyes meant she had an idea, and it had nothing to do with sharing secrets or unspoken pains.

"As many movies as we've watched together, we always get sidetracked before finishing." Dahlia giggled. "Let's cook up a little something and see if we can get to the end credits for a change."

Norris smiled. He was definitely learning to read her well. And the more he learned, the more he liked. "I'm willing to give it a shot," he said, following her to the kitchen.

Memories of this evening replayed in Norris's head. He'd never talked to any woman about his parents, but tonight he'd not only told Dahlia about his folks, he told her about the daughter he hadn't even told his best friend about. And when all was said and done, he felt calm about it. Happy even.

His smile grew wider as he watched Dahlia rifle the fridge for this and that. All doubts evaporated. Hell had frozen over, pigs had taken flight, and the first of Neverary had arrived. The utterly impossible had finally come to pass. Norris Converse had fallen in love.

CHAPTER 5

Dahlia sighed softly and smiled. The unmistakable scent of Norris, a woodsy sweetness with a hint of spice, made the best alarm clock in the world.

Waking to his scent all around her wasn't unusual. The hours they spent together twined in her sheets kept his presence lingering long after he was gone. But this morning brought a difference. It didn't find her nestled in the downy softness of her king-size rice bed, her body satiated and humming with memories of Norris's masterful touch. Instead, she woke with a dull ache in her neck and an amazing feeling throughout her being. Happiness and contentment overwhelmed her from something as simple and innocent as spending an entire night in Norris's arms, on her couch.

She pressed her nose to his chest, breathing him in. She liked Norris being here. She liked that he had chosen to tell her something he hadn't told another soul. But she didn't like that she liked it. She shouldn't like it. They had an arrangement. Sex. Simple and uncomplicated. Just primal urges being met. Feelings weren't supposed to exist in that, outside the orgasmic pleasure realm, but damn if feelings hadn't developed.

Feelings? Maybe she was just confused. She had an intense physical attraction to Norris, and he was upset last night after learning about Reese, so her heart went out to him. Her attraction to him coupled with his emotions made her more susceptible to empathy. Yeah, that's what it was. Empathy.

Dahlia lifted her head to find Norris awake and smiling down at her. "How'd you sleep?" he asked.

"Not as well as I do when I'm in my bed, but okay. You?"

"Best sleep I've had in years."

"How long have you been up?"

"Well, I've been awake for a while, but I've been *up* even longer," he said with a lusty smile, straddling her on his lap.

Dahlia curled her arms around his neck and rolled her hips, smiling. "I can tell." She loosened the buttons of his shirt, exposing the fine dusting of dark hairs covering his chest. Norris had the perfect body. Not bulky and over-stuffed like most of the guys that defined 'fit' on the cover of fitness magazines, but solid and well-defined, beautiful. "I've been *up* for a while myself."

His lips brushed hers. "Thank you for last night."

"I didn't do anything special."

"Letting me be here was special. You listened and you talked. You made me know as uncertain as things look, everything with Reese could be okay."

"I'm glad I could be of help." She kissed him softly and swiveled her hips, eliciting a deep groan from Norris. "I think you have another problem I can help you with right now."

"Uh-hmm." His lips claimed hers, hungrily, passionately. She opened herself to him, welcoming the warmth of his exploring tongue as his hands explored beneath her top. A short gasp fell from her lips when his caressing thumb brushed against the tip of her breast, bringing the tiny nub to immediate attention and shooting every nerve ending in her body to high alert.

The next moments found her top on the floor and Norris's mouth fastened to her breast. His deep moans grew with her sighs of pleasure. He turned his attention to her other breast. Tasting, teasing, and deliciously tormenting her, Norris's hot mouth and skillful touch had her heart racing and body crying for more of him.

Having endured all the foreplay she could take, Dahlia longed for the main event. Sliding her hands between them, she worked feverishly to unloosen his belt and find the button of his slacks. Just as she reached his zipper, the phone rang.

Norris captured her lips in a kiss. "Don't answer it," he mumbled against her mouth, attempting to lower her pajama bottoms below her waist.

The ringing continued.

"It might be the salon."

"Let it wait." He ground against her, and as natural as breathing, her hips responded to his movements. His lips trailed along her neck. "I'll go crazy if I don't have you."

Dahlia nodded in agreement. The answering machine would soon pick up, and if important, the caller would phone again.

"Dahlia, are you there? I'm sorry to call so early, but . . ."

Reese's troubled tones broke the sound of heavy breathing and the sexual tension in the room. Dahlia grabbed the phone.

"I'm here," she said, careful not to mention Reese's name.

"Why are you out of breath?" Reese asked.

"Why am I out of breath?" Dahlia glanced at Norris. "I was halfway down the stairs when the phone rang," she lied. "I raced to the closest phone. Are you okay?"

"Yeah. It's my mom," Reese explained.

"Is she okay?"

"I don't know. Can I come over? I really need to talk to you. I can be there in half an hour."

"Yes, that's fine, come on over."

Norris touched her shoulder. "Come over?" he mouthed.

Dahlia shrugged. She was sorry to disappoint him, and herself, but it was clear Reese needed to talk. And after what Norris had told her last night, she was pretty certain of what was troubling Reese. "I'll see you in a little bit. Bye."

"You'll see her in a little bit?"

"Yes. I'm sorry, Norris, but it's one of the girls I met when I did my presentation at the high school last year. She's interested in attending Columbia and studying business, so we got close. Something's upsetting her and I want to help."

"I can't fault you for that, although . . ." He looked down to his lap. "I didn't expect the morning would end like this."

She kissed his cheek. "Me, either."

Norris buttoned his shirt. "Can I see you tonight?"

"I insist on it. Your place?"

He nodded. "Six o'clock?"

"I'll be there."

Dahlia pulled on her top and walked him to the door. "What are you going to do today?"

Norris opened the door and leaned against the jamb. "I'm going to start the process of getting to know my daughter. I don't know how yet, but that's my big plan for today. Thank you for everything, Dahlia." He pecked her lips. "I mean that."

"You're welcome," she said with a smile, her heart fluttering from his sweet kiss. "I'll see you later."

Dahlia closed the door after Norris drove away in his gray Porsche—his hot man-mobile. She had some thinking to do. The very real and unexpected feelings she had for Norris grew stronger with every second she spent with him, and were beginning to eclipse everything in her life. No strings? Huh! There were plenty of strings, and they had her tied in more knots than she thought she could ever see herself through.

Norris drove straight home and hopped into a cold shower. Though disappointed he couldn't start his day drowning in Dahlia's delight, her selfless desire to help a young friend in need gave him even more reason to love her. *Love?* Norris laughed out loud. He still couldn't believe it. "I'm in love."

When the icy spray of the water jets accomplished the desired effect, Norris dried off and padded to his bedroom. Spotting the number five flashing on his answering machine, he sat on the bed and listened to the messages. The first was from his mother, whom he hadn't heard from in months, stating she'd be coming to South Carolina for a visit in the next couple of weeks. He grunted. That should be fun.

Calls from lady friends wondering when they'd see him again made up the next three messages, and the last was from Lara inviting him over for breakfast. Norris laughed. The poor woman probably didn't get a wink of sleep last night from wondering what he had on his mind. Norris decided not to keep her waiting. Changing into some designer warm-ups and sneakers, he made his way to his friends' house.

Justin, Ryan's ten-year-old son, pulled up on his bike as Norris parked. "Hey, Uncle Norris," he greeted.

"What's up, buddy?" Norris removed his sunglasses. "Where are your folks?"

"In the kitchen with Angelica." Justin looked down the street and reversed the cap on his blonde head. "I see my friends. See ya later."

Norris walked into the house. The unmistakable scent of blueberries filled the air. Muffins or pancakes? He hoped pancakes.

"A beautiful, pregnant lady invited me over for breakfast," he said, strolling into the kitchen. "Is this where I sign up?"

"Uncle Norris!" Angelica leapt from her chair and raced over to him with open arms.

Norris swooped her up and kissed her cheek. Curls of golden-streaked brown hair framed her pretty face. "Is this my breakfast?" He kissed her neck, evoking giggles from the three-year-old. "You're so sweet and good, can I eat you up?"

"No, Uncle Norris, you can't eat me up. I'm going to the park with Sue-Ma," she said, her brown eyes shining bright.

The girl's happiness at spending time with "Sue-Ma," Ryan's former mother-in-law and Justin's grandmother, gave Norris a lot of hope in regard to his parents and Reese. Sue's initial unhappiness with Ryan and Lara's relationship could have inspired legends, but the realization that Lara being a part of Ryan and Justin's life wouldn't rob her of her place in their lives transformed Sue. Not only did she have Justin, but she loved Angelica just as much. They were a wonderful extended family. Complete blood ties had to make a difference for his family with Reese.

"You can eat up Daddy's pancakes," Angelica suggested.

Norris kissed her cheek again. "I guess that's a pretty good second choice."

"Glad you could make it, Norris," Lara said with a smile.

"I'm sure you are," he replied, joining her at the table and propping Angelica on his knee. "I'm sure this breakfast invitation was totally altruistic."

"We love you, Norris. We want to be sure you have a complete and healthy breakfast."

"Uh-huh."

Ryan brought over a stack of pancakes. "How can you question our sincerity?" he said.

"I know you." He looked down at the plate. "What, no sausage and eggs?"

"Your wish is our command." Ryan brought over a platter of bacon, eggs, and sausage. "Have at it."

Lara smiled as Norris poured maple syrup over the pancakes. "Is there anything else we can get for you?" she said.

"How about your firstborn daughter?" he quipped. "You two seem to be falling all over yourselves this morning to please me. How far are you willing to go?"

Ryan removed Angelica from Norris's lap and hugged her close. "Not that far."

Norris laughed as he cut into the pancake stack. "Just checking."

Minutes later a horn blew outside.

"That's Sue," Ryan said. He carried Angelica over to Lara. "Kiss Mommy goodbye."

Angelica gave Lara a loud smack. "Bye-bye, Mommy."

"Bye, sweetie. You have fun with Sue-Ma."

The girl nodded.

Sue knocked on the kitchen door and entered. "I'm sorry I'm a little late," she said. "I had to stop by the ATM." She waved at Norris. "Hello, Norris."

"Good morning, Sue," he replied, before turning his attention to the delicious breakfast.

Sue gave Angelica a big grin as she approached with open arms. "How's my sweet angel?" she said.

"Good!" Angelica jumped into Sue's arms. "Let's go."

"Yes, let's. Carl and I want to take her to lunch, too. Is that okay?"

"Sure," Lara said. "I'm sure she'd have it no other way."

"Great. We'll be back around three-thirty."

"See you then," Ryan said, escorting them to the door.

"Bye-bye, Daddy." Angelica waved.

Ryan kissed her cheek. "Bye, sweetheart. Have fun." Ryan closed the door and turned his attention to Norris. "Okay, now, what's going on?"

"I can't finish my breakfast?"

"You can talk and eat." Ryan sat beside Lara. "I know you better than anybody and I can't figure it out. Your behavior last night had us worried."

"You had no reason to worry. I thought I explained that."

"You explained very little," Lara said. "Now is yesterday's tomorrow, so talk. What is it?"

Norris finished his eggs and popped the last of his third sausage link into his mouth. He wiped his mouth with a napkin, getting a perverse pleasure in keeping them waiting. "Can I have a little coffee?"

"No!" Ryan barked.

"Now, now, Ryan. That's no way to treat me, if you're so worried about me."

Lara stood. "I'll get it," she said.

"No, you stay down," Ryan said, settling her into the chair. "You do enough running around in class with your kindergarteners. I'll wait on His Highness." Ryan retrieved the carafe and poured Norris a cup.

"I hope that's real coffee and not the stuff Lara drinks," Norris said, detecting the scent of vanilla.

"I can't drink it right now, so I at least like to smell it," Lara explained. "It is coffee."

"Humph. I'll be more specific next time," Norris grumbled, adding cream and sugar to the steaming cup.

"Norris, you've been beating around the bush since last night. Spill already," Ryan said.

"All right, all right." Norris drank some of the flavored brew and gave his full attention to his friends. "Yesterday, I found out I have a daughter."

"You what?" Ryan and Lara shrieked.

"I have a daughter," he said again, still getting used to the idea. "How's that for a life-changing event?"

Dahlia changed into jeans and a T-shirt and finished a breakfast of dry toast and scrambled egg whites as she waited for Reese to arrive, grateful this Saturday was one of the two she took off every month. Between Norris and the feelings she didn't want to feel for him and Reese and her troubled tone, she didn't have anything left for her clients and their problems.

The ringing doorbell announced Reese's arrival. Dahlia moved to the door and pulled it open. "Hi, Reese, come in."

"I hope my coming over isn't a problem," Reese said, making her way to the living room couch.

"Not at all. Do you want anything? Juice? Some breakfast?"

"No. I ate a little something earlier."

Dahlia sat. "You sounded a bit out of sorts earlier. What's this about your mother?"

Reese shrugged and pulled on a lock of her curly hair. "I don't know. She talked about my father last night."

Dahlia maintained what she hoped was a noncommittal expression as she listened quietly.

"For years I asked her about him, and she sidestepped every time. It got to the point I stopped asking. But last night she brought him up, and she's anxious we meet. He's in Denburg."

"This isn't a good thing for you? You said you asked her about him. Now's your chance to get to know him."

"I'm confused about the timing. She was very evasive, Dahlia. I think something's wrong with her."

"Wrong? What do you mean?"

"I think she's sick." Tears streamed unchecked down Reese's cheeks. "Why else would she want me to meet him?"

"Hey now." Dahlia pulled a tissue from the box on her coffee table and dried away the tears. "Reese, don't worry yourself needlessly."

"I can't help it." Reese pulled a tissue and blew her nose. "Something's going on."

"I know you're confused, but don't let your confusion stir up needless fears. Do you really think your mother would keep the fact she's sick from you?"

"I don't know, Dahlia. I know something's up."

What was up was Gail hadn't told Reese about her trip to Uganda. She would visit her friend to find out why. "What's up is you're finally meeting the dad you always wanted to know," Dahlia said. "Maybe that might explain her behavior. This is a change for her, too."

"She never told him about me."

"How did you feel to hear that?"

"Surprised. Hurt. I always figured he didn't want to be a part of my life because I'm black, and Mom stayed quiet so I wouldn't feel bad about being abandoned by him. I guess I can't feel that way now."

"You guess?"

"I'm still black. To find out he has a sixteen-year-old is a shock, but the rest of it . . ."

"You think he'll have an issue with your race?"

"Don't you think so?"

Dahlia had to bite her tongue to keep from screaming "Absolutely not!" Race was one problem Reese didn't have to be troubled about where her father was concerned. Dahlia would have to find a way to get Reese to lose that worry without divulging her connection to Norris.

"Your mom wouldn't want you to meet someone who had an issue with you. And if your father had an issue, we'd have nothing to discuss right now, would we?"

"I guess you have a point. Mom said he was a nice guy."

"There you go." Dahlia draped her arm around Reese's shoulders. "It's Saturday, and you don't need to waste this beautiful spring day fretting, as my grandma says. Catch up with Diana and go to the mall or something. Be a teenager. When you get to be an old lady of thirty-six like me, you'll look back at this time and be glad you enjoyed it."

Reese nodded and smiled. "All right, I'll do that." She pulled Dahlia into a hug. "Thank you for talking and listening. It helped a lot."

"I'm glad. You take care."

Dahlia showed Reese out and then placed a call to Gail. The women exchanged pleasantries and agreed to meet for lunch. Gail mentioned something pressing she wanted to discuss with Dahlia. Considering Norris's revelation, Dahlia didn't have to wonder about the nature of the pressing matter.

Following a workout and shower, Dahlia dressed for her lunch with Gail at Corlino's Kitchen. The phone rang as she walked to the door. Dahlia looked over her shoulder, and after a short debate, decided to answer the call.

"Hello."

"Hi, Dee. It's been a while."

Dahlia grunted. She would learn to check the caller ID before answering. "I can't talk now, Leslie."

"Are you saying that because it's me?"

"I'm not particularly interested in talking to you, but I was heading out the door."

"You still sound angry," Leslie said.

Dahlia rolled her eyes, galled by the statement. "You slept with my husband!" She sucked in a breath in an attempt to calm her fury. "I have every reason to be angry with you."

"It's been years, Dee. A lot has happened."

"Not enough. I don't have time for this right now, but I have your number. When I'm ready to talk, you'll hear from me."

Without another word, Dahlia slammed down the phone. Memories of Leslie and Jonah going at it like jackrabbits played in her head. She rubbed her temples. If she needed a deterrent to relationships, that memory provided it. No strings equaled no hurt, and she would never allow herself to be hurt again. Tonight, she would remind Norris why their arrangement worked.

CHAPTER 6

"Don't all speak at once," Norris said, when the quiet around the kitchen table got too loud for him to take.

"You have a daughter?" Ryan said, as Lara stared at Norris unflinchingly.

"Finally, some words." Norris pushed aside the cup of coffee. The vanilla flavor was more than he could stand. "Yes, I have a daughter. I promise, I'm as surprised as you both."

"How could that have happened?"

Norris pursed his lips as he glanced at the belly of his best friend's wife. "I think you know, pal."

Lara touched Ryan's shoulder. "I think what he's saying is that you're so cautious."

"Exactly," Ryan said. "Now you're saying you have a baby."

"No, I didn't say I have a baby," Norris corrected. "What I said is I have a daughter. She's sixteen."

Ryan's eyes widened. "Years old?"

"That's right. Remember back in college—Dr. Gail?"

"Doctor . . ." Ryan's jaw dropped. "Are you serious?"

"Very."

Lara turned to Norris. "Who was this Dr. Gail?" She raised a brow. "You didn't sleep with one of your professors, did you?"

"No, Gail is an M.D. She helped me with a baseball injury."

"And then you helped yourself to something. You were in college and she was a doctor. Your Mrs. Robinson, huh?"

Norris smiled. "Yeah, I guess you could say that."

"How did you find out about this?" Ryan asked. "Didn't she move away?"

"To New York state. But now she's back in Denburg, with my daughter. My beautiful daughter." Norris smiled.

"You've met her?"

"Not yet, but I've seen a picture."

Lara shook her head. "Wow. I can't believe this."

"You could have knocked me over with a feather when Gail told me the news. I don't know what I'm feeling more: happy, surprised, or angry. She waited sixteen years to tell me. And get this, in two weeks she's getting married and she and her new husband are leaving for Uganda for six months to do relief work. Leaving yours truly to be daddy."

"She's giving you time to bond?" Lara said.

"That's the idea, but only if Reese agrees. If not, she'll have someone in place as a guardian and I'll still have freedom to see Reese whenever I want."

"You and Dr. Gail have a child." Ryan paused for a moment and raised an eyebrow. "You told your parents yet?"

"No," Norris answered flatly. "I don't quite know how to break that one to them."

"I would think they'd be happy to know they have a grandchild," Lara said. "Your brother and sister aren't married or seriously involved, and since you're not exactly the settling down type, this news should make them happy."

Norris and Ryan burst into laughter.

"Lara, sweetheart, you have no idea," Ryan said.

Lara looked from Ryan to Norris and back again as the chuckling continued. "What am I missing?" she asked.

"The little fact Dr. Gail is African-American."

Norris nodded as her surprised gaze fixed on him.

"Your daughter's biracial?"

"Yes," Norris answered.

"Hmmm?" Lara rubbed her chin. "What is Reese's last name?"

"Elders," he said.

Lara snapped her fingers. "Ryan, I think we know her."

"You do?" Ryan said.

"Yes. Diana's friend. The one Justin has the crush on. Her name is Reese Elders."

"That beautiful girl? Oh, there's no way she can be Norris's daughter."

"Ha-ha. The fact you acknowledge she's beautiful is all the proof you need to know she's mine," Norris replied. "You say you know her?"

"Unless there's another Reese Elders in Denburg, who's sixteen and has these familiar gray eyes, I think so. We've only met her a couple of times, but since Justin spends so much time at Celeste's with Billy, he sees her quite often..He thinks she's . . . What does he say, Ryan?"

"'All that,' dear," Ryan answered.

"Yep, that's it. Does Reese know about you?"

"I honestly don't know what she knows," Norris answered. "But if Gail is consistent, Reese doesn't know very much. All the more reason I think I should get to know my daughter before I introduce her to the loving grandparents."

Ryan rested a supportive hand on Norris's shoulder. "No wonder you were in such a hurry to leave the restaurant last night," he said. "You've got a lot to deal with."

"And Reese is just a part of it," Norris said.

"A part? There's something else?"

"Sure is, bud. This is the biggest surprise of all."

"Bigger than having a teenage daughter?" Lara said.

"I'd say so." Norris smiled as the mere of thought Dahlia filled his heart with happiness. "I've fallen in love."

"I'm not late, am I?" Dahlia asked as she settled into the chair across from Gail.

"No, I'm a little early," Gail answered, closing the menu. "That's a lovely blouse. Lime green looks great on you."

Dahlia smiled. "Thanks."

"I'm glad we could meet, Dahlia."

"Me, too, Gail. I must admit, I had ulterior motives."

"Really?"

"Yes."

The conversation halted when a waitress approached with a pitcher of ice water. Both ordered chicken parmesan and resumed their discussion when the young redhead left.

Gail sipped her water. "Ulterior motives, huh? What's on your mind, Dahlia?"

"In a word, Reese. She came by my place this morning."

"I see." Gail dabbed her lips and draped the white linen napkin over her lap. "She told you about her father?"

"She did. I can't help but wonder why you didn't tell her about him sooner. She said she'd asked about him."

"Countless times," Gail admitted. "But the timing wasn't right to tell her."

"And it's right now?"

Gail nodded. "For many reasons, yes."

"Are you sick?"

"Sick?" Gail's confusion erased what little doubt Dahlia had in that being the reason for her sudden need to tell Reese about Norris. "No, I'm perfectly healthy. Why would you ask?"

"Because Reese thinks you're sick. You didn't tell her about Uganda, did you?"

Gail's mouth hung open. "How did you know about that?"

Dahlia grunted. Sometimes her mouth got ahead of her head.

"The only person I told was . . ." Gail gave her a pointed look. "You know Norris," she said.

Dahlia nodded. "Yes, I know him."

"Well, well. That's a surprise."

"No more than learning you share a past with him."

"You two must be pretty close for him to tell you about Reese and me."

Dahlia reached for her water glass and drank. The last thing she wanted was to be grilled about Norris and forced to think about feelings she shouldn't be feeling. "It's not what you think, Gail," she said.

"Oh, no? What am I thinking?"

The waitress returned to the table with steaming breadsticks and salad. Dahlia breathed in the scent in of the freshly baked bread. Today food would be a welcome distraction.

She reached for a breadstick. "These are delicious."

"You're avoiding my question," Gail said.

"Not at all. Norris and I are . . ." She thought long and hard as she searched for the right answer. Acquaintances? No. You wouldn't tell an acquaintance a significant secret. Lovers? Uh-uh. Too much information. "We're friends," she said.

"Friends?"

"Well, friendly. He's a friend of a friend. I'm going through an audit, and my client Lara Andrews is married to his best friend, so she recommended Norris to me." That wasn't a lie, she just didn't mention meeting Norris prior to the recommendation. "Now, back to Reese," Dahlia said. "Why didn't you tell her about Uganda?"

"I'm trying to ease into it."

"She thinks you're dying, Gail. Easing isn't working."

"I knew this would be hard, but not quite this hard."

"You have to talk to her."

Gail pushed the salad around with her fork. "I know."

"You said there was something you needed to discuss with me," Dahlia said. "I imagine it's about Reese and Norris."

"Yes." Gail dropped the fork to the plate. "I have a huge favor to ask of you, and as much as I want you to agree to it, I don't want you to feel pressure."

"Sounds serious."

"It is," Gail said. "I might want you to take custodial guardianship of Reese while I'm in Uganda."

"Custodial guardianship?"

"I know this must come as a surprise, but I trust you and Reese adores you. We've known each other for years, and . . ."

"Wait," Dahlia interrupted. "What about Norris?"

"I want him to spend time with Reese, and her living with him would be ideal, but I can't force a father/daughter relationship between them. Their closeness is going to take some time, and if Reese doesn't want to live with him, I wanted her to be with an adult she was close to. Knowing you and Norris are . . ."

"Friends," Dahlia readily said.

Gail smiled. "Friends. I think your presence will be even better. You'll be a bridge for them. Being friends of his friends is a plus. Reese will have more people to help with this transition. So, will you be that second option?"

"This is a big deal, Gail, but I understand the importance of Reese and Norris getting to know each other, and I want to help however I can." She nodded. "Yes, I'll be her guardian if she doesn't want to stay with Norris."

Gail squeezed Dahlia's hand. "Thank you. Worrying about Reese is a given, but now I won't be quite as worried."

"Are you going to talk to her tonight?"

"Yes, I'm going to tell her everything. Now, you tell me everything." Gail smirked. "What's with you and Norris?"

"There's no me and Norris."

" 'The lady doth protest too much.' "

"No protesting. It is what it is. He's helping me."

Gail laughed. "I'm sure."

"The story is you and Norris. How did that happen?"

"It just sorta did."

"He told me you were his E.R. doctor."

"I was. And a few days later we were playing doctor." Gail chuckled. "Bet you didn't expect that from your Sunday school teacher."

"Not at all."

"Norris was so attractive, young and hormone-driven. My biological clock kept me awake nights, and when I saw him that loud tick was silenced. I used him. He was my unwitting accomplice in becoming a parent."

"You didn't feel bad about not telling him?"

"Not at the time. He was twenty, and nowhere near ready to be a parent. I didn't want nor expect him to be."

"You just wanted a sperm donor. You tricked him."

"I'm not going to apologize for wanting a child. And I wanted to see the actual father, not a little vial. I should have told him, but he wasn't ready for the responsibility of fatherhood, and I didn't want to thrust him into the role."

"But you want to now?"

"A lot of years have passed, and I know I was wrong. Norris has grown up, and from what I can tell, he's settled down. When I talked to him yesterday, I knew something in his life had changed, and now I know that change is you."

Dahlia sighed deeply. Was she wearing some invisible sign that said 'mention the feelings I don't want to think about?' "Gail, why do you keep . . ."

"You can deny it all you want, but you and Norris are more than friends, and pretty soon you'll have to deal with it."

Don't I know it. Dahlia pinched off a piece of bread and popped it into her mouth. *Don't I know it.*

CHAPTER 7

Norris bounced the basketball over to Ryan, but what he really wanted was to throw it at his face. From the moment he confessed to falling in love, Ryan had been wearing a goofy grin, and after two hours, Norris was a little sick of it.

"Maybe next time I won't share such pertinent life information with you." Norris frowned at Ryan. "You want to stop grinning already?"

Ryan chuckled as he dribbled around the concrete half-court in the backyard of his spacious two-year-old house. He circled around Norris and tossed him the ball. "Say it again. Say 'I've fallen in love.'" Ryan's smile grew wider. "Mmm, mmm, mmm. There's something about hearing those words coming from you."

"When did Lara say she'd be back?"

"Just before Sue gets back with Angelica. And since Justin's with her, we'll have all this bonding time to talk about your love. Umph." Ryan shook his head. "Your love? I never thought I'd be using those words about you."

"Me, either." Norris shot a midrange jumper that found the bottom of the net with a soft swoosh. "Norris Converse does not fall in love. At least he didn't before Dahlia Sinclair."

Ryan rebounded the ball and laid it back up. "How did that happen?" He passed the ball back to Norris.

"I don't know. The last couple of weeks, I've just been thinking about her more. When I'm awake, when I'm asleep. I want to make up excuses to call her, and I don't need excuses."

"Because of this arrangement you have?"

Norris's shoulders slumped. "Yes."

"Why do you say it like that?"

"Because it's not about sex for me."

Ryan raised a curious brow. Norris tossed the ball back at him and walked over to the picnic table a few feet away. "It's about more than sex," he said, sitting on the edge of the table.

"How do you know?" Ryan rolled the ball under the table and sat on the other end. "How do you know you're in love?"

"I told her about Reese before I told you."

"You were stressed and seeking comfort sex."

"I didn't sleep with her."

Ryan's brow lifted. "Come again?"

"Being with Dahlia last night wasn't about sex. I wanted to talk to her. I needed to tell her about my daughter. Last night was the most incredible experience I've ever had in my life, and I was fully clothed the whole time. We talked, and laughed, and listened to each other. I've never felt so close to a woman. I need Dahlia, and that—that's scary."

"Oh, my—" Ryan's eyes widened. "You are in love."

Norris nodded. "Yes, I am."

"When are you going to tell her?"

"I don't know if I can, or should."

"You love her. Why not tell her?"

"Because our arrangement is what it is. It's not about feelings. It's not supposed to be. I'm in love with her, but I don't know that she's in love with me."

"You think she could be though, right?"

"I want to believe it, but like Lara said, Dahlia's had a lot of hurt in her life. That's why she's turned off on relationships. She's confident, but a little bit afraid. She's lost a lot of weight, and I think a part of her doesn't think she's worthy of love because her husband cheated on her. Talking with her last night told me the pain is still there. I'm not exactly Mr. Commitment. How can I want her to love me, to ask that she love me, when I know it will hurt her?"

"I . . . I can't believe what I'm hearing from you. I never doubted you were capable of love, but I never believed you would realize it. Norris, you love Dahlia, and you need to tell her."

"It's not that simple, Ryan. It's not just me anymore. For Dahlia to be with me the way I want her to be means she has to embrace my daughter. A teenager I've never met."

"But the fact you want Dahlia in your life as more than a pit stop is huge. You know what you want, Norris, and you're not a man used to not getting what he wants. You want to connect with your daughter and you want a real relationship with Dahlia." Ryan grabbed Norris by the shoulder. "For God's sake, man. You go and get it!"

"Go and get it?" Norris sighed. Ryan's impromptu pep rally sounded good, but winning this prize wouldn't be easy. "How am I supposed to do that? I've never had to fight for a woman's affection."

"That's because affection implies feelings, and for you it was never about emotions, just physical gratification. Dahlia is different. You need to change your game plan. It's time for Norris the playboy to meet Norris the romancer."

"Woo her?"

"At the very least. What do you want from this relationship? I'm talking end game."

Norris smiled. "I want . . . I want what you have. A wife I'm madly in love with, wonderful children, and a happy home. Not a bachelor's condo, not a revolving door of women, but a home. Something I've never had. That's what I want. I want it with Dahlia and Reese."

"There you have it. It's yours for the taking, Norris. You just gotta go out and get it."

After a helpful meeting with friend and Attorney Dan Monroe about paternal rights, Norris drove home prepared to talk to Gail about their daughter. He definitely wanted to see Reese, and considering he'd been robbed of years of her life, Gail was in no position to argue with him. The anger he felt when he thought of the time he'd missed with his daughter set him on edge, but he vowed not to be short when he phoned Gail.

The clean scent of carpet powder and wildflower air freshener greeted Norris when he walked into his place. His housekeeper, Mrs. Castanza, had been there. The sixty-year-old grandmother had been in his employ for twelve years, taking care of all the necessities a busy bachelor on the move could not. A note on the desk said she'd gone out for groceries and would be back soon. Maybe he'd have enough time to give Gail a call before Mrs. Castanza returned and got on him about being too thin—any man without a pouch hanging over his belt was too thin to her—and not having a steady girlfriend. Norris realized he would forever be too thin for her liking, but perhaps that steady girlfriend problem could be rectified soon.

Retrieving Gail's business card from the dresser, Norris punched in the numbers to her cell phone and got an answer on the third ring.

"Hello."

"Gail, it's Norris. I think it's time I met Reese."

"That's good to hear. I'll try to arrange something soon."

"I don't want you to try. I expect the three of us to have brunch tomorrow. You pick the location, and I'll be there."

"Norris, look, I . . ."

"No excuses, Gail. I've missed sixteen years, and I won't miss any more. Call me later with the details."

Norris hung up before Gail could offer a protest. If she truly wanted him to have a relationship with Reese, arranging brunch shouldn't be a hardship.

With the first step in getting closer to Reese taken, Norris turned his attention to the important first step with Dahlia. He needed to tell her how he felt, but he didn't want to scare her away. She still had very real pain from her divorce, and getting her to see love didn't have to hurt would be his challenge.

Besides being the first woman to find her way into his heart, Dahlia was the first woman to find her way into his head. She challenged him, made him laugh, and made him want to know every detail about her. She excited him, and not just in the bedroom. The idea of spending a lifetime with her was all the incentive he needed to give winning her over a try. He only hoped she would want to be won.

Reese returned home to find her mother sitting on the couch, looking as strangely serious as she had the night before.

"Were you waiting for me?" Reese asked.

"Yes, I was," Gail answered. She patted the spot beside her. "Join me."

Reese sat. "This is the talk, huh?"

Gail nodded. "I saw Dahlia today," she said, taking Reese's hands in hers. "I'm sorry you thought I was ill. I should have been more up front with you, but I didn't want to pile on too much at once."

"So, you're not sick?"

"I'm the picture of health, baby, really."

Reese sighed in relief. "Thank God. So what's with all this talk about my father?"

"I've mentioned Ben's desire to do relief work in Africa."

"Yeah, and I think it's great."

"It is great. A lot needs to be done over there, and they need all the help they can get. Ben's leaving for Uganda after the wedding, and I've decided—"

"Whoa!" Reese broke in, getting a sinking feeling where this was going. "You're not going with him, are you?"

"Sweetheart, I know this is sudden and unexpected, but I need you to understand."

"Understand what? You leaving me to run off to Africa with your new husband! I guess that explains your sudden urge for me to know my father."

Tears filled her mother's eyes. Regret grabbed Reese by the throat. "I'm sorry, Mom. I should've said that better."

"People don't tend to think when they're angry."

"I know, but I'm sorry I hurt you. It's just . . . You have to know how this looks to me. You're leaving the country at the exact time you decide it's time for me to know my father."

"You're right, Reese, this looks one way, but my decision to go to Africa came after I decided it's time you met Norris."

"That's his name? Norris?"

"Yes, Norris Converse. He's an accountant in town. You need to know coming to this decision wasn't easy. I struggled with this, but I realized it was something I had to do." Gail pressed her hand to Reese's cheek. "I'm so selfish when it comes to you," she said with a kiss to Reese's forehead. "For sixteen years I had you to myself, and even when you asked about your father, I fought you. I didn't want to share you. I realize I was wrong, but it doesn't make sharing you easier."

"Mom . . ."

"No, let me finish. Self-reflection can be very hard, especially when you find things you don't particularly like. I've made some mistakes in raising you, in keeping your father from you, and I'm trying to make that right. You need to know Norris, and I need to let that happen without interfering the way I know I would if I were around. Baby, I don't want to do this, but I need to. My saving grace is knowing you'll get to know your father while I'm in Africa helping to save lives."

Reese clasped her hands around her mother's. "Mom, you're working under the assumption that my father, this Norris, wants to get to know me. Maybe he doesn't."

"No, he does. He wants to have brunch with us tomorrow."

Reese sighed. Meet her father tomorrow? She released her mother's hands and eased further down the couch. This was happening way too fast. "I don't know about all this."

"Reese, I would never entertain the notion of leaving you if I thought for one second you wouldn't be in good hands."

"But these hands belong to a stranger, Mom. You only knew him for a short while, and I don't know him at all."

"You're right, my time with Norris was short, but it was profound. It gave me you." Gail smiled. "As nervous as you are about this meeting, I'm sure Norris is feeling the same."

"I guess he might be feeling more. I always knew he existed, but he never had a clue about me."

"That's another reason I think my going away is important. Six months won't make up for the sixteen years he's missed, but it will give you both some much-needed time alone."

Reese groaned as butterflies flitted in her stomach. "This alone thing, Mom. Do you really think that's a good idea? If we're both nervous and tentative, how are we going to get any bonding done? Will we be living together?"

"I've thought about that. I do want you to spend time with Norris, and living together is a consideration, but if you're not comfortable with that, I've made arrangements for you to stay with Dahlia. But you have to make yourself readily available to Norris. That's the deal. You okay with that?"

"Do I have a choice?"

"No."

"I enjoy being with Dahlia, so I guess I can live with those terms. When are you leaving for Uganda?"

"Right after the wedding."

"And you'll be gone for six months?"

"Yes."

Tears filled Reese's eyes. "Oh, Mom."

"It's okay, baby." Gail brought Reese into an embrace. "I'll miss you, too. But the time will fly by. It'll be through summer and I'll be back soon after you get settled into your senior year. I hate I'll miss your birthday this year."

"But you'll return a few weeks later, and that'll be the best belated birthday present ever."

"So, you're okay with all this?"

"I can't say okay, Mom, but I'm willing to try." Reese sighed. "I guess there's only one thing left to ask."

"What's that?"

"What time is brunch tomorrow?"

CHAPTER 8

Wearing her sexiest dress and most winning smile, Dahlia pushed Norris's doorbell and waited for him to answer. The approval-filled eyes and big smile that greeted her moments later confirmed the powder blue sundress with its deep neckline and high hem as the perfect choice.

Dahlia smiled. After hearing Gail's conviction that Dahlia had more than friendship with Norris, she wanted something that would bring their relationship back to its basis. Norris's reaction to this outfit told her she'd done just that.

"You going to invite me in?" Dahlia said, when it appeared Norris would keep her standing outside as he shamelessly ogled.

Norris blinked the lust from his gray eyes. "I'm sorry. Yes, come in." He took her hand and escorted her inside. "Have I told you how incredible you look?"

"Not with words." Dahlia laughed. "I'm glad you approve." She moved to the comfy leather couch and crossed her legs, exposing even more of her thighs to his unwavering eyes.

Norris growled. "Is it your intent to drive me crazy?"

She beckoned him over with her forefinger, and flashed her most provocative grin. "You tell me."

The role of aggressor wasn't unfamiliar in her arrangement with Norris, but in her only other physical relationship, the one she'd shared with Jonah, she had never been so brazen. With Norris she could be this uninhibited woman, but just chaste enough to come across as an innocent temptress.

Smiling seductively, Norris joined her on the couch. The warmth of his breath tickled her neck as his fingers slowly trailed along her cheek, eliciting tingles down her spine and a soft moan from her lips.

Desire darkened his smoky eyes. "Dahlia, I've been thinking about you all day." His lips nuzzled her neck while busy hands slid up the skirt of her dress, caressing her thighs. "You smell so good, and you feel even better."

His lips claimed hers in a slow, intoxicating kiss. Her tongue met his, willingly surrendering to the quiet demand of shelter in his warm mouth. Cinnamon flavored his tongue, making his fiery kisses even more so.

"Mmm. Mmm." Norris pulled away. "This is really nice," he murmured, "but I want us to talk before things get too intense."

Dahlia groaned. That was the last thing she wanted to hear. It was talking that got them into trouble. "We talked last night, Norris. Tonight is about the arrangement."

"I want to talk about that, too."

His finger brushed her cheek and he gave her that disarming smile. Those damn tingles returned. She shouldn't be feeling tingles from a smile and a touch. She wanted to tell him that, but the way her heart raced made her doubt she could get a word out. Then, again, she didn't want to talk.

Dahlia curled her arms around his neck, bringing his lips crashing down to hers. No more talking. Talk was overrated. She kissed his neck, loosening his shirt buttons.

Norris moaned. "Dahlia," he said, reaching for her hands. "I want to tell you something about my daughter."

Dahlia left his neck and met his gaze. "What is it?"

"I talked to her mother today. With any luck, I'll be having brunch with them tomorrow." He grinned. "I'll finally get to meet my daughter."

Dahlia smiled at his happiness. "That's great, I know how important this is for you."

"It really is."

Norris's excitement about meeting Reese made it clear to Dahlia she had to tell him about her relationship with the girl and her mother. "I need to tell you something," she said.

"You can't wait to have your way with me?" He laughed. "Ms. Sinclair, you've not made that a secret."

"Guilty." She laughed. "But there's something else. I suppose I should have told you this last night, but it didn't feel right."

Norris rested his arm along the back of the couch, drawing the heat of his body closer to her and giving his magnetizing aftershave the opportunity to weaken her like an invisible gas. "What is it, Dahlia?" His gaze held hers with an intensity she'd never seen before. "You can tell me anything."

Dahlia's heart pounded so hard she thought she would pass out. *Get yourself together, girl. Vulnerability is not your friend.* She pulled away, pressing her back flush to the couch. "I know them," Dahlia said. "I know Reese and Gail."

Norris blinked. "What?" he said just above a whisper.

Dahlia couldn't tell if he hadn't heard what she said or was surprised by it. "I said I know Reese and Gail. They're clients and friends."

"Wait a second. You knew about her and didn't tell me?"

"No, no, no. I didn't know you were her father until you told me last night. I wanted to say something, but I didn't want to put myself in the awkward position of answering questions for you that I had no answers to. The call I got this morning was from Reese. And after learning what I had, I needed to talk to her. I wanted to make sure she was all right."

"You two are close?"

She nodded. "We are. She's like another niece to me. My brother's children are in their teens, but since Quentin's a serviceman and constantly moving, I don't see them very often. Reese is such a sweet girl. It was easy to get close to her."

"She was upset when she called you. How is she?"

"She's good. Better. Dealing with everything and what it means. I told her to go out and have some fun."

"With Diana Monroe."

Her eyes narrowed. "How did you . . ."

"Lara mentioned they were friends. I saw her father later on, and he told me they were together."

"I'm sorry I didn't tell you about my connection to them, Norris, but it just felt like the best thing to do."

"It's okay. I understand."

"Do you?"

"Yes." He smiled. "You're Switzerland—-neutral ground."

"That's exactly what I am. I'm glad you understand."

"Sweet Dahlia, it's easy to understand things with you."

Norris pulled her from the couch and crushed her body to his, kissing her like a man possessed. Never breaking the kiss, he directed her to his bedroom. Dahlia drew closer to him, drowning in his scent, reveling in the majesty of his touch. Her heart might be in a battle with her head, but her body knew exactly what it wanted. And in this moment, that was all that mattered.

Only when they reached the bed did Norris release Dahlia's mouth. He watched, transfixed, as her tongue slid against kiss-swollen lips. His flesh tingled. How he wished at that moment those lips were his. He pressed his hand against her face, staring deeply into her eyes. "You take my breath away."

Dahlia sighed softly. The expressiveness of her brown eyes got him every time. They said so much more than she ever allowed her words to say. For the last several weeks, he'd been struggling with how to deal with the feelings he'd developed for her. Now, as he gazed into those telling eyes, he saw the truth she seemed determined to keep secure deep within herself.

Norris recalled earlier in his living room when for a split second he thought Dahlia would speak the words he'd been longing to hear. She didn't make that much hoped for confession, but instead admitted to having a relationship with his daughter. The woman he loved already loved his daughter. All the ingredients they needed for a happy future were laid out before them. Friendship, respect, attraction, and the deep but unspoken love they had for each other. Everything he wanted was within his reach, he just had to hold out his hand, and convince Dahlia it wouldn't hurt to take it.

Norris slipped his fingers under the straps of Dahlia's dress and slid them off her shoulders. He had to make her see that acknowledging those ingredients, this relationship, wasn't a bad thing. Tonight, he would show her that it wasn't.

Easing the straps further down her arms, Norris watched the delicate fabric fall away from her body, exposing her full breasts to his feasting eyes. Dahlia stepped out of the heap around her ankles and kicked four-inch heels from her feet. Only a scrap of lace he could hardly call panties rested about her hips.

Norris engaged in a shameless sweep of her body. From the bright red polish coating the toenails of her pedicured feet, to her luscious, long legs, curvy hips, ample breasts, and saucy smile. His arousal throbbed desperately in his slacks, aching for the relief he would find in the heaven between her thighs.

Dahlia took a couple of steps forward, loosening the buttons on his shirt. Her sweet lips trailed along his chest, greeting every inch she exposed with a feathery soft kiss. Norris managed to keep his buckling knees from giving way when her palms brushed his straining arousal in an attempt to relieve him of his belt. Her every touch turned him on more and more.

Yearning to feel Dahlia's soft body pressed against his, Norris stripped the clothes from his body and crushed her to him, kissing her hungrily, passionately.

He lowered Dahlia to the bed, raining kisses along her neck and shoulders. She moaned his name. He trailed lower, taking an erect nipple between his lips, suckling one and then the other, enjoying her blissful cries. Led by his tongue, Norris continued on his journey. He poked inside her belly button and then lingered around the waistband of her sexy underwear.

Peeling the panties from her waist, Norris lowered the scant material down her legs and to the floor. Dahlia's knees bent and her thighs parted in silent invitation. He grew harder as her spicy sweetness beckoned to him. Heeding her call, he reached inside his nightstand drawer and pulled out a condom.

"Let me help you," Dahlia said, removing the foil package from his hand.

Deep moans rumbled in Norris's throat, the feel of Dahlia's soft hands against his raging length driving him crazy. With the condom in place, Dahlia guided him into her waiting heat, inch by inch, until he filled her completely. Her arms curled around his back.

Norris stayed motionless inside for a long moment, enjoying the feel of her velvety warmth all around him. Dahlia whimpered beneath him, but he wouldn't move. He closed his hands about her waist, halting her desire to move.

"Norris, please."

He nuzzled her neck, remaining embedded inside her. "Please what?" He pushed inside her. "This?"

Dahlia closed her eyes, moaning. "Oh, Norris."

He thrust again. "This?"

"Yes!" Her short fingernails dug into his back.

"Yes?" He delivered another long stroke.

"Oh, yes, Norris. Yes."

Norris freed her waist and their bodies moved together, finding an immediate rhythm in the age-old lover's dance. Dahlia's legs closed around his waist, pulling him in deeper with every thrust of his hips. Norris smiled into her neck. She wasn't about to let him stop now.

Their bodies moved with expert precision. Dahlia held fast to his backside, meeting his every thrust as though she knew his movement before he made it. As many times as they'd been together, it had never been like this. They were joined as one, moving as one, loving as one.

Norris turned on his back, holding Dahlia in a close embrace as their bodies continued to stroke. Dahlia's whisper soft kisses dusted his neck and trailed down his chest. His body trembled with the feel of her tongue against his nipple. He whispered her name. His movements increased.

Dahlia buried her face in his neck, gently nipping at the skin. His hands cupped her backside, maintaining the tempo of their bucking hips. He brushed his lips over her shoulder, his trailing tongue mopping the tiny beads of sweat salting her skin. Release neared with every thrust of their hips, and when he reached nirvana, Norris wanted Dahlia with him.

His hands on her hips, Norris flipped Dahlia to her back and entered her with renewed urgency. His lips found hers, squelching her cries with a deep kiss. Their tongues connected, mating as frantically as their joined bodies.

Dahlia nipped his lips and arched her back, bringing him as far as he could go. Norris pushed into her once more, crying his release as Dahlia did the same. Their bodies crashed to the bed, their breathing heavy, labored.

Minutes later, his body still tingled from his earth-shattering release. If he knew this was what love did, he would have been open to the idea a lot sooner.

"Somebody took vitamins," Dahlia said between breaths.

Norris laughed. "So it was good for you, too?"

"Good?" She closed her eyes, purring like a content kitty. "Good doesn't begin to describe it." She snuggled against him, kissing his chest. "That was so much better than good."

"For me, too." His fingers combed the flattened curls of her hair, while the fingers of his other hand twined with hers. "It was different this time." He kissed her nose.

"You can say that again."

"No, I mean it was *really* different. The most incredible and unexpected kind of different."

Dahlia's body ·tensed against him. She released his hand and eased up, holding a pillow to her chest. "Norris, the sex was wonderful, but . . ."

"Sex? Dahlia, I know you've been fighting what's been happening between us for a while. I have, too, but what just happened here was more than sex. We connected on a totally different level tonight. We made love."

"Norris—"

"No, Dahlia, you said it. What we just shared was incredible. Can you imagine how much more incredible it would be if we stopped pretending things haven't changed?" His fingertips slid along her arm. "Things have changed."

Dahlia jerked her arm away. "Stop it, Norris! I don't want to do this. I'm not pretending anything. I like things the way they are, and I want them to stay that way."

"What way? It's not no-strings sex anymore, Dahlia. I can't undo this and make it something else. I love you."

"Damn it, Norris! Why did you have to say that?"

He shrugged. "I don't know, because it's true."

Dahlia shook her head. "You ruined it." She left the bed and reached for her clothes.

"Ruined it?" Norris pulled up, stunned by her reaction. "What are you talking about? Dahlia, where are you going?"

"Home." She slipped on her panties and pulled on her dress. "You changed our arrangement, Norris. It was supposed to be two consenting adults giving and receiving physical pleasure."

"Having sex!" he barked.

"Okay, having sex. Whatever it was, it didn't entail feelings." Dahlia stepped into her shoes and trailed her fingers through her hair, bringing life to the curls of her short style.

"I didn't plan to fall in love with you, Dahlia. I never expected to fall in love with anyone. You think it was easy for me to say those words to you?"

"It seemed pretty easy to me."

"Couldn't have been too easy. I didn't hear you saying them back! But that's okay, because you showed those words to me in this bed. We were of one mind when we were of one body. You can deny it all you want, but I know the truth."

"That's your truth, Norris, here's mine. We're over!"

Norris left the bed and stepped into his slacks, shaken by her words, but not deterred. "You don't mean that," he said.

"I do."

"You say a lot of things, but your eyes give you away."

Dahlia dropped her head. Teardrops fell to the floor.

"You're crying because you know I'm right. You care about me. Hell, you love me. I know you're scared to trust and you've shut yourself off to relationships because of what Jonah did, but . . ."

"No buts, Norris." Dahlia's teary gaze met his. "You're right. I'm turned off on relationships. I never denied that. We were on the same page when we started this. Because

you want to confess feelings doesn't mean I do. I don't."
New tears filled her eyes. "I can't."

"Dahlia." He reached out to brush away the tears, but
she stepped back.

"We're over, Norris."

"Uh-uh." Norris shook his head. "I won't accept
that." He said the words calmly, but felt anything but
calm with the threat of tears burning his eyes.

"You don't have a choice!" she shouted, racing out of
the room before he could offer a rebuttal or get his feet
to move. Moments later the front door closed behind her.

Norris dropped to the bed. *What just happened here?*
Ryan's words of advice seemed to mock him. Norris
mumbled an expletive and fell backward on the bed. Hot
tears burned down the sides of his face. So much for
telling Dahlia how he felt.

Dahlia raced up to her bedroom, tossed her purse on
the bed, and headed straight for her Jacuzzi tub. If ever
there was a time she needed the comfort of the bubbling
jets and steamy water, it was now. She should have
stopped by the grocery store and gotten some chips, too.

Why did he say it! Dahlia groaned as the tub filled
with hot water and foamy suds from the drops of
lavender bubble bath she added. *Why did he have to say
it!*

Dahlia slid into the frothy water and rested her head
on the bath pillow. She closed her eyes, trying to enjoy

the constant force of water pounding against her body, but thoughts of Norris and his pounding force inside of her kept interfering. Their sex life had never been bad, but tonight . . . Tonight he had loved her. And she'd felt loved. Cherished. Desired. The same things she'd felt with Jonah that had left her devastated. Love hurt.

Why did he have to say the words? Why did hearing them make her feel so good? Who was she kidding? She knew why.

A romantic at heart but a realist in practice, the idea of love made her happy and hopeful, but the pain of love kept her feet firmly planted. Waves of euphoria didn't define love, and tingles of pleasure didn't sustain it. Love equaled pain. Trusting someone with your heart meant it could be smashed to smithereens. She didn't want that anymore, and Norris had never wanted it. At least that used to be the case.

Believing Norris could have feelings for her when she stood deep in denial about the feelings she'd developed for him was one thing, because moments of hypothetical what ifs didn't matter. But hearing these words straight from his mouth made it a truth she didn't want to deal with, because as much as she tried to fight it, Norris was right. This man who loved African art and leather furniture and who doted on himself and his best friend's children had stolen her heart. She had fallen in love with him, too.

CHAPTER 9

"Norris, this is a surprise." Lara's bright eyes dimmed when she peeked out the door around him. "You're alone?"

"More than you know," he answered, stepping into the house. "Your *husband* around?"

Lara chuckled. "My husband? Ryan is giving Angelica a bath. What's with the tone?"

"I have a lot on my mind."

"As well you should. I haven't been able to stop smiling since I heard about you and Dahlia. Why didn't you bring her?"

"Why? That would be your husband's fault."

"There's that word again. Are you angry at Ryan?"

"Yes." Norris plopped to couch. "I should have never listened to him."

"Listened to him about what? What's wrong?"

"Everything," he said, the word coming out strangled as he fought the resurgence of tears.

"Ryan!" Lara cried, waddling over to the couch and sitting. "Ryan, come out here!" She took Norris's hand in hers. "What happened?"

Ryan raced into the room with an underwear-clad Angelica padding behind. "Lara, are you okay?" he asked as Justin rushed in behind him equally alarmed.

"Mom, what is it? Are the babies coming?" said Justin.

"No, Justin, I'm fine. It's Norris."

Ryan placed his hand over his heart. "Babe, are you trying to scare me to death? I thought you'd gone into labor."

Justin nodded. "Me, too," he added.

"I'm sorry I scared you, but Norris has scared me. He's upset about something." Lara touched his shoulder in an offer of comfort. "I've never seen him this sad."

"Sad?" Justin grunted. "With a hot daughter like Reese?" Justin plopped next to Norris on the couch. "Mom told me all about this great news. Uncle Norris, could you get her to stop treating me like a little kid? It's really annoying."

"Justin, you are a little kid," Ryan said. "And now is not the time to bother Norris with this. Go to your room."

"Aww, Dad. He can make her . . ."

"Justin," Ryan said more firmly.

"Oh, all right." Justin groaned, dragging off to his room.

Norris pressed a kiss to Lara's hand. "Thanks for your concern, Lara, but I don't want you worrying about me," he said. "I'll be fine."

Angelica walked over and touched his knee. "Uncle Norris, do you have boo-boo somewhere? You look like you have an owie."

Managing a smile, Norris brushed his finger against her nose. "I have a bit of an owie right in here," he said, poking his finger in his chest, "but a kiss from you can make it feel a lot better."

"All right." Angelica reached up and kissed his cheek. "You feel better now?"

Norris nodded. "I sure do."

Angelica smiled brightly. "Good."

Norris gave Lara a hand as she struggled to her feet.

"I'll finish dressing Angelica and give you guys some time to talk." She whispered something in Ryan's ear and then gave him a kiss when he nodded. "Angelica, tell Uncle Norris goodnight," she said over her shoulder.

"Night-night, Uncle Norris." Angelica waved.

"Goodnight, sweetheart. You sleep well."

Angelica walked over to Ryan. "You still going to tell me a story, Daddy?"

"Sure will, precious. I'll be there in a little bit."

She nodded and took Lara's hand. "Come on, Mommy."

Ryan made his way over to the couch after Lara and Angelica left. "I take it things didn't go well tonight," he said.

"Considering your three-year-old figured out I had an 'owie' just by looking at me, I'd say that's a pretty good assumption."

"What happened?"

"I followed your advice. Dahlia came over, we were together and everything was so . . . It was fantastic."

"So?"

"I told her how I felt, and she flipped. She said we were over and she left."

"You just let her walk away?"

"Let her? I didn't *let* her. I poured my heart out to her. I said things I can't believe were coming out of my mouth. And she didn't take it well."

"Oh, man, I'm sorry."

Norris grunted. "You ought to be. It was your rotten advice that caused this."

"I guess that's what Lara was talking about. You blame me for this."

"So that's what the whispering was about. Humph. I should have known."

"She was worried about you and wanted to give me a heads up. You're in pain right now, so I'll take your anger, but you can't tell me you're sorry you told Dahlia how you feel."

"I'm not sorry, but had I known what her reaction would be before I told her, I think I might've reconsidered." Norris took a deeper dive in the pool of self-pity he'd been swimming in for the last two hours. "I lost the woman I love before I even had her. Now I don't have anything."

Ryan groaned. "Please, spare me an invitation to your pity party, Norris. You're hurting right now, but your pain will lessen. In the meantime, you still have a lot in your life."

"Yeah? Name one thing. And don't say money. I'd give every dime I have if it meant I could have Dahlia."

"I'll tell you what you have, Norris," said Lara, returning to the living room and settling on the couch between him and Ryan. "You have a daughter, you have us, and you have two, soon to be four, godchildren who love you. As for Dahlia, I think you should give her more time."

"That all sounds good, Lara, and I do appreciate you, Ryan, and your family. But my daughter is still a stranger to me, and Dahlia seems content to live the rest of her life without me being a part of it."

"Has love made you a quitter, Norris?" Ryan asked. "I've never seen you give in so easily."

"And I've never had what feels like a Mack truck slam into my chest. Experiences change people."

"They do indeed, and people are also responsible for seeing if those changes are positive or negative. You can control that. Don't you want to try? Or maybe you don't think Dahlia's worth it. Maybe all that talk today about wanting Dahlia and your daughter in your life was just talk."

Reverse psychology. Norris smiled in spite of himself. "I know what you're doing, Ryan."

Ryan grinned as he curled his arm around Lara's. "Is it working?" he said.

Norris expelled a breath. "Dahlia's response today didn't make me happy, but I think a strong measure of her anger was from the fact she returns my feelings, and doesn't want to face it. I'm not going to give up on her." He smiled. "And I hope to have brunch with Reese tomorrow, so all is not lost. Thank you both for helping me to remember that."

Lara kissed his cheek. "You don't have to thank us, Norris. We love you and we want you to be happy."

"I know," he said, feeling better than he thought he could after the blowup with Dahlia. "I've not quite reached the level of happiness you and Ryan have, but I won't give up until I do."

"That's what I like to hear," Ryan said with a big smile. "You hungry? There's a pot of chicken stew on the stove."

"Chicken stew?"

"My wife wanted chicken stew, she got chicken stew."

Norris shook his head. "No thanks, bud, I'm good. What I would like is to read that bedtime story to Angelica."

"I'm sure she'd love it," Lara said.

Norris stood. "Good. My daughter isn't three, but it's good to know there's a sweet little girl who cares about me without reservation."

"Angelica knows you. When Reese gets to know you, she'll be as crazy about you as Angelica is."

Norris chuckled. "There's something to aspire to." He made his way into Angelica's room, stopping at the edge of the bed when his cell phone rang. His breath caught. *Dahlia?* "Uncle Norris needs one minute, Angelica," he said to the waiting girl.

She nodded and sat up in her bed.

Norris reached into his pocket and found Gail's number on the caller ID. Perhaps this was some good news. "Hi, Gail."

"Hello, Norris. I talked to Reese and she's willing to meet tomorrow at ten-thirty."

Norris smiled. "Okay. That's good," he said. "Thank you for this, Gail."

"Thank Reese. I wanted her to do this, but she's the one who's making it happen."

"I'll be sure to thank her tomorrow." Norris borrowed some drawing paper and a crayon from Angelica, jotted the address and directions to Gail's house, and folded the sheet into his pocket. "I'll see you both tomorrow."

Norris dropped the phone back into his pocket and made his way to Angelica's bed.

"You look real happy, Uncle Norris," Angelica said. "Your owie must not hurt anymore."

"To tell the truth, it does still hurt. But I think that owie and all the others will be all better real soon."

"Maybe this wasn't a good idea," Reese said, closing the curtain after peeking out the window for the third time in the last five minutes. She jammed her thumbs in the back pockets of her jeans. "I don't think I'm ready for this, Mom."

"You are ready, Reese." Gail placed her arm around Reese's shoulders and ushered her to the couch. "Norris is your father. You don't need to be nervous."

"Norris is a stranger. And father or not, I don't know him. I don't know if I'm ready to play nice."

"You shouldn't have to play. Norris has done nothing wrong. He just found out about you, and he's wasted no time in trying to get to know you. That should mean something."

Reese grunted. "It probably means he's expecting sixteen years' worth of Father's Day presents. He'd better not expect me to call him Dad."

"I think his only expectations are getting to know you and being friends."

Reese rushed over to the window when she heard a car pull up. She grunted. "He drives a Porsche?" She moved from the window and back to the couch. "Great. My father is some old dude who's trying to recapture his youth by driving a flashy sports car."

"Uhm, Reese, about that. Norris is . . ."

The doorbell rang in the middle of her mother's words. Reese held up her hand. "You don't have to say another word, Mom. I'll get it." She walked to the door and pulled it open. The tall, handsome, smartly dressed man standing on the other side was nothing like the balding, pot-bellied youth chaser she imagined, and not nearly as old. "I'm sorry, are you lost?"

"No," the man said. The sparkle in his gray eyes grew brighter by the second. "Reese, you're even more beautiful than your picture suggested. I'm Norris. I'm your father."

The butterflies in Norris's stomach grew more restless. He thought he'd feel less nervous after meeting Reese, but nothing could be further from the truth. Dressed casually in jeans and a pink pullover, Reese looked like the typical teen. But she wasn't typical, she was his, and that made her different. This tall, slim, beautiful girl was his daughter. His daughter.

The door opened soon after he rang the bell, but the look on Reese's face and her question to him made him think she was expecting someone else. *Was I lost?* What was that about?

"Is something wrong?" Norris asked. "I'm not early, am I?"

"No, you're not early, Mom just neglected to tell me something." Reese fixed unhappy eyes on Gail. "Isn't that right, Mom?"

Gail flashed a tight smile as she walked over to the door and welcomed Norris inside. "Let's sit down so we can talk."

Reese moved wordlessly around her mother and sat on the couch, her eyes trained on her lap.

"If you have any questions you can ask away," Norris said, settling into the end chair nearest Reese, watching her ignore him. "I'm anxious for us to get to know each other."

Intense quiet engulfed the room. Norris turned to Gail for some assistance.

"The albums," Gail said, walking over to a large, wine-colored bookshelf built into the wall. "I have lots of pictures of Reese growing up."

"Great. I bet you were a beautiful baby, Reese."

"You'd win that bet," Reese said.

"Reese!" Gail chastised.

"It's all right, Gail. She's just being honest."

"Here we go." Gail returned with three large albums and placed them on the brown leather ottoman that served as a coffee table and complemented the modern style wine-colored sofa and end chairs. "I think these would be a great starting off point in the journey of you two getting to know each other," she said. "In the meantime, I'll be in the kitchen preparing brunch."

"Wait!" Reese stood abruptly, taking her mother's arm. "You're leaving?"

"I'll only be a few feet away. I'm not needed here."

"Of course you are," Reese said, wrapping a finger around a lock of curly, long hair.

"No, I am not. You and your father need some time alone." Gail turned her attention to Norris. "Do you want anything to drink? Water, coffee, juice?"

"No thanks, I'm fine," he said.

"All right. Brunch should be ready in about an hour or so." Gail pressed her hand to Reese's cheek. "It'll be okay, baby."

Reese ambled back to the couch and sat, sighing.

Norris cleared his throat. "I understand how you feel."

"I don't think so," Reese said, still avoiding his eyes.

"Well, I suspect you're feeling ill at ease and a bit uncomfortable about being alone with a close family member you were formally introduced to only five minutes ago."

She looked at him and nodded. "I guess you do know."

Norris moved over to the couch. He thought to take Reese's hand, but decided that might be taking things a little too far too fast. At least she was looking at him now.

"Reese, when I found out about you I was surprised. Stunned, in fact. But after the shock wore off, it made me happy. Now, I don't have any preconceived notions for us and how our relationship will evolve, but I do know I want to be a part of your life, and I'm willing to take things at whatever speed you want."

"Real accommodating kind of guy, huh?"

"I like to think so."

If only he'd been that way with Dahlia last night. She still might have run, but at least they wouldn't have had a fight. He shouldn't have been so pushy, so insistent of her feelings for him. Somehow he would make this right. She hadn't answered his phone calls, but if he leaned on her doorbell, she would have to let him in. He loved her, and he couldn't give up without a fight. But first he had to make headway with Reese.

Norris tried to read her expression, but it remained noncommittal. "Are you willing to give me a chance?" he asked.

"I guess," Reese said. "I don't know what to call you."

"Norris is fine."

"May I ask you a question?"

"Of course. You can ask me whatever you want."

"How old are you? My mother is fifty-two. I don't think she looks it, but she's fifty-two. I find it suspect you both could defy time."

"How old do I look?" he asked, a bit surprised by her question, but hopeful her response to his wouldn't hurt his feelings.

"About thirty-five. I truly hope that's not right."

"It's not, but it sounded good." He laughed. "I turned thirty-seven a few months ago."

She gasped. "Thirty-seven? How did you meet my mother?"

"Gail didn't tell you?"

"My mother hasn't told me much about you, although I have asked more than once over the years."

"I got hurt playing baseball, and she was the doctor on call. I thought she was the most stunning woman I'd ever seen, and we ended up spending some time together. Time that brought me a beautiful daughter." Norris reached for an album. "Would you like to narrate the pictorial of your life to me?"

A dubious smirk curled her lips. "Is that your attempt at changing the subject?"

Norris laughed. Just sitting with Reese provided some insight into her. She was playful, just like him, and a little bit vain. "Yes and no," he answered honestly. "I don't have a problem telling you more about that time, but I think it would be better coming from your mother. I'm sure Gail will be more forthcoming with you now."

Reese nodded. "I guess you're right." She pulled the album onto her lap. "This is me from day one to age five."

"Reverend," Dahlia said with a smile as she reached her pastor, who was waiting at the church door.

"Dahlia, I was so glad to see you at services today. It's been a while," said Reverend Myles Leonard, pastor of Sweet Zion Baptist Church for the past forty years.

She hadn't stepped through the doors of the sanctuary in months—since Christmas service, to be exact. But after things imploded with Norris last night, she'd deemed the Lord's house the best place to be. It also provided an opportunity to escape the urge to return the numerous phone messages Norris left, insisting they talk.

"I'm sorry it's been so long, Reverend," Dahlia said.

He closed his hands around hers. "The tithes you send in every month are welcome, but we much prefer your presence."

"I know, Reverend. I've been . . ." *What? Busy? Fornicating like nobody's business with a man I didn't plan to fall in love with, and ending things immediately when he admitted he loved me?* That definitely wouldn't go over too well. "I've been caught up in a lot of things," she finally said. "But I realized when things get crazy in life, there's no place better than church."

"Amen, sister. Your parents and grandma should be coming in for the second service. They'll hate they missed you."

Dahlia nodded. She knew for sure her grandmother would hate she missed her, but her parents would just use the opportunity to get on her about Leslie. And she didn't want to have those hostile feelings in church. She would contact her grandmother later, but being 'talked to' by her parents didn't give her any thrill.

"I'll be sure to see them later."

"Will I be seeing you again soon, or should I just expect you the next quarter?" he asked.

Duly chastised, Dahlia managed a little smile. "I'll be better, I promise."

"Very good. May the Lord be with you, child."

Dahlia nodded and proceeded down the brick steps to her car, a black Jaguar she'd brought as a present to herself after she lost the weight. If she hurried, she could make it out of the parking lot before her parents pulled in.

"Dahlia!"

Oh, no! Dahlia turned in the direction of her approaching mother. With her bright yellow suit and feathered yellow hat, the small-framed Nona Sinclair looked more like a giant canary than vice president of the local community bank.

"This is a surprise." Nona kissed Dahlia's cheek. "You can sit with us. Your daddy is helping Mama out of the car."

"Actually, Mama, I was in early services, and was on my way home."

"Nonsense," Nona said, fanning her hand at Dahlia's words. "You'll join us for services and we'll have dinner together. It's been so long since we've shared Sunday dinner."

"Mama, I don't . . ."

"Dee, baby," said seventy-eight-year-old Flora Best, strutting down the blacktop parking lot with open arms and a black pillbox hat topping her snow white hair. "Come give me some sugar."

Dahlia moved around Nona to give Flora the requested hug and kiss. Her father, Wilson, approached from Flora's rear. "Hi, Daddy," she said, as she released her grandmother.

"Dahlia," said Wilson, his baritone voice, like rolling thunder, somewhat out of place in his average-size body, but perfect for the principal of the middle school. "Considering you're at church, I guess you must know."

"Know what?" she asked, looking from her father to her mother. "Okay, what's going on? Grandma?"

"I don't think she knows, Wilson," said Nona.

"Know what?"

"It's your sister," Flora said, taking Dahlia's hand into her wrinkled ones. "She's having some problems."

Dahlia laughed, loud and overly obnoxious laughter. "Are you surprised?" she said. "She hooked up with Jonah. What did she expect?"

"What she's expecting is a baby," her father said. "She's in her fifth month and she's having some medical problems."

Dahlia's head swam and her knees buckled, but somehow she managed to keep herself from kissing the pavement. She backed up to her car, leaning on it for support.

Children had been a dream of hers for a long time, and when things ended with Jonah, she'd convinced herself not having them had been for the best. But learning her sister was having the family she wanted with the husband she'd lost . . . It hurt more than she cared to admit.

"How long have you known?" Dahlia asked.

"A few weeks," Wilson said. "Leslie wanted to tell you on her own. In her own way."

Tears burned the backs of Dahlia's eyes, but she willed herself not to cry. Now she knew why Leslie had called. "So, uh, what's wrong?"

"Stress," her father said. "Her blood pressure has been erratic and she's been placed on bed rest."

"I'm sorry to hear that, but what do you want me to do?"

"Be her sister."

"Dahlia, I know you and Leslie have your problems," Nona added, "but . . ."

"Problems? Problems, Mama? I caught her in bed with my husband, in my house. The house I invited her to live in while she went to school. A house, I suspect, she's still living in. Now she's pregnant with said husband's baby and having problems. How is that my business? If you ask me, I think her chickens have come home to roost."

"Dahlia!" her mother shrieked.

"No, it's the truth. I could come up with dozens of clichés that would fit this situation, but I'm not going to be ugly. I have somehow found a way to move past this, and I'm not going to get sucked back into it. Leslie has made her choices, now she has to live with them."

Certain she'd recovered her balance, Dahlia walked over to Flora and kissed her cheek. "It's good to see you, Grandma. I'll be sure to visit more often."

"I look forward to seeing you." Flora pressed her hand to Dahlia's cheek, forcing their eyes to meet. "I understand, baby," Flora whispered, the intensity in her gaze reaching straight into Dahlia's soul, reading and feeling all the hurt and anger she tried so desperately to keep to herself. "I understand."

The emotions Dahlia thought she'd bottled up threatened to explode. Grandma Flora could break through her defenses like no one else, a big reason she'd opted for phone calls and not face-to-face visits since hooking up with Norris. Her grandma would call her on her emotions and dare her to lie. She didn't have to say a word, and her grandma knew how she felt. And she didn't judge or have expectations. She just cared.

"Thank you, Grandma," Dahlia choked out, before racing to her car and speeding out of the parking lot.

CHAPTER 10

"So, am I an only child?"

Norris almost choked on the coconut cake Gail had served for dessert. After a drink of water, he looked over at Reese, who stared unflinchingly at him. "I'm sorry?" he said.

"Do I have any siblings?" Reese clarified. "A little brother or sister?"

"As far as I know, you don't."

"You're not married?"

"No."

"Divorced?"

"I've never been married," he answered, suddenly wondering if he could rescind his 'ask anything' offer. He'd learned Reese had an interest in business, but with her ability to ask the tough questions, journalism seemed more appropriate. He'd also learned they both liked sports, specifically basketball and baseball, and shared a dislike of liver.

"Thirty-seven and never married. Do you have a fear of commitment? Hmm?"

Norris scratched his neck. "Actually, I . . ."

Gail held up her hand, halting his words. "Norris, please." She turned to Reese. "Honey, give it a rest."

"Mom, he said I could ask him whatever," Reese explained.

"Perhaps, but I don't think he expected you'd ask everything in one day."

"Am I being intrusive, Norris?" Reese asked, her bright eyes as sincere now as they were intense moments before.

"No. I don't want you to have any questions about me. It's just a little strange being asked so many in rapid succession."

"The lights getting a little hot, huh?" Reese laughed. "Don't worry, this can be a stopping point. I actually have other plans for today."

Though happy to be freed from the hot seat, Norris couldn't deny his disappointment at the thought of her leaving. They had made some progress, if that was the right word, and he wanted to spend more time with her. "You're going somewhere?" he said.

"Yeah. I . . ."

The doorbell rang in the middle of her words. "That's my ride now."

Gail stood. "You didn't tell me you had plans, Reese."

"When I got home yesterday, we got into some deep stuff, and I just forgot to mention it. Diana and I are going to catch a matinee." Reese opened the door. "Come on in, Diana. I just have to run to my room to get my purse."

"Okay," said Diana, entering the living room. She smiled at Gail. "Hello, Dr. Elders. I noticed the car outside and wondered . . ." She looked to the side. "Mr. Converse. Hi. I knew that car was familiar."

Norris waved. "Hello, Diana."

The oldest of the Monroe children, the pretty seven-teen-year-old had her mother's tall, slim frame, her father's honey brown complexion, and their shared love for the practice of law. Norris couldn't be happier his daughter had such a good friend in Diana.

Reese halted her trek to her room, and turned around, wide-eyed. "You two know each other?" she asked, wagging a finger between Norris and Diana.

"Yeah," Diana said, smiling. "Mr. Converse is a family friend. He's Ryan's best friend, and practically an adopted cousin." She laughed.

"Ryan?" said Reese. "Mr. Andrews?"

"Yeah." Diana moved to the couch and sat next to Norris. "What are you doing here?"

"I'm here to see Reese," he answered, clasping his hands and turning his attention to Reese, waiting for her to say more.

"Norris, uh, he's my father," Reese explained.

"What?" Diana shrieked, gazing from Reese to Norris and back again. "Mr. Converse is your long-lost father?" She turned back to Norris. "You?"

Norris smiled. "Surprise," he said.

"Reese, when you told me your father was in Denburg, I never thought for a second he was someone I knew."

"It gave you a leg up on me. At least you knew him. I only met him today," Reese said, shooting a stinging glare at her mother. "I'm going to get my purse, and then we can go." Without another word, she disappeared down the hall.

The room grew instantly quiet. Norris looked over at Gail. She tried to put on a stoic face, but her shiny eyes and quivering lip gave her hurt away. His heart went out to her. He understood Reese's anger, as he had some of his own, but . . .

He moved over to Gail and placed a comforting hand on her shoulder. "She's upset."

Gail nodded. "I know. Upset and angry. I've been with her for sixteen years. I know her temperament. She gets things off her chest, feels bad for lacking tact when she's doing it, and then apologizes. Reese is the most passionate and emotional person I know. She's also quick to apologize when she's wrong."

"Reminds me of myself."

"You two are a lot alike. And when it comes to this situation, I suspect you're both feeling a lot of the same things. I know you're still angry."

"I am, but I'm working through it. I know, and I know Reese knows, you did what you thought was best. It's hard to deal with, but being angry won't help."

"You are so grown up, Norris. But our daughter is sixteen, and as mature as she is, she's still young, and she has to work through her issues her way. Are my feelings hurt? Sure. But I think I hurt more because I know I deserve it, and in two weeks, I won't be here to take this anger she needs to get off her chest. I'll be in Africa with my new husband." Gail clicked her tongue. "I told you this wouldn't be easy."

He nodded. "Yes, you did."

Reese returned to the living room and walked over to Gail and Norris. Regret filled her sad gray eyes. "Mom, I'm . . ."

"It's okay, sweetheart," Gail said.

"No, it's not. I was out of line, and I'm sorry. This is all so much to take in at once, but I'm trying, I really am." She turned to Norris. "It was good meeting you. Maybe we could catch up again soon. Finish our Q&A." She smiled.

Norris returned her smile. "I would really like that. I enjoyed our time today."

"Me, too." Reese took her mother's hand. "I should be home around six or so."

"Okay. Do you have your phone?"

Reese touched her purse. "It's in here. And, yes, it's charged." She kissed Gail's cheek. "See ya later."

Norris found himself holding his breath when Reese turned to him and their eyes locked for an extended moment. For an instant he thought she would kiss his cheek, too. He wanted that, but instead she waved and said goodbye. He released the breath, feeling a bit foolish for wanting something he knew was too soon to hope for.

"You girls have a good time," he said.

"And be safe," Gail added.

"Will do," the girls chimed in unison.

Norris stared at the door after it closed behind Reese and Diana. "I wonder if I can do it," he said.

"Do what?"

"Get to know Reese as well as you. Earn her love."

"You will, Norris." Gail gathered the dessert plates. "It'll just take time. Today was a good start."

"I guess," he said, helping her with the dishes.

"I know," she replied. "You two hit it off pretty well. It'll only help more when she finds out about you and Dahlia."

The saucer in Norris's hand crashed to the shiny wood floor, breaking in four pieces. *Me and Dahlia?* He quickly gathered the shattered dish. "I'm sorry, it slipped."

"Uh-huh," Gail grumbled, her arms folded at her chest and doubting eyes boring into him.

Norris dumped the broken pieces into a waste can in the corner. "I'll buy you a whole new set of dishes."

"It's not the dish I was talking about."

"Then what *are* you talking about?"

"Norris, please. Dahlia and I had lunch yesterday."

Norris shrugged. "Dahlia?"

Gail groaned, exasperated. "Do you see the word 'stupid' stamped across my forehead?"

Norris moved to the couch and sat. He could continue this cat and mouse game, but as the running mouse, he could feel the cat's hot breath on his back. Gail appeared dead set on discussing this, but before he offered information, he had to know just what she thought she knew.

"You say you had lunch with Dahlia?"

"I did," Gail said, joining him on the couch. "And she was as mum about this as you, but the less she said, the more she told me. She mentioned Uganda. You and my fiancé were the only people who knew about that, and Ben and I decided to keep quiet until I squared things with you. Making you the only person who could have told her."

"Okay, I told her. I needed to share it with somebody."

"Somebody not Ryan?" she said, lifting a curious brow. "I know you two are still close, our meeting at my office said as much. So, not telling your best buddy this news first tells me there's someone very significant in your life."

Norris released a breath. *Caught.* He didn't even feel like denying it anymore. "Yes, Dahlia is important to me."

"How important?"

"Important enough for me to tell about Reese."

Gail tucked herself in the corner of the couch, crossed her arms, and stared with those questioning eyes. "Why are you two being so quiet about this? Dahlia is a wonderful woman, and you . . . My goodness, Norris, you are such a good, grounded man. Why are you guys being so hush-hush?"

"It's the way Dahlia wants it. As a matter of fact, she doesn't even want that anymore." Norris's guts clenched as he thought of the way they'd left things last night. He'd needed to tell her how he felt, and for that moment in time, her relationship issues didn't exist. They were of one mind. At least he thought they were. "She ended things," he said.

Gail shook her head. "That doesn't sound right."

"It might not sound right, but it's what happened."

Gail clasped his hands. "Norris, she cares about you. She didn't tell me so, but I know she does."

"I agree, but she doesn't want a relationship."

"I don't understand. Weren't you already in one?"

Norris stood, feeling the conversation going to a place he didn't feel comfortable going with Gail. "I should be going."

"Norris, I'm sorry if I pried, it's just . . . The idea of you and Dahlia . . ."

He held up his hand, stopping her words. "Look, Gail, there's no Dahlia and me. I'm not happy about it, but that's the way it is. I would really appreciate if you didn't mention this to Reese. I know she and Dahlia are close, but what we had . . . There's no point in talking to her about it. And don't talk to Dahlia about it, either."

"I won't mention it, but it might be a bit hard to keep it secret when Reese will be living with Dahlia."

Norris hid his disappoint at the announcement. "She will?"

Gail nodded. "She felt it would be best to stay with someone she knew, but she knows being available to you is the criteria. I hope you're okay with this."

"I'm a little let down, but I want Reese to be happy and I want to know her. So, if she wants to live with Dahlia, I'm okay with that." Norris made his way over to the door. "Thank you for brunch and allowing me the opportunity to meet Reese. Let her know I'll call her tomorrow." He turned around, eyeing the albums lying on one of the end chairs. "You think I could . . ." He motioned to the stack of books.

Gail walked over to the albums and gave them to him. "They're yours. I have duplicate copies of every photo she's ever been in."

Norris clutched the albums to his chest like the prized possessions they were to him. "Thanks, Gail, I'll be in touch." With a wave goodbye he got into his car and made his way to Dahlia's. Now it was time to make things right with her.

"I hope you don't mind skipping on the movie, Diana," Reese said, as she and her friend sipped strawberry lemonade at the Burger Barn. "I don't think I could've concentrated on the screen with everything going on in my head."

"No kidding. Mr. Converse is your father." Diana shook her head. "That blows my mind."

"How well do you know him?"

"Pretty well, I guess. He and my parents are friends, and I've been around him enough to gather he's a cool guy. Just never thought of him as the fatherly type, although he's great with Lara and Ryan's kids, and my brothers think he's a riot."

"Your family likes him?"

"Yeah. He's a friend." Diana made a hissing sound as she sucked in a breath. "I can't imagine him and your mother, though. How did that happen?"

Reese shrugged. That was one of the many questions she still needed an answer to. "I really don't know," she said, sipping more lemonade. "I know he's fifteen years younger than my mother and they met when she helped him after he hurt his hand. Mom never told him about me. Not until a couple of days ago. What kind of guy is he?"

"Run of the mill, I guess, except he's loaded."

"Loaded?"

Diana rubbed her fingers together. "He's rolling in it, but he's not overly flashy. He works at his accounting firm downtown, he has a condo, a Porsche, and a Benz. I can't think of much else."

"Is he dating anybody?"

"I don't know his personal business, but to hear my folks talk, he likes the ladies, and lots of them. And for an old guy, he's kinda hot. So, that makes sense."

Reese bristled. "Diana! What are you saying?"

"I don't want to jump his bones or anything. I'm just saying he's a nice looking old dude." Diana laughed. "You know, you look like him."

"That's kind of impossible. I'm black."

"No, you're more a warm honey pecan," Diana quipped.

Reese frowned at her friend. "You're having too much fun with this," she said. "I'm serious."

"What are you trippin' about?"

"I don't know." Reese groaned. "For so long I wanted to know about my father. Different scenarios of what he'd be like played in my head, but what I've thought and what I'm getting is . . . My mom is getting married in two weeks, and then she and Ben are leaving for Africa for six months. Leaving me alone to bond with my father. My white father. This man I don't know."

"That's where the bonding comes in. You get to know him. And why are you making race an issue?"

"I'm not making it an issue. I've always known my father was a white guy, but I never had to deal with that. My family has always been my mother's family. Black people. Now I'm going to have to address this other side of me."

"That's where Mr. Converse comes in. He's not just white, he's your father. You haven't known him your whole life, but he's always been a part of your life. And now you get to know about that part. Think of it as journey to another world."

Reese scoffed. "It's another world, all right."

"You met him today, what's your first impression?"

"He's okay, but he's trying too hard. He can't be himself if he's trying to make himself somebody I'll like."

"Does that mean you like him or not?"

"I don't know. I don't think he's a weirdo, but I do think he wants us to be some happy insta-family. Add Reese and stir."

"What's wrong with him wanting that? You're his daughter. You don't think he should want you to be a part of his life? You always wanted to know your father. Now you do. Don't look for ways to ruin it before you get a chance to enjoy it."

"Easy for you to say, you've always known your father."

Diana groaned, took a long sip of her lemonade, and then pushed the cup to the side. Reese sighed. The intensity and irritation in her friend's dark eyes told her she wouldn't like whatever Diana was about to say.

"You know what, saying you couldn't watch the movie was the only sensible thing you've said today. Your head is all over the place. Who are you angry with? Your mom for keeping Norris from you, or Norris for wanting to be a part of your life?"

"Both of them. Why couldn't they be like your folks, and have children when they were married, huh? That way I would've had the option of meeting them at the same time. But me, I know my mother sixteen years, and then I meet my father, who I'll have the pleasure of spending the next six months with, without my mother, getting to know."

"I think your parents are handling this the best they can. I promise you this: If I had cut Celeste Monroe the look you shot your mother before you went for your purse, my teeth would be on the floor, and the rest of me would be in the middle of next week. What were you thinking?"

"I wasn't." Reese toyed with the straw in her cup. "I was upset, and I apologized for that. I already feel bad, and you're making me feel worse."

"No, what I'm trying to do is make a comparison. You get away with a lot because your mother, for whatever reason, kept your father's identity from you. And because of that, I suspect she feels obligated to take your smack. That wouldn't fly in my house, because neither of my folks have any guilt in regard to their children. I'm your friend, so I don't feel bad about telling you what I see. You need to cut your parents some slack, and at least try to see things from their point of view. It's obvious they're bending over backwards to do that for you."

"I should be more open?" Reese said.

"Try. This isn't just new for you. At least you've always known your father was out there. Mr. Converse never had a clue you existed. And look at him; he's trying. That's got to count for something. Plus, I'm here for you. He knows me, and all my family in Denburg. We're all connected. Heck, we're practically family now, Reese. Getting to know your dad will be a good thing."

"You make it sound like it could be."

"Take my word for it." Diana smiled. "Something else you can take my word for." She nudged her head toward the door. "Jack Armstrong is crushin' hard on you."

Reese's heart pumped triple time. *Jack Armstrong!*

"No, no," Diana said, grabbing Reese's hand before she turned around. "Don't look."

"Don't look?" Reese whispered. The cutest, smartest, most popular boy in school had just walked into the restaurant, and her best friend had confirmed a hope she'd harbored for weeks, him to be interested in her, and now she couldn't look at him? "Why can't I look?"

"Because he's coming over." Diana brushed her hand over her long ponytail. "Just stay cool," she said.

A brief shadow covered the table and then Jack came into view beside Diana. Six feet, one hundred seventy pounds of beautiful, brown muscles showcased wonderfully in a tank shirt and knee-length shorts. Full smiling lips displayed perfectly straight pristine white teeth, and hazel eyes sparkled against his sweat-glistened skin. Reese reached for her cup, taking a long sip of the fruity lemonade. If she didn't know better, she'd swear she was having a hot flash.

"Hello, Diana," Jack said, his unwavering gaze on Reese.

"Hi, Jack," she said, grinning at Reese before reaching for her cup. "I'm going to get a refill."

Without breaking eye contact, Jack slid into Diana's chair. "Reese, how are you doing?" he said.

"Good," she squeaked out. "You?"

"Okay, just getting in a run. Decided to dash in for a cold drink. That's been my best move all day." He smiled.

Reese's heart leapt into her throat. Her lips curled in response. If Jack taking a first step toward her could make her feel this good, meeting her father halfway in their journey to forming a familial bond could only make things easier for them. She couldn't make any promises, but with Jack's smile urging her on, she was certainly willing to give her father a try.

Two hours of homebound solitude provided Dahlia the opportunity to shed her tears, shout out her frustrations, and dive headfirst into a bag of chips. It all helped, but now she had to deal with the guilt. She sighed. Why was she the only female offspring of Wilson and Nona Sinclair who had a conscience? Dahlia tossed the empty bag and the mountain of crumpled tissues into the trash. "Treadmill, here I come."

The doorbell rang as she made her way upstairs to change out of her church clothes and into workout clothes. Her heart slammed against her chest. That was Norris. She could feel it. A part of her, a huge part, wanted to pull open the door, leap into his arms, and never let him go. But a smaller part, the more vocal part, reminded her of how she'd spent the last two hours, and why seeing Norris wouldn't be a good idea.

Norris knocked on the door. "Dahlia, I know you're in there. Please let me in. We need to talk." He knocked again after a few moments. "Please."

After arguing with herself about the many reasons she shouldn't open the door, Dahlia pulled it open and stepped back. She immediately regretted her decision upon seeing him standing there. Norris was too handsome and her emotions way too rocky to deal with him now.

His face lit up, making her want to slam the door even more. She was not strong enough to deal with him now.

"I knew you were in there," he said.

"You were right," Dahlia said, fighting her natural response to smile back, well aware encouraging him would not be wise. "I really don't think this is a good idea."

"I do." He moved forward, but she blocked his way. Norris sighed. "You're not going to let me in?" His gaze swept over her. "Why are you dressed up? You going somewhere?" He looked closer. "Were you crying?"

"Norris."

"No." He bullied himself in. "I'm not leaving until you tell me what's wrong."

Dahlia closed the door and followed him to the couch. "What are you . . . You can't just barge into my house!"

"I've already done it." He sat. "Are you going to tell me what's wrong, or am I gonna have to pry it out of you?"

"Oh, like that love I'm supposed to be feeling for you after you bared your soul last night? You can't make me do or feel anything, Norris."

His face reddened. "Okay, okay. Maybe I deserve that. But as well as I know something's bothering you, I know you love me. I don't doubt that for a second."

"Is that why you're here? To get some heartfelt confession out of me?"

"Only in my dreams," he said, settling back on the couch. "No, I came here to apologize. I was a bit brusque last night."

"Is that what you were?"

"I'm not apologizing for what I said. I'm apologizing for how I said it. I never imagined I would tell any woman I loved her. It just wasn't something I thought was in me. But, Dahlia, for the past couple of weeks, there's been a change."

She held up her hand, using her open palm as a force field to shield her from Norris's words and everything he made her feel. "Norris, please. We've done this."

"No, we haven't. When we were together in my office on Friday, I wanted to say it then. I felt the words bubbling in you, too. I kept quiet for one reason, the same reason I've forced myself to be quiet for so long. Because I didn't want to have my words push you away. I know you've been hurt, and you've sworn against relationships and love, but we have a relationship, and we *are* in love."

"Damn it, Norris! Stop it! I cannot do this today." She stomped to the door and whipped it open. "Leave!"

"No." Norris moved to the middle of the floor, his arms crossed. "What's bothering you? I want to believe it's just me, and what happened between us last night, but not even I am that vain. Something's hurting you, and I'm not leaving here until you tell me what it is." He waved his hand in a motion for her to close the door. "If you want to share your air-conditioning with all of Denburg, feel free. But I'm not going anywhere."

Dahlia stayed motionless for a long while. Hearing Norris, but not wanting to hear him. Needing him, and hating she did. Loving him, but wanting to scratch his eyes out for making her deal with love when she didn't want to. Loss of control. That's what love did to her. And she was supposed to be happy about it?

The clack of Italian loafers against her hardwood floor signaled Norris's approach. Dahlia stiffened when she caught a whiff of his cologne, even before the heat of his body burned against her back. His breath tickled her neck as he reached around her and pushed the door closed. Her knees buckled. If he touched her, she would crack. She would lose the last bit of strength keeping her together and fall completely apart.

"You're going to talk to me, Dahlia."

Her body trembled when his hand slid down her arm, and the dam holding back her tears broke completely. Instead of fighting and fleeing, she gave in. Turning into Norris's open arms, Dahlia wrapped her arms around him and took comfort in his soothing words. His arms tightened around her. Dahlia drew closer. And for the first time since hearing her sister's news, even through her wracking sobs, she felt happy.

CHAPTER 11

"I made you some tea," Norris said when Dahlia returned from changing out of her Sunday finest and into the customary jumbo T-shirt and spandex joggers that made up her workout gear. "It's that mint and lemon flavor you like." He offered her a steaming mug. "I didn't add anything to it, but I brought out a couple of those yellow packets you use."

"Thank you, Norris, but you didn't have to do this. I told you I was fine."

"Yes, you said that, but I wasn't totally convinced."

"It's the middle of the afternoon on a warm spring day, and you're offering me hot tea. Who's the one having issues here?"

Norris smiled. In hindsight, maybe the tea wasn't his swiftest move. "It sounded like a good idea when I did it," he said. "I thought it would calm you."

"I'm calm now."

"Why can't I believe that?"

"I don't know. Don't I look calm to you?"

"You look resigned."

"I am." Dahlia stood and kicked up her left leg, holding it against her backside and stretching. She reversed the action with her right leg. "Now, I'm going to work out."

"Burn off the chips, eh?"

"You were rifling through my trashcan?"

"Didn't have to rifle. The empty bag is barely covered by that half box of tissues you have piled on top of it. Tears and chips? Not a good combination for a self-proclaimed chipoholic."

"Sometimes a girl's got to do what a girl's got to do," she said, leaning into toe-touches.

"Hey." Norris took her hand and brought her beside him on the couch. "I don't want to keep you from your workout, but I'm not leaving here until you talk to me. I know you don't want me to care, but I do. The sooner you tell me, the sooner you hop on your treadmill."

"Fine, fine." Dahlia expelled a breath. "This morning I went to church and my parents told me my sister is pregnant."

"Sister? You've talked about your brother, your Grandma Flora, and your folks, but you've never mentioned a sister."

"We aren't close."

"That's fine, but to never mention her?"

Dahlia sighed, loudly.

"Look, I'm sorry. I'm just surprised to learn—"

"That I have a sister? That's just it, Norris. We don't really know anything about each other."

"We know quite a lot about each other, and I don't only mean what we like in bed."

"Norris, you were hit with some unexpected news. You have a daughter, and all of a sudden you want to be daddy and confess love. This is a phase."

Norris shook his head. "No, no, no. I'm not going there with you. I know what I'm feeling, so I'm not going to argue with you about that. Besides, we were talking about you and your sister. Why is her being pregnant upsetting to you?"

"She's having problems. Hearing about it made me feel bad."

Norris waited. There had to be more to it. "And?"

"*And?* That's it. I felt bad."

"Bad enough to come home, cry, and eat a six-ounce bag of chips, but not bad enough to get on the phone and call her to make things better?"

"What makes you think I didn't call her?"

"Because had you called her, the fact she's having a problem pregnancy wouldn't be what's bothering you, it would be that you had a fight."

She frowned. "You think you know it all, don't you?"

"Not yet," he answered with a smile. "But I am a quick study of all things Dahlia Sinclair, and I won't be satisfied until I have my Ph.D. Why don't you and your sister get along?"

Dahlia shook her head and walked to the door. "Sorry, that's a class for another day. You wanted to know why I was upset, and I told you. Now, you have to stick with your end of the deal." She pulled open the door. "I'm fine."

His eyes raked over her. "Yes, you are that," he said, getting the smile from her that he wanted. "I'm done pushing." He held up his finger and leaned into the doorjamb. "However, I also came by to let you know I met Reese today."

Dahlia's face brightened. "That's right! You said you hoped to meet her today." Dahlia's hands wrapped around his, making him wonder why he didn't share this news sooner if this was the response he would get. "What do you think?"

Norris looked at their joined hands and then into her eyes. "I think she's as wonderful as you said she would be." Dahlia smiled and he smiled back. "We still have some getting to know each other to do, but we're both willing to try."

"That is good to hear."

"Gail told me Reese will be staying with you."

"I didn't know it was finalized, but you'll be able to see her as often as you want. You'll have complete access."

"I appreciate you saying so." Norris pulled her hands together and held them between his. Dahlia's happiness for him and Reese was sincere, but pain still lurked in her eyes, and it broke his heart. "Is there nothing I can do for you? I hate seeing you upset."

"I'll be all right, Norris." Dahlia freed her hands from his. "Don't worry about me."

"Too late." Norris leaned forward and softly kissed her lips. "I can't help it."

"Norris." Agnes stuck her head in his office door. "I'm about to go grab some lunch. You want anything?"

"Do I want anything?" Norris sighed and turned his attention to the window behind his desk. Happy couples and playing children filled the corner park across the street. It made him both hopeful and miserable. "Agnes, I want so many things, but nothing you can get me from a lunch counter."

Agnes groaned. "Oh, for goodness sake." She closed the door and bounded over, blocking his view. "What is wrong with you? Ms. Sinclair doesn't need any more consultations?"

He frowned. "Not funny."

"It wasn't meant to be. I don't think I've ever seen you so pitiful."

Norris clicked his tongue and faced the desk. "I'm not pitiful."

"No, just in love." Agnes moved around the desk and sat on the edge. "Are you ready to admit it?"

"I thought I was when I did it Saturday night, but Dahlia has me all but convinced I was wrong about that."

Agnes's green eyes lit up. "You told her?"

"Yep. She was incensed. She's not interested in being in love."

"That may be, but she does love you. I can tell."

"You can tell? You've only been in her company once."

"I saw how she looked at you, and I'm not a fool. I know full well what was going on in this office. I've known you for fourteen years, and I've never seen you captivated. Not until this past Friday when I watched you watching her. And that look didn't just happen. How long have you been seeing her?"

"A couple of months," he confessed.

"You're not giving up on her, are you?"

"No way." Norris thought of the twelve bouquets of flowers he had arranged to be sent to Dahlia's salon today, and the twelve messages explaining why he loved her and always would. Dahlia being the beautiful contradiction she was, he could see her frowning on the outside, but beaming on the inside with the arrival of every colorful display and its heartfelt words. Ryan had said woo, so he would woo. "She's worth fighting for."

"Is that why you were out yesterday? Working on ways to win her favor?"

"No, actually, yesterday I was working on winning the favor of another beautiful woman." He reached in the breast pocket of his dress shirt and extended a recent picture of Reese. "Congratulate me. It's a girl. Her name is Reese."

Agnes gasped. "Well, shut my mouth! She's such a pretty thing. And she has your eyes."

Norris smiled proudly. "Yes, she does."

"How did . . ."

"Compliments of Dr. Gail Elders," he explained, receiving the picture. "She told me Friday. That's why she wanted to see me. I saw a designer yesterday and got some work started on a room for Reese. Gail's getting married next weekend and leaving for Africa right after. She'll be gone for six months, giving me time to get to know my daughter better."

"Reese will be living with you?"

He sighed. "No. But I want to be prepared in case she decides to sleep over. I'm a little nervous about it all, but I'm looking forward to it. She's a wonderful girl, Agnes."

"I bet so. You're just so proud, Norris."

"I am. I'm just getting to know her, but she reminds me of myself."

Agnes raised a brow. "She's not vain, is she?"

Norris erupted in a loud, telling laugh.

"Oh, Lord. Two of you?" she grumbled in good humor.

"What can I say? She appreciates her great genes."

"It's good to see a splash of happiness in your eyes, Norris. I'm glad your daughter can do that for you, and I know Ms. Sinclair will be doing it for you soon, too."

"I don't know about soon, but I'm willing to keep at this until I make her mine forever."

Because without "u," beautiful would not exist in my world.

Dahlia wanted to roll her eyes at the cheesy scrawl beneath the eleventh flower card titled "Why I Love You," but she couldn't help being affected. No one had ever done anything like this for her, and as touched as she was, she couldn't show her emotions in front of the salon ladies. She could imagine the talk at dinner tables tonight. Especially Mrs. Flo's.

"You know, some man sent Dahlia a million flowers today. Some secret admirer. I bet it's Baxter the product distributor. He's always grinning at her."

Baxter was definitely sweet on her, but if the idea of a twenty-something hunk of dark chocolate showing interest could get tongues to wagging, learning about Mediterranean-meets-Midwest millionaire Norris Converse would bring on the vapors.

Dahlia tucked the card in her purse, along with the other ten, and breathed in the fragrant mix of roses, lilies, and peonies in crystal vases on her desk. The news of her sister having her ex-husband's baby still had her reeling, but Norris transforming her beauty shop into a flower shop definitely gave her a needed lift. Even when she didn't want him to, which was most of the time, he found a way to lift her spirits. She sighed. *Why did he have to be so wonderful?*

A knock on the door jostled Dahlia from her thoughts. "Come in," she said.

Lara peeked her head inside. "Hey. You up for some company?"

"Of course." She smiled, waving Lara in.

"Wow," Lara said, taking in all the flowers. "Most people would ask who died, but I know better."

"I'd say you do." Dahlia helped her pregnant friend into a chair. "You've talked to Norris, right?"

Lara nodded. "He came over Saturday night. Dahlia, he . . ."

"Lara, I know what you're going to say."

"Okay. And?"

"I can't do this. I have too much going on, and a relationship is not something I want distracting me."

"Love is never a distraction, Dahlia. And Norris does love you. The idea of saying love and Norris in the same breath is mind-blowing. I've known him for almost five years, and I see a change in him."

"Yes, there's a change. He's a father now."

"It's not only Reese, and you know that. He's happier, and it's because of you. Everything has come together for him."

"See, that's it. I can't be a part of his everything." Dahlia put on her best straight face and prepared to give the speech she'd been unsuccessful at getting Norris to listen to for more than a second. "I don't want a relationship. I never promised Norris anything, and I can't."

"Can't or don't want to? You've been pretty happy, too. Except before, I didn't know Norris was the reason why."

"We had an understanding, Lara."

"Sometimes the heart has its own ideas."

"Heart. Love. Relationships." Dahlia looked at all the flowers and remembered Norris's sweet words. Her stomach did the fluttery thing that reminded her of how weak she was and how being weak invariably led to pain. She sucked in a breath and met Lara's gaze head-on. "I've had my fill of these things, Lara, and I don't want any more."

"Love is sweeter the second time around."

Dahlia scrunched her face. "I think that's generally used when you fall in love with the same person twice."

"Blech!" Lara shuddered as if she'd been offered a plate of fish guts. "Let's change what it means for this instance, okay? What I'm saying is, if you allow yourself to feel, in spite of your fears, it could be a wonderful thing."

"And it could be devastatingly painful. I'm not knocking love, Lara, it's just not for me."

A rap on the door broke the conversation. "More flowers," said Marci, bringing in a vibrant bouquet of tiger lilies and setting them on the file cabinet. "I do believe your secret admirer has purchased every flower in the city of Denburg and possibly a few surrounding counties." She smiled at Lara. "Hello, Mrs. Andrews."

"Hi, Marci. How are you?"

"The question is how are you?" Marci touched Lara's belly. "It must be exciting expecting twins."

"Double the pleasure, double the fun."

"Double the pain and double the diapers." Marci shook her head. "No thanks. But you do look wonderful."

"I feel wonderful. Thanks."

"Oh, before I forget." Marci handed over the card. "Here you go." She waved good-bye and went about her way.

Lara pulled herself out the chair. "Hmm. You might think love is not for you, but I think Norris is going to do everything in his considerable power to change your mind. I, for one, hope he succeeds," she said, smiling. "Take care."

Take care? Dahlia groaned as she stared at the unopened card. How was she going to do that with Norris drowning her in flowers and singing her praises? Why couldn't he just be angry and ignore her like any other man in his position would?

She snatched open the card. "I chose these flowers for their fiery color, and sent them last because I knew you'd be feeling pretty angry right now. Beautiful and fiery—note the symbolism here." Dahlia rolled her eyes at his smiley face. "I know you're angry, and I'm sorry, but I love you, Dahlia, and you're going have to deal with what that means. N."

A single tear slid down her cheek. She knew what it meant. And that's why she couldn't do it again. She just couldn't do it again.

Norris checked his watch. Four-thirty. His fingertips tapped an anxious beat on the desk. He thought Dahlia would have called by now, for if nothing more than to tell him to give it up after all the flowers, but she didn't call. His tapping increased. She couldn't ignore him. He snatched up the telephone handset. He wouldn't let her ignore him.

Just as he'd punched in the first six digits, there was a knock at the door.

"Norris," said Agnes, sticking her head inside, "you have a visitor."

The goofy grin on the woman's face had to mean one of two things: Reese had arrived or . . .

Dahlia appeared at the door, looking very cute in blue jeans and a yellow baby-doll shirt. Norris's agitated anxiousness dissipated. Smiling, he walked over and ushered her in. "Thanks, Agnes, that will be all," he said, closing the door on his beaming assistant before turning all his attention to Dahlia. He wanted to take her in his arms and kiss her until her toes curled, but figured that response might be a bit strong after everything that had happened. So he smiled at her, feeling like a lovesick schoolboy.

"I'm so glad you're here," he said. "You look calmer than you did Sunday. Have you talked to your sister?"

"No, I haven't, but I don't want to talk about that. Norris, about the flowers and the cards . . ."

"I wanted to do something nice for you, and tell you again how I feel."

She dragged her hands over her face, groaning. "That's just it. I don't want to hear about feelings. I don't want to read about them . . ."

"You don't want to think about them. I know, I know," Norris broke in, feeling as frustrated as she looked. "But guess what, you have to. Because they exist, and not talking about them won't make them go away."

"Norris, what we've shared these last couple of months has been great, but . . ."

"No buts. It's been great. It is great."

"It was great. It's past tense now. You made it so."

"By saying I love you?"

"You don't love me, Norris. You're caught up in a moment. For over two months we've been enjoying each other's company. A no strings, carefree physical relationship. *Physical.* It was sex. That's all it was supposed to be."

"Things changed, Dahlia."

"You just think they have. It's understandable. You have this new responsibility with Reese, you're a father now, and it makes you want to create this life you think she should have."

"You think I told you I love you because of Reese?"

"Nothing else makes sense. We have what can only be described as earth-shattering sex, and the next minute you're professing love to me the day after you find out you have a daughter. Woman plus child equals family."

Norris laughed. "You must've stayed awake all night thinking up that one. My question is, do you believe it?"

Dahlia stuck out her chin and crossed her arms, looking a lot more confident and determined than Norris believed she felt. "It's the truth," she said. "Why wouldn't I believe it?"

"Why? I'll show you why."

Norris pulled her close and claimed her lips in an intoxicating kiss. He expected to find resistance, but she offered none. Dahlia melted in his arms. The soft curves of her body molded against his. Desire stirred in his loins. It never took much effort for her to get him in the mood, and now was no exception.

Dahlia's hands slid over his back, moving to his backside. A moan rumbled in his throat as her lips left his and moved to his neck. She nipped at his earlobe before bringing it between her warm lips and suckling softly. His moans grew louder and his knees weaker. He closed his hands around her waist, pulling her closer to him. Letting her feel what she stirred in him.

"I miss being with you, Norris, and I know you miss me," she murmured against his ear. "Admit you were caught up in the thrill of the moment and let's get back to the way things were."

As if shut down by a power failure, Norris's "On" button flipped off. As much as he wanted Dahlia, and he wanted her, he wouldn't deny his love for her to make it happen. He stepped back and sat on the edge of his desk, arms folded across his chest. "I'm sorry, Dahlia. I don't want things to be the way they were. I want more than that."

She closed her eyes, groaning. "Why are you doing this?"

"Why are you? Why are you so insistent I don't feel what I feel? What I know you feel?"

"It's attraction, Norris. It's what it's always been."

"Argh!" Norris scratched his fingers through his hair and stomped back to his chair. "You are the most infuriating woman I've ever met in my life. Norris doesn't like aggravation. And if I didn't love you so much, I would not put myself through this. But I do love you. I love you, Dahlia. I love you! I'm not going to stop saying that. One day, when you're not afraid to own up to it, you're going to say those words back to me."

"It's not going to happen."

"I beg to differ. And until you're ready, I'm going to be right here, thinking of new ways to show you every day how much I do love you. You'll just have to deal with it."

Dahlia sighed. Her dark eyes smoldered with anger and frustration, two feelings Norris had in surplus.

"You know, I think it's best we limit our contact to my audit," she said.

"Can't do it. You're going to be my daughter's guardian."

"Reese is sixteen and has a cell phone. We won't need to see each other for you to see your daughter. I really believe as little contact as necessary is for the best."

"Of course you do. You're running away. You can run, but I have lots of sneakers and plenty of money to buy more. I'm going to catch you, Dahlia. And I don't mind spending the rest of my life and all my money doing it. Norris always gets what he wants, and this will be no exception."

CHAPTER 12

Dahlia glared at Norris, both flattered and infuriated by his arrogance. She used to get a kick out of his ego and the way he referred to himself in the third person. She knew he believed it, but before it hadn't come off as conceited more than it had funny. Now, it wasn't funny, it was scary, because she knew he was serious. He was not going to give up on having her, and the more she resisted, the harder he would fight.

"Why are you doing this, Norris?"

"Why do you keep asking that? You know why. I've said it over and over again. If you think this is fun for me, you'd better think again. I don't think it's fun handing my heart to you and you smashing it with a mallet and handing it back to me. 'No, thanks, Norris. This isn't the part of your body I want.'"

"You think I'm a tramp?"

"Far from it, Dahlia. In fact, I'm willing to bet you've only been with two men your entire life, and I'm lucky number two. Am I right?"

She stuck out her chin, saying nothing.

"Question answered." Norris clasped his hands and stared at her, smiling. "I think you're the most amazing woman I've ever met, and definitely the most beautiful. It would take such a woman to steal the heart of Norris

Converse." He flashed his biggest smile. "Gosh darn it, you're special."

The laugh escaped before Dahlia could stop it. Norris did that. He made her laugh. He made her care. He made her feel. *Damn!* He made her sick because he could do these things. She didn't want to love him. Why did he keep making it impossible not to? She frowned. "Stop it, Norris!"

"Stop what?" he said, leaving his desk and making his way over. "Breathing? That's what I'd have to do to stop loving you. And you don't want me to stop breathing, do you?" He grinned.

She glowered at him. "Don't tempt me."

"Ouch." Norris laughed. "I'll let that slide, because I know you don't really mean it."

He walked behind her and trailed his finger along her cheek. Her body trembled and a soft gasp fell from her lips. Norris pressed his nose to her hair, breathing deeply. As usual, she'd become putty in his hands. She missed his touch. She missed his company. She missed him.

"Just say it, Dahlia," he said. "I'm not Jonah. I won't betray your love."

She turned to face him. "How can you say that when you've betrayed our arrangement? We said no strings. Love is strings, Norris. I didn't want that. I don't want that."

"But it's what we have."

"No, what we have is a great understanding. We like being together and we have fun. I miss that, Norris. I miss you. But if you insist on bringing love into it . . ."

"I didn't bring it, it showed up. It developed, it grew, it did whatever love does. I'm happy about this, and Gail thinks Reese will be happy about it, too."

"Gail? You told her?"

"She figured it out when you two had lunch."

Dahlia groaned. She should have known. "You know what, it doesn't matter. There's no us, Norris, and I don't want Reese to know about this."

"Why not?"

"Our relationship is sex."

"That's what it was."

"*Was* is correct, because now it's over. There's nothing for you to tell Reese, and I don't want her to know about that."

"I don't want her to know about that either. The arrangement you keep alluding to is not what I want my daughter to celebrate with us. I don't regret our beginning, it led to our love—"

Dahlia rolled her eyes. Was every other word out of his mouth going to be *love*?

Norris closed his hands around her face, his smoky eyes serious, intense, and filled with the love he had no problem expressing. Dahlia wanted to look away, to avert her gaze, but she was drawn to the look in his eyes. "Our beginning led to our love, but I won't tell her about us until I can mention my love for you to you without an eye roll and groaning," he said. "Dahlia, you can say whatever you want with your words, but until I look into those beautiful brown eyes, beyond the exasperation and frustration, and not see the love I feel staring back at me,

I'm not giving up. Reese is going to know about us, but it will be when it's time. When you can say you love me and not feel like your world will fall apart." He pressed a kiss to her forehead. "I'm expecting Reese at any moment. We're having dinner over at Ryan and Lara's. You are welcome to come."

Dahlia shook her head as she willed her heart to stop racing from the memory of his innocent but powerful kiss. "That's definitely not a good idea."

"Fine, I won't push." He held up his finger and returned to his desk. "I would like your opinion on something, though. I had a designer come over yesterday to work on a room for Reese. I don't know what teenage girls like, but Ms. Stone came highly recommended." He slipped on the reading glasses that made him look too sexy for words, and extended several sheets with photos and fabric swatches. "What do you think Reese would like? I want her to be comfortable if she ever decides to sleep over."

Dahlia pulled her eyes from his bespectacled face and looked through the samples. "These are very nice," she said.

"They are," he said, moving next to her. "I especially like this one."

"That's the one I like, too. I'm sure Reese will love it."

Their fingers brushed when Dahlia handed over the samples. She looked up, seeing the same longing in Norris's eyes that his nearness stirred in her. She trailed her tongue against her lips, leaning forward as Norris did the same.

Buzz! Buzz!

They both jumped at the sound of his phone buzzing.

"Excuse me," Norris said, picking up the handset. "Yes, Agnes. She is?" He removed his glasses. "Please, send her in." He hung up the phone and smiled. "It's Reese."

Norris held up his hand as Dahlia started to talk. "Don't worry," he said, "I won't say anything to her. You should know Agnes figured it out, but she won't say anything, either. So, you can relax."

She smiled. "Thank you."

Agnes and Reese entered the office sharing an easy laugh.

"Hi, Reese," Dahlia said.

"Dahlia." Reese smiled. "What are you doing here?"

"Norris is helping me with my audit," she answered.

"Do you know?" Reese asked, motioning to Norris.

"Yeah. Your mother mentioned it when we had lunch."

Norris cleared his throat. "Since it appears you already know Ms. Sinclair, I want to formally introduce you to someone else," he said, walking behind Agnes and placing his hands on her shoulders. "Reese, this is Agnes Ross, the best assistant and surrogate mother a guy could ask for."

"Surrogate mother, huh? I guess that makes you my surrogate grandmother." Reese extended her hand. "It's nice to formally meet you, Mrs. Ross."

Agnes closed Reese's hand between hers. "Please, everyone calls me Agnes, and it's my pleasure. I'm looking forward to getting to know you better."

Reese smiled. "Me, too."

"Agnes, you can take off now," Norris said. "I'll see you tomorrow."

"Getting off a whole ten minutes early. Whatever will I do with all that time?" Agnes quipped. "Is there any wonder I enjoy working with him so much?" She patted Norris's cheek.

"Good-bye, Agnes." Norris ushered her to the door.

"Bye-bye, Reese, Ms. Sinclair."

"Good-bye, Agnes," Dahlia and Reese replied.

Norris closed the door behind Agnes and turned to Reese and Dahlia with a smile. "She's fun, isn't she?" he said.

"She is," Reese answered. "I think she's cool."

"Cool? I'm sure she'll be happy to hear that."

"So, what's this about an audit?"

Dahlia readily spoke up. "The I.R.S. wants to keep me on my toes," she said. "Norris is taking care of it for me."

"I guess it's good you two know each other already."

"You think so?" Norris said.

"Yeah. I mean, I'm going to be living with Dahlia, so it would be helpful for you two to be acquainted."

Norris nodded and smiled at Dahlia, leaving her squirming in discomfort.

"Are you okay with my decision, Norris?" Reese asked.

"Absolutely," Norris said. "You'll still have a room at my place, but if Dahlia's is where you want to stay, that's fine."

"You really are accommodating."

"This is true, Reese. I've learned you can't force things, and you have to give in a little. Being accommo- dating goes a long way in helping one achieve desired goals. I want us to be close, and I'm willing to do what I must to make that happen. You understand that, don't you, Dahlia?"

Dahlia nodded, all too aware his words were as much for her as they were for Reese. This would be the hardest six months of her life. "Yes, Norris, I understand per- fectly."

The following days brought little improvement to the relationships Norris wanted with the two most important women in his life. Women generally bent to his will, but not Dahlia and Reese. They were the exception to the rule.

School, extra-curricular activities, and friends kept Reese busy. He did talk to her on the phone and had a couple of meals with her, and in a significant move, his name had finally been added to Reese's birth certificate, but things were nowhere close to what he wanted.

Dahlia had all but made herself incommunicado to him. He'd call, but she'd be too busy to talk. He'd go to her place, and she'd always be about to head out. An easy go of this was the last thing he'd expected, but he hadn't thought it would be this hard. She didn't even mention her gifts or the catered lunches he'd provided her and her staff over the past week and a half, or the huge donation to the community center where she provided free appointments to low-income women.

On one of the few occasions he'd managed to reach Dahlia, he invited her to ride with him to Gail and Ben's wedding. She turned him down, but since she'd be there, he vowed not to let this opportunity to be in the same place with her slip away.

The intimate wedding ceremony went off without a hitch. Norris mingled with the Monroes during the reception at the Denburg Inn ballroom, but Dahlia had all his attention. In a soft yellow cocktail dress that showcased her lovely shoulders and gorgeous legs, Dahlia looked absolutely stunning.

Apparently one of the male wedding guests thought so, too, as he made it his business to stay in Dahlia's orbit as if she were the president and he was Secret Service. The two spun around the dance floor like Ginger Rogers and Fred Astaire, laughing and chatting like old pals.

Jealousy boiled in Norris's belly as he watched the scene unfold. When an attractive Asian woman, who introduced herself as Mai Lee, asked him to dance, Norris agreed without hesitation. Dancing with beautiful women wasn't foreign to him, but this dancing felt strange, because spite fueled it, and not some preamble to seduction as it used to be. *Love.* The things it led him to do.

An hour or so later, after the customary reception rituals, more dances with Mai, and a gentle rebuff of her invitation to go out for a drink, Norris rejoined the

Monroes at their table. He watched intently as Dahlia engaged in animated conversation with Reese and Diana at a corner table. Dahlia's dance partner, as well as the other two dozen guests, left soon after Gail and Ben addressed the assembled friends and relatives and thanked them for sharing in their special day. Now Norris wanted to address Dahlia and ask what the heck was going on between her and Mr. Twinkle Toes.

"This was a lovely day, wasn't it? Norris?"

A hand on his shoulder shook Norris from his trance. "I'm sorry, Celeste, were you saying something?" he asked.

"I was commenting on how lovely the wedding was. Much like your daughter. I see Reese has all of your attention."

"My attention?"

"Yes. That table has you rapt."

"I guess I am a little sidetracked."

"Reese is a delightful girl." Celeste chuckled. "She definitely doesn't lack self-esteem."

Norris smiled. "She is something else, isn't she? When I look at her and realize she's mine, it's overwhelming."

"Go over and talk to her," Dan said. "You didn't have a chance earlier with the picture-taking and reception line keeping her occupied. Go on and catch up. The reception is over, and I'm sure Dahlia and Diana won't mind."

Maybe Diana wouldn't mind, but he had a feeling Dahlia would. But she wouldn't make a scene, not here. "I think I'll do that, Dan. You guys excuse me."

The chatter at the table stopped when Norris arrived. Diana smiled. "Hi, Mr. Converse," she said.

"Hello. If I haven't said so already, you three ladies are looking quite fetching today."

"Fetching?" said Reese. "What is that, one of those eighties terms? You have got to get with the program, Norris. 'Fetching' sounds like what you do for bonding time with you obedient dog." They all laughed. "Did you need something?"

"No, I just came over to talk." He grabbed a chair from the next table and sat beside Dahlia. "You all seemed to be having a very enjoyable conversation before. What's the topic?"

"Guys," Diana answered without hesitation. "The good and the bad of them."

"I see." He smiled at Dahlia before turning to the girls. "As the lone representative of my species at this table, I hope the good has been outweighing the bad."

"Mostly, I guess," Reese answered. "We're waiting to see what Dahlia thinks."

"Hmm." Norris turned his chair toward Dahlia and folded his arms. He'd arrived just in time. "So, what do you think?"

Reese stood and pointed before Dahlia could answer. "There's Mom and Ben," she said. "Come on, Diana. They'll be leaving soon." The girls left the table to greet the newlyweds, who had changed into their 'getaway' clothes.

Norris returned his attention to Dahlia. "Aren't you going to answer the question?" he asked.

"No."

"Okay. Answer mine. Who was that guy you were so caught up with during the reception?"

"None of your business." She crossed her arms. A shadow of annoyance darkened her pretty face. "I find it amazing you could notice my goings-on with your hands full of Ms. Mai."

Norris smiled. The animosity in her voice like music to his ears. "You do care," he said. "I always knew it."

Dahlia scoffed. "I have a question for you, Norris. What are you doing?"

"What do you mean?"

"What do I mean? The donation to the community center, the extravagant catered lunches for everyone in my salon for a week, the roses on Wednesday, candy on Thursday, and the sapphire earrings on Friday. That's what."

"So, you did get all of that. You've been avoiding me so much, I thought maybe there was some other Dahlia Sinclair in Denburg who got all those things."

"I want you to stop it."

"I know. Did you like it? The gifts and the food?"

She sighed. "What does it matter?"

"It matters to me." He smiled. "You did like it. I can tell in your eyes."

"You seem to see a lot in my eyes."

"They talk to me when you won't. Emily Dickinson calls eyes the windows to the soul. I see your soul, Dahlia. I see you."

"What you see is what you want to see." She rubbed her forehead and expelled a sharp breath. "I'm tired of talking about this. I'm leaving."

He grabbed her hand, feeling that familiar spark pass between them. Their eyes met and held, the attraction between them palpable. Dahlia snatched her hand away and stormed off. Norris followed. He wouldn't let her get away that easily.

They hadn't gotten very far before being stopped by the happy couple and Reese.

"I'm glad I caught you two together," said Gail, sliding her hand into that of her new husband. Norris liked Ben. He showed himself to be a stand-up guy who clearly loved Gail and Reese a great deal. "We're about to leave, but we wanted to stop and talk for a minute."

"You don't have to worry about Reese, Gail, she'll be in good hands," Dahlia assured her.

"I know that." Gail brought Reese's hand to her lips. "It's still hard. We've only been away from each other a few days at a time. My conventions and her weekend slumber parties, but never six months." Tears filled her eyes and slowly trailed down her cheeks. "I don't know how I'm going to make it without my baby for that long."

"Mom, I don't want you to go, and I can't pretend I do, but I understand why you need to," Reese said, glancing at Norris and then turning back to Gail. "I'm going to be okay, and you have Ben. I know he's going to take good care of you."

"I haven't even left you and you've already grown up so much in the last minute." Gail pulled Reese into a hug. "I'm going to miss you so much."

Reese sniffled as she clung to Gail. "Me, too."

Norris watched the tearful goodbye, becoming more aware of what it meant for him. Gail and Reese shared a closeness he and Reese did not, and even with six months, he wondered if they could get anything near that. Reese was willing to try, but would missing her mother, who was leaving specifically to give them time alone, lead her to resent him for making Gail feel the need to leave?

Reese ended the embrace and wiped Gail's tears. "It's going to be okay, Mom. We're going to email each other every day, and you're going to call whenever you can, right?"

Gail nodded. "That's right. And Norris and Dahlia will be on you just like I would. So you'll hardly miss me."

"No, I'll miss you, but I get the point."

Ben checked his watch. "I hate to break this up, but we need to get to the airport. The flight to New York is leaving in less than two hours."

"It's true dedication for you all to set aside a honeymoon to help the less fortunate," Norris said. "I like to think I'm magnanimous, but I don't think I'd be willing to do that."

"We'll have years together, we just want to make sure the people in Uganda get another day. And our flight to Africa leaves tomorrow morning, so we'll have a few hours." Ben's dark eyes lit up and his full lips turned into a bright smile. "Just being in Gail's presence is a honeymoon in itself."

Norris's gaze cut to Dahlia as Ben gave his new wife a kiss. He envied Ben in being able to show his love for the woman he loved, and not have her get upset about it. Dahlia averted her gaze. Norris sighed. Dahlia's stubbornness tried his patience, but he refused to fold. He saw this as a challenge he could meet. The prize was worth it.

Hugs abounded as the happy couple said their final goodbyes. While Ben chatted with Monroes and Dahlia, Gail took Norris by the hand and led him to a quiet corner.

"Are you ready for this, Norris?"

"I'm ready to know my daughter. I understand this is hard for you, Gail, but you don't have to worry about her."

"I'm not so much worried as I am at a loss. I hate leaving her." Her voice wavered and new tears filled her eyes. Gail expelled a breath. "But I know I need to do this, and I will be doing a lot of good while I'm away." She squeezed Norris's hand. "Now you. Are you sure you're all right with Reese staying with Dahlia?"

"I was a little hurt to find out she wouldn't be living with me, but I'm okay with it. Like I told Reese, I want her to be comfortable. If there's strain between us, we won't get close, and I want us to get close."

"There seems to be a little strain between you and Dahlia. What's up with that?"

"We have different opinions on some things, but we both agree when it comes to Reese's best interests, so don't worry about anything."

"A mother always worries."

"That may be, but in regard to Dahlia and me, you have no reason. Try to enjoy your short honeymoon and concentrate on helping the people of Uganda. Reese will be fine."

"And you and Dahlia? I know you love her."

"Gail . . ." he groaned.

"All right, I won't press."

"And you won't discuss this with Reese?"

"I haven't and I won't. You just take care of my baby."

"Our baby," Norris reminded her. "And I will."

CHAPTER 13

Dahlia kicked off her clear pumps and tossed her purse to the couch. With Reese sleeping over at Diana's, she could curse the girl's father without having to answer a million questions.

A workout was what she needed, but a bag of chips what she wanted. She padded to the kitchen and rifled the cabinets for the box of single-size packs she kept for emergencies. She reached far in the back and found the box empty. She shouldn't have been surprised. Norris had provided plenty of emergencies lately with his calls, gifts, and general sweetness. She'd have to make a run to the store.

Sliding the pumps back on her feet, Dahlia pulled open the door to find Norris standing on the other side.

"My, you're in a rush," he said.

Dahlia demanded her wobbly knees stop shaking. Norris always had an amazing effect on her, but in the light beige suit and white linen shirt, he looked even more delectable than usual. Might explain why Mai couldn't keep her hands off him.

"What do you want, Norris?" she asked, finding the strength to meet his hypnotic eyes.

"It's your house, and I know Reese isn't here. It should be obvious. You going to invite me in?"

"No."

"Thanks, I'd love to," he said, pushing his way in.

"You've got to stop doing this."

"Dahlia, if I believed for one second you didn't want me here, I wouldn't be here." He moved to the couch and sat. "I won't stay long, but there are some things I need to say."

"I didn't imagine you would stay long." Dahlia grunted. "I'm sure Mai is waiting."

He grinned. "Most women are waiting for Norris to enter their lives, so she's in good company."

Dahlia rolled her eyes. She'd walked into that one. "What's on your mind?"

"A few things." He patted the space on the couch. "Sit."

"I'd rather stand."

"You insist on being contrary, don't you?"

"Is that why you're here, to give me a tongue lashing?"

"A tongue lashing?" Norris's lips curled into the sexy smile that tossed more kindling on the fire he burned in her. Maybe she should have sat. At least then she could look straight ahead and not be drawn in by his male prowess and devastating good looks. "Something about giving you one sounds rather appealing," he said.

"Norris, please, just get to it."

"Okay, fine. You made a couple of digs about Mai. That gives me hope. Confirms what I already know— you care about me. Why do you have such a problem admitting that?" He held up his hand. "Don't answer, I know why. It's your divorce. I can't imagine how that hurt, especially when you believed everything was fine, but I don't want you to give up on love and happiness because of Jonah."

"*You* don't want me to give up. That's just it. This is not for *you* to decide. I liked us the way we were, and you want to change it."

"For the better, Dahlia. What we have could be so much better if you let it be."

"How do you know it can be better?" Dahlia thought of the days and nights she and Norris had spent together laughing, talking, watching movies, and being in each other's arms. It was heavenly. "Was it so bad before?"

"No. It was wonderful. The most wonderful time of my life. It made me fall in love with you."

Dahlia whipped her fingers through her hair. *Why does he keep saying those words?* "Norris, damn it!"

"We've got to deal with this, Dahlia. Watching you in some other guy's arms today drove me crazy. On the one hand I wanted to punch his lights out, and on the other I wanted to be him. I wanted to be the guy you were dancing with and laughing with in front of everyone at that reception. I wanted them to see you were there with me. But I didn't get that. He did. I'm in love with you and we have never once gone out on a date."

"That's just it, Norris. We don't have a dating kind of relationship. We didn't want it, remember?"

"Is that my punishment? Being without you because I happened to fall in love with you?"

"You don't have to be without me." Dahlia moved to the couch, taking his hand in hers. She wanted Norris, but it had to be on her terms. She was being selfish and she knew it, but being selfish kept her in control, and admitting to her feelings would make her lose all control. She couldn't do it. "Norris, I miss you. I miss your company, your voice, your touch, your scent, I even miss your vanity. You make me laugh. I want that back, I do, but I don't want a relationship with you."

"Dahlia, what do you think you just described?"

"What makes us good," she answered without hesitation. "Norris, we are good together." She nuzzled his neck, breathing in his intoxicating scent, feeling the pulse points pound furiously against her. "I excite you." She kissed his jaw. "You excite me." She kissed his nose and straddled his waist. The bulge in his slacks pressed against her panties. A roll of her hips elicited a deep groan from him. His hands palmed her backside, holding her against his throbbing arousal. She didn't have to speak her feelings, and she was more than willing to pretend he didn't. He just had to want it, too. "Let's forget about emotions and think about needs for a while."

Her lips covered his in a deep, urgent kiss. Their lips parted as eager tongues explored. Norris's hands moved up her back and around to her breasts. His thumbs teased her taut, sensitive nipples, sending shivers throughout her body. Blissful moans fell from her lips when he buried his head in the valley of her breasts, sliding his warm tongue along her cleavage. She closed her arms around his head, rocking her hips in time with his moving pelvis. Norris's moans grew deeper, stronger. But all of a sudden his sounds ended and his movements ceased.

Dahlia struggled for breath as she gazed at him, confused. "What's wrong?"

"I can't do this, Dahlia," he said between haggard breaths, sliding her back to the couch. "I love you. I love you too much to settle for half of you. As much as you know and can feel I want your body, I want your heart even more."

She pressed her kiss-swollen lips together as she fought the threat of tears. "I'm sorry, Norris, you can't have it."

"No, I'm sorry, because I disagree. You love me, I know you do, you're just not ready to say so. That's something I can't help you with, and I'm not going to force you to say it. But what I will do is wait for however long it takes for you to finally say those words to me. In the meantime, I want to amend our arrangement."

"You've already amended it." She glowered at him. "That's the problem."

Norris shook his head, grunting. "Again, I'm not going to argue with you about that. Here's my suggestion. We'll still see each other, but instead of meeting for romps, we have dates. We go to the movies and out to dinner. We go dancing, we go to the beach, and take walks in the park. We get to enjoy each other's company outside the confines of our homes and bedrooms. I want to court you."

"What does Norris Converse know about courting a woman?"

"Nothing. But I want to learn with you."

Norris seemed sincere, and Dahlia believed he loved her, but she also knew Jonah had loved her once, too. She'd thought Jonah was true, but he'd cheated with her sister. Norris had an affinity for the ladies, which was a big part of the reason she was drawn to him. She liked that he found her attractive, and she enjoyed the idea of being with him without the situation being clouded by feelings. He couldn't hurt her because she wanted what he wanted—no ties. Norris used to be safe, and now he wasn't.

He was a lifelong playboy. Sure, he loved her now, but how long would his love last? Her wounded heart didn't buy into longevity. And as much as she loved Norris, she didn't think she could trust her heart to him, and doubted she ever would.

"I'm sorry, Norris, but I don't want to be the guinea pig in your dating experiment. I suggest we forget our previous arrangement and this dating idea and keep things all business. You'll handle my audit and I'll be guardian to Reese. You'll still have complete access to her, but not to me. That's the way it has to be."

Norris stood and shrugged. "Okay."

Okay? That was it? No protestations? "I'm not going to change my mind," Dahlia said, waiting for more from him.

"All right," he said, heading for the door. "I'd like to have lunch with Reese tomorrow, if that's okay."

She nodded without saying a word. Of all the responses she's gotten from Norris when they talked about this relationship he wanted, this was the strangest of all. Had he really given up on her? Dahlia followed him to the door.

He pulled the door open and turned around. "Dahlia?"

"Yes," she answered quickly, certain he was about to offer his last ditch effort.

"I've been reviewing your paperwork, and I should have a report for you in a couple of days."

"Th-thank you."

"No problem. Take care."

"Yeah, you, too."

Dahlia closed the door behind him, needing those chips more than ever.

Norris returned to his condo, feeling particularly happy considering Dahlia had shot him down yet again. But this brush-off gave him hope. He'd changed his game plan, and it appeared to be working. *Be accommodating.* He would give Dahlia what she thought she wanted, and in the long run he'd get what he wanted, a long and happy future with her.

He tossed his suit coat to the couch and clicked on the television. Norris Converse at home alone on a Saturday night. He dropped to the couch and flipped through the channels. He'd thought last week was a fluke, but two weeks in a row presented an unlikely pattern. He'd worked late last Friday, had dinner with Ryan and Lara last night, but another Saturday night found him watching cable news. He groaned. Dahlia had to get past her issues soon.

Thirty minutes into a special on the economy, Norris heard a knock on his door. He smiled, feeling a strong sense of validation. Dahlia had come to her senses quicker than he'd expected. He moved to the door and pulled it open. "I knew you would . . ." He stopped abruptly. "Mom."

"You remember me," she said, walking past him and into the living room. "You might want to close the door, son. Those horrible bugs that fly around the light fixtures might find their way inside."

Norris closed the door and gazed at his mother, who was getting way too comfortable on his couch. Genevieve Converse was a woman who liked things her way, and when she didn't get it, she wasn't happy. From an old-money Greek family, the sixty-three-year-old socialite was a curt, overbearing snob. And that was on her good days. "What are you doing here?"

"Don't you check your messages?"

"Yes."

"Then you know I said I was coming for a visit." Genevieve sniffled, probably from the painful-looking extra-tight bun she had her dark hair pulled into. "Your father and I are having problems," she said, dabbing at misty gray eyes.

"I'm sorry to hear that, Mom," he said with as much feeling as he could muster, "but you won't be able to fix them when you're here and he's . . . Where is Dad?"

"The Riviera, the last I heard. Probably lying on the beach with some naked tart at his side." She shook her head, as if clearing the image from her mind. "We are officially separated, and times like these I need my children."

"You have two other children," Norris reminded her, none too pleased with being the chosen child on this occasion.

"Yes, but Lane is out of the country on business and your sister is . . . I don't know where your sister is. I always know where you are. It's the one good thing about you living among commoners in South Carolina."

"Commoners. Weren't you and Dad the ones who insisted Lane, Julia, and I live amongst the 'commoners' as we grew up?"

"No, no, no, that was not my idea, it was your father's. Had I my druthers, you and your siblings would have stayed in Greece with my family and the power and position you deserve."

"You had no say in it, huh?"

"I was raised to respect my husband's wishes."

"So, this separation is Dad's idea and you're just going along with it?"

Genevieve sighed. "Norris, really, I don't need this from you right now."

A horn sounded outside.

"That's the taxi driver," Genevieve explained. "I don't have any cash, so could you take care of that for me and bring in the luggage?"

"Honestly, Mom, I think you'd be more comfortable at a hotel. The Inn is very nice."

"I've stayed there before, Norris, and it's nice for what it is, but I want to stay with you. Darling, really, the meter is running," she said, shooing him on his way. Norris bit back the testy words resting on his tongue as he made his way to the waiting cabbie. Why would she care about a few dollars when she wasn't paying the bill anyway? And ordering him around in his house . . . this could not last.

With the promise of a ten-dollar tip, Norris got the impatient driver to help him lug in what looked to be several months' worth of luggage. Roughly five minutes later, after he brought in the last suitcase, Norris immediately noticed his mother wasn't in the living room and his art pieces had been removed from the walls.

His face grew hot. "Mother!" Norris shouted. "Mother!"

Genevieve strolled into the living room. "Norris, must you shout? What is the problem?"

"Where is my art?"

"Art? Oh, you mean the hideous masks you keep on the walls. I removed them. They're scary, and just not appropriate for a man of your means. The leather furniture isn't so bad, but those masks . . ."

"What the hell are you talking about?"

"You're a wealthy man, and you have a lovely home, but your taste in art? Son, what is it with the jungle motif?"

"It is not a jungle motif. I happen to like and appreciate African art, and it is very expensive. And considering this is *my* house, I want *my* art back on *my* walls. I don't want you touching anything in here. As a matter of fact, I don't want you staying here."

"I'm going through so much right now. Why are you being hostile towards me?"

Norris covered his eyes. His temples pounded with the threat of a monster headache. "Mom, I'm not being hostile, I'm just tired and I don't like my things being disturbed."

"Fine, I'll put the masks back up."

"You do that." Norris sat on the couch and closed his eyes, wanting to block out the fact his mother was standing in his living room. She needed a place to stay. "Mom, I don't mind having you a few days, but just until you find your own place. Your luggage suggests you'll be in town for a while."

"I don't know how long I'll be here, but I wanted to be prepared for whatever I might decide. Thank you for allowing me to stay. I'll try to be out of your hair as soon as possible." Genevieve pointed towards the hallway. "Why did you change your spare bedroom? It seems a little feminine for you, but it's very nice. I should be very comfortable in there."

Norris sat up. "Oh, no. You can't stay in that room."

"It's your guest bedroom."

"It was, but it's no longer for a guest. I'll crash on the couch while you're here and you can take my room, but the other room is off limits."

"I understand you don't want me here, but the dresser drawers in that room are empty, so unless your guest is invisible, that explanation doesn't work."

"Mom, I don't have to give you an explanation of what goes on in my house, and, again, I don't want you going through my things." Norris sighed heavily. His mother would not stop snooping and the sooner he told her about Reese, the sooner he could prepare Reese for meeting her. "Since you will not leave this alone and you're going to find out anyway, I guess now is a good time for me to tell you something."

"What?"

"That room belongs to my daughter."

Genevieve's eyes widened. "Your daughter?"

"Yes. Her name is Reese and she's sixteen years old." Norris paused. "And there's more."

"More than that?"

"I guess in addition to is more appropriate."

"I don't think you can surprise me more than you have."

"Guess again. My beautiful daughter, your grand-daughter, is biracial. Her mother is African-American."

CHAPTER 14

Early the next morning, Dahlia left her bed and dragged down to the kitchen. She wanted to feel happy that Norris had finally given in and realized a relationship wasn't in the cards for them, but disgust led the field in the emotions department. Disgust with herself for keeping him at arm's length, and disgust with Norris for allowing her to do it. Why did he have to have all or nothing? Why couldn't he just let things stay the way they were?

Dahlia forced herself to eat her breakfast of three scrambled egg whites, dry toast, half a grapefruit, and skim milk. She wanted to work out before going to church and needed fuel to make it happen. Plus, she'd eaten two of the single bags of chips she'd bought last night, making two workouts today essential. Determined not to succumb to her salty, crispy weakness, Dahlia emptied the remaining four bags into the trash disposal. If push came to shove she knew she would buy more, but at least the temptation was not in her house.

Two hours later, Dahlia sat at the bar in her home gym drinking water and wiping the sweat leaking from every pore of her body. Her clothes stuck to her skin, and a quick glance in the mirrored wall behind the bar showed her hair matted to her head, but she felt good.

She'd needed that workout. It had kept her mind off of what's-his-name.

The sound of the ringing phone quickened Dahlia's still-racing pulse. *Norris!* She pushed aside the water bottle and grabbed the cordless phone. "Hello," she said, trying not to sound as anxious as she felt.

"Dee, baby, you okay?"

"Grandma," she said, always happy to hear from Grandma Flora, but feeling the slightest bit let down. "I'm fine. I just finished working out."

"You do a lot of that."

"I have to."

"You going to church today?" Flora asked.

"I'd hope to, yes, ma'am."

"Think you can pick up your old grandma?"

Dahlia smiled. "You'll never be old, and I'd love to."

Her parents had gone to Atlanta to visit the ailing Leslie. The last she'd heard, her sister was doing better, and she was glad, but even after a couple of weeks, accepting that Leslie carried her ex-husband's baby was hard to take.

Dahlia drew a breath and concentrated on the moment. She hadn't spent as much time with her grandmother as she'd wanted to, but today could change that. Maybe they could grab a bite together after church, too. "I was planning to attend the first service. Would you rather I wait for the second?" she asked.

"No, no, first is fine. I can be ready in an hour."

"Okay, I'll see you then, Grandma."

Dahlia smiled as she made way out of the gym. The endorphins from the workout had her body humming, and talking to her grandmother always did her heart good. She'd be lying if she said Norris wasn't still on her mind, but she felt a lot better than she had when she woke up this morning.

"Hey there."

Dahlia jumped at the sound of Reese's voice. She covered her racing heart. She'd finally caught her breath after exercising and now she couldn't breathe again.

"I'm sorry," Reese said, coming out the kitchen with a glass of orange juice. "I didn't mean to scare you."

"It's okay," Dahlia said, still gasping for breath. "I thought you were staying at Diana's until later."

"I was, but I needed to unpack a few things and study for a test. Last week was crazy with preparing for the wedding and bringing some of my things over here, but now it's back to the real world. This is the last test before finals. Can't get into Columbia if I let my A average slip." A curious smile played at the corner of Reese's lips. "So, what were you so happy about just now, Dahlia? Did your guy keep you company last night?" She giggled. "Is he the hottie from the wedding?"

Dahlia lowered her gaze. Reese's easy-going questioning was a lot more painful than fun.

"Uh-oh. Have I stuck my foot in my mouth again? Did you and your guy have a fight or something?"

"I never said there was a guy, Reese."

Reese crossed her arms, clearly not believing that line for a second. "Or something, huh?" she said.

Dahlia nodded. "Yeah. Or something." She rubbed the towel through her damp hair; she'd go with the flat look today. "I'm heading up for a shower and then going off to church."

"Okay, we can talk later," Reese said, her twinkling eyes and coy smile reminding Dahlia more and more of Norris.

Dahlia flashed a tight smile. "Right, later."

"That was quite a sermon from Rev. Leonard," Dahlia said, opening the passenger side of her car and helping Flora inside. "He had a little extra fire and brimstone this morning."

"He's a good God man," said Flora, swinging her legs inside. "He has a way of bringing the word to people in the way he feels they need it."

"Right." Dahlia closed the door and got in on the driver's side. "How about some lunch, Grandma? We can go to Martin's."

"You don't need to spend all your money when you can come to my house and eat."

"I know, but I'd like to do something special for you, and have somebody cook for you for a change."

"Child, while I still got two good arms and legs, I'm going to do whatever I can for myself. 'Sides, I want us to talk, and I don't want a bunch of strangers around when we do it."

Dahlia nibbled on her bottom lip. The unsettling feeling she got from Reese's questions this morning returned to her stomach. Dodging Reese's questions was one thing, but Grandma Flora was a different story.

"You know what, Grandma, I just remembered something I . . ."

Flora waved her hand. "Don't even try that with me, girl. You've been keeping away long enough. I woke up early this morning and baked a ham, made some macaroni and cheese, perlo rice, collard greens, cornbread, and pound cake, and you will talk and eat this food with me today."

"Grandma," Dahlia practically whined, not sure if she was more upset about the idea of facing her grandmother's questioning or eating her delicious and extremely fattening food. She allowed herself to eat what she wanted, but she always had trouble turning down seconds from her grandmother's table.

"One good meal will not hurt you, and I'm ready to hear about this man you haven't told me about."

Dahlia froze. *Grandma knew.* Denial was an option, but after so many months, she really needed to unburden herself to someone. "How long have you known?"

"A while now." Flora closed her warm, wrinkled hand around Dahlia's. "Go on and drive. We'll talk at the house."

About an hour later, Dahlia sat at her grandmother's kitchen table with a steaming plate of the Sunday lunch/dinner before her. Flora sat across from her and offered the blessing.

"Amen," they both said at the conclusion of grace.

"You can eat and talk," Flora said, waving her fork at Dahlia's plate.

Dahlia had a bite of the macaroni. The distinctive flavor of the three cheeses her grandmother used enlivened her taste buds. She smiled. "It's even better than I remember."

"There's more than macaroni on your plate."

Dahlia took a bite of everything. Soul food definitely had the right name. She hadn't even started talking yet, and her soul felt better already.

"All right, now. Tell me about him," Flora said.

"I don't know where to start." Dahlia ate a few more bites of food. "It's complicated, Grandma."

"One thing's not complicated. Do you love him?"

Dahlia pushed back the plate and nodded as the first of her tears streamed down her cheeks. "Yes, Grandma, I love him."

"Now, child." Flora used a paper napkin to dab at Dahlia's tears. "Does he love you?"

"He said he does."

"Then why are you so upset?"

"I don't want to love him," Dahlia said between sobs. "I don't want to love anybody. Love hurts too much."

"Baby, love doesn't always hurt. This man can be the one to show you that."

"No, he can't show me that. He says he loves me, but I don't think I can trust that."

"Why not?"

"Because our . . . The way we got together is not what you'd call traditional."

"What you mean, child?"

Dahlia reached for her glass of tea, gulping the sweet beverage until it was gone. She lowered the glass to see her grandmother's unflinching brown-eyed gaze.

"Are you really going to make me say it, Grandma?"

Flora shook her head. "Uhm, uhm, uhm. My Lord, my Lord."

"You're disappointed in me, aren't you?"

"I'm surprised. You're not a loose woman. You were raised in the church. Why do that?"

"I can't explain it, Grandma. It just happened."

Flora moaned. "Go on with your story, Dee."

"I guess you can figure out the rest. I met him at the movie rental store back in February. I thought it would only be one time, but one time turned to two, and two multiplied. We agreed it would be what it was."

"You were some man's bootie call?"

Dahlia gasped. "Grandma!"

"That's what you're saying, ain't it?"

"He was mine, too, okay? We understood each other. And then he had to ruin it by saying he loves me." Dahlia scoffed. "Jonah said he loved me, too."

"You can't measure every man by Jonah. I never really liked that boy, but I tried for you."

"I remember." Dahlia laughed. "You were right about him."

"Maybe I'm right about this man, too. What's his name?"

"Norris Converse."

"The Norris Converse with that business downtown?"

"Yes, ma'am."

Flora's eyes widened. "Dahlia, he's white."

Dahlia nodded. "Yes, he is." She didn't have to address the comment again. Flora had told many stories about the inequity she faced growing up in the Jim Crow South, but she didn't hold hostility, insisting hate was taught and she wouldn't allow the unfairness she faced to compel her to treat people she didn't know the way she had been treated. If she showed hostility toward anyone, it was because they brought it on themselves. "He's also Reese's father," Dahlia said.

"The girl staying with you?"

"Yes, ma'am. I don't know who was more surprised by that revelation—Norris, Reese, or me."

"My Lord, my Lord." Flora drank some tea. "Why do you doubt his love? Did he say the words at a time you'd have reason to doubt them?" Flora asked with a raised brow.

"Grandma!" Dahlia dragged out in stunned disbelief. "No, he didn't. Goodness." She shuddered, shocked at her grandmother's implication and even more by the level of detail she'd shared. Talking about her sex life with her grandmother. These were definitely some strange days.

"Then what's the problem?"

"Norris. He has a reputation with the ladies, and he's not the committing type. To keep saying he loves me when he freely admits he'd never said the words to another woman troubles me. He's like Jonah in a lot of ways. I didn't find Jonah with lots of women, but I'm not so foolish as to believe Leslie was the only one. I know Norris has a reputation with women."

"Is that the problem?"

"Yes." Dahlia nodded. "That is the problem. I chose to get involved with Norris because he didn't do relationships, and I didn't want to do them anymore. He was safe. When I fell in love with him, I knew it didn't matter, because I still didn't want a relationship, and I believed he felt the same. But then he said the words. And he keeps saying them, and he says them with such conviction."

Dahlia sighed. "How could I fall in love with a man exactly like the one I left? And not just love him, but like him, care about him, want to share everything with him. Grandma, I don't want to be like those women who leave one abusive relationship only to fall into the same kind of relationship with a different man. I'm not stupid, but I feel that way. How could I let myself fall in love again?"

"The heart knows what it wants."

"But sometimes your heart wants the wrong thing. I can't get with that 'It's better to have loved and lost' ideology. I could have gone my whole life without feeling that pain. Why would I willingly put myself in the position to feel it again?"

"Because you love him. You love him and it scares you to death. You can't keep this truth from me."

Dahlia held Flora's hand in hers. "Okay, you're right, Grandma, I am scared. But I can handle the fear I've placed on myself a lot better than I can the hurt somebody places on me. I chose this fear, and it keeps me alert. That's why I know, as hard as it is, I can live with the decision I've made to end things with Norris. It's the best thing I can do for myself." She kissed her grandmother's cheek. "Thank you for letting me talk, for listening, and for not judging me."

"It's not for me or anyone else to judge you. I only want you to be happy."

"I am." Dahlia bobbed her head from side to side. "Mostly." She kissed Flora again. "Thanks for the food and everything, Grandma. I really appreciate it."

"You're welcome, but I'm worried about you." Flora moved over to the counter and sliced several large pieces of cake. "You talk big, but I know you. You feel things deeply, child. Hurt, sadness, happiness, and love. You won't be able to pretend you don't feel what you feel. And if this man loves you as much as it appears he does, he'll see your feelings in your eyes. Just like I do."

Dahlia said nothing to that. Norris always said he could see her love for him in her eyes, but then he gave up on her. Maybe it was just words. Another man feeding her lines. Dahlia wanted some chips. She needed her comfort food.

Flora wrapped the cake in aluminum foil and handed it to Dahlia. "This is for you and Reese," she said.

"Thank you."

Flora pulled Dahlia into a hug. "You take care, child."

Dahlia nodded and managed a smile. Once she got hold of some chips, she'd be able to take care of herself very well.

"Right over there," said Norris, directing three guys wearing green polo shirts stitched with "Denburg Inn" to his mother's luggage. "Make sure you don't leave anything."

"Yes, sir," answered the larger of the three men.

Minutes later, the men, the bags, and all traces of his mother were gone. Norris thought back to last night and his mother's reaction to hearing about Reese. She had said very little after repeating, "This isn't funny, Norris," several times. Once convinced it wasn't a joke, Genevieve had grabbed her purse, explained she would send for her things, and stormed out. Norris hadn't expected her to take the news well, but it didn't lessen the hurt he felt at being right. She had a granddaughter and couldn't care less.

Dahlia had wondered if his parents' reaction to Reese would be any different than what they'd shown Lara. He'd thought it would. He had thought blood would be the difference. So far with his mother, he'd been proven wrong. And countless calls to his father went unanswered, showing the separated spouses were probably of one mind when it came to this issue. Norris shrugged it off. Their loss.

At least his siblings were excited. He'd engaged in an impromptu conference call with Lane and Julia the night of the brunch, and they couldn't wait to meet Reese. He'd even told them about Dahlia. Plans for an extended visit were in the works, and they'd ended the call with a promise to get better at keeping in touch.

Norris picked up his phone. Who better to keep in touch with than his daughter? Maybe Reese was up for lunch.

"Hello," she said.

"Hi, Reese, it's Norris."

"Oh, hi." Norris heard paper rattling in the background. "What's up?" Reese asked.

He tried not to be put off by her lack of enthusiasm. "Are you busy?" he asked. "You seem distracted."

"I'm studying. Got a big test on Tuesday."

"How long have you been at it?"

"It's a little after noon now, so about fours hours."

Norris whistled, impressed. "Aren't you the studious one?"

"I have to be. Columbia's within my sight."

"How about food? When was the last time you ate?"

"I had some OJ when I got back to Dahlia's this morning."

Norris's ears perked up. "You're back at Dahlia's? I thought you were staying over with Diana."

"I can hang out with her later. I needed to study."

"Is Dahlia helping you?" he asked, playing sly in his attempt to gather information.

"No, I'm studying alone. Dahlia went to church."

"Church?" Probably praying for escape from her love for him, Norris reasoned. "She's not back yet?"

"She called to say she was having lunch with her grandmother. Why are you wondering about Dahlia?"

"I'm . . . I'm not," he stammered. "I just don't like the idea of you being alone in a new place."

"I've been here before. The visit is just longer now. Besides, I'm sixteen, not six. I can be alone."

"I know. I'm sorry. I just . . . Do you want to go out for lunch? I know you're studying, but you have to take a break sometime. And orange juice isn't a meal. You can't study on an empty stomach. We'll go wherever you want."

Reese said nothing for several moments. "I guess we can have lunch," she finally said.

"Great. I can be over in half an hour."

"Half an hour?" Reese scoffed. "I'm going to need longer than that. Beauty takes time."

"You're already beautiful, Reese."

"I know this," she said, her confidence never wavering. "Still, I have an image to maintain. I can be ready in an hour."

Norris smiled. "Okay, you win. I'll be there in an hour." He hung up the phone. *One hour.* With any luck, Dahlia would be home when he arrived, and he could see for himself if she still wanted to keep things all business.

"Everything smells so good," Reese said.

Norris nodded in agreement. "I think Corlino's Kitchen has some of the best food in town," he said.

Having been shown to a table near the front of the restaurant, Norris and Reese sat and perused the menus in companionable silence. Gail's wedding, exams, and Reese's plans for the summer had dominated conversation on the ride over, but bummed by Dahlia not being home, Norris did more listening than talking.

He stared blankly at the menu, his thoughts on Dahlia. She had a close relationship with her grandmother. Could their lunchtime conversation be about him? Gladness peppered his dour demeanor. He could see that taking a long time. Norris smiled, feeling a lot better. That could definitely be the hold up.

"What are you grinning about, Norris?" Reese asked, her voice shaking him from his reverie.

"Happy thoughts," he said. "You know what you're having?"

"Yeah. I think I'll go for the fettuccine alfredo."

Norris closed his menu. "I think I'll have the same."

A blue-eyed, brown-haired waiter arrived at the table with two glasses of ice water and a smile. Introducing himself as Mike, he offered the customary Corlino's Kitchen greeting and proceeded to give Reese all of his attention. Norris could understand young men finding his daughter attractive, but he wasn't at all happy with the lustful look in Mike's eyes.

"Do you have our orders, Mike?" Norris asked, hearing the testiness he'd tried to keep out of his voice.

Mike cleared his throat and met Norris's gaze. "Yes, sir," he answered nervously. "Two fettuccine alfredos." He placed the order pad in his pocket and retrieved the menus. "I'll be right back with some breadsticks."

"Thanks." Norris draped the napkin over his lap as Mike retreated to the kitchen.

Reese frowned. "That was mean."

"What?"

"You intimidated him. I don't think I've ever heard 'thanks' sound like an insult."

"I asked about our food."

Reese groaned. "Gimme a break."

"That boy was practically drooling on you."

"It's a natural response." Reese tossed her straightened hair over her shoulder. "He can't help it. I've discovered I have that effect on men."

"You were flirting with him. And don't try to deny it, because I know flirting when I see it."

"Flirting is harmless fun."

Norris shuddered. The more time he spent with Reese, the more of himself he saw in her, and the more he wondered if that was such a good thing.

"Men are like dogs in a lot of ways," Reese said. "And Mike's young, so he's like a puppy dog. You pat then on the head, make them feel valued, and then they'll trot off with a wagging tail. It's like paying a compliment. My public service to the male population." She laughed. "Besides, I've seen Mike around school and he's nice enough, but I'm not interested in him. So, don't worry, Norris, I have it under control."

Mike returned with a basket of hot breadsticks and placed it in the center of the table. "Here you go," he said, flashing Norris a tight, nervous smile.

Reese touched the boy's shaky hand. "Thanks, Mike."

The tightness disappeared from Mike's smile as his gaze met Reese's. "You're welcome," he said.

Norris cleared his throat, loudly. "That'll be all," he said.

Mike moved on to another table.

Reese shook her head. "You can't help yourself, can you?"

"No, I guess not." He plucked a steaming breadstick from the basket and dropped it on his plate. "Look, this fatherhood thing is new to me, so you'll have to bear with me."

"Having a father is new for me. We still know so little about each other."

Norris reached across the table, closing his hand over hers. "That's why we're doing this. We've learned some things already. I know you're smart as a whip, you like basketball, and you're not short on feelings of self worth." He laughed. "That's a start. You've met my closest friends, you've been to my condo and office, and you know a few of my likes and dislikes. We're on our way." Reese pulled her bottom lip into her mouth. "What? Is there something you want to ask me?"

"Yeah, there is. Mom's accused me of lacking tact on occasion, so I'm going to apologize before I ask this if the question comes out wrong."

Norris took a bite of the breadstick, not crazy about that preface. "Okay," he said, drinking some water.

"Is my mother the only black woman you've dated?"

"No," he answered, not overly stunned by the question.

"Are you one of those white guys who have a thing for black women?"

Norris blinked. That question surprised him, and Reese didn't even know about his feelings for Dahlia yet. He drank more water.

"Look, I'm only asking because, well, it begs to be asked," Reese said. "Your place is loaded with African art. You're European blueblood, not exactly a commonality there, and your best friend is married to a black woman. Birds of a feather."

"You're straight to the point, aren't you?"

"I try to be," she said, nibbling on a breadstick.

"I didn't expect your question, but since you asked it, I'll answer it. The simple answer is no, I don't have what you call a 'thing' for black women. But I do have a thing for women. Beautiful women. And that runs the gamut of race, creed, and religious orientation. I have not been a saint in my lifetime, and that's mainly because of my fascination with the fairer sex." *That's why your flirtation worries me so much,* he wanted to say, but thought better of it. "As for Ryan, he followed his heart. He fell in love with Lara, so he married her. Just like he fell in love with his first wife, who was white, and married her. Race had nothing to do with it."

"So, Ryan's motivated by love and you by lust. Is that what you're saying?"

Norris detected irritation in Reese's voice. "I don't think I can answer this question without you getting angry with me. What do you want me to say, Reese? I was a heel back in the day? Okay, I was. I freely admit it."

"Did you love my mother, or was she one of many conquests?"

Norris drained his glass. "I thought you were going to ask Gail about that," he said, twirling the misty, cold glass.

"I never got around to it." Reese sat back and folded her arms. "So?"

"Is it my imagination or do I hear something in your tone?"

"You hear curiosity in my tone. I asked a question and I'm waiting to hear the answer. You're beating around the bush, so I'm going to assume the latter is the answer." She shook her head, grunting in dismay. "I don't get what my mother saw in you."

Norris bristled, as if slapped by an unexpected backhand. "You really think a lot of me, huh?"

"I don't know what I think of you. That's just it. I barely know you, and what I do know leaves me with more questions. You're confusing."

"What's so confusing? I'm doing everything I can to be as open and accessible to you as possible. What more can I do?"

Mike took this moment to return with the food. "Two fettuccini alfredos," he said, placing steaming plates before both of them. "Enjoy."

Neither Norris nor Reese responded. Mike left.

They ate in silence for the next few minutes.

"I deserve some answers," Reese said, halfway through her meal. "My mother is gone, and she didn't say much. You can shed some light on things for me."

"Reese, there's not much light I can shed for you. Gail and I were together for a short while. I thought she was a fantastic woman, and she made quite an impression on my life."

"But you didn't love her?"

"I cared a great deal about her, and as the mother of my only child, she will always have a special place in my heart." Anger flashed in Reese's eyes. She wanted an answer, and he had to give her one. "No, Reese, I wasn't in love with her," he said after another bite of pasta. "If it's any consolation, she didn't love me, either." He continued eating, hoping he'd appeased her and she would end the questioning.

"It's not." Reese pushed back her plate and met his gaze. "Have you ever loved any woman, or has it always been about sex?"

Norris lowered his fork. Suddenly the pasta didn't taste so good. He wanted to tell Reese about his feelings for Dahlia, but her hostility and Dahlia's being upset made him second-guess making the disclosure.

"Norris Converse!" Tawny Fisher, one of his many old acquaintances, approached. He hadn't seen the leggy blonde since before he met Dahlia, but Tawny's many phone calls had left no doubt about her desire to see him. "Have you been avoiding me?"

Yes! "I've been busy," Norris said, glancing nervously at a very unhappy-looking Reese.

Tawny gazed at Reese. "She's pretty enough, Norris, but a bit young, don't you think?"

"This is my daughter, Tawny."

"Daughter?" Tawny eyed Reese up and down. "That's a surprise." She tapped Reese on the head. "Why don't you be a sweet little girl and run off and play while I have a little fun-time with Daddy."

Norris frowned. "Wait a minute!" He glared at the nervy blonde. "Reese isn't going anywhere, but you are!"

"No, I am," Reese said, standing. "We have nothing more to discuss. My question has been answered." She glowered at Tawny. "Thank you."

"Reese, wait! If you want to leave, I'll take you home."

"Fine. I'll be outside."

Norris dropped a fifty-dollar bill on the table, and pushed past Tawny.

"Wait, Norris." Tawny grabbed his arm. "You going to call me later?" She smiled brightly, leaving no doubt in Norris's mind about what she had planned for later.

Norris jerked his arm away. Having his randy past thrown into Reese's face didn't make the list of things he wanted to share with her, and celebrating the event was even further off the list. He said nothing to the woman and continued on his way, praying he hadn't lost his daughter for good.

CHAPTER 15

"Reese, talk to me. Tell me what you're feeling."

Dahlia pushed her bag of chips to the side and stood from the sofa as an upset Norris followed Reese into the house. "What's going on?" she asked, looking from father to daughter.

"Ask him," Reese said, glaring at Norris. "I'm going to finish studying." She bounded up the stairs and locked herself in her bedroom.

Dahlia turned to Norris. "You want to explain that?"

Norris shrugged. "She's a teenager. I've yet to become adept at deciphering teen."

"Something caused her to react like this."

"Me. I'm not the man she imagined her father to be."

"Has she told you what kind of man she expected her father to be?"

"Not in so many words, but she's made it pretty clear I'm not it." He looked toward the stairs and shook his head. "I don't know what more I can do."

The hurt in Norris's eyes said as much as his words. Dahlia had never seen him so miserable. She ached to bring him into her arms and comfort him, but realized holding him would not be wise for many reasons. "Come into the living room and sit down for a while," she offered instead. "I can make you some tea." She smiled.

Norris smiled back. "Tea?" he said.

"I understand it's very comforting." She followed him into the living room. "It'll only take a sec to put on the water."

He gently tugged on the back of her jumbo T-shirt, halting her trip to the kitchen. "Don't bother with the tea, Dahlia. Just talking to you is comfort enough. Is everything all right with you?"

"Me? Sure. Everything is great with me," she lied, settling into the left corner of the couch and tugging on the ends of her leggings.

"Really?"

Dahlia nodded.

"Then why are you eating these?" Norris asked, retrieving the bag of chips from behind the pillow. "Your comfort food. Grandma Flora didn't help things?"

"How did you . . ." Dahlia sighed. "Reese?"

Norris nodded as he sat. "Yeah. She told me you went to church and then had lunch with your grandmother. Is everything okay? Are things better with your sister?"

"Leslie is better. My parents are with her."

"Something's wrong. You don't eat chips for nothing."

Dahlia rolled her eyes. That's what she got for sharing. "I don't really need an excuse to eat chips. They aren't my weakness for nothing."

"Maybe. But you usually have a reason for diving headfirst into a bag. You don't want to tell me what it is, do you?"

"Not particularly," she said, finding it difficult to look at him as something other than misery flickered in his eyes.

"All right. I won't pry," Norris said. "I hope it gets better soon, whatever it is."

There's no chance of that if I keep seeing you. "Thanks," she said. "I'll talk to Reese for you."

"And say what?"

"Whatever it takes. A girl needs her father."

"Thanks, I appreciate it."

"No biggie."

Dahlia followed Norris to the door. Their hands brushed as each reached for the knob. Dahlia's breath caught, the power of his touch awakening every nerve ending in her body. Norris swallowed loudly, not unaffected. His thumb brushed her lower lip. Dahlia trembled, wanting more of his touch. Norris leaned forward. His warm breath tickled her lips. Dahlia closed her eyes, anticipating his tantalizing kisses, but heard only a pained whimper. Her eyes opened just in time to see a flushed Norris pull away.

"I'm sorry." Norris opened the door and stepped outside. "Tell Reese I'll call later." He dashed to his car without looking back.

Sighing, Dahlia closed her eyes and pressed her back against the door. *Would this ever get any easier?*

"Is he gone?"

Dahlia jumped, startled for the second time today by Reese's voice.

"I scared you again?" Reese said.

"Surprised me. I thought you were studying."

Reese shook her head, descending the stairs. "Just wanted to get away from daddy dearest."

"What happened at lunch today?"

"I saw the master at work."

"The master?" Dahlia said curiously.

"Mr. Lover Man. Some blonde bimbo sauntered over to the table and practically threw herself at him."

Dahlia managed to maintain what she hoped was an even expression. "What was his response?"

"He made an attempt at outrage, but I wasn't buying it."

"Why not?"

"Because just moments before he admitted to being a womanizer."

"He told you that?"

"He said he had a thing for beautiful women, and lots of them. He said he cared a great deal for my mother, but he didn't love her, and when I asked if he'd loved any woman, he . . ."

"What?" Dahlia asked. "What did he say?"

"Nothing. That's when the bimbo showed up. At that point I'd had enough, and that's when we left."

"The whole time was bad?"

Reese's shoulders slumped. "It wasn't bad. It was actually kinda fun, but that's the problem. He's too free, if that's the right word. He's not the fatherly type."

"But he is your father, Reese, and nothing is going to change that. You really need to take it easy on him."

"I am, Dahlia, but I can't pretend I'm okay with the kind of person he is. He never loved my mother. She was just a warm body for him."

"Is that what's really bothering you? The fact he didn't love your mother?"

"I guess. It was just a moment in time, and now he wants to step into the parenthood role. He doesn't have to do that, and I'm not up for it."

"You can't punish him for not knowing about you. He wants to know you, Reese. It stands to reason he would have stepped up to the plate if he had known about you all along."

"I wouldn't be so sure. He was a playboy then, and he's a playboy now. I honestly don't know what my mother saw in him."

Dahlia grunted to herself. She could list countless reasons why Gail would've been into Norris. A purely shallow and very obvious reason, he was drop-dead gorgeous. "You seem to have your mind made up about him," she said.

Reese nodded. "Mostly, yes."

"I really think you should give him another chance. He was really upset when you ran upstairs."

"He's not used to a woman not falling at his feet." Reese moved to the couch and sat. "He'll get over it," she said, munching on Dahlia's chips.

"What are you going to tell your mother?"

"Mom? What do you mean?"

"She left town to give you the opportunity to spend time with your father, a decision she didn't reach easily.

And now you're just giving up without giving Norris a chance."

"Dahlia, what do you want me to do?"

"A good start would be not to expect him to be Ward Cleaver."

"Who?" Reese asked curiously, digging for more chips.

Dahlia chuckled to herself. What was she thinking? "You shouldn't expect him to be the perfect father," she restated in simpler terms. "He's feeling his way through this just like you. Just keep that in mind the next time you see him. And you will see him again, right?"

After some reluctance, Reese nodded. "Yeah, I guess."

"Good."

"I think I'll finish studying now," Reese said, traipsing up the stairs with Dahlia's bag of chips. "I'll see you in a couple of hours."

Dahlia watched with longing as her chips disappeared behind Reese's door. She knew she should have bought another bag. *Mr. Lover Man?* Who was this blonde Norris had encountered at lunch?

Norris smiled as the hostess escorted Dahlia to the private room at Martin's Lakeside Restaurant. He hadn't seen her since the day he dropped Reese off after the luncheon gone wrong over a week ago. After much fast-talking, he'd managed to get Dahlia to agree to meet him for a business dinner. Of course, business was the last thing on his mind, but he needed an excuse to see her, and her audit made one readily available. Seeing her in the black dress that displayed her every perfect curve and a sexy twist to her stylish hair confirmed he'd done the right thing. She was too gorgeous for words.

He stood when Dahlia approached the table. "I'm glad you could make it." Norris excused the hostess and helped Dahlia into her chair.

"You made it sound important, so I'm here." Dahlia looked around the room. "The private dining room at Martin's?" She shook her head. "I shouldn't have come. This isn't business."

Norris grabbed her hand before she could get away. "Dahlia, wait. Look." He reached under the table and produced his briefcase, a weak attempt at compensating for the roses, candlelight, and elegant dinnerware decorating the room. "See? This is business," he said, returning the case to the floor.

"We could have done this over the phone."

"I think this calls for a face-to-face meeting."

"You have an office."

"Yeah, but Martin's is so much nicer."

"Your office is very nice."

"Yeah, it is. I have great taste." Norris smiled as she rolled her eyes. "But this is more . . ."

"Romantic?"

"I guess that's a word, not that my office hasn't had moments of romance." He shook his head as his gaze swept over her. "You look sensational, but you always do."

"Norris."

"Dahlia, how much longer are we going to keep doing this tap dancing? I have been trying so hard to do things your way, but I can't keep this up. I swear, I put Mario Andretti to shame when I left your house. Cold showers have become for me what ripple chips are for you. I miss the feel of your soft skin against mine. Your sweet smell. The way you moan when I take you there."

"Norris . . ."

"I miss all of that. But what I miss most is you. Being around you. Talking to you. Laughing with you. Cold showers are a comfort, but they're also a bitch. I'd much rather have you keeping me company than thoughts of you."

"What's wrong, Norris? The nameless blonde isn't taking care of your needs?"

"Blonde?" He smiled. "Reese told you about Tawny."

"Tawny?" Dahlia drank from the sweating water glass placed before her. "That figures," she mumbled.

"You're jealous."

"Of someone I don't know?" Dahlia scoffed. "You really think a lot of yourself."

"Indeed I do, but you're still jealous." Anger flashed in Dahlia's eyes. Norris laughed. "Okay, I'll rephrase. You're unhappy with the idea of her. I think that's even better than jealousy. It's very sweet, but unnecessary. Tawny means absolutely nothing to me."

"That doesn't surprise me, Norris. She's like all your women, including me. That's what I want you to understand."

He shook his head. "I can't understand that, because it's a lie. Tawny is one of a string of women I've been with. I've had more than my share of lovelies, but none lovelier than you. Dahlia, you are the one lady I never believed could exist. The one I fell in love with."

"No."

"Yes." Dahlia winced and lowered her gaze. Norris couldn't ignore her discomfort, but he also couldn't stop. "I know you don't want to hear that, but at the same time, I think you like hearing it. I see your conflict, Dahlia, and feel your pain. I don't like seeing my love hurt you. The love I know you feel."

Dahlia lifted her head. Tears streamed down her cheeks. "What do you want me to say, Norris?"

"You know what." He brushed away her tears. "But I'm not going to pressure you." He saw this struggle with winning Dahlia's love as the price he'd have to pay for the hedonistic life he'd lived. So he would suck it up. "I want to hear the words from those sweet lips, but I see them in those beautiful eyes every time I look at you, and that's enough for me. It will continue to be enough until you're ready to speak them."

Norris chuckled. "When I say these words, I can barely believe it's me. Ryan's been on me for years about settling down, and telling me one day the love bug would take a bite out of me, but I never believed it." Norris settled his hand around hers, and to his great happiness, Dahlia didn't pull away, shout, or bolt. She looked at him, quiet but attentive. "Ryan was right. The love bug has bitten the hell outta me, Dahlia, and I don't mind saying it to you. I don't mind saying anything to you. I'm at ease with you. And I think our beginning is the reason why. We kinda just happened, and it's the best thing to ever happen to me."

Dahlia's tears refreshed. She pulled her hand away. "I need—I need to go," she stammered.

"Before you run off, I have a couple of things to say."

"Haven't you said it all?"

"Not quite. Dahlia, I'm in this for keeps. I've not been with any other woman since I met you, and I don't want to be with anyone else . . . ever."

"What do you mean *ever*?"

Norris thought of the five-carat diamond ring he'd picked up today and locked away in his home safe, and the day he could finally present it to Dahlia. "It's what you think I mean," he said. Norris released her hand. "I'm done."

After several moments of intense quiet, Dahlia cleared her throat. "What about my audit?" she said.

"Audit?" he repeated.

"Yes. That appointment with the IRS. What brought me here."

"Oh, yeah, that. It's fine. Everything is going great. Don't worry." The aromas from Martin's many tantalizing dishes wafted into the room. Norris's mouth watered. "Are you hungry?"

"No."

The growl from Dahlia's stomach brought a smile to his lips. "It's a good thing your body always tells me the truth your mouth won't. I had the chef prepare some of your favorite foods. He even prepared some ripple chips for you, loaded with cheese, bacon bits, and a ranch dip. Delicious."

"You shouldn't have done that.".

"I like doing things for you. I only wish you would let me do them more often. You're hungry, Dahlia. Stay. It's just one meal, and we've had them before."

"This feels different."

"It might be. If you stay, I'm liable to consider it our first date."

Dahlia frowned. "It's not a date, Norris, it's business."

Norris couldn't help smiling at the insincerity he found in her angry scowl. "Whatever you say," he said.

Dahlia and Norris conversed over the decadent cherry cheesecake that completed their delicious dinner. She'd have to spend days on her treadmill after the food she ate, but she didn't have any regrets. She was having a good time with Norris, being a sounding board for him.

"And you haven't talked to your mother since?" she said.

"Not a word." He pushed his empty dessert plate to the middle of the table and drank some water. "I shouldn't have been surprised by her reaction, but I was. Surprised and hurt."

"I'm sorry, Norris, but I tried to tell you."

"I know. I've had a hard time making headway with Reese, and to explain her grandmother, and most likely her grandfather, have issues with her race . . . I doubt we'll ever have the kind of relationship I want for us."

"Don't give up on Reese. You two have spent some time together over the last few days. She hasn't said much about it, but I didn't get the impression it went badly."

Norris shrugged. "Not bad, but not exactly good. We're pleasant with each other. Like we're interviewing each other and afraid to say the wrong thing."

Dahlia finished the cheesecake and lowered her fork to the plate. "It's only been about two weeks since Gail left, Norris. Things will get better between you two." She laughed. "I think the biggest problem is you're both so much alike."

"I agree with that. Reese is even more beautiful than I am. She's very aware of that, and so are the boys who can't keep their eyes off her."

"Did you hear yourself?"

"What?"

"She's even more beautiful than you are? I find it amazing I can like two people who are as vain as you and Reese."

"You like me?"

"I've never denied that."

"No. You just never say you love me. Then, again, you haven't said you don't." Norris brushed his thumb along the corner of her lip. "You missed a bit of topping," he said, licking the red glaze from his finger.

Dahlia's heart pounded furiously in her chest. They'd enjoyed a delicious dinner and stimulating conversation mostly free of the "L" word, and then Norris went and ate food from her face, making things tense again. She sucked down some water. "You could have used a napkin."

"Yeah, but what's the fun in that?"

A trio of strolling violinists made their way into the room. Dahlia couldn't believe this evening. Norris had spared no expense.

He extended his hand across the table. "Dance with me."

"I don't think that would be wise."

"Ah, come on, Dahlia. Throw caution to the wind. I won't tell anyone you danced with me, and I'm sure the entertainment won't, either." Norris kept his hand extended. "Come on."

Against her better judgment, Dahlia took his hand and took to the floor with him. Their bodies moved in a gentle sway to the music. Norris brought her closer, clasping his fingers around the small of her back.

Dahlia draped her arms around Norris's shoulders, and nestled her head in the crook of his neck. A soft sigh passed her lips. She missed being in his arms. This didn't feel scary. Even on that first night, as wrong as it was, it had felt right. Her fingers combed through the soft curls at the nape of his neck. Norris moaned and held her closer. His pounding heart thudded against her breast, as an altogether different pounding thumped against her thigh.

Dahlia lifted her head to the reward of Norris's kiss. His supple lips caressed hers with the softness of a feathery touch. Her lips parted at the insistence of his warm tongue, welcoming his sensual invasion to her mouth. Dahlia clung to him, savoring this moment she had gone without for so long, with the thought of allowing it to continue back at his place. But she knew he would have none of that, and as much as it drove her crazy, it also made her feel incredibly special.

The kiss came to an end. The sound of heavy breathing joined the sweet melody of soft strings. Passion-laden gray eyes stared down at her.

"I would love nothing more than to take you home with me," Norris said, stroking her cheek and reading her thoughts, "but you know why that can't happen."

She nodded. "You've made it clear."

"This is killing me, Dahlia, but I can't allow my carnal urges for you to override my hope for our future. It's too important to me. I think this was a pretty good first date."

Dahlia smiled. He was right, but she wouldn't allow herself to say the words. She had some serious soul-searching to do. "Good night, Norris."

"Good night, Dahlia."

CHAPTER 16

"Hi." Norris kissed Lara on the cheek and made his way into the house. "Angelica ready?" he asked.

"Just about. Ryan is helping with her sneakers."

Norris brought his hands together. "Great. This should be fun. I know Justin went to the movies with Billy, but I'll be sure to find him something he'll like."

"Why do you want to take Angelica to the mall again? I'm certain using her as your chick magnet isn't it this time."

"You wound me, Lara. I'm a chick magnet in my own right." He grinned at Lara's pursed lips. "She's my god-daughter and I love spending time with her. And I don't think you and Ryan will mind having some time alone."

Lara pressed her hand to the side of her ever-widening girth. "I think Ryan and I have spent more than enough time alone. Today, we'll spend our time alone writing thank you notes for last week's baby shower." She grimaced.

"Oh." Norris touched the top of Lara's tummy. A thrusting movement bumped against his hand. "Oooh. Is that a foot?"

"I think they're playing Twister. You don't want to know where those other feet are."

Norris shuddered. "I think you're right."

Angelica raced into the room with Ryan following closely behind, urging her to stop running.

"Uncle Norris!" Angelica leapt into his arms, hugging his neck. "Will you buy me a baby doll?"

He kissed her nose. "Absolutely."

"Don't spoil her, Norris," Ryan said, draping his arm around Lara's shoulders.

"I think you've already beat him to it," Lara remarked.

"He's worse than me, babe."

"What worse?" said Norris. "Buying this sweet child a doll is not spoiling her." He pressed his cheek to Angelica's. "Just look at that face. Who can say no to that face?"

Lara raised her hand. "I can," she said. "It's hard but possible. Don't go crazy, Norris."

"And that's crazy by our standards, not yours," Ryan said.

Norris smiled as the precious little girl. Spoiling this angel came as easily for him as breathing. How he wished he'd known Reese at this age. If he didn't call Reese, he would probably never hear from her. She didn't freeze him out, but she definitely didn't overextend herself, and the school year had ended a couple of weeks ago. Things had to get better for them, but first he had to convince her he'd shed his title of lady-killer.

"So, is Dahlia joining you and Angelica on the mall excursion?" Ryan asked.

"No. As far as I know, she's working," Norris answered.

"As far as you know?"

"That's right. You ask me the same question all the time, and the answer is the same. There's no relationship."

"You guys had that great date a couple of weeks ago."

"Yes, weeks, Ryan. More than a month. The last significant conversation we had was when I informed her about the success of her audit, and that was business. I'm not pushing the personal issue anymore. Dahlia knows how I feel. I'm giving her space to deal with what she's feeling."

"I saw Dahlia yesterday," Lara said. "She asked about you."

"Did she?"

"Uh-huh. She's weakening."

"Really? She hardly says more than hello to me when I phone for Reese."

"That's what women do," Lara said. "Dahlia can't let you know she's thinking about you."

"But you just told me."

"That's right, because she wanted me to."

"Huh?" Norris said, switching Angelica to his other side. "Did she ask you to tell me?"

"No, she didn't. But trust me, if you were to—I don't know—pay her a visit, I bet she'd be glad you did." Lara smiled broadly. "Just something to think about."

"Things better with Reese?" Ryan asked.

Norris grunted. "Let's just say they aren't any worse."

"She's a teenager, and you're both still adjusting," Lara said. "She just needs . . ."

"More time," Norris said. "I know." He jiggled Angelica. "You ready to go?"

"Yep!" she answered.

"All right."

Lara kissed Angelica's cheek. "You keep your eye on Uncle Norris, okay?"

Angelica nodded. "I will, Mommy."

"Don't spend more on her today than Lara and I make in a week," Ryan told him, kissing Angelica's forehead. "We want her to grow up to appreciate things and not just expect them because Uncle Norris can buy them for her."

Norris frowned. "Killjoy."

"Norris."

"All right, all right," he said. "I won't overindulge."

Ten minutes and one toy store after arriving at the mall, Angelica had two new babies to play with. Norris walked through the mall with Angelica holding one hand and a bag with her two new dolls and a video game for Justin in the other.

"I have two babies just like Mommy is going to have," Angelica said proudly. "Thank you, Uncle Norris." She beamed.

"You're welcome, sweetie." Norris wondered if he could ever get a big smile like that out of Reese. "I was happy to get them for you."

"Uncle Norris, look!" Angelica pointed across the way to the music store. "Diana and Reese."

Norris looked over to find his daughter and her friend engaged in jovial conversation with two young African-American men, one of whom had his arm around Reese's waist, an act she didn't seem to mind, but one he minded a lot. Her flirting with a guy made him uneasy, but touching made him worried.

"C'mon!" Angelica pulled him toward the girls, but Norris didn't need any prodding. Angelica tapped on Diana's leg, finally getting her cousin's attention from the young man who had her all smiles. "Hey, Diana," she greeted cheerfully.

"Angelica, Mr. Converse, hello," Diana said.

"Hello." Norris gazed at his daughter. "Hello, Reese. Who's your friend?" he asked of the young man who seemed somewhat familiar to him, but way too familiar with Reese.

"This is Jack," Reese said, sliding her hand into her friend's.

"Jack? Like Cher?"

Reese frowned, but Norris held his ground. She didn't have to tell him her darkest secrets, but he deserved to know of her interest in some guy and what his full name was.

"No, sir, Mr. Converse, I'm Jackson Armstrong," said the young man, extending his hand. "My father works at your firm."

Norris shook Jack's hand. "David," he said, remembering Jack's face from a photo on David Armstrong's desk. A good man and great accountant, David had joined the firm a couple of years ago when several area non-profit organizations approached Norris for services. David had taken up the paying customers Norris found it beneficial to accept to keep a flow of capital on hand for financial planning classes in different communities. So far, things had been going great. In fact, he entertained the idea of hiring a couple more accountants to help with David's burgeoning clientele. But being fond of David was one thing, and having his son hanging all over Reese quite another. "How long have you two known each other?"

"Since Reese moved to Denburg. We're classmates," Jack explained. "She told me about finding out you were her father."

"Amazing, she hasn't said a word to me about you. You two dating?"

Reese glared at him through narrowed eyes. "Why are you here, Norris?" she said, her words intensely measured.

"He bought me new dollies," Angelica happily shared, swinging Norris's hand. "Wanna see 'em?"

"Maybe some other time, Angelica," Reese said, managing to give the little girl a smile before fixing her angry frown back at Norris.

Quiet settled around them. Norris couldn't understand why Reese didn't tell him about Jack. She asked him all sorts of personal questions, but she'd never once mentioned she liked a guy. Why had she kept this a secret? Wondering why only served to anger him. She had some explaining to do.

Diana cleared her throat. "Jack, why don't you and Barry go over to the food court, okay?" she said. "Reese and I will meet you over there in a bit."

The guys nodded and went on their way.

"Mr. Converse, I'm going to take Angelica to the bathroom."

"But I don't have to go," said Angelica.

"Then we'll go to the carousel." Diana flashed a tight smile at father and daughter and reached for Angelica's hand. "You two go on and discuss whatever it is you have to discuss. We'll be over there," she said, making tracks to the merry-go-round.

"You want to explain your behavior!" Reese blasted, once Diana and Angelica were out of earshot.

"That's my question, young lady. That boy was all over you."

Reese folded her arms. "Boy?"

"Don't you dare do that to me!" he barked, not happy with her insinuation. "You know exactly what I'm talking about."

"He's a friend of mine."

"Diana's your friend. How come I've never heard about him?"

"How come I never heard about Tawny before she graced us with her presence at lunch?"

"That was over a month ago."

"Doesn't matter. The point is, I don't know all of your friends, and you don't know all of mine."

"When said friend is hanging all over you, I need to know about him."

"Says who?"

"Says me. I am your father."

Reese grunted. "Don't remind me."

"You don't want me to care about you?"

"What I don't want is you interfering in my life."

"You're sixteen years old. You don't have a life yet." Norris drew a breath and lowered his voice that had grown progressively louder. Patrons in the music store started to stare. He took Reese by the arm and led her to a quiet spot near the mall entrance. "Jack may be a nice kid, but he's a young man with hormones. And watching him touching you made me uneasy."

"You act like he was groping me. His arm was around my waist. I held his hand. Not exactly baby-making stuff."

"That stuff leads to the baby-making stuff."

"I'm not an idiot. I know where babies come from and how to keep them from happening." She stuck out her chin. "Something you at twenty and my *doctor* mother at thirty-five apparently had no clue about."

Norris dragged his hands over his face. "You will slip in that dig every chance you get, won't you?"

"It's true."

"What's true is I care about you and I don't want to see you getting in over your head."

"For showing interest in a guy? Norris, Angelica is the three-year-old, not me. Now you can practice parenting on her as much as you want, she seems to like it, and you seem to be quite good with her, but I don't need that from you. And I don't want it."

Norris gritted his teeth. Once charmed by Reese's spirit, it now served only to test his patience. "You don't have a choice," he said. "I am your parent, and while your mother is thousands of miles away in another country, I'm going to be that to you. In my quest to get closer to you, I've been too accommodating with you. I wanted to be your friend, but I have to be your father first. You need to tell me where you're going to be, when, and with whom. You can tell Dahlia, too, but you *will* tell me. You will call me at least once in the morning and check in with me by eleven at night. And before you go out with *Jack* again, you will ask my permission."

"What?" Reese blasted, her eyes as wide as saucers.

"You heard me. Things are going to be different with us."

"Because *you* say so?"

"Yes." He nodded. "Because *I* say so."

"This is because you saw me with Jack, isn't it?"

Hell yeah! "I think we need to establish some structure in our relationship," Norris said. "The old way isn't working."

"You can't control me."

"I don't want control, Reese. I want inclusion. Through no fault of my own, I missed sixteen years of your life. I'm not missing any more. I will be actively involved in your life from now on. You don't have to like it, and your pouting tells me you don't, but it's the way it's going to be."

"Can I leave now?"

"What are the rest of your plans for the day?"

"We're going to the movies."

Norris checked his watch. Three-thirty. "Which showing?"

"Four-fifteen," Reese answered.

"And after that?"

"We might get something to eat."

"Call me after the movie when you know for sure."

Reese rolled her eyes. "This is how it's going to be from now on?"

Norris folded his arms. "Yes, it is," he said sternly.

"Great," she grumbled. "Are we done?"

"Sure."

Reese walked away, saying nothing.

"And, Reese?"

She turned back to him. "What?"

"It wouldn't be wise to make me have to call you," he said, giving her pause if she had any notions of disobeying him. "I don't think you'd like the outcome of that."

"Good night, Mrs. Lee. I'll see you in two weeks." Dahlia waved good-bye to her last client for the day and dropped her smock in her chair. "All right, ladies, I'm done," she said to Marcie and Mrs. Flo, who each had a client to finish.

Marci waved goodbye.

"You leaving a little early tonight, Dahlia. You got big plans?" asked Mrs. Flo, mindlessly flipping through the current issue of *Jet* magazine as she went about her business of snooping into Dahlia's business while her client dozed under the drier.

"No, ma'am, I don't have any big plans. I'm just going to go home, make some dinner for Reese, and get ready for church in the morning."

Mrs. Flo raised an eyebrow. "That's all?"

"That's enough."

"After the flowers, presents, and good food your secret admirer sent over here, I would think you'd be busy trying to keep that man happy." Mrs. Flo closed the magazine and dropped it in her lap. "Maybe staying home and doing nothing might explain why those presents stopped coming, hmm?"

"Or maybe he just brings them to my house when he comes over, hmm?" Dahlia flashed the nosey woman a tight smile. "Or maybe not. That's where 'private' comes into 'private life.'"

Mrs. Flo squared her shoulders and grunted. "Humph. I'm sorry I asked."

"No, you're not. But it's okay. You can't help yourself." A gifted cosmetologist with dozens of faithful clients, Mrs. Flo knew hair like the back of her hand. Too bad she had to know everybody's business the same way. Dahlia grabbed her purse from her station cabinet. "I'll see you all on Tuesday."

The phone rang as she made her way to the door. "I'll get it," she called out to the ladies, picking up the phone mid-ring. "DBS."

"Dahlia, it's Josette Lee. There's a white man sitting in a Mercedes outside your shop. I asked him if he was lost, and he said no, but he didn't leave. I thought he might be waiting on that pretty blonde girl Marci is working on.

That's why I called you. He really liked my hair," she said, with a giddy laugh.

Dahlia smiled. *Could it be?* Over the past month she'd done little more than think about Norris, and now it seemed he sat a few feet outside her shop. "Is the car gray?" she asked.

"Yes."

Norris. "Thanks for telling me, Mrs. Lee. I'll take care of it," Dahlia said.

"All right. Bye now."

Dahlia hung up the phone and pulled her cell phone from the waist clip on her jeans. She pressed and held the number five on her keypad, the speed-dial button to Norris's cell phone, and walked out the door.

"Hi. This is a pleasant surprise," Norris said.

"How long have you been waiting outside my salon?" She approached the car and tapped on the passenger side window.

Norris laughed. "About ten minutes. But I've been driving around the perimeter for the past hour or so." He ended the call and opened the door. "How did you know?"

"I have my sources," she said, sliding inside.

"The sweet old lady with the nice hairstyle, right?"

"Your compliment made Mrs. Lee's day."

"That's the Norris touch."

Dahlia couldn't help smiling. "You waiting outside also concerned her, so she called to give me a heads-up. Why are you out here? Is something wrong?"

Norris shrugged. "I don't know. Maybe. Can we go somewhere and talk?"

Dahlia nodded. They definitely needed to talk. "Sure. How about my place?"

"I'll follow you."

Norris remained quiet as he walked into her house. He sat on the couch, sighing wearily.

Dahlia sat beside him and touched his arm. "What's wrong, Norris? Is it your mother?"

"No. Reese."

"What about her?"

"I saw her at the mall earlier. I think—hell, I know she's not happy with me."

Dahlia groaned. "What happened?"

"I found her all hugged up with some boy."

"Found her? Was she hiding?"

Norris grunted. "Not hardly. I couldn't believe my eyes."

A horrible image of Norris ripping a poor kid to shreds flashed before Dahlia's eyes. Reese had mentioned his snippy attitude toward the waiter at Corlino's Kitchen for showing interest, so to have a young man actually touch her, probably the guy Jack she'd mentioned she liked, Norris probably went ballistic. "What did you do?" Dahlia asked, almost afraid to hear the answer.

"What's with the accusatory tone I hear in your voice? You're supposed to be on my side."

"I'm Switzerland. I'm not on anyone's side. Now, you tell me what you did."

"Dahlia, my sixteen-year-old daughter let some kid practically paw her in front of everybody in the mall. I reacted as any parent would."

"I'm not a parent, so why don't you break it down for me."

"I talked to her."

"To her or at her?"

Norris shook his head, looking as if she had suddenly started speaking in a foreign tongue. "I don't understand."

"No, you don't. You've only known about Reese for a couple of months, but she's not a baby, Norris. Why do I have the feeling you treated her like one today?"

"I know she's not a baby, but she is *my* baby. I don't think I'll ever get used to the idea of boys looking at my daughter and seeing a woman. She's not a woman yet, and I don't want boys looking at Reese and thinking the thoughts boys her age think."

"Like the thoughts you had at their age?"

"Yes!" He shook his head. "No."

Dahlia laughed. "Uh-huh." She tapped his knee with her hand. "Finish telling me what happened with Reese."

"When I saw her hugging this boy I never even heard about, I was a little angry."

"A little?"

"A lot angry. I was with Angelica and she spotted Diana and Reese and they were with these jock types. Completely taken, I might add. We talked alone, and Reese rebuked me for my less-than-warm reception of her friend Jack. I, in turn, shared my unhappiness about her not telling me about him. That went on for a while, and when all was said and done I let her know I expected to hear from her twice a day every day, and she is to tell me of any plans she makes before she makes them."

"How did Reese receive that?"

"She was angry. And I'm sorry she's angry, but I'm not sorry I said what I did."

"I think you're sorry about something. Your sullen expression before you began to explain said as much."

"I guess I could have delivered my words in a gentler manner. It's just . . . seeing her with this kid. He seems nice enough, and his father works at my firm, but . . ."

"But your daughter with a guy makes you see red."

"No, it makes me see fear. You've said Reese and I are a lot alike, and I have to agree with that. That's what scares me. She flirts with young men."

"You flirt with women. Young and old. Mrs. Lee."

"Yes, but I know what I'm doing. And I'm a man."

"You did not just say that."

"Dahlia?"

"Norris, Reese is a very smart girl. She's not advertising or suggesting anything when she flirts. It's just her way. It's a part of her charm, like it is yours. As for 'finding' her with this young man, you really need to choose another term. I don't think she was hiding anything."

"Maybe she wasn't, but I still want to keep closer tabs on her, and I definitely want to spend more time with her. Gail's been gone over six weeks, and Reese and I have spent little significant time together."

"You're definitely within your rights as her father, but you don't want to come across as a tyrant. Go easy with her. I will see that she follows your rules."

"Thank you, Dahlia. I appreciate your support."

"Gail wants you and Reese to get closer, and I'm here to help that along."

"How are you getting along?" Norris asked. "We haven't really talked since Martin's."

Dahlia nodded. "I know. I've been—I've been thinking about things."

"And where are your thoughts?"

"Right now, I'm thinking how glad I am to see you." She closed her hands around his. Her heart swelled from the warmth in his touch and light in his eyes. "I've missed you a lot, but that's the norm."

"I know. I've missed you, too. You know it's not about . . ."

"I know, Norris. You said a lot that night at Martin's, and I've thought a lot about it." Dahlia wondered if she'd be able to explain the battle she'd been waging since she realized she'd fallen in love with him. How her desire to give him the loving relationship he wanted wrestled with her desperate need to keep her heart safe from harm from a man so much like her ex-husband it would be foolish to believe he could be different. How could she explain it? "I know what you want from me, Norris, and I think I should tell you that—"

The phone rang in the middle of her words.

Norris gave her hands a gentle squeeze. "Let it ring."

"I can't. It might be Reese." Dahlia reached for the phone. Her father's cell number appeared on the caller ID display.

"Is it Reese?" Norris asked.

"No," she said, placing the phone to her ear. Norris sat back on the couch with his arms folded. "Hi, Daddy."

"Dahlia, baby, I know you have issues with your sister, but things are bad right now."

"What do you mean, bad?"

Norris leaned forward, watching her intently.

"Her blood pressure is extremely high and she's gone into early labor. They're giving her medicine to slow down contractions and lower her pressure, but they still might have to take the baby. She has six weeks to go. It's too early, Dahlia, and she's scared. She needs her big sister."

A knot formed in Dahlia's throat. Tears slid down her cheek. Norris reached for her hand, the comforting squeeze like an embrace for her whole body. She drew a breath, gaining strength from his touch.

"Will you come to Atlanta?" her father asked.

"Yes, Daddy, I'll be there as soon as I can."

Norris retrieved the phone from her shaky hand. "Dahlia, what's wrong?"

"Leslie's in the hospital. Her pressure is up and she's having contractions."

"I'm sorry."

"I have to go to Atlanta." She clasped her shaky hands. "I need to book a flight. Arrange a rental car."

"I'll take care of that. Do you want me to come with you?"

Yes! But she couldn't say that. Norris's presence would be a comfort, but it would also be a huge distraction. She had enough of her own questions without having to deal with those of her parents. "I think it might be best if I go alone," she said.

"I'm worried about you, Dahlia. You and your sister have issues and the pregnancy is upsetting to you. You shouldn't go to Atlanta alone. Your folks are going to be too upset about your sister to concentrate on you."

"It's okay, Norris. I can take care of myself."

"I know you can, but you don't have to." He closed his hands around her face. "I want to take care of you."

"I know." The emotions in his eyes overwhelmed her. New tears slid down her cheeks. "Thank you."

"Don't thank me for that. It's not a favor, Dahlia, it's an honor." His thumbs brushed away the warm streams. "I love you. Give me your hurt and I'll take it away. Believe in me and what I feel for you. I promise you can, and you won't ever regret it."

"Don't believe anything he says, Dahlia!" Reese bounded into the living room. "Norris, you just couldn't wait to . . ." Her eyes widened and words stopped. "Dahlia, what's wrong?" Reese moved to the space next to Dahlia on the couch, glaring at Norris. "He hasn't been feeding you lies about me, has he?"

"No, Reese, he hasn't," Dahlia said, wiping her eyes.

"You're back early," Norris said.

"Yeah, I was too mortified to sit through the movie." Reese rolled her eyes and turned to Dahlia. "If he didn't say anything, why are you upset?"

"Her sister has been hospitalized," Norris answered.

"I need to go Atlanta," Dahlia explained. "I hope you understand."

Reese nodded. "Absolutely. I'm so sorry to hear that, Dahlia. I hope everything will be okay. I'll call Diana. I'm sure her folks won't mind me staying over until you're back."

"That won't be necessary," Norris said. "You'll be staying with me until Dahlia returns."

"No, I won't."

"Yes, you will! And it's not up for discussion. You have a room at my place, and you will be using it. Now go upstairs and get your things." He held up his finger. "And do it without saying another word."

Reese shot off the couch and stomped up the stairs.

Dahlia slowly turned to him. "What happened to gentler?"

"I'm being firm. I have to take this stand."

"All right, Norris. I want you two to get closer while I'm away. Just be careful."

"You be careful." His finger glided against her cheek, stirring the butterflies that grew restless in her stomach whenever he touched her or fixed those gray eyes on hers. "I'll be thinking about you the whole time you're gone."

Dahlia nodded. "Me, too," she murmured.

"I'm glad to hear that, but here's a little something that might help along the way." He leaned forward, claiming her lips. Their mouths moved in concert, softly, tenderly. "Call me if you need anything at all, or even if you don't, okay?"

"Okay."

"I'll stay down here and make your arrangements. You go up and pack."

"Thank you, Norris."

"Stop thanking me. Go on, I'll take care of everything."

Dahlia believed he would take care of everything. And maybe, just maybe, that included her heart.

CHAPTER 17

Dahlia stepped off the elevator. The pungent scent of alcohol and disinfectant made trying to forget she was in a hospital impossible. Not that she could forget even if she wanted to, with personnel in scrubs of every color of the rainbow scurrying here and there, with hip-clipped pagers and stethoscope necklaces enhancing their medical look.

After two and a half years away from the city, returning had its difficulties. Dahlia had never wanted to come back after that horrible winter day. Her attempt to surprise Jonah with an early return from Denburg had yielded a shocking and unexpected surprise that ended her marriage and destroyed life as she knew it. She'd always thought herself lucky to have a husband so understanding about her spending three to four days a week in another state, but she wasn't lucky, just blind.

Familiar laughter caught Dahlia's attention. She looked up to find her ex-husband in cheery conversation with a pretty nurse with dark brown micro-braids and deep dimples. Jonah brushed his hand against the nurse's cheek and whispered something in her ear. Dahlia shook her head, surprised, yet, not. Too good-looking not to notice, Jonah had a way of demanding attention, even when you didn't want to give it to him. Always perfectly groomed and stylishly dressed, Jonah Baron, of the Baron Bourbon dynasty, used his winning smile, athletic body, and excess charm with the finesse of a snake charmer. You didn't know you were under his spell until it was too late. Maybe she could save this unsuspecting nurse before she became the newest casualty of Baron magic.

"Dahlia."

Her mother's distraught voice stopped Dahlia's approach toward her ex. She turned to see her mother's face stained with tears, and her father, holding tight to her mother, looking older than she'd ever seen him. Her heart dropped to her stomach. Tears blurred her vision and thoughts she didn't want to think filled her head.

"What—what is it?" Dahlia asked, managing to speak through the knot in her throat.

"Her blood pressure, the contractions. There was a se—seizure," Wilson said, clutching tight to Nona's hand as the woman sobbed uncontrollably.

Warm tears raced down Dahlia's cheeks. "She's not . . ."

"I don't know. They rushed us out of the room." Wilson walked his distraught wife to the waiting area.

Dahlia sat beside her mother and took her other hand. "Try not to worry, Mama. Leslie's strong, and she's strong-willed. She's going to make it."

Nona snatched her hand away. "And it would be no thanks to you," she hissed.

"Nona, don't do this," Wilson said.

"Why not? You know it's true. She stopped talking to her sister. Even when Leslie first had problems, she didn't bother to come see her."

"Mama, I . . ."

"No. She kept asking for you in that room before she started shaking so uncontro—She wanted her sister, and you were nowhere to be found. You gave up on her."

Dahlia drew a breath, trying mightily not to respond with the anger growing inside her. "Mama, I know you're upset, but this is not my fault, and I refuse to take the blame for it. I'm here now, and I do care. Why is it you refuse to recognize what Leslie did to me? Why I have reason to be upset with her?"

"There is never a good reason to be upset with your sister. All you have is family, and you turned your back on yours."

"What did she do to me? What are you doing to me now?" Dahlia shot up, desperate to get away from her mother before she said the wrong thing. Her tone was already a lot louder than she knew it should be. "I have to get out of here."

Dahlia rushed out of the waiting area and encountered that blasted laughter again. She stomped over to the nurses' station and grabbed Jonah by the arm. "Excuse him," she said to the nurse, who didn't look at all happy with the interruption.

"Dahlia?" Jonah jerked his arm away when she dragged him into a waiting area down the hall. "What are you doing?"

"The question is what the hell are you doing! My sister is near death in a hospital room having—God help her—your baby, and you're hitting on some nurse."

"I'm here, aren't I? I have tons of paperwork on my desk, but I'm at this hospital."

"Tasting the dish of the day."

"Dahlia." Jonah chuckled. "Are you jealous, baby?" His eyes roamed over her body, and approval brightened his dark brown eyes. "You're looking really good."

"Too bad you'll never know just how *good* I feel now."

He frowned. "Why did you pull me in here?"

"Mostly, to give you a piece of my mind. When I walked in on you and Leslie in our bed, I . . . I hurt more than I thought there was pain in the world to feel. You were my life and Leslie my best friend and my sister, and you two betrayed me."

"We've had this discussion. One very long discussion."

"Yes, we have, but I see it didn't stick with you. Can you commit to any woman?"

"I don't have to." He smiled. "There's enough of me to go around. I can't allow any woman to be selfish and keep me all to herself, but you were special enough to be Mrs. Baron. I loved you as much as I can love any woman. That makes you a cut above the rest. And, damn, woman, you are looking mighty fine."

Jonah brushed his thumb and forefinger against his perfectly trimmed goatee and smiled his winning Baron smile. Dahlia hated his guts, but couldn't deny his attractiveness. Not that Jonah would let anyone do that.

"You're still hot for me, aren't you, Dahlia?" he said.

Anger rose up in Dahlia from Jonah's gall. "I'm feeling some heat, all right," she said.

He beckoned her with his finger. "Why don't you come on over and give the Baron some of that brown sugar."

"Oh, I have something for the Baron." She walked over and slapped him so hard she swore she saw sparks from the contact. "How's that fire for you, Baron?"

Jonah rubbed his face. An impression of her hand-print appeared on his smooth-shaven, chestnut brown cheek. "Damn it, woman, have you lost your mind?"

"Not at all." Dahlia rubbed her burning hand against her thigh. "In fact, my thinking has never been clearer. If you don't want a matching look for your right cheek, I suggest you be quiet and let me talk now."

Rubbing his cheek, Jonah backed to a chair and sat.

"I was so in love with you, I didn't see all your faults. There you were, this attractive man from a successful family with a bright future ahead of him, and you wanted to be with me. Back then I thought you were a prize. Booby prize is more like it. My sister is near death having your baby, and you're grinning in some nurse's face and trying to hit on me. There was a time I believed Leslie deserved whatever she got for what she did to me, but nobody deserves the devastation being involved with you leaves behind."

"You're just full of compliments and good will today."

"The truth hurts, Jonah. And truth is what I had to face when our marriage ended. I took a good look at myself and saw the need for change. I made the changes and am all the better for them. It wasn't easy, but necessary. You could use a few changes in your life, too. You're a heel, Jonah, but you can better yourself and at least try to be a good example of manhood for your child."

He laughed, his derisive laughter making Dahlia wonder why she had tried to reason with him in the first place.

"Good thing your thoughts of me don't matter, Dahlia. I like myself, and I have no plans of changing me. Of course I'll take care of the baby, but I never promised Leslie anything."

"It wouldn't matter if you did. You promised to keep only unto me, and we saw how well you kept that promise. I guess you said 'I do' with your fingers crossed."

Jonah's mouth twisted into an annoyed frown. "You left me, remember?"

"I never had you, Jonah. I found that out the hard way. Were you ever faithful to me?"

"What do you mean?"

"It's a straightforward question. Were you ever faithful?"

"New York is a big city. So, yeah, I saw other girls when we were together. But when I was with you, I was with you."

"Out of sight, out of mind, right? Keep going."

"When we first got married, I was golden. For the first three years, there was no one else. It was all about you."

"Am I supposed to be excited about that?" Dahlia closed her eyes for a long moment, calming her growing anger at Jonah's nerve. "What changed? What made you start cheating again?"

"You. Me. We were moving in different directions. When we got married, I was happy, but once we finished grad school and moved to Atlanta, your days grew longer, as did my hours alone, and I had to find something to keep myself occupied. You weren't there. You were always in Denburg."

"Don't you dare give me that!" Dahlia sucked in a breath. "My clientele was in Denburg. I had to get established. Did I not ask you over and over again if you were okay with my long hours? If you wanted me home more? You always said, *'No, babe, it's fine. I support your dream. I know how important this is to you.'* So don't you dare make your philandering my fault! I guess that's why you insisted on living in Atlanta and not moving to Denburg. You've never been faithful to me, and you cheated because you wanted to. Be man enough to say so!"

"Fine. You're right, I did. I got sloppy. You were in the dark for years, and then just blew my game completely."

Dahlia frowned. "Yeah. I came home. And my life changed forever."

"That was your choice. You wanted a divorce, so I obliged you."

"I also wanted a baby, but you couldn't make that happen."

"I made it happen for Leslie."

"Yes, and this baby will connect you to my sister forever, but I hope with all my might she'll see you for the loser you are and drop-kick your rotten ass out of her life."

"I take it you don't want to be friends."

"With friends like you?"

Jonah shrugged. "Your loss. Is there a guy?"

Dahlia's thoughts went to Norris. How she wished she'd taken him up on his offer to come along with her. She really needed one of his hugs right now. She met Jonah's gaze, but said nothing. She wouldn't discuss her personal life with him.

"Is that a no?" he asked.

"That's a none of your business."

He nodded and smiled. "It's a no."

"I've said all I need to say to you, Jonah, and heard all I need to hear. Try to act like you give a damn and go check on Leslie and your baby."

Dahlia left the waiting room and rode the elevator to the chapel. She lit a candle and sat in a middle pew. Words of prayer filled her head and softly spilled from her lips. She prayed for her sister and the safety of her little niece or nephew who may have already entered this world, for Norris and Reese to grow closer with their time together, and finally strength for her family and herself to deal with all the things they had coming their way, all the time wondering if she were crazy for coming back here.

"It was crazy to make her come back here." Norris looked in the direction of Reese's bedroom, where she'd been unpacking her things for the past two hours, as he spoke with his sister on the phone. "I know she's angry,

Julia, but I'd rather her yell at me than give me the silent treatment."

"Norris, I'd be giving you the silent treatment, too. I used to think you were up with the times," Julia said.

"I've heard this speech from Dahlia. You don't have to give it to me again."

"Oh, so you talked to Dahlia. How is she?"

"She's been better. Right after we talked she learned her six-and-a-half-months pregnant sister was hospitalized."

"I'm sorry to hear that. Is her sister okay?"

"I don't know. Dahlia flew to Atlanta this evening. Her plane landed about an hour or so ago."

"That's too bad about her sister, but I'm glad you two are talking."

"I wouldn't get too excited. She's still not in confessing mode."

"But talking is good. Soon everything will be just the way you want it. One of us will finally have that elusive family."

"Let's hope. So, what prompted your call?"

"We promised to work on keeping in touch, so I'm doing it."

Norris laughed. "And what else?" he asked.

"Okay, I called for another reason, too. I talked to Lane earlier, and our visit is set. We're coming to Denburg. We'll finally get to meet Reese."

"That's great, Jules. When?"

"We should arrive early Wednesday afternoon and stay for ten days."

"I can't wait to tell Reese."

"No, don't tell her. Let's surprise her. You can take her out to lunch somewhere, and we'll show up. A wonderful little family reunion."

Norris laughed, thinking of his mother's face at the idea of such a gathering.

"What are you laughing about?" Julia asked.

"Mom at a reunion with the three of us and Reese."

Julia scoffed. "Please. Who's inviting her? That woman has been blowing up my phone. Do you know what she wants?"

"Uh-huh. You. She wants her time with you."

"Just one more reason she's not invited. I'll see you in a couple of days."

"See ya, Julia."

CHAPTER 18

Norris knocked on Reese's door. She had said all of two sentences to him since arriving at his place Saturday night. Her request to attend church services with the Monroes had turned into an all-day vacation from his company. When she returned before six Sunday evening, she had locked herself in her room for the rest of the night. Ten o'clock Monday morning, she still remained in her room. Times like this he wished her bathroom was down the hall and not adjoined to the bedroom. At least then he'd see her.

"Reese, are you going to come out today?"

"I don't know," she answered. "I don't feel good. I think I'll just stay in bed."

Don't feel good? Norris knocked again. "Reese, I'm coming in." She pulled the covers over her head when the door opened. "What's wrong?" he asked, approaching the bed. "Do you have a fever?"

"It's my stomach."

"You need an antacid or something?"

"No, I just want to be left alone." She curled into the fetal position under the covers.

"Have you eaten anything?"

"Norris, I'm not hungry."

"You're still angry with me, aren't you?"

Reese said nothing.

Norris sighed. He had to get her from under those covers. If he saw her, he could try to gauge how sickly she felt. "I know you don't believe it, but I only have your best interests at heart," he said, knowing Reese wouldn't take those words too well and would no doubt let him know in no uncertain terms, providing him the opportunity to assess her well being.

"My best interests?" Reese roared.

As expected, she popped out from under the covers, the curls of her dark mane flying here and there. Norris watched her closely. Though anger flashed in her eyes, they weren't glassy and she didn't look flushed, so he ruled out a fever.

Reese glared at him. "Trying to dictate who I spend time with and treating me like I'm a little kid is in my best interests? Jack is a nice guy, and you were rude to him."

"All I saw was that kid's arm around my little girl."

"I'm not a little girl!" Reese whipped her fingers through her hair, frowning. "And what's with this possessiveness? Your little girl? When I was a little girl, you weren't around."

Norris grunted. He hated when she made him out to be some absentee father, when nothing could be further from the truth. "That wasn't my fault."

"It doesn't matter. You can't make up for lost time now."

"I can try. I know you are a young woman. Intellectually, I get that. But when I see you, after looking at picture after picture of you growing up, I see what I missed. You are my little girl, and no matter how old you get, you'll always be that to me. That precious little child I didn't get the chance to know. I love you, Reese. I just want us to be closer."

"You love me?"

"You sound surprised."

"How can you love me?" Reese winced and slid back under the covers, curling once more into the fetal position. "You don't know me."

"I know you're mine. I know you hate to be told what to do, I know you still blame me for your mother not being here, and I know you're still upset with me about what happened at the mall on Saturday. I get all of that, but I also get you don't feel well, and I just want to . . ."

"There's nothing you can do for me, okay? I just want to be left alone."

Irritability. More than usual. She was right. He couldn't help her. "Fine. I'll be in the living room if you need anything."

"Whatever," she mumbled, cozying further under the covers.

Norris left the room and walked over to the phone. She wouldn't talk to him, but she had to talk to somebody, and he knew it needed to be a woman. "Hi, Lara, it's Norris. Think you can come over here for a bit?"

Reese moaned into her pillow as severe menstrual cramps continued to rip through her lower abdomen. A heating pad or a Midol, was that so hard to ask for? Why did she have to be stupid and suffer in silence? Times like this she missed her mother even more. She didn't have to say anything, her mother just understood. It seemed Norris would never understand her or what she needed. Were all fathers that dense? Thinking of his reaction to Jack made the cramps more severe, but she couldn't stop thinking about it. When would he realize she wasn't a little kid?

He loves me.

Reese fought the smile that bubbled in her with thoughts of his declaration. Something about having the love of her father made her feel good, but she still didn't like his interference in her life. If he loved her, he'd want her to be happy. She wasn't happy right now, and that was his fault.

Another knock rattled on the door.

Reese groaned. "Norris, please, leave me alone."

"Reese, it's not Norris, it's Lara. May I come in?"

"Sure," Reese answered, sitting up in the bed.

Lara waddled into the room and lowered her blossoming body to the edge of the bed. "How are you feeling, sweetie?" she said, lowering a beautiful summer handbag off her shoulder.

"I'm okay."

"Norris doesn't think so. He was so worried about you, he called me over."

"He worries about everything and nothing. Lara, he treats me like I'm six. I have cramps, okay? Sometimes they're pretty bad. I figured if I told him, he might have me rushed to the emergency room in an ambulance or something."

Lara laughed. "Is he that bad?"

"I think so."

"He's trying, Reese. Norris is used to being a single guy, and now he has a beautiful teenage daughter. It's a daunting experience for him, but he's making some progress." Lara reached into her bag and handed Reese a box of menstrual pain reliever and a bottle of Gatorade. "He gathered your troubles might be of the female variety, so Ryan stopped by the drug store on the way over. I got the Gatorade because it worked for me, and I figured it wouldn't hurt if you gave it a try."

"Mom gave me the same thing. Norris figured this out?"

"Uh-huh. He mentioned you were upset with him, too."

"He didn't explain why?" Reese said, opening the bottle of pills and washing two down with the fruit-flavored beverage. "Maybe he realizes how foolish he behaved and is too embarrassed to talk about it."

"What exactly should he be embarrassed about?"

"His behavior at the mall on Saturday. He saw me with a friend and lost his mind. He acted like a total—"

"Father, I suspect," Lara said. "Was this friend a male?"

"Yes. Lara, he's so nice. His name is Jack and he's captain of the basketball team, and was just elected president of the student body. He's an A student, and he's so gorgeous. He has dark brown eyes and the most beautiful full lips." A fluttery feeling filled Reese's heart. She sighed. "I doubt I'll ever get the chance to kiss them now."

"What did Norris do?"

"What didn't he do?" Reese hugged a pillow to her chest. "Besides being horrible to Jack, he all but accused me of engaging in foreplay in the mall. I held Jack's hand, Lara, and he had his arm around my waist. That's all."

"Norris had a fit, huh?"

"I couldn't believe it. Then, he laid down all these new rules. Call me at this time, ask before you do this and go there. He's got such a tight leash on me, I doubt I'll make it to the front door before being yanked back."

Lara laughed, and tugged at one of Reese's curly locks. "I don't think he's that bad," she said.

"He's not your father."

"No, but he is *a* father. His behavior doesn't sound any different than my father's. And I got it worse, because I had two older brothers, twins, and they were just as bad as Daddy."

"Are all fathers like that?"

"Mostly, yes. I can just imagine Ryan when Angelica and baby girl number two here," Lara touched her belly, "are your age. I think over-protectiveness is just a good father gene."

"You think Norris is a good father?"

"I've seen him with my children, and whether he knows it or not, he has a knack, so I'll have to say yes. Right now, your opinion is the one that matters. He wants a good relationship with you. Think you can meet him halfway?"

"Dahlia and my mom are always telling me that."

"They are very smart women. I think it's good advice."

"I'll take it under advisement, but I think Norris could take a few steps, too."

Lara smiled. "Point taken. I'll talk to him."

"Thank you, Lara. For everything."

"You're welcome." Lara cupped Reese's cheek, with the touch of a caring mother. "Feel better."

Reese snuggled under the covers after Lara left. *Meet Norris halfway.* She could do that. For as much as he tried her nerves, she did love him, too.

Norris stopped talking to Ryan when Lara returned to the living room. "How is she?" he asked, as Ryan helped Lara to the sofa.

"You made a good call. She's better," Lara answered.

Norris sighed. "Thank you, Lara. I'm not familiar with all that female stuff, but she kinda reminded me of my sister at select times of the month, so it made me wonder. So, uh, you were in there for a while," he said, curious to know what prompted the delay.

"We were talking," Lara said.

"So I gathered. You want to elaborate?"

"I can, but I think you already know."

Norris grunted.

"She's still ticked about Big Daddy Pops over here going uber-paternal at the mall Saturday, huh?" Ryan said, slapping Norris's shoulder, laughing.

Norris frowned. "I'm glad I can amuse you, Ryan. You just wait until Angelica is sixteen."

Lara nodded. "I told Reese the same thing," she said.

"I won't dog some kid for being interested in my baby girl," Ryan said. "But this is all hypothetical, because Angelica's not going to start dating until she's thirty."

Lara kissed Ryan's cheek. "Keep believing it, sweetie." She turned to Norris. "I kinda think you might have gone a little overboard Saturday."

"What is overboard? Lara, she was—"

"Innocently holding a friend's hand."

"Did she mention his arm was around her waist, and she was wearing hip-hugger jeans and a shirt missing its bottom half?" Norris grunted. "Her skin exposed to his molesting hand."

"Molesting hand?" Ryan erupted in boisterous laughter. "Norris, do you hear yourself? Can you imagine how you would be if she'd been on the beach with this guy and not in the mall?"

Norris shuddered. "I don't want to think such thoughts."

"I understand where you're coming from, Norris, but Reese is not a little girl, she's a beautiful young woman. As such, as much as you might hate it, boys are going to find her very attractive, and they will flock to her like moths to a flame. Justin's ten, and thinks she's the best thing since PS3."

Norris covered his face, groaning in his hands. He didn't need to hear Ryan validating his thoughts.

"You see yourself in Reese, Norris, but you also see yourself in the boys who like her, and it scares you to death, because you know what everybody's thinking. Except Justin. And he'd better not be thinking it. You can't protect her from life, but you do have to trust her to do the right thing."

"I do trust her, Ryan, it's these boys I don't trust."

"That can be remedied," Lara said. "Reese talked a little about Jack, and she really seems to like him. Give him a chance, and don't put a stranglehold on her. You can't hold on too tightly, because doing so will only make things worse."

"You're right, you're both right, and I'll try. I really will." Norris rubbed his forehead, groaning. "I knew stepping into fatherhood with a teenager wouldn't be easy, but it's even harder than I imagined."

"It's going to get easier, Norris," Ryan said. "Trial and error and give and take, that's what it's about."

"I'll keep that in mind."

"Good." Ryan tapped Lara's knee. "We gotta get going, babe," he said, helping Lara to her feet.

"What's the rush?" Norris asked.

"Doctor's appointment." Ryan rubbed Lara's tummy. "Once a week every week until delivery day. Fifteen days and counting, or less."

"Less?" Norris questioned.

"Twins usually come early, but everything looks good, so it's wait and see," Lara said. "I'm going to stop by the bathroom before we go. I'll be right back."

"Can you make it?" Ryan asked as she waddled down the hall.

"Yes, Ryan. You guys talk."

"She wanted to give us a minute, right?" Norris asked, when he heard the bathroom door close behind Lara.

"She did, but lately she stays in the bathroom, so she would have made that run anyway. How's Dahlia? What's the word on her sister?"

"Dahlia is trying to be strong, but she sounded tired when I talked to her last night. Her sister is still in a coma, but the baby is holding his own. He weighed only four pounds, but his lungs were fully developed, so doctors are cautiously optimistic."

"That's good."

"Yeah. I really want to see her. Dahlia puts up a good front, but I know being there is very hard for her. The relationship with her sister is strained, and with the emergency C-section, the coma, and the baby's health, I'm just very worried about her. I want to be there for her."

"Has she talked to you about this issue with her sister?"

"Not really. Just enough to know whatever it is, it's very painful for her."

"Hmm." Ryan paced around the couch. "I wonder if Lara fell in." He laughed nervously.

"It hasn't been that long." Norris watched Ryan curiously. "You know what it is, don't you?"

"Not it, they. A boy and a girl. You know that, too."

"I'm not talking about the babies, pal. You know what happened between Dahlia and her sister."

"Lara mentioned something to me, yes. I could tell you, but you don't want to hear it from me."

Norris nodded. "You're right." He could have hired any number of detectives to unearth this secret, but he wanted to hear it from Dahlia. So, he would wait for her to tell him, just like he would continue to wait to hear her say she loved him. Two things he had no doubt she would tell him soon.

Lara returned from the bathroom. "I'm ready to go," she said. "I looked in on Reese, and she's resting peacefully."

"Thanks, Lara." Norris kissed her cheek and draped his arm around Ryan's shoulder. "You guys are the best," he said, hugging them to close his side. "I must be rubbing off on you."

"Oh, boy," Ryan grumbled. "That's our signal to leave." He pulled open the door to find Genevieve on the other side. "You have company, Norris."

Genevieve flashed a tight smile. "Hello, Ryan." Her eyes widened when they dropped to Lara's distended abdomen. "Oh, hi, Lori. I . . . I didn't see you there."

"It's Lara, Mom!" Norris spat, not at all happy to see his mother darken his doorstep. "This is not a good time."

"No, Norris, it's a great time," Ryan said. "And, look, your mother just paid Lara the ultimate compliment. I've been telling her for the longest she hadn't gained that much weight, considering she's having twins. Now it's been confirmed."

Norris and Lara laughed as Genevieve stood fuming outside the door.

Ryan wrapped his arm around Lara. "Come on, babe."

"Bye, guys." Norris closed the door and turned to his red-faced mother who now sat on the couch. "Why are you here?"

"You didn't tell me Ryan's uh-"

"Wife. She's his wife."

"You didn't tell me his wife was pregnant."

"You didn't ask. However, I did ask a question. Why are you here? I thought you'd said it all when you said nothing."

"I needed some time to think."

"What's changed? My daughter is still biracial."

"How do you know?" Genevieve said.

"What do you mean how do I know?"

"Not that's she's biracial. If you say she is, there's no disputing that. My question is how do you know she's your daughter. Have you done a paternity test?"

"I don't need to do a paternity test. I can count and I've seen her. I've also been added to her birth certificate. There's no question of her paternity."

"Norris, you have a lot of money. Maybe her mother is . . ."

"Her mother is a doctor. A happily married doctor, married to another doctor, who doesn't want or need my money."

"You obviously underestimate the power of money. Being a doctor can't compare to your wealth. You can't be that blind."

"I'm not blind at all." Norris walked to his desk and retrieved Reese's picture. "Look at her." He thrust the picture into his mother's hand. "This is your grand-daughter. Your beautiful granddaughter. She's Katsoros, your family, our family, through and through. You might not want to see it, but the proof is right there."

His mother's gaze stayed on the picture. Tears filled her gray eyes. An unexpected pang of emotion pricked Norris's heart as he watched his mother's tears. Was this the breakthrough he'd hoped for in her? "Mom?" he said. "Are you all right?"

Genevieve reached into her purse and pulled out a lacy handkerchief, dabbing at her misty eyes. "How can I be all right? Pay the woman off, Norris. Your life doesn't have to be ruined by a mistake. The world won't have to know about this."

Norris wanted to kick himself. Once again he wanted to expect the best from his mother, and like every other time, he got the worst. He picked up Reese's picture and pointed to the door. "I want you to leave."

"We need to discuss how to handle this."

"We have nothing to discuss."

"Norris, I really think . . ."

Genevieve stopped talking when Reese walked into the room.

"Sorry," Reese said, tugging on a gray T-shirt that almost totally covered red and black plaid shorts. "I thought Ryan and Lara were still here." Norris watched as his daughter waved at the woman she didn't know was her grandmother. "Hi."

Genevieve's angry face became the picture of pleas-antness. "Hello, dear, how are you?" she said warmly.

Norris eyeballed his mother suspiciously. Genevieve's cordial greeting and bright smile worried him more than her unexplained suggestion on how to deal with his "mistake." *What the hell is she up to?*

"I'm fine, thank you," Reese answered.

Norris cleared his throat. "You need something, Reese?" he asked, more than ready to get her away from his unpredictable mother.

"I got a little hungry. I thought I'd have some cereal." Reese pulled her dark mane of curls behind her ears, glancing from Genevieve to Norris. "Why do I feel like I've walked in on something?"

Norris glared at his mother. Reese had definitely walked in on something. Something his daughter might be better off not being exposed to.

Reese continued to stare. Her eyes widened with realization. "Oh, wait a minute. Is this . . . is this your mother?"

Norris nodded grudgingly. "Yes."

"You weren't going to tell me?"

Norris had no idea how to answer that question. He wanted Reese to know her family, but more often than not his mother didn't feel like family.

"You weren't, were you?" She shook her head. Her humorless chuckle pierced his heart. "I don't warrant an introduction to my own grandmother. You're more disappointed in me than I thought."

Norris looked at his mother. The makings of a smile tugged at her lips. The heat of rising anger burned his face. She wanted this. Norris turned to his daughter. "Look, Reese . . ."

"Forget it. I'm hip to what's going on here. I'll go back to my room. I see it's where you prefer me." She stormed off.

"Reese!" Norris started after her.

"Let her go, son."

Seconds later Reese's door slammed.

He turned angry eyes to his mother. "Did you see the look on her face? She thinks I'm ashamed of her."

Genevieve nodded. "Appears so. It's for the best, really."

"Best? So, that explains the sweetness and light show." Norris rubbed his face, not knowing if he felt more angry or frustrated. "You pretend to be some kind old lady for Reese, instead of presenting yourself as the barracuda I know you to be, so I look like the bad guy who's too ashamed to introduce my daughter to her nice grandmother, when all I'm trying to do is protect her." Norris dropped to the couch. "I've been bending over backwards to get close to her, and look what you've done."

"This way she can go back to her family—her own kind—and not have any residual feelings where you're concerned. It will be a clean break."

"I don't want any clean break! She's my daughter, and I love her. And her kind is us, whether you like it or not!"

"I don't like it!"

"You've made that crystal clear." He pointed to the door. "I suggest you leave before I say something no son should say to his mother."

Genevieve picked up her purse and turned to him when she reached the door. "Think about what I said. I'll set up a nice trust fund for the girl, she'll never want for anything, and . . ."

"Mother!"

"Fine, fine, but this problem must be dealt with."

Norris looked toward the hallway when the door closed behind his mother. How could trying to do the right thing for his daughter always turn out so wrong? He drew a breath and walked to her room. "Reese?" he said, knocking on her door.

"Leave me alone."

"I thought you were hungry."

"I lost my appetite."

He twisted the knob. Locked. "Look, honey, I want to . . ."

"I'm not your honey and I don't want your explanations. I may be black, but I'm not stupid."

Norris flinched. "Reese, do not do that to me. You know me better than that."

"Do I?"

"You know you do. Open the door so we can talk."

"There's nothing more to talk about, Norris. I'm through with this bonding crap. We tried it, and it didn't work. As soon as Dahlia is back from Atlanta, I will be out of your hair, and you can continue to keep your dark child a dark secret from your family."

"Reese, it's not what you think." He knocked on the door. "Reese?"

Loud music smothered his words, making it clear she had little use for anything he had to say. Norris pressed his forehead to the door. He needed to see Dahlia.

He pulled out his cell phone and returned to the quiet of the living room. "Hi, Agnes, it's me. I need a favor."

CHAPTER 19

Dahlia entered her nephew's room in the NICU to find her father sitting in a rocker near the incubator staring down at his youngest grandchild. Dahlia touched her father's shoulder and gazed at the tiny, wrinkled little baby with tubes running from his little body to the machines all around him.

"How is he?" she asked.

"He's doing okay. He's a little fighter," Wilson said.

"He's so tiny, Daddy." Dahlia dragged over the other rocking chair and sat next to her father. "I know Mama is upset with me, but you have to know I never—I never wanted this," she said, her voice cracking with emotion.

Wilson closed his hand around hers. "I know, Dahlia. I know. And so does your mother. She's upset, but she knows you would never wish your sister any harm. She's with Leslie now."

"I know. I just left the ICU. I stayed in the observation room. I don't think Mama even knew I was there."

"She's very worried."

"What are the doctors saying?"

"They feared she might have had a stroke, but the tests show she didn't. Which is good. Her body is tired. They hope maybe in a few days she'll wake up."

"And if she doesn't?"

"We're not claiming that. Prayer works, and God will answer our prayers."

Dahlia nodded. "You're right. He will."

"You know, times like this allow you to do a lot of reflecting. This situation is bad, but I can't . . ." Wilson stopped talking and shook his head. "No."

"What is it, Daddy?"

"I can't help but wonder if somehow—somehow Leslie brought this on herself. Is that mean for me to say? I'm her father."

"Can't be mean if it's true. Daddy, I want Leslie and this precious baby to be okay, and I pray for that every day. I have since I heard about this pregnancy. But I can't pretend this is easy for me, or say I didn't think these difficulties were a result of the bed she made when she got into mine with my husband. And as angry as I am with her, and I'm angry and disappointed, I don't hate her, and I don't want her to die."

Wilson brushed away Dahlia's tears. "I'm sorry, Dahlia."

She sniffled. "Why are you apologizing?"

"Because I've not been very understanding of your feelings, and neither has your mother." Wilson squeezed Dahlia's hands between his. "We always tried to stay out of personal grievances with you kids, but this thing with Jonah—we shouldn't have stayed quiet. And we definitely shouldn't have expected you to fall into line and move on like it was nothing. Maybe if we had dealt with this as a family two years ago, this wouldn't be happening now."

"No, Daddy, we can't do what if. We can only go by what is. Right now, we have to think about Leslie and her baby."

"We can think about you, too. You look tired, Dahlia. When was the last time you had some sleep?"

"I caught a few Z's in the waiting area," she said, stifling a yawn.

"Not nearly enough of them. Go to your hotel and rest up. I'll call you if there's any change."

"Daddy, I want to . . ."

"Shhh. Don't argue with me. I'll call you."

"Fine." Dahlia smiled. She couldn't remember the last time she felt so daddy's girlish, so certain her daddy would make everything okay for everyone. "I'll get some sleep."

"Come here." Wilson opened his arms, bringing Dahlia into a tight embrace she readily returned. "I love you, sweetheart. I don't say it enough, but I don't want you to forget that."

"I know, Daddy. I love you, too."

He kissed her cheek. "You go on now."

Dahlia walked out the door, smiling broadly. For the first time in days, she didn't feel weighed down around her family. She drew a deep, cleansing breath. *What the . . .* She sniffed the air. Why did she smell Norris?

Like a trained bloodhound, she set out to find out. Then just as quickly stopped. Even with countless millions, Norris didn't have a lockdown on cologne, just one on her heart. She decided to call. Maybe things with Reese had turned a corner the way they had with her and her father.

Dahlia reached in her purse for her cell phone as she walked toward the elevator. Rest would come a lot easier after she talked to Norris. She activated the speed dial and stepped into the empty car.

Moments before the doors closed completely, she heard a ringing phone and saw a hand and leg spread the doors apart. In the next second, Norris slipped into the elevator, looking like a slice of heaven in a soft yellow shirt and dark slacks. She couldn't believe her eyes. "Norris."

He showed her his phone, smiling. "You rang?"

After getting an earful from Diana on how foolish she was behaving and listening to her friend's steadfast refusal to bring over a burger and fries, Reese tossed her cell to the bed and stared at the door. She couldn't avoid Norris forever, and he had left her alone as she'd asked. She sighed. If listening to whatever explanation he offered meant she could get something to eat, she'd have to listen.

Reese hopped off the bed and walked into the living room, surprised to find her surrogate grandmother, and not her infuriating father, on the couch poring over some papers. "What's up, Agnes?"

"You, finally," Agnes said, straightening the papers on the coffee table. "I understand you were under the weather."

"I'm better now. Is Norris around?"

"No, he's not."

Reese frowned. "You're not babysitting, are you?"

"Aren't you the first to remind Norris you aren't a baby?"

"That's the problem, Agnes. I have to keep reminding him. Did he call you over to watch me?"

"No, he called me over to let you know he had to go out of town to take care of some unexpected business. Since you were under a self-imposed lockdown, he didn't want you to wonder where he was. That's why I'm here. And now that you know, I'm going to go back to the office for a while."

Reese watched as Agnes gathered files from the coffee table. "You're really leaving?"

Agnes nodded. "I'm really leaving."

"And you're not coming back?"

"Not unless you want me to. Why?"

"Norris is leaving me alone?"

"He shouldn't be gone too much longer. I expect he'll be back early evening. Eight at the latest." Agnes pressed her hand to Reese's cheeks. "He trusts you."

Reese dropped to the couch, shoulders slumped. Norris continued to confuse her.

Agnes sat beside her. "What's going on in your head?"

"I don't know. Norris is so hard to read. One minute I think he's a cool guy, and the next I . . . I don't know what to think." Reese groaned. "He makes me crazy."

Agnes laughed. "That's what fathers do," she said, pushing the hair from Reese's shoulders. "He was a little upset when he asked me to come over. Want to talk about it?"

"He didn't tell you?"

"No."

"His mother was here."

Agnes pursed her lips. "I see."

"I know he's not close to his folks, and he doesn't see his siblings as often as he'd like, but they're my family. My grandmother was here, and he didn't introduce me to her."

"Did he tell you why?"

"I didn't give him a chance. What could he say?"

"I'm sure he has his reasons for what he did."

"Humph. I know he does. That's the problem."

"I would suggest you not read into things. Norris loves you. I can say that without hesitation. You remember that, and don't let anything cloud what you know is true, okay?"

"You sound like everybody else."

"Everybody?"

"The Andrews, Diana, Dahlia. Everybody."

"There you go. We can't all be wrong," Agnes said with a smile. "You need anything before I leave?"

"No. I'll reheat the lasagna Mrs. Castanza made yesterday. Her cooking is one of the best things about coming over here."

"That's progress. It means something besides her cooking makes being here enjoyable."

Reese lowered her gaze. *Cold busted.*

Agnes smiled. "Call me if you need anything, and you can always reach Norris on his cell phone."

"Thanks for coming by, Agnes."

"No problem. You take care."

Reese looked around the living room, taking in all the quiet. Even after his reaction at the mall, Norris actually trusted her alone in his place. And he'd said he loved her. Maybe he was meeting her halfway after all.

Dahlia led Norris to her room at the hotel. "I can't get over you being here," she said.

Norris grabbed her hand as she inserted the key card. "I know we wanted a quiet place to talk, but how wise is this?" he said, not trusting himself to be alone with her in a hotel room.

She smiled. "You want to go down to the lounge?"

"I don't, but . . ."

"We're just going to talk, Norris."

His gaze swept over her. Dahlia looked absolutely breathtaking in a tangerine-colored halter shirt and white slacks. The vibrant orange shade contrasted beautifully with her rich brown skin. His lips ached to kiss hers, and trail along those beautiful shoulders and so many other places. It had been so long since he'd been with her, and never had that reality been more obvious than at this moment.

"Talking might be the plan, but things can change."

"Only if we both want them to." She tilted her head, smiling. "At present, we both want to talk, right?"

Norris nodded and smiled. "Right." He'd been strong so far, and he would continue. He couldn't allow his carnal urges to get him off his plan. *Heart before body. Heart before body.*

Dahlia opened the door. Though strengthened from his personal pep talk, Norris sighed in relief to see she had a suite, with the door leading to the bedroom closed. There was no point in tempting temptation.

"It was good to see you smiling," Norris said, sitting on the couch. "Considering how upset and tired you sounded yesterday, I didn't expect a smile today."

"I had a talk with my father. An unexpected but really good talk."

"I'm glad one father and daughter had a good talk today."

"So, a spat with Reese brought you here?"

"I was concerned about you, too."

Dahlia gave his hand a little shake. "You don't need to be. I'm a lot better than I thought I would be. How are you?"

"I . . . I'm great. Fantastic at being a failure as a father. Reese thinks I'm Attila the Hun."

"You know she doesn't think that."

"She's probably thinking something worse. My mother came by my place today, just as Ryan and Lara were leaving."

"You didn't go to work today?"

"No. Reese wasn't feeling well, girl stuff, so I asked Lara to come by. Mom learned I was home when she called the office, and decided to drop by to bend my ear about my 'mistake,' " he said making air quotes, "and how to fix it."

"Oh, no," Dahlia groaned.

"Oh, yes. After Ryan and Lara left, Reese walked in, felt the tension, and realized whom she'd walked in on. I didn't want to subject her to my mother. I don't know that I would've never introduced them, but I didn't want to today. Reese took my lack of acknowledgement to mean I was ashamed of her. I tried to explain, but she blasted her music and completely tuned me out. She hates me, Dahlia."

"She does not hate you. Reese is sixteen. Girls are all over the place at sixteen, and her hormones are a little out of whack right now. I can talk to her for you."

"And say what? 'How can you possibly hate your father, Reese? I'm madly in love with that man, and he's just more wonderful than words can express.' " Norris smiled. "Something like that?"

Dahlia laughed. "Not quite."

He snapped his fingers. "Darn."

"Norris, be serious."

"I am serious."

"More serious." Dahlia reached into her purse. "I can call her right now."

Norris pulled her hands out of the purse. "Don't bother, Dahlia. Thank you, really, but it won't be necessary."

"I want to do this."

"Why?"

She shrugged and walked over to the window. "Because."

"Because why?" Norris followed her to the window, taking in the breathtaking view it offered of the city.

"Talk to me, Dahlia," he said, dragging his fingertips against her arms. Her soft sigh hummed in his ears. Maybe he'd finally get a confession out of her. "Why do you want to help so much?"

"Because I promised Gail I would."

"Is that the only reason?" Norris lowered his head, breathing in her sweet fragrance. She trembled against him. "Why are you so shaky?"

"It's cold in here."

"No, Dahlia, it's hot in here." Norris brushed his lips against her neck and clasped his hands around her waist. Dahlia's moan grew into a whimper as her backside settled against his growing arousal. "What are you thinking?"

"Maybe we should have gone to the lounge," she said, her tone low, words breathy.

"You were about to tell me something before you got the phone call about your sister." He continued his assault of her neck. Her pulse points throbbed wildly against his lips. "What was it?"

Dahlia breathed heavily. "I can't—I can't remember."

"You can't remember?"

"No."

"Maybe this will help refresh your memory." Norris turned Dahlia around, crushing her body to his, stifling her gasp of surprise with his fervent kiss. Her lips relaxed and parted, welcoming his tongue into her mouth. Norris drew her closer, deepening the kiss. Her muffled sighs grew deeper. She curled her arms around his shoulders, holding him against the soft curves of her body, driving him crazy. Too crazy. He couldn't lose control. It wouldn't help matters. "Dahlia." Norris slowly, painstakingly pulled away. "Dahlia, I'm sorry." He licked his lips, holding on to the memory of her sweet mouth. "I shouldn't have done that." He stuffed his hands into the pockets of his slacks, trying to alleviate the pressure in his groin from pants that suddenly felt too tight.

"You have to stop apologizing when you kiss me."

"I'd like to. It's impossible to act like I'm not attracted to you, or that I don't want to take you in my arms every time I see you, but I don't want to be led by my physical need for you. Dahlia, what I feel goes so much deeper than that."

"As you keep saying."

"What do you say? And don't tell me nothing. You had something on your mind before."

"Don't tell me. You saw it in my eyes, right?"

He nodded. "I did, and I felt it in your kiss just now. You're not tired of denying it yet?"

"Norris, I—"

Her cell phone rang before she could answer the question.

Norris rolled his eyes. "This is like déjà vu."

Dahlia walked over to her purse and fished out the phone. "Even more than you think," she said. "It's my father."

Norris returned to the couch and sat.

"Hello, Daddy." Her eyes brightened. "Really!" she exclaimed. "That's great. No, it's no problem. I'll be right back. Bye-bye."

Norris smiled at her joy. "Good news, I suspect."

"Great news. Leslie woke up." Dahlia expelled a breath. Her expression sobered. "She woke up." Dahlia dropped next to him on the couch. "Oh, boy."

"Stop jumping for joy, Dahlia, I insist," Norris quipped.

"I'm happy, I am, it's just . . ."

"This strife with your sister, right? Seeing her means you'll have to deal with it."

"Yes." She sighed, wearily. "I don't know if I'm ready to deal."

"Are you ready to tell me about it?"

After several moments of silence she nodded. "Yes, I am."

CHAPTER 20

Dahlia looked into caring gray eyes as she searched her heart for the right words. She didn't want to sound as bitter as she'd been feeling for the last two and a half years, especially with her ill sister back in the conscious world. But finding the right words and then getting them out without the bitter undertones would be the real challenge. She groaned. This was so hard.

Norris squeezed her hand, providing much-needed support. "I take it this isn't about a pair of pumps she borrowed without your permission," he said.

"No. It's about a husband she slept with behind my back. A husband she just had a baby for. The baby I wanted but Jonah could never give me."

Several quiet moments passed.

"Maybe Jonah wasn't meant to be the father of your children." Norris pressed his hand to her belly, the look in his eyes one of love and hope. "I would love nothing more than to give you a child." He shook his head, as if clearing away his wonderful dream and coming back to reality. "But we can talk about that later. Finish telling me about Leslie."

"Leslie." Dahlia sighed, dismayed. "Leslie and I were so close. We're ten years apart, but she was like one of my baby dolls come to life. I loved her from the moment

Mama brought her home from the hospital." Tears blurred her vision. "She was the maid of honor at my wedding. Twelve years old." Dahlia sniffled. "That sweet baby girl, my sister, gave birth to my ex-husband's baby, and almost died doing it. She almost died."

"Hey." Norris brushed her tears away. "She didn't die."

"Thank God." Dahlia closed her eyes. "I don't know what I'm going to say to her."

"What do you want to say?"

"I don't know. That I'm glad she's alive, that her baby is tiny, but beautiful."

"And what about the not-so-cordial stuff?"

"I can't be cross. It wouldn't be good for her."

"You think pretending you aren't feeling what you feel will be? She's not stupid, Dahlia. You haven't seen her in years. You think she's going to expect you to be happy that she had your ex-husband's baby? Pretend like nothing's happened?"

"She could. I talked to her very briefly a few months ago. She seemed surprised that I sounded angry."

"You didn't tell me about that."

"You didn't know about her then. I didn't see the point."

"How did the conversation go?"

"I'd hardly call it a conversation."

"How do you feel about the baby?"

Dahlia smiled. "I love him. He's incredible, and so beautiful. Heartbreakingly so." The burn of new tears stung Dahlia's eyes. She closed them tightly, waiting for the sensation to pass.

"You really love that baby."

"I do. In spite of his father." She sighed deeply. "This situation is so difficult. I love the baby. I love my sister, and though I can't stand his guts, a part of me will always care about Jonah. He was my husband. My first love."

"But not your last. The last is always the best. Especially when that love's name is Norris." His eyes twinkled.

Dahlia smiled, appreciating the sincerity cloaked in levity Norris provided. She didn't need to comment, and knew he didn't expect her to. He was just being his wonderful self.

"Seriously, now, talk to me." Norris squeezed her thigh, his touch one of concern and caring. "What are you feeling? Tell me everything you want to tell your sister."

Dahlia returned to the window. "I can't do that," she said, knowing giving too much thought to those feelings would open a floodgate of emotions she wouldn't be able to control.

Norris followed and closed his hands around her shoulders, massaging her tense muscles. "If you don't want to share this with me, it's okay. Shout it out to yourself on your way back to the hospital. You need to do what you did a couple of years ago, Dahlia. Shed the weight that's holding you down. Deal with this anger that's keeping you and your sister apart. This anger that drives the fear that's keeping you from admitting your feelings for me."

Dahlia turned around. The intensity in his eyes all but dared her to deny his words. She sighed. "Norris."

"Shhh." He pressed his finger to her lips. "Don't say anything. You have so much going on right now. You take care of you, and when that's done we'll take care of us." He kissed her left cheek, her right cheek, her forehead, and then softly kissed her lips, managing to find a way to erase all the reasons she had for running from her love for him from her head. "Thanks for listening to me about Reese and offering to help."

"I can still call her for you."

"No, it's okay. I'm hopeful things will be better in a couple of days. Julia and Lane are coming for a visit. Reese will get to meet some family I actually like." He chuckled. "It should help."

"Sounds like it." Dahlia stared at Norris, her heart full and heavy. She didn't want him to go, but she couldn't ask him to stay. He had to get back to Reese. "Call me when you land."

"I will." Norris brushed his finger against her cheek, stirring those always-restless butterflies in her stomach. "I love you so much, Dahlia."

Norris brought her into his arms. Dahlia held him tight, breathing him in, not wanting to let go. *I love you, too.* Would she ever allow herself to say those words to him without fear of destroying herself in the process?

"Call me if you need anything."

"Will you come with me?" she heard herself say.

Norris pulled away, gazing into her eyes. "What?"

"Will you come with me to the hospital? I would really like you there."

Norris smiled. "With your family and everybody?"

"My brother is still in Japan, but, yes, with my family and everybody." She closed her hands around his. "I want you with me, Norris."

"I want me with you, too." He kissed her hand. "Let's go."

Norris and Dahlia walked hand in hand into the entrance of the hospital. Curious glances and stinging glares came from all sides. Even with the stares, Norris had never felt happier. His hand closed tighter around hers. Dahlia gave him a smile he readily returned. She still hadn't said she loved him, but he was even more convinced that she did. They'd reached an unspoken understanding that buoyed his hope for things to come. She'd extended him an invitation to be with her family, and coming from Dahlia, that was a big step.

The elevator hummed as they rode to the fifth floor. "Are you okay?" Dahlia asked.

"Never better," he answered. "You?"

"I'm a little nervous about Leslie." She whimpered softly and squeezed his hand. "Maybe I should have unburdened myself to you like you suggested."

"It's not too late. This elevator has a stop button."

She laughed. "Don't you wish everything in life did?"

"Sometimes." He smiled. "I can press the button. Give you more time."

"No, I'm good. I have you."

"Yes, you do, and you always will."

Their lips came together the moment the elevator doors opened at the fifth floor.

"What the hell!"

Norris pulled away at the sound of an irate man. Fuming eyes and flaring nostrils distorted the face of the tall, African-American man.

Dahlia frowned. "What are you shouting about, Jonah?"

Jonah? Norris gave Dahlia's ex a once-over. The infamous cheating louse ex-husband. He shouldn't have been surprised to see the man there, as he'd just become a father thanks to Dahlia's sister, but surprised he was.

"I'm shouting about this." Jonah motioned his finger toward Norris. "Who's your friend, Dahlia?"

"That's really none of your business, Jonah, but if you must know, his name is Norris Converse." Dahlia slid her hand into Norris's as they stepped out of the elevator. "Were you going somewhere?"

"Yes," Jonah answered, glaring at Norris.

"Where could you go that's more important than being here?"

"That's my business." Jonah pressed the elevator button and waited for the car to return.

Norris did not want Jonah to get away without having a few words with him. "Dahlia, I can't go into the ICU with you, so I'm going to go make a few phone calls. Call me when you're ready," he said. "I won't be far."

"Norris, where . . ."

The elevator dinged, signaling its arrival.

"I won't be far." He kissed her cheek. "Hold that elevator!" he called to Jonah, backing toward the open car.

"Call me when you're ready." Norris slid into the closing elevator and met Jonah's unhappy gaze. "We need to talk."

"I have nothing to say to you."

"So you'll just have to listen, because I've got plenty to say to you."

Norris crossed his arms, studying Dahlia's ex. He could see her finding the man intriguing. Jonah had style, flare, and intelligence marked by a Columbia MBA. And though no Norris Converse, he wasn't a bad-looking guy, either. In fact, Norris saw a lot of his qualities in this man, which didn't make him feel too good.

The men stepped out of the elevator and walked outside to a sitting area a few feet away from the hospital.

"Talk. I don't have all day," Jonah said.

"I'll make this quick. I don't think you're aware of how much you've hurt Dahlia, but I'm making this clear. I won't let you hurt her again, and that includes whatever you do in regard to her sister."

"Oooh." Jonah trembled in mock fear. "Is that my cue to get scared?"

"I'm just making a statement of fact. I don't know if you ever truly loved Dahlia, but I'm letting you know I do. She's the most incredible woman I've ever known, and she deserves some real happiness."

"And you think you can give that to her?" Jonah's derisive laughter rang in Norris's ears. "You are fooling yourself. Dahlia is angry with me for cheating on her, but she loves me. She'll always love me. And, yes, I did love her." Jonah folded his arms and met Norris's gaze head-on. "I know she doesn't love you. She can't."

"You'd like to believe that, wouldn't you?"

Jonah laughed. "Come on, man. I don't doubt Dahlia likes you, but she *loves* me. She has a lot of anger. I saw Dahlia once after she found me with Leslie, and that was the next day when she arrived to pack her things and chew me out. Throughout the divorce, it was just her lawyer. She refused to see me."

"That should tell you something. I've been with Dahlia for a while, and you have done a serious number on her. But I think her biggest problem is you hurt her with her sister. I know Dahlia loved you once, but she loves me now."

"Has she said so?"

Norris stared at Jonah for a long moment and said, "What do you think?"

"I think you didn't answer my question. You'll be waiting a long time to hear those words from her, because she can't say them to you. My name is seared on her heart, and no white-bread stud is going to change that."

Norris laughed. "That's funny—white-bread stud. You know, you don't sound very convincing when you talk about what Dahlia's not feeling for me. But it's understandable. You're still steamed from the kiss you saw. You can't deny the emotion in it, no matter how much you want to. Dahlia's moved on, and she's done it with me. She's a special woman. Something you either never knew or chose to forget until it was too late. That mistake will never happen with me."

"I'm done talking." Jonah stood. "I'm outta here."

"Wait a minute." Norris walked in front of Jonah, blocking his path. "What are you going to do about Leslie and the baby?"

"I'm not going to do anything about Leslie, but I'm going to take care of my son. That's what I'm off to do now, stud. I have nannies to interview." Moments later Jonah peeled out of the parking lot in a maroon Aston Martin.

Norris expelled a breath. That went about as well as he had expected. He knew where Jonah stood with the baby, and Jonah knew where Norris stood with Dahlia. He looked toward the hospital, wondering if Dahlia was reaching a similar understanding with her sister.

Dahlia stared at the elevator long after it closed. *A few phone calls.* Humph! More like a meeting of the minds with Jonah. Could such a thing even happen with those two personalities?

"Dahlia, I'm glad you're here."

She turned to her father's voice. "Yeah, Daddy, I arrived a few minutes ago."

The two walked in silence to the ICU.

"Leslie's been asking for you," Wilson said when they reached the observation room.

"What did the doctors say?"

"She's turned a corner. She's still weak, but her pressure is down. They plan to move her to a regular room later today."

Dahlia smiled. "That is good news." She looked through the window to see her mother fussing over her sister. Dahlia's resolve faded. "Daddy, I don't know."

"You're going to be okay. Leslie's weak, but she's not fragile. And you're a smart woman." Wilson pressed his hand to Dahlia's cheek. The warmth of his strong, gentle hand was the push she needed. "You'll do what needs to be done. Just trust yourself, Dahlia."

She nodded and walked into the room.

Nona left Leslie's side and made her way to Dahlia. Earnest remorse had softened the fear and worry that had once hardened Nona's face. Nona closed her hands over Dahlia's shoulder. "I owe you an apology," she said. "Even my worry for Leslie was no excuse to lash out at you the way I did."

"You don't need to apologize, Mama. It's been a tense few days for everyone. I understand."

"Thank you for that. It's more than I deserve." Nona pulled Dahlia into an embrace and kissed her cheek. "Are you two going to be all right?" she asked, looking from one daughter to the other.

"Yes, Mama," Leslie answered, her voice soft and a little shaky, but sounding good for someone who'd just come out of a coma. "I need to talk to Dahlia alone." She tucked her long, dark hair behind ears. "We'll be fine."

"Your daddy and I are going to leave and get those items you wanted for yourself and the baby, and give Quentin a call to catch him up with everything that's been going on. We'll be back in a couple of hours." Nona waved good-bye and left.

Dahlia gazed at her sister. Alone with Leslie for the first time in years, she didn't know what to say first. 'I'm glad you're okay' or 'Why did you do it?'

Leslie motioned to the stool at the side of her bed. "Sit down, Dahlia."

Dahlia walked over and sat.

"You really look incredible," Leslie said. "Not that you weren't beautiful before, but you've lost so much weight."

"Eighty pounds," Dahlia said.

"I know. Mama and Daddy told me. They've been keeping me in the loop. I love your haircut, too. You look wonderful."

Dahlia pulled back her hand when Leslie reached for it. "I don't think I'm ready for that yet," she said.

Leslie nodded. "I understand. I owe you a lot of explanations and a lot of apologies."

"Visiting hours will be over in five minutes, so why don't you skip the apologies and get to the explanations. I'm dying to hear this," Dahlia said, trying not to sound snarky, but certain she did anyway.

"I thought I loved him," Leslie said. "The first time it happened, he was just there when I needed someone. I had lost out on yet another job and I was still reeling from the break-up with Walt. Jonah came home and found me crying on the couch. He wiped my tears, lifted my spirits, and propped me up. One thing led to another."

"And another and another."

"The day you found us was supposed to be the last time. We had been together about three months, and I felt horrible. I had convinced myself I loved him, but the guilt was killing me. I told him it had to end. Jonah said one more time, that you'd never know. He's so attractive and was so persuasive. I gave in. But you came home early from Denburg, and that was that."

"So, you decided to keep seeing him."

"When you found us, Jonah said we didn't have to end things. You disappeared, Dahlia. You kicked me out of your house and the next thing I knew you were gone and Jonah was getting divorce papers. I thought I was special. He told me I was special. But after two years, when he still refused to consider marriage, I discovered there were special women in every corner of the world. I had to know more than business kept him away. I'd lost my big sister and best friend for a man who was never worth my time." Tears streamed from the corners of Leslie's eyes. "I had hurt you, the person I loved and admired more than anyone in this world, for nothing."

Dahlia dried Leslie's eyes and wiped her nose as she had so many years ago. "We both fell under the spell of Baron magic," she said, understanding how her sister could succumb to Jonah's considerable charms. "Thankfully, the spell wears off."

"Do you think you'll ever forgive me, Dahlia?"

Dahlia tossed the damp tissue onto the bedside table. "I can't promise anything, Leslie, but I think I'd like to try. Nearly losing you really shook me up. It shook us all up, but it's also brought this family closer together. I don't want to be the weak link in this chain. I can't lie, watching you raise Jonah's child will be a challenge."

Leslie dropped her head. "I'm sorry, Dahlia."

"I know, but that doesn't make this any easier. I always wanted a baby."

"I know."

"Which makes this even harder. Jonah may be a heel, but he was also my husband, and I loved him. This is going to be tough, Leslie, but your baby is so incredible. I already love him. I will always love him, and I want to be a part of his life—a part of your life."

"You forgive me?" Leslie murmured.

"I didn't say that," Dahlia said, "but I'm willing to try."

"Dahlia." Norris walked over to her the moment she emerged from the unit. "How did it go?" he asked, unable to read her expression.

"It went." Dahlia released a breath. "We have a long road ahead of us, but I think we'll make it."

"That's good to hear." Norris smiled. "Have you eaten?"

"I had an apple earlier." She rubbed her stomach. "Much earlier."

Norris offered her his arm. "How about a late lunch/early dinner?"

"Sounds good." Dahlia curled her arm around his. "And while we're eating, you can tell me all about the conversation you had with Jonah."

CHAPTER 21

Norris arrived home just before eight to find Reese curled on the couch watching TV. He tossed his keys to the coffee table and smiled. "Glad to see you out and about," he said. "You feel better?"

"I do, thanks." Reese pulled up the blue bed sheet wrapped about her knees. "How did things go with your work?"

"My work?"

"Yes. Agnes told me you had to leave town to take care of something."

"Oh, that." Norris walked to his desk and browsed through the mail he'd asked Agnes to pick up. "It went fine."

Norris hated not telling Reese about his feelings for Dahlia, and honestly didn't know how much longer he could keep it up after what happened today. They'd grown so much closer. He'd learned about Leslie and Jonah and been introduced as a 'dear friend' to her parents. It wasn't a ringing endorsement for a relationship, but he'd met Dahlia's parents, and that was huge. He didn't think he'd ever stop smiling.

"What did you do today?" Norris asked.

"Listened to music, ate, slept, thought," she mumbled. "I left you some of Ms. Castanza's lasagna. Want me to heat it up?"

"I'm not hungry right now, but thanks." Norris picked up the newest edition of *Sports Illustrated* and joined Reese on the couch. "What have you been thinking about?" he asked, dropping the magazine to the coffee table.

"What happened earlier." Reese clicked off the television and gave him all of her attention. "I'm ready to listen now."

Norris studied his daughter closely. He didn't detect any anger in her expression or tone. She seemed curious and interested in whatever he had to say, a strange but welcome metamorphosis. "You're not angry anymore?"

"I'm learning fathers and daughters don't always see eye to eye, and it's normal. So, I guess we're doing something right."

"You're not giving up on me?"

Reese tugged on a curly lock. "Dahlia, Lara, Diana, and Agnes won't let me."

Norris smiled. "I guess it's a good thing so many people care about us." Norris reached for Reese's hand, and much to his amazement, she didn't pull away. "These past few months have been like none I've ever experienced. They've been the hardest and best of my life, and a big reason for that is you."

Reese scrunched her face. "I guess there's a compliment in there somewhere," she said.

He laughed. "There is. Reese, when I say I love you, I mean it, and I am not ashamed of you. I want to shout to the world I have this beautiful and bright daughter."

"To the world, but not your mother?"

"My mother and I don't see eye to eye on a lot of things, and today was no different. As you suspected, you caught us in the middle of something. Introducing you to this pain in my butt didn't enter my head as something to do."

"You call your mother a pain in the butt?"

"It suits her. I bet you've said the same about me."

"I haven't. You're more a pain in the neck." She laughed.

Norris dropped his jaw in feigned outrage.

"Yes," she said. "I've learned it's a condition most fathers give their daughters. I'm trying to become immune to its annoying effects, but it's a challenge."

"There are a few conditions daughters give their fathers, too. Gray hairs, sleepless nights, indigestion."

"Indigestion?" Reese laughed.

He nodded. "Fathers get it from worrying about the boys that have this amazing way of lighting up daughters' eyes. It's enough to make them sick to the stomach."

"From what I've heard, you lit up your share of eyes in your day."

"My day? You make me sound like I'm a hundred years old."

"May as well be. You're played out."

"Pl—Are you kidding?" Norris stood and pranced around like a fashion model. "Look at this. I'm just hitting my stride. There's a lot of gas still left in Norris's tank."

"When the indigestion isn't taking its share." Reese grinned.

"Touché." Norris returned to the chair, laughing.

Talking, joking, dare he say it, bonding? After the rocky start to the day, he and Reese had somehow managed to salvage the evening and get closer. He didn't feel the tension that seemed to always linger just beneath the surface. It felt good. After months of struggle, in one day he'd made some real headway with the two most important women in his life.

"Tell me, how much do you like Jack?" Norris asked.

Reese's eyes took on the glossy shine he'd mentioned earlier. His stomach twisted in knots. He would probably never get used to seeing that look in her eyes. He groaned.

"What?" Reese asked.

"What? That's my indigestion groan. You can't see how bright and shiny your eyes are right now."

Reese smiled, "But I can feel my happiness." She curled into the near corner of the couch and clutched the throw to her chest, sighing. "Jack is wonderful. He's considerate, kind, smart, athletic, and so fine. Mmm." She fanned her flushed face.

Norris rolled his eyes. "Tell me how you really feel."

Reese chuckled. "You asked," she said.

"I did." Norris paused for a moment. "That day at the mall, I might've been a bit . . ."

"Might've been?"

"You didn't let me finish."

Reese held up her hands. "I'm sorry. Please continue."

"Maybe I was a little rough on him, but I want to know any guy you go out with. I guess my thoughts on this aren't very high on your list, but it's important that I know. Call it another one of those father things. I want my daughter to have the best of everything. That includes potential boyfriends."

Reese gave his hand a pat. "Don't worry about that, Norris. Jack is a great guy. You know his father. Chip/block."

"I guess. Invite him over soon. Maybe he can give me pointers on how to make you so giddy and happy."

"You have your own ways of doing that," she said, bringing a moment of companionable silence between them. "Now, enough about my personal life. What's going on with you? Is this drought about me?"

"Drought?"

"All the ladies. I see 'em checking you out, but it's like you're blind to them. What happened to the legend? Or has the torch been passed on to me? You know, I do have my charms."

Norris shook his head at Reese's beaming smile. She was too much. "There's been no passing of anything, young lady. I've just grown."

"What does that mean?"

"It means I'm not interested in a string of women. I'm beyond that now. I want something better than the life I had." He smiled, imagining the future he could have with Dahlia and Reese, and seeing it so clearly he could almost reach out and touch it. "I really think I can get it." Dahlia had to deal with her demons, and after their discussion today, he felt strongly she'd be professing her love soon. He knew she felt it, but she had to be okay with feeling it.

"What are you talking about? You never go out. All you do is work and spend time with the Andrews and me." She raised an eyebrow. "Wait a minute. You seeing somebody on the sly?"

The ringing phone postponed Norris's debate on how much of the truth he should give Reese to her question. "I'll get that," he said. "Hello."

"Norris, it's Ryan. I'm at the hospital. Lara's in labor!"

"Is she?" Norris smiled. "How's she doing, pal?"

"Pretty good so far. The real party hasn't started yet."

"I'll be right over."

"You might want to wait," Ryan said. "It could be a while."

"Or maybe not. I'll be over soon." Norris ended the call. "Lara's in labor," he said. "I'm heading to the hospital."

"Cool." Reese stood. "Mind if I tag along?"

"You want to?"

Reese nodded.

"Feel free."

"I need to change first. I won't be long," she said, heading to her room.

Norris smiled. Closer to Dahlia, closer to Reese, and this much closer to having new godchildren. This had definitely turned into a pretty good day.

He dropped to the couch and leafed through his *Sports Illustrated*. Another thing he'd learned about his daughter, when it came to getting dressed, not long usually meant an hour.

Twelve hours later, Norris and Reese returned home. "Who would've thought two six-pound babies would take so long being born. I was beginning to wonder if they were coming by Pony Express," Norris said.

Reese laughed. "They are the cutest little things." She cooed. "Brianna Evelyn and Christopher Boyd. I could actually look forward to babysitting."

"I'm sure Lara and Ryan would love to hear that." Norris stretched. "I'm beat."

"So am I." Reese yawned. "I'm gonna crash for a while."

"Go ahead. I'll turn in after I check in with Agnes."

"Good night, then."

"Good morning," Norris corrected, smiling as Reese disappeared down the hall.

Two minutes after Reese went into her room, Norris ended his call with Agnes. His body was so tired, he wondered if he could make it to his bed. In the middle of taking the first step toward his destination, the doorbell rang. Norris turned to the offending sound. *What damn cruel trick is this?*

He checked the peephole to discover the cruel trick to be a hellish nightmare. His mother. He pulled open the door, desperate not to hear that ringing again. His heart pounded with fury and hands shook with exhaustion. "What do you want?"

"We needed to finish talking."

"We were finished yesterday. Mom, I'm tired. I've had a very long night, and I want—I need—to go to sleep."

"Sleep? Norris, it's nine o'clock in the morning."

"I was at the hospital for the past twelve hours. Ryan and Lara's babies were born earlier this morning."

Genevieve grunted and brushed past Norris. "I see."

"No, you don't see." Norris rubbed his hands over his face, feeling the rough overnight stubble. "I want you to leave. You're not going to destroy the life I'm trying to make."

"It seems to me you're destroying your own life. You're drowning in a sea of bad choices. I'm throwing you a life preserver, and you won't take it."

"Getting me to disown my daughter is your way of helping me? No thanks, Mom, I'm not interested."

"She's not interested in you. What is it, Norris? You want to be so much like Ryan, you're going to take in this brown child to make it happen?" Genevieve's face reddened. "I bet the next thing you'll be telling me is you're going to marry some black woman!" She folded her arms. Her face an angry scowl of disapproval.

Norris looked at Genevieve, the woman who had given him life, and saw her for the first time. His eyes were tired, burning for sleep, but he'd never seen a clearer picture of his mother than he did at this moment. She wasn't misguided; she was lost. He didn't have the desire to lead her from her darkness. But he would prepare her for this worst-case scenario she'd already dreamed up in her head.

"It's funny you should mention marriage, Mom. I have some news that should make you really happy."

The light of happiness dissipated the anger in her eyes. "You've met someone?" Genevieve said. "Our kind of woman?"

"She's definitely my kind. She's beautiful, successful, an Ivy League graduate. MBA."

Genevieve clasped her hands. "Norris, this lady sounds perfect," she gushed.

"I think she is. She's also African-American." He smiled. "Is she still perfect, Mom?"

Genevieve recoiled. "No." She backed away, shaking her head. "This isn't true. You wouldn't do this to me."

"I'm not doing this *to* you. I'm doing it *for* me. For years I've gone from woman to woman, seeking cheap thrills and nothing more. Commitment wasn't in the cards for me, until I met this woman. She's shown me a happiness I didn't think existed, and if she'll have me, I'm going to spend the rest of my life with her, and hopefully populate this earth with more brown babies."

Tears streamed down his mother's face. Norris shook his head, not the least bit affected.

"Why do you want to hurt me like this?" Genevieve said.

"Get it into your head, Mom, this is not about you. But perhaps the reason it's taken me so long to find someone to love is because the first woman a boy should love, his mother, was missing from my life. You were too busy jet-setting to be a parent. Hired help raised Lane, Julia, and me. And when we got used to one set, they were gone and new workers came in. Had it not been for Ryan's folks, I wouldn't have known what a real, stable family looked like."

"And you think this girl and your Ivy League woman will give you a real family?"

"I know they will. I'm going to be a good spouse to my mate, and a good parent to my child. Two things you and Dad have never been." Norris pointed to the door. "I want you out of my house, out of my life, and I don't want you to come back."

"You . . . you don't mean that."

"No, Mom, I mean it. You've made it clear you don't think my daughter is good enough to be a part of your family. Well, I've decided you're not good enough to be a part of mine." Norris walked to the door and pulled it open, bringing in the muggy heat of outdoors, making him more exhausted. "It's not bad enough you've insulted my closest friends, but you refuse to accept your one and only grandchild because her skin is darker than you'd like. That's pitiful, you are pitiful, and I want you gone."

Genevieve stuck out her chin and grabbed her purse. "Fine. You know how to reach me when you change your mind."

"My mind won't change. Good-bye." Norris closed the door behind his mother and waited for devastating sadness to fill his heart. No sadness came, but he did feel the weight of a boulder leaving his shoulders.

"Norris?"

He turned around to find Reese in a pink nightshirt, wearing the devastating sadness missing from his heart on her face. A knot formed in his throat. "How—how much of that did you hear?" he asked, fearing the answer.

Tears filled Reese's sad eyes. "All of it," she said.

"Oh, baby." Norris held his crying daughter in his arms as the shards from his broken heart fell with his tears. "I'm so sorry, Reese. I'm so sorry you had to hear that."

Reese's arms curled around his shoulders, alerting him of a most ironic fact. His mother's stupefying ignorance had provided his first embrace with his daughter. Thanks to his mother, he was hugging Reese.

Minutes later Reese pulled away. "I'm sorry about this." She sniffled.

Norris brushed away her tears. "Why are you apologizing?"

"Because I was a fool yesterday. You were trying to protect me, and I accused you of being ashamed of me." Reese hunched her shoulders. "She seemed nice yesterday."

"That's what she wanted you to believe. My mother is not a nice person." Norris cupped Reese's face, forcing their eyes to meet. "I want you to understand, Reese, when it comes to you, there's nothing I won't do. I want to protect you from everything harmful. I know I won't always be able to, but I'll try. You mean the world to me, and I want you to be happy."

"I am." She walked to the couch and sat. "You come off a bit gruff sometimes, but I believe you do things with my best interests in mind. You really do love me, don't you?"

"Absolutely." He moved to the couch and cupped her chin. "More than anything."

"Even that Ivy League woman you've fallen in love with?" Reese smiled. "You're in love with Dahlia, aren't you?"

Norris nodded and smiled. "Yes. I love her very much."

"I should have known. Her interest in Tawny, your interest in her whereabouts, always finding you two huddled together. And then her phone call yesterday."

"She phoned?"

"Yeah. The usual talk she gives me. I should cut you some slack and try to see things from your point of view. Yesterday, with everything going on with her sister, she calls me to sing your praises. You went to Atlanta, didn't you?"

"I wanted to give you some space."

"And you wanted to see Dahlia, too, right?"

He nodded. "That, too."

"I knew there was a guy, but Dahlia denied it every time."

"You knew there was a guy?"

"Of course." Reese nodded. "She was always smiling or looking sad. Only a man could give a woman such high highs and low lows. How long have you guys been together?"

"We met on Valentine's Day."

"Why did you two keep it a secret?"

"It's rather complicated, but it's what Dahlia wanted."

"She loves you, you know."

"I do know, but she doesn't want to own up to it."

"Neither did I, but you kinda make it hard not to. Dahlia's going to come around, just like I did." Reese kissed his cheek. "I'm going to try to get some sleep, old man."

Norris touched his stubbly cheek where Reese had placed her kiss. His daughter loved him. His lips curled into a wide smile. Reese loved him.

Norris drew a breath and grabbed the colorful bouquet of tulips from the passenger side of his car. How hard could this be? He was doing an unasked favor for Dahlia. Checking in on Grandma Flora. Dahlia had made it clear the older woman was self-sufficient and hated the idea of people checking up on her, but he could tell Dahlia was concerned, and he wanted to reassure her. After being away from the office for two days, he couldn't get away yesterday, but visiting today topped his "To Do" list.

He walked up the brick steps of the large white house, but before he could ring the doorbell, he heard a voice from the right side of the wrap-around porch.

"Over here, child."

Norris made his way around to see Mrs. Best watering the colorful flowers growing around the base of the porch.

"Mrs. Best, I'm . . ."

"I know who you are," she said, interrupting his words but never deviating from her task at hand. "Took you long enough to get here. Put the flowers next to the lemonade on the table and sit yourself down. When I finish with my flowers, we'll talk."

About two hours later, Norris was waving goodbye and making his way back to his car. He couldn't remember when he'd enjoyed a conversation more. He was in no way ready to give up on Dahlia, and after the talk with Grandma Flora his convictions remained strong.

It had surprised him to learn how much Dahlia had told her grandmother about him and their arrangement. Flora confessed the details surprised her, but she wanted to draw her own conclusions about Norris, and all in all he seemed like a pretty good man, and she could see why Dahlia loved him. When he admitted being inconsistent in attending church, she made him promise to attend with her the coming Sunday.

A smile stayed on his face as drove to the office. Things in his life had definitely taken a turn for the better. Reese met his siblings yesterday and they were hitting it off, and he and Dahlia kept the telephone lines burning. Absence definitely made the heart grow fonder, and he was counting the days until he could hold her in his arms again and never let her go.

CHAPTER 22

"I gonna miss you, Sammy."

Dahlia smiled down at her sleeping nephew, tucked nice and cozy in his crib at Leslie's apartment. Leslie had given her the honor of naming the newest Sinclair, and considering his entry into the world and his amazing strength through it all, the name Sampson seemed ideal. Sampson Aaron Sinclair. Aaron after Grandma Flora's beloved husband, and Sammy's great grandfather. Jonah was none too pleased he didn't have a junior, but managed to keep his disappointment to a minimum in order to hash out an agreeable visitation schedule with Leslie.

Dahlia brushed her fingertip against Sammy's soft little cheek. Her love for him filled her heart.

"You're a natural, Dahlia," Leslie said, brushing the downy thatch of black hair on her son's head.

"He makes it easy."

Leslie sat in the nearby rocker, hugging a blue teddy bear to her chest. "I can't believe how fast the last two weeks have gone. I don't know how I'll make it without you."

"You'll be fine. You're amazing with him. You've found your greatest love."

Leslie nodded. "I have. And what about you? I didn't get to meet Norris, but Mama and Daddy think he's made quite the impression on you."

Dahlia managed a tight smile. She and Leslie had gotten closer, but she was nowhere near ready to discuss her personal life with her baby sister.

"You don't want to talk about him with me, do you?"

"No, Leslie, I don't," Dahlia answered, refusing to lie. "I'm trying, but we're not there yet. I'm sorry."

"No, I'm sorry. It's going to take some time, and I understand that. I hope you find the happiness you deserve. Maybe Norris can be that for you."

"Maybe." Dahlia checked her watch. "I need to head to the airport. My flight leaves in a couple of hours, and I have to turn in the rental car."

Leslie stood with open arms. "Take care of yourself."

Dahlia accepted her sister's hug. "I do love you, Leslie."

"You just don't like me the way you used to, right?" Leslie shrugged. "It's my own fault. I'm glad you're willing to try to get us back to where we were."

"I am, and I'm going to keep trying." Dahlia hugged her sister. "You take care of Sammy, okay?"

Leslie nodded. "You know I will. And I'll send lots of emails with pictures."

"Thank you. I would love that. I'll visit when I can."

"Will you?"

"We can't get closer if we don't see each other." Dahlia grabbed her purse and smiled down at Sammy. "Auntie Dahlia loves you." She kissed her finger and pressed it to his cheek. "Bye-bye, sweetie."

Leslie followed Dahlia to the front door. "This has been good, right?"

Dahlia smiled. "It's been tense at times, but it's been very good." She embraced Leslie once more.

"Be happy, Dahlia. That's all I hope for you."

Thoughts of Norris's smiling face and gentle touch filled Dahlia's head. "I think I'm on my way, Leslie," she said, already counting the minutes until she landed in Denburg. "I'm on my way."

"Whoa!" Norris rushed over to the door as Reese and his sister, Julia, stumbled inside loaded down with packages. "Should I ask for my credit card or is it too hot to touch?" he asked half-jokingly.

"You can touch it," Reese said, "but using it might prove to be a little embarrassing." She smiled.

"Tell me you're kidding."

"I'm kidding."

Norris tilted his head and crossed his arms.

"I'm kidding," Reese repeated with conviction. "I used some of the ridiculous amount of cash you call allowance. The operative word being *some.* I can still go out and buy the Hope Diamond if I want."

"So long as that's still an option." Norris laughed. "You guys had fun?"

"Did we." Julia plopped into the chair, expelling a loud breath of exhaustion. "You've got a champion shopper on your hands, Norris."

"Considering her aunt is the reigning title holder, I'd say she got that skill honestly."

"You hear from Lane?"

"Yeah. He should be here in a few minutes."

"Oh." Reese sat on the arm of the chair, her mouth turned down. "I wish you guys didn't have to leave."

"Aww, me, too." Julia gave her a squeeze. "But we'll keep in touch. And who knows, maybe before the summer ends you can come visit me in Paris. That is, if you can stand being away from *Jack* that long."

Reese's face lit up like a megawatt bulb. Norris wanted to think excitement about spending time in Paris with Julia had brought on her happy glow, but he knew better. Reese could have found a worse kid to be interested in, and in the last few weeks, Norris had found Jack to be a likeable young man, but he still got cold sweats at the idea of some boy being interested in his daughter.

Julia tapped Reese's cheek, laughing. "Looks like I'll have to come back to Denburg, 'cause this girl is going nowhere this summer."

Norris rolled his eyes, not finding the least bit of humor in Julia's teasing.

The doorbell rang. Norris jumped up, anxious to get away from his daughter's grinning and his sister's giggling. "I'll get that," he said. "It's probably Lane."

Norris pulled open the door to find the brother he expected looking a lot like Dahlia. He blinked, believing the beautiful vision in strawberry red to be a figment of his imagination, until the scent of her intoxicating, sensual perfume erased all doubt. Visions did not smell this good.

He brushed his finger against her smooth cheek and softly whispered, "Dahlia." Norris gathered her into his arms, kissing her softly, yet thoroughly, savoring the sweetness of her ruby lips like a glass of vintage chardonnay as his hands reacquainted themselves with her soft, supple body.

"Mmm, mmm." Dahlia moaned. "Norris," she mumbled against his lips. "Where's Reese?"

He continued to kiss her, drowning her words with his tongue. He didn't want to talk. He wanted to touch, to taste, to kiss, to hold her the way he'd wanted to for months. Dahlia combed her fingers through his hair, her touch an active accelerant to the fire stirring in his loins. He held her closer, allowing her to feel his need. Her body molded against his like a hand in a tailored glove. She wanted him, too.

"Ahem!"

The exaggerated cough broke the kiss, but the Jaws of Life would have to pry his hands from her body. Norris turned toward the sound to see Reese front and center and his sister a few steps behind.

"Welcome back, Dahlia," Reese said. "I can't give you the kind of greeting Norris did, but it's just as heartfelt."

Norris licked his lips, recalling Dahlia's sweetness, fighting the urge to taste those lips once more. He nuzzled her neck, breathing in her delightful perfume.

Dahlia pulled back, eyeing Norris curiously. "Why doesn't she sound surprised by this?" she asked.

"Telepathy?" he said with a coy grin.

"Norris?" Dahlia frowned.

He chuckled. "Okay. I told her." Norris ushered Dahlia inside and closed the door. "Reese overheard me talking about the woman I love, and when she asked I confessed." His fingertips trailed from her waist to her hip. "You're not angry, are you?"

Dahlia smiled. "No. I'm not angry."

Julia made her way over with her right hand extended. "Hi, Dahlia, it's nice to finally meet you," she said.

Recognition shone bright in Dahlia's eyes. "You must be Julia, Norris's baby sister," she said, taking Julia's hand. "I can see the resemblance."

"See, that's the highest compliment anyone can get. Looking like me." Norris grinned.

Julia gave his shoulder a sportive shove. "How do you put up with this guy, Dahlia?" she said.

Dahlia shrugged. "I don't know." Her gaze met his. "He makes it hard not to."

As always, Norris found so much more in Dahlia's eyes than she ever allowed herself to verbalize. They needed to talk. The sound of three quick raps turned his attention to the door.

Lane popped his head inside. "No time for long good-byes, Jules, we need to hit the road," he said.

Norris waved him in. "Come inside for a second, I want you to meet someone."

Three inches taller and forty pounds heavier, Lane personified the term 'big brother.' With straight black hair and ice blue eyes he had a look that made many a woman take a second glance. However, unlike his younger brother, Lane didn't suffer egocentric tendencies.

"What's up?" Lane rested his sunglasses atop his head and walked in, smiling broadly when he spotted Dahlia. "Uh-huh! Now I see," he said. "You must be the amazing Dahlia."

Dahlia raised a brow. "Amazing Dahlia?" she said.

"Hey, this guy is talking love, that's amazing." Lane kissed her hand. "It's a pleasure."

"It's all mine. I see charm is in surplus with the Converse men."

"Some of us have more than others." Norris grinned.

"Norris told us about your sister," Lane said. "I'm glad she's doing better."

"Thank you. She is so much better, and baby Sammy is growing like a weed."

"Glad to hear it." Lane checked his watch. "I hate to do this, but we have to get going. You know these airports, and we can't miss our connections at O'Hare." He pulled Reese into a big bear hug. "Favorite niece, don't be a stranger."

Reese smiled. "I won't, and I'm your only niece," she said.

Lane snapped his fingers. "That's right."

Following more hugs and kisses, Julia and Lane departed for the airport.

"Your siblings are really nice."

"I think so, too, but there are some new siblings I believe you'll think are even nicer."

Dahlia smiled. "Lara's babies."

"They are something else."

"The most darling little angels," Reese added.

"Can we go see them?" Dahlia asked.

"Sure. You're not too tired after the trip?"

"No, I'm great. I would like to drop my car off first."

"We can follow you. Maybe after we see the babies, the three of us can grab some dinner."

Dahlia nodded. "That sounds good."

"I agree," Reese said. "I'll need about five minutes to take my bags into the room and freshen up."

"Freshen up? You look great."

"You're stating the obvious, Norris, but it's hot out, and I'm sure you can see your reflection in my face. It'll only be five minutes," Reese said, grabbing her shopping bags and dashing toward her room.

Dahlia laughed. "She is definitely your daughter."

"She is that." Norris smiled as he pulled Dahlia into his arms. "Alone at last." He kissed her neck, hugging her close. "I missed you."

"I missed you more." Dahlia smoothed the hair along his temples. "We need to talk."

"I know." He kissed her cheek. "After dinner?"

She nodded and settled back into his arms. Norris held her closer, breathing her in, luxuriating in the feel of her against him. Moments like this would fill his future, because tonight promised to be the night he'd longed for. The night Dahlia would finally confess her love for him.

Dahlia brushed her finger against Christopher's soft golden cheek. His blue eyes fluttered open for the briefest moment, and after a long yawn, they closed.

"Ahh," she cooed. "Ryan, he is so handsome."

"You won't hear me disagree with you," Ryan said. "I'm a card-carrying proud papa."

Dahlia smiled as Christopher's tiny hand wrapped around Ryan's finger. "I can see. How are Justin and Angelica taking their new siblings?"

"Very well. Justin's offering to change diapers, and Angelica's chomping at the bit to play dress-up with a live dolly. They really love their new little brother and sister."

"That's great."

"Something else is great," Ryan said, smiling. "Seeing you here with Norris. I hope this means I'll be seeing you two together a lot more often."

Dahlia smiled. "You just might."

"I'm carrying a very dry and very beautiful little princess," Norris said, returning to the living room with Lara following behind. "And Reese has Justin and Angelica enthralled with the video game she brought over for them."

"Happy and quiet kids. I'm not complaining," Ryan said, relinquishing his spot on the couch to Norris.

"You two look right at home with babies in your arms," Lara said, smiling brightly at the duo. "Don't you think so, Ryan?"

"I do," he said, wrapping his arm around Lara and settling in the loveseat across from the couch. "It's a great picture."

Dahlia pressed her lips together to keep from laughing out loud. Lara and Ryan were definitely not keeping their opinions on her and Norris as a couple to themselves.

"You guys want to cut it out?" Norris said.

Ryan and Lara shrugged. "What?" they said in unison.

"You know what."

The married couple smiled brightly but said nothing more.

Brianna's olive complexion reddened as wails filled the air and distressed tears filled her brown eyes.

"I think somebody's hungry," said Dahlia.

Norris walked over to Lara and handed her the crying baby. "Here you go, Lara. I think this is a job for Mama."

"Yes, it's feeding time for them, and if I know my son, he's going to . . ."

Christopher's wails broke into Lara's words.

"Just as I expected," she said.

"Chris doesn't like his big sister Bri to dine without him," Ryan said, gathering the baby boy from Dahlia's arms.

"Speaking of dining, it's time I get some food into this beautiful lady," Norris said, taking Dahlia's hand and helping her from the couch. "I'll get Reese."

Lara moved over to Dahlia when Norris left, gently shaking a quieter Bri. "Should I be hopeful? I know Norris is."

Dahlia smiled and said, "Yeah, I think you should."

"You've been pretty quiet since we left Ryan and Lara's, Norris," Dahlia said, finishing the last bite of her grilled salmon. "What's on your mind?" As if she didn't already know. The look in his eyes spoke volumes.

"Guess." Norris reached for her hand. "Reese deciding to stay at Ryan and Lara's wasn't by chance," he said. "My daughter could tell I wanted to be alone with you."

Dahlia wiped her mouth and drank the last of her tea. Zixby's Surf & Turf had some of the best food, but the iced tea was even better. She lowered the glass to find Norris staring. She smiled. Deciding to open her heart to him hadn't come easily, but she wanted to do just that. What she didn't want was to have this long-awaited conversation in public.

"I can handle some alone time with you." She gave his hand a squeeze. "My place?"

Norris nodded. "Let's go."

Dahlia said very little on the ride back to her house, her thoughts on how to say words she never thought she'd say to another man. She practically floated inside her house. Her cheeks hurt from smiling so much.

Norris followed her to the couch. "You always accuse me of vanity, but I can't help but think I have a little something to do with that smile you can't wipe off your face tonight."

Dahlia chuckled. "Maybe a little something."

"Tell me what's on your mind."

"I think you can guess."

"I can. I've just—I've waited so long for this."

She nodded. "I know."

Norris pulled her into his lap, curling his arms around her waist. "All right, Ms. Sinclair, you have my undivided attention." He pecked her lips. "Talk to me."

Dahlia trailed the back of her fingers against Norris's smooth cheeks, tracing the lines of his handsome face. She lowered her head, breathing in his scent. Her lips repeated his soft kiss. "There's only one thing left to say, Norris. I love you. I've loved you for so long. Fighting it was hard, but fighting you was even harder. Being in Atlanta helped me. The place my life came crashing down turned out to be the place where you helped me build it back up. Confronting my sister and Jonah and putting all that anger, hurt, and fear where it belonged— it cleansed me. You gave me strength to deal with all that. And not just in Atlanta. Every time I needed you, no matter what I said to the contrary, you were there. Supporting me and loving me. When you left Atlanta, I knew I was ready to embrace my love for you. Can you ever forgive me for making you wait so long to hear what you already knew?"

"Oh, my sweet, beautiful Dahlia." Norris kissed her cheeks, forehead, chin, nose, and then softly kissed her lips. "You are the love of my life, my one and only love. There is nothing to forgive. You and Reese. I love two of the most stubborn, beautiful women in the world. I've learned patience." He brought her into a warm embrace. "We're an 'us' now?"

Dahlia nodded. "Yes."

"We get to go on real dates, too?"

Dahlia chuckled. "Yes, we do. And, if you don't mind, I want to just date. You know?"

"No more arrangement?" he said ever so slowly.

She nodded. "Yeah. No point in confusing things. It was your suggestion, and I think it was a good one. We know what we're great at. Let's see if we can eclipse that."

"No arrangement. I said that. I did. Well, uh, I guess the place I want us to go for our first date as a couple is very appropriate."

"Where's that?"

"Sweet Zion tomorrow. I have a standing date with Grandma Flora."

CHAPTER 23

Soft sighs and low moans joined the faint sounds of love songs playing on the stereo. Norris held Dahlia closer to him and deepened their kiss. Nearly two months into their courtship and almost five months into a life of abstinence, Norris hadn't been happier or more frustrated. Dahlia's soft backside on his lap made things that much harder. Oh, so much harder.

He broke the kiss and nuzzled her neck. "Dahlia, sweetheart, I think we need to amend our amended arrangement."

Dahlia's butterfly kisses on his neck deepened his moans and his need. "I thought you were the master of restraint," she said. "Weren't you the one always apologizing and rushing off when I kissed you?"

"That was before. We've come so far since then. I love you so much, Dahlia. I want to show you."

"I love you, too, Norris, and you've already shown me."

"I can show you so much more." He kissed her softly and pulled away, looking into her eyes. "You know by now this is not just a physical thing."

"I've known that for a while, Norris."

"We want the same thing, don't we?"

Dahlia nodded. "I think we do," she said, curling her arms around his neck and joining her lips with his.

"You two!" Reese groaned, bringing an end to their kiss and a disappointed moan from Norris. "Aren't you supposed to be planning my party?" She closed the front door and made her way over. "This looks to be a two-person party, and not the ideal planning session I expected for my blowout birthday bash."

"You're back early, Reese," Dahlia said.

"Early? It's eleven-thirty. I would like a later curfew but . . ." Reese turned her gaze to Norris.

"Eleven-thirty is late enough," Norris said. Especially when the time was spent with smile-inducing Jack.

"Where did the time go?" Dahlia wondered.

"I can only imagine." Reese laughed as Dahlia stayed perched on Norris's lap. "How's my party planning going?"

"Great." Norris answered. "In fact, we're done."

"Really?"

"Yes," Dahlia piped in.

"Cool. Then you two can go back to whatever you were doing." With a wave of her hand, Reese went off to her room.

"Think she's excited about the party?" Dahlia giggled.

"Maybe just a smidge," Norris said. "If it's not everything she hopes, she's gonna let me hear about it."

"You have nothing to worry about. She's going to be blown away. You have some big surprises for her."

"I might have one or two for you, too."

Dahlia raised a perfectly arched brow. "For me? What?"

Norris shrugged. "You'll see in two weeks."

Dahlia grabbed her purse and raced for the door. Reese's party started in an hour and a half, and there were a few last minute details she needed to check at Sandy Run, the banquet facility they'd booked for the party.

She swung open the door to find an attractive, tastefully dressed brunette woman, who seemed to be a young sixty-something, about to ring her bell.

"May I help you with something?" Dahlia asked.

"I think you just might," the woman said. "My name is Genevieve Converse."

Dahlia blinked, surprised to learn her visitor was Norris's mother. She wanted to be cordial, but after what she'd heard from Norris and Reese and given the fact she was running late, playing nice to this woman wasn't much of a priority. "I was just on my way out," she said.

"It will only take a few minutes."

I don't have a few minutes! Dahlia flashed a tight smile. "Fine. Do you want to come in?" she asked.

Genevieve peeked around Dahlia as if to check the place for armed felons. "Perhaps that would be okay." She slowly walked inside, taking in the house from ceiling to floor. "This is a charming little place you have. Amazingly well-kept."

Dahlia had never considered her twenty-five-hundred-square-foot house little, and the comment about it being well kept . . . She sucked in a breath. "What's on your mind, Mrs. Converse?"

"You and my son. The last time we spoke, he threatened—" Genevieve cleared her throat and started again. "He intimated you two were seriously involved and contemplating marriage. Is that true?"

Dahlia folded her arms, annoyed by the woman's presence and her initial choice of words. "Ask Norris," she said.

"Norris tends to *color* the truth for me. He's always been ungrateful for everything he's had, all the privilege my family's wealth afforded him. As a result, he does things to get attention, be it truth or lies. I want to hear this from you. Are you going to marry my son?"

"What if I am?"

"Is that your answer?"

"No, ma'am, that's my question to you. What would be the attention-grabber in Norris marrying me?" Dahlia asked, curious if the woman would answer the way she expected.

Genevieve wrinkled her nose and sighed, exasperated. "You people are so touchy. I asked a simple question."

"You people?" Dahlia repeated. "What people? Columbia graduates? Business owners? Or would it be the common black woman kind of people?"

"You know precisely what I mean. Norris mentioned you've managed to make something of yourself, but it doesn't make you right for him. That is, if he's really interested in you. I have my doubts about that."

Mrs. Converse had her doubts. Dahlia grunted. Why didn't that surprise her? Never had she been more empowered by her complete love for Norris than she was in this moment. Dahlia met Genevieve's bitter gaze.

"You know, you stand here and talk about all you've given to Norris, and the only things you've given him are money and grief. You and your husband never gave him the love and attention he wanted and still craves, so he's learned to live without it. Just like he has to live with the fact that you refuse to accept your granddaughter. It is the ultimate example of gall for you to come to *my* house and presume to tell me the kind of man your son, and, yes, *my* future husband, is."

Genevieve's face burned bright red with anger. Dahlia smiled, pleased with the reaction. "Norris is smart, funny, sweet, caring, gentle, loving, and just the slightest bit vain, a wonderful array of qualities that made me fall in love with him. You have missed out on so much with Norris. And for a woman who's supposedly so worldly, it's a shame you haven't realized that yet." She opened the door and turned to Genevieve. "Now, if you'll excuse me, I have someplace to be." Dahlia stood at the door and waited for Genevieve to pass.

The woman's silence and angry glare said everything. Dahlia locked the door and raced to her car when Genevieve's limo drove away, ready for all the surprises and happiness the evening promised to hold.

Reese's party was back in full swing after an unexpected glitch with one of her surprises, a live performance by a chart-topping male R&B superstar, which had prompted six girls and one boy to faint from shock and excitement. Norris sighed in relief when he joined Dahlia and the others in the adult corner.

"Everybody has come to, thank God," he shouted above the loud music. "I was beginning to worry about the young man."

Dahlia curled her arm around his. "Worry no more. Things are back to normal and Reese is enjoying her party. Look at her and Jack." Dahlia smiled at the dancing duo surrounded by their cohorts and Agnes and her husband, Bob, who were threatening to steal the show. "Everyone's having a great time."

Norris nodded. The one good thing about the headache-inducing music was it kept Reese out of Jack's arms. He'd slipped the DJ an extra fifty bucks to ensure no slow songs got played tonight. She could have as much fun as she wanted so long as the songs stayed fast. Norris smiled at Jack's parents. He had invited David and Margo as a show of goodwill for Reese in regard to Jack, and to drop a hint to David about more responsibility at the firm. Both seemed to be working.

Minutes later, after hearing a humorous earful from the Andrews, Monroes, and Armstrongs about the loud music and their need to escape it, Norris decided to present Reese's other surprise as soon as possible so the over-thirty crowd could go home and still rescue some of the evening. Spotting his smiling siblings flashing thumbs up, Norris knew now was the time. Hopefully, things would die down quickly thereafter and the party would wrap up. He still had a surprise to give to Dahlia.

"It's time for Reese's next present," Norris said.

Following a quick meeting with his siblings, Norris got the DJ to cut the music, and he called Reese to join him on stage. He wrapped his arm around her shoulders and pressed a kiss to her temple, his love for her filling his heart to overflowing.

"Five months ago, I discovered this beautiful young woman was my daughter. And as some of you know, that was quite a time for the both of us."

Chuckles and murmurs of affirmation echoed about the room.

"You can say that again," offered Diana.

Norris smiled. "When I think of how far we've come, it makes this moment all the more special. Today is Reese's seventeenth birthday, but for me it's her first. I thought long and hard about all the things I didn't get to buy for her birthdays as she was growing up, and one gift stuck out in my mind. A pony. A white pony with a red ribbon."

Reese squinted. "A pony?" she whispered. "Don't you think I'm a little big for a pony?"

"She asked if I thought she was too big for a pony," Norris said to the crowd. "Yes, I do, sweetie. So, I thought outside the box. You're too big for a pony, but you're just the right size for a horse. Three hundred of them—inside the engine of a brand new Mustang." Norris pulled the key from his pocket and dropped it in her hand. "Happy birthday, Reese."

"You got me a Mustang!" Reese squealed and leapt into Norris's arms. "I don't have to drive Mom's ten-year-old Honda anymore!"

"I take it you're happy." Norris laughed.

"Beyond words." Reese kissed his cheek. "Thank you, Daddy! Thank you."

Norris froze. Had his ears deceived him? He pulled back, looking at Reese through a haze of tears. "Did you call me Daddy?"

"I did. You are my daddy. And I love you."

"I love you, too, Reese."

Norris looked out in the crowd as he held his daughter and met Dahlia's teary, love-filled gaze. Perhaps before his daughter's birthday was over, he'd have his greatest wish. A promise from Dahlia that she'd be his wife.

Norris collapsed onto Dahlia's comfy couch. "What a day."

Dahlia dropped down beside him, blowing out a long breath. "Yes indeed." She curled against up against him. "But wasn't it a great party?"

"Yes, it was. Thanks for all of your help, Dahlia. I couldn't have done this party without you."

Dahlia pecked his lips. "You're more than welcome. Reese is a special girl, and she deserved a special birthday."

"This day surpassed all of my hopes. Reese enjoyed all of her gifts, from the video call with Gail and Ben this morning to her brand new car. She's out on a date with what's his name and I'm not going too crazy. And she called me Daddy." Norris closed his eyes, the memory of that moment still fresh in his mind. "She called me Daddy, Dahlia. I can't describe how wonderful it is to hear that word directed at me."

Dahlia smiled. "You're describing it pretty well right now." She brushed her fingertips along his temple. "Something happened to me today I find a little hard to describe." She chuckled. "I was paid a visit by your mother."

Norris blinked. "You what?"

"She came by just as I was leaving for Reese's party. She's every bit the way you described."

He groaned. "I can't believe this. I told her about you, but I never mentioned you by name."

"She wears her money very well. I guess she used some of it to do some digging. It's not like we've been a secret these past months. She was particularly curious about your—she caught herself before calling it a threat—desire to marry me."

Norris grunted. "Well, she would call it a threat, but it's only my greatest wish. I do want to marry you, Dahlia."

"That's good to know, because I want you to marry me, too."

He smiled. "Are you asking?"

Dahlia chuckled. "Are you?"

Norris eased off the couch and dropped to one knee. "I am indeed." He reached into his pocket and pulled out the ring he'd purchased for Dahlia so many months ago.

"I've had this ring for a long time, and now I want you to have it on your finger. Dahlia, will you marry me?"

She nodded. "Yes, Norris, I will. I love you so much."

"I love you, too." Norris slipped the ring on her finger and then asked his newest burning question. "When?" he asked.

"Is two weeks soon enough?"

"One will be better."

"Rev. Leonard won't marry us without at least three marriage counseling sessions, and there's only two per week. I married Jonah on his family's estate with a judge. This time is for keeps, and I want the blessing of the church for us."

"And you'll have it. Sweet Zion in two weeks?"

"It's a date," she said, sealing the promise with a kiss.

Norris followed the scent of scrambled eggs and sausage into the kitchen, just in time to see Reese place a platter of the breakfast items on the table. They'd come so far. She still grumbled when he reminded her of curfew, but she respected him in his role as her father, and they loved each other. They were a family. And before the day was over, he'd have a wife.

He walked over and kissed her cheek. "What a fine way to start off my wedding day," he said, sitting down and digging into the food. "Thanks, sweetie."

Reese smiled. "You're welcome, Daddy." Her eyes widened as he scarfed down the scrambled eggs and sausage. "I can't believe in a few hours you'll be standing in Sweet Zion about to get married. You don't even seem nervous."

"I'm not. I do feel bad for the slew of women who are going to be crying into their pillows tonight, but they'll get over it—in about five or ten years." He laughed.

Reese rolled her eyes. "And people think I'm bad," she said, popping the last of a sausage link in her mouth.

Norris continued laughing. "Seriously, I'm over the moon." He ate the last of his toast. "I'm hours away from marrying the woman of my dreams, and my beautiful daughter is here to share it with me. What more could I ask for?"

"That your beautiful daughter won't steal your thunder when she walks down the aisle in her-to-die for bridesmaid dress." She smiled broadly. "You might want to ask for that."

Norris laughed with Reese. "I'll keep that in mind."

"Would you stop fidgeting!" Ryan said, trying to tie Norris's bow tie. "You're worse than Justin and Angelica. And she wanted to sleep in her flower girl dress."

"I can't help it." Norris couldn't contain his smile. "In a few minutes, Dahlia is going to be Mrs. Converse. I'm going to have a wife. I'll be a husband."

"Now all you have to do is lose the leather furniture."

"Nothing doing, pal. I like my leather, and so does Dahlia." He smiled brighter. "She likes everything about me."

"Oh, whatever." Ryan finished with the tie. "All done." He grabbed Norris's shoulders. "How do you feel?"

"Loved." Norris groaned. "Damn, I sound like a greeting card," he said, checking his reflection in the mirror.

"The right woman does that. You start humming love songs and smiling all the time."

Norris nodded. "Yeah. Yeah."

"I'm sorry your parents aren't here to share in this."

"It's their loss. They've missed most of my life. This is nothing new. I haven't seen my father in almost five years, and he's not returned any of my calls. Lane and Jules haven't heard from him either. I guess separating from Mom freed him from parenthood, too. Not that either of them were there before. I met Reese less than six months ago, and I can't imagine not being in her life. I don't care how old she gets."

"You're a real parent. Do you miss your folks?"

"It's hard to miss something you never truly had. I have what I need now. What I've been searching for. A family. The people I love and who love me are here. That's what matters."

Ryan slapped Norris's arm. "You ready to get married?"

"Am I ever." Norris smiled. "Best man, let's do this."

Norris lay in the bed, his arms folded behind his head and cool satin sheets against his bare skin, in anticipation of Dahlia's warm body taking the place of the slinky bedding. His gaze stayed on the bathroom door she'd disappeared behind five minutes earlier. With the lighting set to a romantic glow and instrumental songs of love piping in from the surround-sound stereo speakers, the only thing missing was his new wife.

"Mrs. Converse, do I need to come in there and get you?"

Dahlia stepped out of the bathroom wearing a super sheer white gown that left very little to the imagination. "Somebody's impatient."

Norris sat up, transfixed. The nearly six months he'd waited for her to come to him like this had been well worth it. He'd seen her with nothing on before, but the teasing transparency sheathing her luscious form added a level of mystery to the body he'd come to know so well and increased his already intense desire to get to know it all over again, a fact made evident by the tenting of the sheet covering him.

Dahlia smiled. "I see you like your present," she said.

He swallowed audibly. "I really do. But I think I'd like it even better on the floor."

"As you wish, husband."

The shining diamonds comprising Dahlia's engagement and wedding rings sparkled like stars in the dim light as she pulled the tiny straps off her shoulders and allowed the gown to fall in a heap at her feet. Norris's gaze raked over every beautiful inch of her, intensifying his need. He pulled the sheets back, welcoming her into the bed. His body trembled when she slid in beside him.

The hot, hard tips of her full breasts brushed against his chest. A deep groan rumbled in his throat.

They lay face to face on their sides. Norris pressed his hand to her cheek. A brand new platinum band shone on his finger. "This has been the happiest day of my life." He nipped her lips. "I want to make you as happy as you make me."

"You already have."

Norris nestled closer to her. His raging hardness pressed against her abdomen. Dahlia's soft moans filled his ears. "I think I can whip up a little more happiness before the night is over," he murmured, touching his mouth to hers.

Their lips moved together, slowly caressing and then parting, allowing their tongues to join in. Norris turned on his back, bringing Dahlia against him. The moist heat between her parted thighs lay flush against him, pulsating against his mid-thigh. His erection throbbed against her belly. He moaned into her mouth, gripping her firm bottom, holding her swiveling hips against him.

Dahlia's lips left his, trailing a searing path from his chin to his neck, to his sensitive and taut nipples. Norris closed his eyes, groaning his pleasure, every nerve ending in his body craving her magic touch. Her tongue flicked one nipple and then the other while her hands splayed in the darks hairs covering his chest. Her soft lips made their way back up his body, nuzzling his neck and then connecting with his.

Sliding his hand into Dahlia's hair, Norris held her closer, kissing her with a gentle hunger, a longing emanating from a place deep inside himself, a desperate need to be one with her. He ended the kiss and turned Dahlia on her back.

He kissed the puckered chocolaty tips of her breasts, laving the stony peaks, drawing one and then the other into his mouth. "I want to love every inch of you, Dahlia." He kissed his way down her body. His lips trailed down one long, silky leg. He suckled each of her French-tipped toes into his mouth. He repeated the action with the other leg as he made his way back up, concluding his journey at the meeting of thighs. As he lapped at her sweetness, her blissful cries echoed about the vast bedroom of the penthouse suite of the luxurious New York hotel. Her fingers threaded in his hair as she held him there. He slipped a finger between her slick folds, increasing her pleasured sighs.

Dahlia spoke his name, a clear and obvious request in her low, breathy tone. Norris ended his sensual kiss. The beauty of her body under the glow of the soft lighting, with the silent pleading in her dark eyes and the invitation of her open arms and parted thighs, became too much to resist. Rising up on one arm, Norris guided his twitching erection into her velvety heat. Dahlia cried out as he filled her completely. Norris closed his eyes, reveling in the pleasure of being one with Dahlia, his beautiful wife.

Dahlia's legs curled around his waist, her slick, heated walls squeezing and holding him in a sensual embrace, giving him pleasure like he'd never known. Her hands explored the planes of his back and traveled to his bottom, urging his thrusts. Answering her call, Norris drove deeper inside her, delivering slow, measured strokes. Filling her, loving her, making her his forever.

Their mouths came crashing together, kissing hard and desperately until the need for air demanded a respite. Dahlia buried her face in his neck, licking and kissing him, throwing his body into an erotic tailspin. No woman had ever touched him like Dahlia. She went beyond his physical body and reached his very soul.

Directing Norris to his back, Dahlia mounted him, her pelvis grinding against his. She leaned forward, teasing his taut nipples with hers. Norris cupped her backside, pressing her hard against him, filling her deeper.

Dahlia pulled upright, trailing her finger against his chest, sending shivers throughout his body. Folding her hands around his neck, she bounced atop him, a saucy grin on her beautiful face. Norris groaned. She was driving him wild.

Norris reached for her breasts, squeezing the fleshy mounds as she moved against him. He pushed them together and leaned forward, rolling each nipple in his mouth. Dahlia moaned her pleasure, but it was all his pleasure, her delicious pebble tips better than any hard candy. Norris gently nipped at her dark mounds. Feasting on her, enjoying her.

He grunted sadly when she pushed him back to the bed, but had little time for disappointment when she arched her back, taking him deeper into her pulsating core. A guttural moan ripped from Norris throat. Stars flashed before his eyes.

Closing his arms around her waist, Norris brought her onto the bed, filling her with his need. His thrusts grew harder and faster, Dahlia's cries louder and deeper. He pinned her legs against him, driving deeper into her throbbing heat. Norris expanded in her depths, drawing closer to his release. Dahlia clutched his bottom, holding fast to him as he continued to push inside her. They moved together, faster and faster, until their bodies seized and then exploded in mutual ecstasy.

Norris's body trembled against Dahlia's as his seed erupted deep in her womb, filling it with the promise of family from the home her love provided. When his movement ceased and their rapturous moans silenced, Norris turned to his side, staring lovingly at his spent wife. Grandma Flora wouldn't have liked the way Dahlia took the name of the Lord in vain when she reached her peak, but it certainly made him feel good.

"How was it for you?" He smiled, brushing beads of sweat from her forehead.

With a coy smile, Dahlia tapped her hand to her mouth, yawning.

"Hey!" Norris said, tickling her sides when she broke into uncontrollable laughter. "You better recognize me, Mrs. Converse. That was my very best work."

"Okay, okay," she said, still laughing. "I have to find ways to keep that ego in check." Norris stopped his tickling. "Seriously, I've never felt more loved in my life. It was beyond incredible." She kissed his chest. "You always said we could be this way together, and you were right."

"Of course." Norris smiled brightly and covered her body with his. "Norris is always right."

EPILOGUE

Norris tried not to cry as Reese placed the last of her things in the back of Ben's SUV. He couldn't believe how fast the last year had come and gone, and now his daughter was leaving for college.

"Please try to smile, Daddy."

Norris attempted to get his lips to curl, but failed. "I can't do it, Reese. I don't feel very happy right now."

"I'm going to college, not prison. Columbia's not so far."

"Maybe not the state capital, but this university is hundreds of miles from Denburg. Hundreds. In New York City."

"Just over an hour and a half by plane. That's not bad."

Norris whimpered.

"Daddy." Reese pulled him into her arms and kissed his cheek. "You're not losing me, you're just letting me grow. I'll be home for holidays, and you can come up and visit." She pulled back and held up her hand in warning. "But not all the time. Not that I'm too worried about that, considering Dahlia is gonna make you a daddy again in about what, two minutes?"

"Three weeks," Norris said, ecstatic about welcoming his son but heartsick to be losing his daughter.

"I'll be home for that, too."

A very pregnant Dahlia waddled out of their brand new house. A house with a sprawling green lawn and white picket fence. Their home. Their home in which she should have been relaxing in air-conditioned comfort.

Norris frowned. "Dahlia." He caressed her belly. "You should be inside resting. It's too hot out here."

"I'm fine, Norris. I thought you could use some moral support."

Reese nodded. "I think you're right," she said.

Gail blew the horn. "Reese, we'd better get going."

Dahlia embraced Reese. "I'm going to miss you, sweetie."

"I'm going to miss you, too, Dahlia." Reese glanced over at Norris. "Take care of him."

Dahlia nodded and smiled. "You know I will."

"Well, Daddy, this is it," Reese said.

Norris shook his head sadly. "Yep, looks like." He gave Reese another hug. "If you need anything or just want to talk, you call home."

"I will. Aunt Julia is working on her designs in New York now, and Jack's at NYU, so I won't be alone. I'll be fine."

Norris grunted. "Call if he gets out of line, too."

"Daddy," she whined.

"I'm serious."

"I know." She kissed his cheek. "I love you."

"I love you, too, Reese."

Norris and Dahlia waved until the SUV piggybacking Reese's car disappeared out of sight.

Dahlia squeezed his hand. "You going to be okay, Norris?"

"Yeah." He stooped down and kissed Dahlia's belly. "Just grateful I won't have to do this again for eighteen years."

The End

ABOUT THE AUTHOR

Raised in Denmark, SC, where she still resides, Tammy Williams received her associate's degree from Denmark Technical College and her bachelor's degree from Voorhees College.

Tammy became serious about writing in 2002 when she joined Romance Writers of America and soon thereafter the local RWA chapter, Lowcountry Romance Writers of America. *Blindsided* is the sequel to her debut novel, *Choices*.

When she's not writing, Tammy enjoys reading, watching television and movies, and spending time with her family.

Visit Tammy's website at *www.tammywilliams online.com*, send her an email at *TamWillms@aol.com*, or write to her at P.O. Box 84, Denmark, SC 29042. She always enjoys hearing from her readers.

Coming in September from Genesis Press:

**Chamein Canton's hotly anticipated new
Indigo Love Spectrum romance**

CHAPTER ONE

Alicia Archer looked as if she were about to faint under the hot lights on set. *If they don't wrap this up the soufflé won't be the only thing to collapse.* The show was going on hiatus and it was the last of the block of shows she had to tape. If it were any producer other than her best friend Lauren, Alicia would have had their head. A foodie since childhood, having her own lifestyle/cooking show was a dream realized. The heat on the set, however, made it difficult to remember that.

Alicia checked the clock. "How long are the commercials?" she said impatiently. "It must be a thousand degrees in here today."

"You're back in forty-five seconds," Norman, the production assistant, answered.

"Thanks." Alicia dabbed her brow. *Maybe if I weren't in long sleeves and dark slacks I'd be cooler, but I'm the one who came up with classic image and now I'm paying for it.* She let out a soft sigh.

Hair pulled up in an elegant upsweep, forty-six-year-old full-figured Alicia looked good in her cotton long sleeve shirt and slacks. Born in Amityville, New York, Alicia was the older of Walter and Loretta Carlson's two daughters. Her sister Samantha was two years younger and nearly a half foot taller than her five feet, eight inch older sister. So being a big girl was something Alicia knew about from birth. Her mother Loretta was from a family of big and tall women. Loretta liked to say she had a round butt in a town of square asses and it was a good thing Alicia's father had a thing for circles.

"And we're back in four . . . three . . . two . . . one . . ." The director pointed to Alicia.

"Now that we've completed a perfectly luscious lemon soufflé, all we need to do is garnish it with a little mint." She turned to the camera. "There we go. Doesn't it look great?" She smiled as she picked up a spoon. "Now we'll have a taste." She took a spoonful. "It's lovely, light, and best of all, the recipe is on our website."

Norman gave her the wrap-up sign.

"Well, that's all the time we have for today. Thanks so much for joining me, and remember that it doesn't have to be a special occasion for a little elegance."

"And we're out." Simon, the director, clapped.

Alicia made a beeline for the refrigerator, grabbed a chilled bottled of water and drank deeply.

"Is there another one in there?" Norman asked.

She handed him a bottle. "Here you go."

"Thanks. You feel better now?"

"Much better, thanks." She paused. "It's been a long week."

"Tell me about it."

Alicia looked around. "So where is our erstwhile producer?"

"I'm not sure. Do you want me to page her?"

Alicia checked her watch. "No need. I know where she is." She looked directly into the monitor.

Alicia, Lauren Jules Jones and Gabrielle Blanchard had been friends since ninth grade when they met at boarding school. Three big girls in a sea of skinny girls, they became fast friends and roommates. But they had more in common than just their size. The girls shared a love of classic romance novels by Jane Austen. On Friday nights the Austen Aristocrats met in the boarding school kitchen where Alicia got to indulge her passion for cooking while they discussed love and romance with the likes of Jane's Mr. Knightley, Edward Ferrars and, of course, Mr. Darcy. As adults they would go on a quest to find their own romantic heroes and, for a time, Alicia found hers. Lauren, however, was on her third try.

I know that look on Alicia's face is for me, Lauren thought as she crouched in the corner on her cell phone. *So what if I'm on the phone?*

A shooting star producer in the television industry, forty-six-year-old Lauren Jules Jones was a force to be reckoned with. Born in Bayside, Queens, Lauren was raised by her grandmother. Her father died in a car accident before she was born and her mother decided she couldn't handle life as a single parent. Grandma Lee worked hard to make sure her son's only child grew up well educated. When the opportunity presented itself to get her granddaughter out of Bayside and into a prestigious preparatory school, she made sure Lauren got there.

Miss Porter's Boarding School may have been like life on Mars but Lauren's grades and academic standing got her a full scholarship to Dartmouth, where she majored in film and media studies.

Upon graduation she earned her stripes doing odd jobs in public television. She caught her first break as an associate producer for a local television station in New York. A friend talked her into leaving the security of local television to become an executive producer for In the Mix Productions, an upstart company that wanted to shed its basic cable roots for national syndication. After she led them to a few industry nominations and a couple of awards, they gave her the green light to sign *Everyday Elegance with Alicia,* which became an instant hit. Now Lauren was light years away from the dowdy, drab, boarding school uniforms and flannel shirts and jeans of Dartmouth. She was a top producer who embraced her curves and cut a sexy and sharp image whenever she entered a room in her designer ensembles. However, while terrific at work, her personal life was another story.

Finding her own Mr. Darcy was a challenge. Twice divorced, her third marriage was to former NFL defensive tackle Kenneth Jones. Ken had never really adjusted to civilian life married to a non-sports mortal. He enjoyed the attention playing for the New York Giants got him, especially from women. Nevertheless, there were benefits to being married to a producer. Lauren helped him land a spot as a commentator on the network's highly popular football program, and, combined with his appearances at fan events, Ken wasn't far from the gridiron he loved so much. For a while it had looked as if the third time was finally the charm for Lauren. She and Ken were the golden couple when they appeared at network, charity and sports events. Wherever they went, Ken was bombarded by men seeking autographs and pictures with an NFL great, including many of the buttoned-up network executives she worked with.

Then the New York Giants made Ken an offer he couldn't refuse. They wanted him to be a goodwill ambassador of sorts to their season ticket holders, which meant Ken did a lot more up close and personal meet-and-greets with the fans. Even when the job description expanded to include more travel and later hours Lauren didn't mind. She knew it made him feel as if he were still contributing to the organization. However, when she began to notice more female fans in the mix, she was less comfortable. Ken tried to tell her they were really into football but Lauren knew football groupies when she saw them. While many of them could recite stats, most didn't seem to know a touchdown from a homerun. It didn't take long before it got to be a problem between them. Ken reverted back to his bad boy ways and Lauren got tired of keeping better tabs on him than the secret service did the president, so they got a legal separation. Still, Lauren held out hope he'd come to his senses despite all evidence to the contrary. "Damn! It's his voice mail again," she muttered as she waited to leave yet another message. "Hi, I'm just confirming dinner tonight at Ricardo's at six-thirty. Call me when you get this message." She closed her phone. *God, I hope I didn't sound too anxious . . .*

"Voice mail again?"

Lauren jumped. "Alicia! You startled me. How long have you been standing there?"

"Long enough," she said as she sat down.

"Wait a minute, how did you get up here so quickly? I just saw you on the monitor."

"Wouldn't you like to know?" She smirked.

Lauren didn't want to hear it from Alicia so she changed the subject. "Are you feeling okay? You looked like you were getting a little hot on the set."

"I was getting overheated, but I'm okay now." She took another sip from her water bottle.

"Are you sure?"

"Yes." Her tone was a little short.

"Don't bite my head off. I'm just asking. You do have MS, and I know what heat does to you."

Alicia got up and quickly shut the door. "Announce it to the whole world, why don't you?"

"The whole world isn't up here. It's just you and me. You have to stop being so paranoid."

"I don't want everyone to know my business."

"I know. I don't understand why you want to be so covert about it. You have MS. You don't have the plague."

"I just want to keep it quiet, okay?"

"Okay. So how are things going?"

"Not bad. I just started a new treatment regimen so now I give myself an injection every Friday evening."

Lauren winced.

"See why I don't want anyone to know about this? You've known me over thirty years and you're freaked out."

"I'm sorry, but it wasn't about you having MS. You know I don't like needles."

"Neither do I, but what choice do I have? At least we're on hiatus now so I'll have the summer to get used to this routine while I relax."

"Ha!" Lauren scoffed. "You relax? I give you three days before you start climbing the walls out there in Scarsdale."

"Naturally it won't be total relaxation. I still have magazine, kitchenware and housewares lines to worry about."

Lauren shook her head. "You just said you were going to relax this summer. You're such a workaholic."

"Oh well." Alicia shrugged her shoulders. "Speaking of climbing the walls, did you get Ken?"

Lauren sighed aloud. "No, I didn't get him but you already knew that."

"Don't get snippy. It was just a question."

"I'm sorry. We're supposed to meet for dinner at Ricardo's tonight."

"Dinner at Ricardo's, I'm impressed. They're usually booked up at least a month or more in advance. How did you manage a reservation?"

"Ken made it. The manager is a big Giants fan."

"I see. Membership does have its privileges."

"Yes, it does." Lauren looked at her phone.

"So what's the occasion?"

"I don't know." She flopped into a chair.

Alicia shook her head.

"Don't give me that look, Alicia."

"What look?" Alicia played innocent.

"The look of disapproval. He's still my husband."

"In name only, Lauren. You've been legally separated for a year now."

"I know, but that's not to say we can't work it out."

"That's exactly what it means, Lauren. You've been to marriage counselors, pastors and therapists galore. Hell, you even saw a rabbi! When are you going to wake up and move on with your life? God knows he has."

"Then why did he call me to have dinner at a romantic restaurant like Ricardo's?"

"You've got me there." She shook her head, puzzled. "I still believe you deserve better than the likes of Kenneth Jones."

"Maybe so, Alicia, but this is my third marriage. I've already struck out twice and I'd rather not be a three-time loser."

"It's the twenty-first century, Lauren. No one is going to make you wear a scarlet 'D3' on your chest. Besides, not wanting to get another divorce isn't a reason to stay married."

"Not everyone is as lucky as you were with the perfect marriage."

"Oh please, don't start that again. Kurt and I didn't have a perfect marriage. We had our ups and downs like everyone else."

"Well, it always looked like you had more ups than most people."

Alicia couldn't help but smile. "We had a lot of good times together but we liked a good fight, too. It kept things interesting," Alicia said wistfully.

"Does it get easier?"

"There isn't a day that goes by I don't think about him. Some days I smile and other days I cry. So I guess the answer is yes and no."

Kurt Archer had been the love of Alicia's life. He was a tall, skinny, fair-skinned black man with reddish hair and nearly green eyes. When they met at Dartmouth they took an instant dislike to each other. They were complete opposites. Alicia was an economics major who understood she would have to play the game in order to succeed in business. Kurt, on the other hand, majored in environmental studies. He was 'green' before it was chic. Alicia thought he was nothing but a tree hugger. Kurt thought she was a corporate raider in training. Her one redeeming quality for him was that she was minoring in creative writing. At least three times a week she and Kurt turned the pavilion dining hall into a debate forum. They said they couldn't stand one another but no one believed them. Kurt and Alicia were the last two people to figure out they were in love. They married a year after graduation.

Two years later Alicia gave birth to their only child, Kurt Jr., in the idyllic Westchester suburb of Bronxville.

At that time Alicia worked as a lifestyle editor and contributor for a major magazine, which allowed her to combine her business and artistic side to create features that entertained while keeping her group on task and under budget. Kurt managed a successful landscape design firm. Life was wonderful until Kurt was diagnosed with pancreatic cancer when Kurt Jr. was a senior in high school. Alicia dropped everything to take care of her husband. She knew Kurt wanted to hang on long enough to see their son graduate and she was determined he'd make it to graduation. Her care through the many pain-filled nights was rewarded when he beamed with pride at graduation as he watched his namesake take his diploma. Unfortunately Kurt didn't live long enough to see his son follow in his footsteps at Dartmouth.

After Kurt's death Alicia didn't fold in on herself. She used her grief to fuel her ambition and moved forward to build her own lifestyle media company, Archer Omnimedia, which included cookbooks, her show *Everyday Elegance with Alicia*, and a magazine of the same name. As CEO she took her company public and became the queen of branding with a kitchenware line in two major store chains. The only kink in the plan came when she was diagnosed with MS two years ago, information she somehow managed to keep from the public, press, her magazine staff and her shareholders. Only a select few knew about her condition and they weren't telling. However, the diagnosis meant more than just a change in Alicia's body. If her friends and family had any glimmer of hope she'd try to find love again, it faded. As far as

Alicia was concerned she'd found her own Mr. Darcy and didn't believe lightning would strike twice, nor did she want it to.

"So how's my godson?"

"He's good."

"Is he excited about grad school?"

"I think so. He has a new girlfriend." Alicia rolled her eyes a little.

"What's wrong with her?"

"Nothing, she's a perfectly nice young lady."

"But . . ." Lauren said.

"She's just blah. There's nothing to her."

"What do you mean?"

"She's not ambitious." Alicia sighed. "She seems content being a legal secretary even though she has an associate degree in criminal justice." Alicia shook her head.

"So what's wrong with that?"

"Nothing, I guess." Alicia shrugged.

"Not every woman can be as driven as you, Alicia."

"Now if that isn't the pot calling the kettle black."

"Point taken."

"I'm going to leave it alone. It's his life and he loves her just the way she is."

"Now if you'd only follow that advice when it comes to Gabby and me, we'd be set."

Before Alicia could respond, fifty-two-year-old Ron Wilder, a slim, brown-skinned man, knocked on the door, out of breath. Ron was one of the executive features editor at *Everyday Elegance with Alicia*.

"Ron? What are you doing here?"

He caught his breath. "I wanted to be sure to get these papers to you." He handed Alicia a folder.

"Thanks, Ron, but you could have messengered them up to the house."

"I know, but I think Barbara needs your signature on them now."

Alicia looked the papers over and signed them. "Here you go." She handed them back to him. "Ron, you know Lauren."

"Oh, hi, Lauren. I didn't see you there."

"Obviously. How are you, Ron?"

"Not bad." He took a deep breath. "I guess I'd better run back to the office. Have a good vacation, boss." He turned to Lauren. "Nice seeing you again, Lauren."

Lauren waved as he dashed out. "You know he has a crush on you, don't you?"

"Don't be silly. He likes Barbara. Why else would he run over here to get papers signed for her?"

"I don't think that's the case, Alicia." Lauren shook her head.

"Stop with your speculating already," she said, grinning. Alicia looked at her watch. "I'd better get going. The car will be here in a minute." She paused. "What are you wearing?"

"Do you really want to know?"

"Of course. I might not like him but that doesn't mean I don't want him to drool over the mere sight of you."

"I'm wearing the Goddess Dress by Abby Z in chocolate brown."

"Nice."

"Are you doing anything special tonight?"

Alicia stood up. "Gabby's supposed to come over for dinner. If things wrap up early you're welcome to join us for dessert and coffee. We haven't had a meeting of the Austen Aristocrats in a while."

"Thank you for the invitation. However, if things go well dessert is covered tonight."

"Entirely too much information." Alicia kissed her on the cheek. "Tell Ken I said hello."

"You know you don't mean that."

"Of course I do. I'm nothing if not polite. Even if he is a three-timing bastard who doesn't deserve you."

"Alicia."

"Sorry." Alicia knew to back off. "You know I only want the best for you." She kissed Lauren on the cheek again.

"It's a good thing I love you like a sister."

"I know." She waved as she left the production booth.

Lauren stared at her cell phone. *Do I call him again?* "Oh, the hell with it." She dialed the phone.

Just then Norman knocked.

"Lauren?"

"Yeah, Norm." She closed her phone.

"Simon wants to see you on set."

"I'll be right there." *Simon saved me from myself. I need to relax and get ready to go to dinner.*

It had been a long day at the Blanchard Gallery and it showed on Gabrielle's face the moment she sat down on the sofa in her office. A natural blonde with blue eyes, Gabby was a curvy size sixteen and although she looked more like a benefactress than hip gallery owner in her navy blue suit complete with pearls and an updo to match, she'd made it look sexy all day long. She'd seen fifty up-and-coming artists over two days who were competing to fill a mere fifteen slots for her gallery's annual exhibit of new artists, and she couldn't wait to get some peace.

"Gabby?"

"Yes, Robin?" She pressed the intercom button.

"I have to go into the file room for a few minutes."

"No problem. We're done with artists for the day."

Robin Pope was Gabby's executive assistant of seven years. A beautiful bronze-skinned woman of thirty-four, she was married to a successful architect on the West Side. A graphic designer herself, she'd given it up to take a job that would be more conducive to her ultimate goal, having a baby.

Although she wasn't an artist herself, Gabrielle Blanchard, nicknamed Gabby, had had an appreciation for and love of art since she was a little girl growing up in her family's posh townhouse on the Upper East Side. Yet Gabby was different from the rest of the pretty blonde, reed-thin girls she grew up with. She was always a little more 'voluptuous' as her dad put it. Her mother, however, didn't subscribe to her father's terminology or lax attitude about her size. Bunny Blanchard put Gabby on every diet known to man before she shipped her off to

Miss Porter's Boarding School in Connecticut, where she met her best friends, Alicia and Lauren. They were big girls, too.

"Ms. Blanchard?" a male voice asked.

Gabby opened her eyes. "Yes?"

Her assistant Robin rushed in. "I'm sorry, Gabby. I told him you were done seeing artists and he snuck back here anyway."

Gabby's eyes focused on the man who'd interrupted her solitude. He was very tall and thin with a rich dark cocoa brown complexion but he didn't fit the usual artist mold. She was used to seeing artists in chic bohemian clothes and not expensive Italian suits.

"Are you representing a new artist?" she asked, puzzled.

He laughed as if he'd heard this question before. "No. I am the artist."

Her assistant Robin looked equally puzzled. "Really?"

"Yes."

Gabby was intrigued. "It's okay, Robin."

"I'll be at my desk if you need me," Robin said as she walked out.

Gabby stood up and straightened out her suit. "So Mr . . . ?"

"Clark. My name is Nigel Clark."

"It's a pleasure to meet you, Mr. Clark," she said, putting her hand out.

He shook it. "Please call me Nigel."

"Okay, Nigel. You can call me Gabby, but I'm still sorry to say that I've already picked the artists for our exhibit."

"I know I'm late getting here but I would really like you to look at my work. I brought one of my paintings with me."

"I don't know what good it will do. Our next new artists' exhibition is next year."

"Maybe so, but I would really like it if you took a look. I've heard terrific things about your gallery, and your reputation for having a good eye for the next big thing precedes you."

Gabby smiled in spite of herself. "Flattery will get you everywhere, Nigel." She picked her glasses up from the desk. "Bring it in."

"Thank you," he said as he left the room.

I hope I don't regret this, she thought, crossing her arms.

The minute he walked through the door her eyes were drawn to the canvas. It was a scene depicting life in Africa with all its hustle and bustle. Gabby was captivated by the vivid way he captured his subjects with color. The painting spoke to her.

"Is this Cotonou, Benin?"

"Yes." He seemed genuinely surprised she recognized it.

"My ex-husband and I visited West Africa many years ago and Cotonou was one of our stops. It's quite a city. Is that where you're from?"

"No, I was born here. My mother is from Cotonou. She came to the States to study and then she met my father."

"I see. Do you often go back to visit?"

"I used to visit my grandparents every spring but they passed away when I was in college." He sighed. "I can still see the place in my mind."

"I can see that." Gabby pressed the intercom button. "Robin."

"Yes?"

"Call Victor and tell him we have one more artist for the exhibit."

"Okay, but you know he's going to complain."

"Victor complains if it's Tuesday. He'll get over it."

"Okay."

"Thank you." Nigel flashed a megawatt smile.

"You're welcome. Just be sure to see Robin on the way out and she'll give you the details."

He put his hand out. "You won't regret this."

"I'm sure I won't." Gabby leaned back in her chair.

"I guess we'll be in touch. I'll see you."

Gabby watched him leave. *He's good looking, talented and charming. He should do well with our patrons, particularly the female ones. He can brush my canvas anytime.* Gabby raised her eyebrow. *This is business, Gabrielle,* she chided herself. *What would Bunny think?*

The car pulled into the winding driveway of Alicia's little piece of heaven in Scarsdale. At over 4,500 square feet, the stone/stucco Tudor style home suited Alicia's image even if it was too much house for her with its six bedrooms, six bathrooms, powder room, gourmet kitchen, pantry and every other amenity imaginable. It was private, sort of, with the exception of the Becker place next door.

Harrison opened the car door. "Hello, Alicia. How did it go today?"

"Not bad. It's hard to believe we're going on hiatus."

He closed the car door. "Time does fly by."

At sixty-four, Harrison Kendall was Alicia's executive personal assistant, which as far as he was concerned, was a glorified way of saying butler. The only hint of Harrison's age came from his silver hair. He was average height with just a hint of post-middle-age spread around the middle. He had a tan complexion, which he credited to his Italian mother. Alicia met Harrison and his late wife Martha, who'd had a more progressive form of MS, at her neurologist's office just after her own diagnosis. It didn't take long for them to become fast friends, and, with no children of their own, they treated Alicia like a daughter. When Martha passed away, Alicia invited Harrison to live with her under the guise of being her second set of feet and hands in the house.

They walked into the foyer. "So how are you feeling?"

Alicia looked at her watch. "Wow, you went a whole three minutes before you asked. You're getting better," she said facetiously.

"I know you like to make light of it, Ms. Alicia, but your neurologist did say you need to be mindful of your body and rest every now and then."

"I am resting. We are on hiatus for the summer."

"You know what I mean."

"Of course I do. I'm fine. I promise." As she walked into the living room her right foot dragged a little. She plopped onto the sofa. "That's much better."

Harrison zeroed in on it. "I'll get your cane."

"What for?"

"You're beginning to drag your foot because you're doing too much."

"What am I doing now if it isn't resting? Leave the cane where it is."

Harrison ignored her and took it out of the closet. "I'm leaving it right here for when you get up." He set it next to the sofa.

"Fine. Has my son called?"

"Yes. He's coming up this weekend."

"Great. Is it just him or is she coming, too?"

"Her name is Sally."

"Yes. Sally. Is she coming?"

"He didn't say."

"So there's hope." She grinned.

Harrison shook his head. "No woman is ever good enough for a woman's son."

"You got that right."

"But your late husband's mother loves you."

"That's because I'm special." She smiled as she flipped the television on.

"Your parents called today."

"They did? Why didn't they call the studio or my cell phone? They knew I was at work."

"They're roaming the countryside in that Winnebago you and Samantha bought them."

Her father was a seventy-year-old retired school teacher and her sixty-nine-year-old mother was a retired cafeteria lady. They had been married forty-eight years. While most of their friends had sold their homes to move into expensive retirement communities or down South, they'd stayed in their home in Amityville. Alicia's parents still had quite a bit of zip left in their step and enjoyed being on the move but they didn't trust the cleanliness of hotels or other people. Therefore a Winnebago seemed the perfect gift to give them the comfort of home while allowing them to have an adventure.

Alicia laughed. "It's what they wanted."

"I know."

"Where were they calling from?"

"They were at the Grand Canyon."

"That sounds nice. I bet they're having a great time."

"They are, but they really called to check on you."

"You told them I'm fine."

"Yes. However I wouldn't be surprised to see their Winnebago pulling into Scarsdale sometime this summer."

Alicia chuckled. "Oh, won't the neighbors love that."

"Oh yes." Harrison picked up her briefcase. "Can I get you anything?"

"Just a seltzer with a twist."

"No problem. What about dinner? I'm planning steaks."

"Good. Gabby's coming for dinner."

"Great. What about Lauren?"

"Lauren is having dinner with Ken at Ricardo's."

Harrison's ears perked up. "Dinner at Ricardo's. Is there something going on you haven't told me?"

"Nope."

"Well, even I know Ricardo's is known for its romantic ambiance. Is reconciliation in the air?"

Alicia shrugged. "Who knows? Your guess is as good as mine."

"I'm asking what you think."

"To tell you the truth I know that's what Lauren wants, but I have a bad feeling about it."

"You don't like Ken."

"No. I don't like him, and I don't think he's the one for Lauren. I've never made any bones about it."

"She loves him."

"The Beatles did say love is all you need. Who knows? Maybe he'll surprise me."

"Maybe." Harrison was about to walk away when he said, "Oh, there is one thing I forgot to tell you."

"What's that?"

"Your favorite neighbor is back in town."

Alicia's face fell. "Why did you have to go and ruin my dinner? When did he get back?"

"I'm not sure exactly. All I know is the parade of women has already begun."

"Great." She hung her head in disgust. "I manage to find a half acre of quiet and it has to be next to Scarsdale's own version of the Playboy mansion."

For any other woman, living next to Dr. Nathaniel Becker would be a treat. A confirmed bachelor at age forty-eight, he was six feet, four inches tall with an athletic build, a full head of wavy dark hair and crystal blue eyes. It also didn't hurt that he came from old WASP money, and, though he didn't need to worry about making a living, Nathaniel was an Ivy League educated doctor who was a part of a thriving medical practice in Scarsdale. What wasn't commonly known was his involvement in pediatric AIDS research and Doctors Without Borders, through which he traveled the world helping impoverished communities get the care they needed. He also gave his time to several clinics throughout the five boroughs. Most people, including Alicia, believed he was an international playboy and he did nothing to discourage it. He gave parties and always seemed to have a parade of women in and out of his place whenever he was in town, which annoyed Alicia to no end. So to say he delighted in pulling her chain was an understatement.

Harrison walked back in the living room. "Here you go." He handed her a glass.

"Thanks." She took a sip.

"So what's on the agenda for the Aristocrats tonight?"

"I don't think we're going to have a meeting tonight since it's just Gabby and me."

"You can't fill Lauren in later?"

"No. It's one of the rules we set up for our little club. In order to have a proper meeting of the Austen Aristocrats all three of us have to be there."

"I guess that means you're sort of the charmed ones of classic romantic literature."

"Yes, it's the power of three." She chuckled.

Even though it had been thirty-two years and a few divorces later, they still had meetings, although now they had the added choice of movie DVDs of their favorite author's work.

"Are you going to show the footage from your last trip to England for the next meeting?"

"I was thinking about it. I had a lot of fun touring Austen's stomping grounds."

He chuckled. "You mean The Virgin Suicides Tour."

"Oh, that's not nice. Jane Austen died of Addison's disease."

"She lived in the eighteenth century, same difference."

"You might have a point." She laughed.

He looked at the clock. "I'll go fire up the grill."

"Thanks." *Hopefully this is only a pit stop for Nathaniel. The idea of that man being here for the entire summer is more than I want to think about.*

Dressed to kill, Lauren nursed a martini alone at her table. She checked herself in the reflection of the silver. *Glad I decided to wear my hair down. It looks better with the dress.* She ran her fingers through her dark, shoulder-length hair. Everywhere she looked there were happy couples and groups enjoying the modern yet romantic elegance of Ricardo's. She stared at her cell phone. *Why he hasn't he called? Where is he?*

The waiter interrupted her thoughts. "May I get you something else?"

"No." She picked up the menu. "I'm sure my husband will be along soon and then we'll order together."

"Very good." He walked away.

Lauren continued to stare at the entrance, hoping to see Ken walk through the door.

"Pardon me?"

She looked up to see a nicely attired gentleman standing next to her table. He was tall, broad-shouldered, with dark good looks. In fact, he was just the type of man she usually was attracted to, but she was in no mood to be hit on.

"May I buy you another drink?"

"No, thank you, I'm waiting for someone."

"Okay then. How about an appetizer while you wait?"

Is this guy for real? "Listen, I'm waiting for my husband."

He smiled. "And I will extend the same offer to him. I'm Randy Rivera. This is my restaurant."

Lauren turned red. "Oh, I'm sorry. I thought you were . . ."

"Trying to pick you up? Not at all, although you are a very attractive woman."

"Thanks." She paused. "Aren't you the executive chef, too?"

"Guilty. I'm usually behind the scenes, but the manager called in so I'm front of the house tonight. Speaking of being a good host, may I ask your name?"

"I'm Lauren Jones."

"It's very nice to meet you, Lauren Jones." They shook hands. "So how about that drink?"

"Why not? I'll have another pomegranate martini."

"You got it." He called the waiter over. "She'll have another one of these."

"No problem." The waiter scurried away.

"Do you mind if I have a seat?"

"Please do."

"Thanks." The minute he sat down he looked as if he'd taken a load off. "I thought it was tough being on my feet in the kitchen, but the front of house is no picnic either."

The waiter brought her martini back.

"Thank you." She took another sip. "It's good."

There was awkward silence between them.

"Are you hungry? We have the best tapas."

"I know."

The sound of a little commotion grabbed their attention.

"I wonder what's going on," Randy said as he strained to see.

There was Ken signing autographs with a group of people around him. At six feet, five inches tall and 275 pounds it was hard not to miss him, surrounded by fans or not.

"It looks like my husband is here." She beamed.

"You're married to Kenneth Jones? I'm a big fan of his. He's one of my favorite defensive tackles."

"Mine, too."

Randy stood up as Ken approached. "Mr. Jones, I'm a big fan."

"Thanks." He smiled and shook his hand. Kenneth looked good in his custom made Armani suit. He bent over and kissed Lauren on the cheek. "You look great, babe. Is that a new dress?"

"Thanks, and as a matter of fact it is new. You like it?"

"It looks great on you."

Randy held the chair for Ken. "Can I get you something from the bar, Mr. Jones?"

"I'll have a scotch, neat."

"Coming right up. I hope you two have a pleasant evening. Enjoy."

"Thank you." Lauren grinned like a school girl.

Randy walked away. A minute later the waiter returned with Ken's drink.

Ken took a gulp and set the glass down. "You look good, Lauren."

"You already said that but I won't complain."

Ken fidgeted in his seat.

Lauren found it endearing. "What's the matter, Kenneth? You look as nervous as you did on our first date."

"Do I?"

"Yes. It was cute then and it's still cute." She sipped her martini.

Ken rubbed his forehead. "I guess there's no easy way to do this."

"Easy way to do what?"

He reached into his pocket, pulled out an envelope and put it in front of her on the table.

"What's this?"

"Divorce papers."

Lauren's heart fell. "What?"

"It's been a year since the legal separation and now I'd like to proceed with the divorce." He waited for a response from Lauren, but she was dumbfounded. "All the terms are still the same. You can have the apartment lock, stock, and barrel. You don't have to buy me out. I think that's only fair."

"Do you?" she asked, still stunned.

"Yes. We had our moments but it didn't work out. I have no hard feelings."

"So what is it you want in return?"

"It's in the papers." He pointed to the envelope.

"I don't want to look at the damn papers, Kenneth, just tell me." She tried to control her anger.

"All you have to do is sign off on the no spousal support clause and we're done."

"That's stated in the prenup agreement I signed before we got married."

"You know how lawyers are. They have to prove they're earning their fee." He gave her a weak smile.

Lauren tore open the envelope and unfolded the document. "Do you have a pen?"

"Don't you want to read it?"

"You're kidding me, right? It's obvious you invited me to this romantic setting so I wouldn't make a scene. Well, you're getting your wish. Give me a damn pen before I change my mind and start bucking for the cover of the *New York Post*."

Ken handed her a pen.

Lauren quickly signed it and threw the pen down. "Are you happy now?"

"Of course I'm not happy. My lawyer told me to use a process server but I thought you deserved to hear it from me directly."

"Why? So you could see my humiliation up close and personal?"

"No. Maybe I shouldn't have asked you here." He put the envelope in his jacket.

"You think?" she asked sarcastically. "You're a real piece of work, Kenneth."

That was Ken's cue to get up. "I'm sorry. I know you don't believe me but it's the truth. Dinner is on me tonight."

"That's the least you can do." Lauren felt herself choking up.

When Ken tried to kiss her on the cheek, she turned away. "I am sorry, Lauren. You're a great lady. You deserve better than me." He walked away.

Lauren sat in stunned silence. *How could I have been so stupid? I'm such a fool.*

Randy walked over. "Will your husband be coming back to order?"

"No, I'm afraid not. You're stuck with little old me."

Although he didn't know her personally Randy could see something was different. "Is everything okay?"

She gulped down her martini. "Everything's just fine. Can I get another one of these?"

"Sure." He stopped a waitress who was carrying a tray of martinis and took one off. "Just get another one for your table and tell them this round is on the house."

"Okay, boss."

"Here you go."

"Now that's what I call service." She took a big gulp.

"How about some appetizers, something to wash it down?" He smiled.

"You're the chef. I'll follow your lead."

He called the waiter back over. "Trey, we'll have the *pincho de datiles* and *patatas bravas*."

"Don't forget another martini. I'm almost finished with this one." Lauren was beginning to get a buzz.

"Yes, bring her another drink and a seltzer with a twist."

"I'll have you know I can handle a few martinis. I'm not a 110 pound model who gets drunk from fumes. I'm a big girl, in case you haven't noticed."

"All I see is a beautiful woman who deserves to have a good time. The seltzer is for me. I'm still working."

She smiled.

"Now that's more like it."

"Don't you have to run your restaurant? You shouldn't be babysitting patrons."

"What's the point of being the boss if I can't switch it up every now and then? Someone else will just have to take over my duties for a little while."

"If you say so."

"Are you staying for dinner?"

Lauren looked at her watch. "Sure. I don't have any place to go, except for my apartment." Her martini buzz was fast becoming a martini haze. "I'll have you know I have a great big three bedroom apartment and it's all mine."

"Terrific."

"It was a real bargain, too. You know what it cost me?"

"No, I don't."

"My dignity, that's all. It doesn't get any cheaper than that."

Trey brought the drinks back.

Randy raised his glass. "Here's to you and what I hope is a new friendship."

They put their glasses together. "Cheers," Lauren said as she sipped her martini. *Here's hoping the martinis can cover my humiliation or at least get me drunk enough so I don't notice it anymore. Ken may be retired, but he still knows how to get a quality sack. I didn't see it coming.*

2009 Reprint Mass Market Titles

January

I'm Gonna Make You Love Me
Gwyneth Bolton
ISBN-13: 978-1-58571-294-6
$6.99

Shades of Desire
Monica White
ISBN-13: 978-1-58571-292-2
$6.99

February

A Love of Her Own
Cheris Hodges
ISBN-13: 978-1-58571-293-9
$6.99

Color of Trouble
Dyanne Davis
ISBN-13: 978-1-58571-294-6
$6.99

March

Twist of Fate
Beverly Clark
ISBN-13: 978-1-58571-295-3
$6.99

Chances
Pamela Leigh Starr
ISBN-13: 978-1-58571-296-0
$6.99

April

Sinful Intentions
Crystal Rhodes
ISBN-13: 978-1-585712-297-7
$6.99

Rock Star
Roslyn Hardy Holcomb
ISBN-13: 978-1-58571-298-4
$6.99

May

Paths of Fire
T.T. Henderson
ISBN-13: 978-1-58571-343-1
$6.99

Caught Up in the Rapture
Lisa Riley
ISBN-13: 978-1-58571-344-8
$6.99

June

Reckless Surrender
Rochelle Alers
ISBN-13: 978-1-58571-345-5
$6.99

No Ordinary Love
Angela Weaver
ISBN-13: 978-1-58571-346-2
$6.99

2009 Reprint Mass Market Titles (continued)

July

Intentional Mistakes
Michele Sudler
ISBN-13: 978-1-58571-347-9
$6.99

It's In His Kiss
Reon Carter
ISBN-13: 978-1-58571-348-6
$6.99

August

Unfinished Love Affair
Barbara Keaton
ISBN-13: 978-1-58571-349-3
$6.99

A Perfect Place to Pray
I.L Goodwin
ISBN-13: 978-1-58571-299-1
$6.99

September

Love in High Gear
Charlotte Roy
ISBN-13: 978-1-58571-355-4
$6.99

Ebony Eyes
Kei Swanson
ISBN-13: 978-1-58571-356-1
$6.99

October

Midnight Clear, Part I
Leslie Esdale/Carmen Green
ISBN-13: 978-1-58571-357-8
$6.99

Midnight Clear, Part II
Gwynne Forster/Monica
    Jackson
ISBN-13: 978-1-58571-358-5
$6.99

November

Midnight Peril
Vicki Andrews
ISBN-13: 978-1-58571-359-2
$6.99

One Day At A Time
Bella McFarland
ISBN-13: 978-1-58571-360-8
$6.99

December

Just An Affair
Eugenia O'Neal
ISBN-13: 978-1-58571-361-5
$6.99

Shades of Brown
Denise Becker
ISBN-13: 978-1-58571-362-2
$6.99

2009 New Mass Market Titles

January

Singing A Song…
Crystal Rhodes
ISBN-13: 978-1-58571-283-0
$6.99

Look Both Ways
Joan Early
ISBN-13: 978-1-58571-284-7
$6.99

February

Six O'Clock
Katrina Spencer
ISBN-13: 978-1-58571-285-4
$6.99

Red Sky
Renee Alexis
ISBN-13: 978-1-58571-286-1
$6.99

March

Anything But Love
Celya Bowers
ISBN-13: 978-1-58571-287-8
$6.99

Tempting Faith
Crystal Hubbard
ISBN-13: 978-1-58571-288-5
$6.99

April

If I Were Your Woman
La Connie Taylor-Jones
ISBN-13: 978-1-58571-289-2
$6.99

Best Of Luck Elsewhere
Trisha Haddad
ISBN-13: 978-1-58571-290-8
$6.99

May

All I'll Ever Need
Mildred Riley
ISBN-13: 978-1-58571-335-6
$6.99

A Place Like Home
Alicia Wiggins
ISBN-13: 978-1-58571-336-3
$6.99

June

Best Foot Forward
Michele Sudler
ISBN-13: 978-1-58571-337-0
$6.99

It's In the Rhythm
Sammie Ward
ISBN-13: 978-1-58571-338-7
$6.99

2009 New Mass Market Titles (continued)

July

Checks and Balances
Elaine Sims
ISBN-13: 978-1-58571-339-4
$6.99

Save Me
Africa Fine
ISBN-13: 978-1-58571-340-0
$6.99

August

When Lightening Strikes
Michele Cameron
ISBN-13: 978-1-58571-369-1
$6.99

Blindsided
Tammy Williams
ISBN-13: 978-1-58571-342-4
$6.99

September

2 Good
Celya Bowers
ISBN-13: 978-1-58571-350-9
$6.99

Waiting for Mr. Darcy
Chamein Canton
ISBN-13: 978-1-58571-351-6
$6.99

October

Fireflies
Joan Early
ISBN-13: 978-1-58571-352-3
$6.99

Frost On My Window
Angela Weaver
ISBN-13: 978-1-58571-353-0
$6.99

November

Waiting in the Shadows
Michele Sudler
ISBN-13: 978-1-58571-364-6
$6.99

Fixin' Tyrone
Keith Walker
ISBN-13: 978-1-58571-365-3
$6.99

December

Dream Keeper
Gail McFarland
ISBN-13: 978-1-58571-366-0
$6.99

Another Memory
Pamela Ridley
ISBN-13: 978-1-58571-367-7
$6.99

Other Genesis Press, Inc. Titles

Other Genesis Press, Inc. Titles (continued)

Other Genesis Press, Inc. Titles (continued)

Ebony Angel	Deatri King-Bey	$9.95
Ebony Butterfly II	Delilah Dawson	$14.95
Echoes of Yesterday	Beverly Clark	$9.95
Eden's Garden	Elizabeth Rose	$8.95
Eve's Prescription	Edwina Martin Arnold	$8.95
Everlastin' Love	Gay G. Gunn	$8.95
Everlasting Moments	Dorothy Elizabeth Love	$8.95
Everything and More	Sinclair Lebeau	$8.95
Everything but Love	Natalie Dunbar	$8.95
Falling	Natalie Dunbar	$9.95
Fate	Pamela Leigh Starr	$8.95
Finding Isabella	A.J. Garrotto	$8.95
Forbidden Quest	Dar Tomlinson	$10.95
Forever Love	Wanda Y. Thomas	$8.95
From the Ashes	Kathleen Suzanne	$8.95
	Jeanne Sumerix	
Gentle Yearning	Rochelle Alers	$10.95
Glory of Love	Sinclair LeBeau	$10.95
Go Gentle into that Good Night	Malcom Boyd	$12.95
Goldengroove	Mary Beth Craft	$16.95
Groove, Bang, and Jive	Steve Cannon	$8.99
Hand in Glove	Andrea Jackson	$9.95
Hard to Love	Kimberley White	$9.95
Hart & Soul	Angie Daniels	$8.95
Heart of the Phoenix	A.C. Arthur	$9.95
Heartbeat	Stephanie Bedwell-Grime	$8.95
Hearts Remember	M. Loui Quezada	$8.95
Hidden Memories	Robin Allen	$10.95
Higher Ground	Leah Latimer	$19.95
Hitler, the War, and the Pope	Ronald Rychiak	$26.95
How to Write a Romance	Kathryn Falk	$18.95
I Married a Reclining Chair	Lisa M. Fuhs	$8.95
I'll Be Your Shelter	Giselle Carmichael	$8.95
I'll Paint a Sun	A.J. Garrotto	$9.95

Other Genesis Press, Inc. Titles (continued)

Other Genesis Press, Inc. Titles (continued)

Meant to Be	Jeanne Sumerix	$8.95
Midnight Clear	Leslie Esdaile	$10.95
(Anthology)	Gwynne Forster	
	Carmen Green	
	Monica Jackson	
Midnight Magic	Gwynne Forster	$8.95
Midnight Peril	Vicki Andrews	$10.95
Misconceptions	Pamela Leigh Starr	$9.95
Moments of Clarity	Michele Cameron	$6.99
Montgomery's Children	Richard Perry	$14.95
Mr Fix-It	Crystal Hubbard	$6.99
My Buffalo Soldier	Barbara B. K. Reeves	$8.95
Naked Soul	Gwynne Forster	$8.95
Never Say Never	Michele Cameron	$6.99
Next to Last Chance	Louisa Dixon	$24.95
No Apologies	Seressia Glass	$8.95
No Commitment Required	Seressia Glass	$8.95
No Regrets	Mildred E. Riley	$8.95
Not His Type	Chamein Canton	$6.99
Nowhere to Run	Gay G. Gunn	$10.95
O Bed! O Breakfast!	Rob Kuehnle	$14.95
Object of His Desire	A. C. Arthur	$8.95
Office Policy	A. C. Arthur	$9.95
Once in a Blue Moon	Dorianne Cole	$9.95
One Day at a Time	Bella McFarland	$8.95
One in A Million	Barbara Keaton	$6.99
One of These Days	Michele Sudler	$9.95
Outside Chance	Louisa Dixon	$24.95
Passion	T.T. Henderson	$10.95
Passion's Blood	Cherif Fortin	$22.95
Passion's Furies	AlTonya Washington	$6.99
Passion's Journey	Wanda Y. Thomas	$8.95
Past Promises	Jahmel West	$8.95
Path of Fire	T.T. Henderson	$8.95
Path of Thorns	Annetta P. Lee	$9.95

Other Genesis Press, Inc. Titles (continued)

Peace Be Still	Colette Haywood	$12.95
Picture Perfect	Reon Carter	$8.95
Playing for Keeps	Stephanie Salinas	$8.95
Pride & Joi	Gay G. Gunn	$8.95
Promises Made	Bernice Layton	$6.99
Promises to Keep	Alicia Wiggins	$8.95
Quiet Storm	Donna Hill	$10.95
Reckless Surrender	Rochelle Alers	$6.95
Red Polka Dot in a World of Plaid	Varian Johnson	$12.95
Reluctant Captive	Joyce Jackson	$8.95
Rendezvous with Fate	Jeanne Sumerix	$8.95
Revelations	Cheris F. Hodges	$8.95
Rivers of the Soul	Leslie Esdaile	$8.95
Rocky Mountain Romance	Kathleen Suzanne	$8.95
Rooms of the Heart	Donna Hill	$8.95
Rough on Rats and Tough on Cats	Chris Parker	$12.95
Secret Library Vol. 1	Nina Sheridan	$18.95
Secret Library Vol. 2	Cassandra Colt	$8.95
Secret Thunder	Annetta P. Lee	$9.95
Shades of Brown	Denise Becker	$8.95
Shades of Desire	Monica White	$8.95
Shadows in the Moonlight	Jeanne Sumerix	$8.95
Sin	Crystal Rhodes	$8.95
Small Whispers	Annetta P. Lee	$6.99
So Amazing	Sinclair LeBeau	$8.95
Somebody's Someone	Sinclair LeBeau	$8.95
Someone to Love	Alicia Wiggins	$8.95
Song in the Park	Martin Brant	$15.95
Soul Eyes	Wayne L. Wilson	$12.95
Soul to Soul	Donna Hill	$8.95
Southern Comfort	J.M. Jeffries	$8.95
Southern Fried Standards	S.R. Maddox	$6.99
Still the Storm	Sharon Robinson	$8.95

Other Genesis Press, Inc. Titles (continued)

Other Genesis Press, Inc. Titles (continued)

ESCAPE WITH INDIGO !!!!

Join Indigo Book Club©
It's simple, easy and secure.

Sign up and receive the new
releases
every month + Free shipping
and
20% off the cover price.

Go online to www.genesis-
press.com and click on Bookclub
or
call 1-888-INDIGO-1

Order Form

Mail to: Genesis Press, Inc.
P.O. Box 101
Columbus, MS 39703

Name _____
Address _____
City/State _____ Zip _____
Telephone _____

Ship to (if different from above)
Name _____
Address _____
City/State _____ Zip _____
Telephone _____

Credit Card Information
Credit Card # _____ ☐Visa ☐Mastercard
Expiration Date (mm/yy) _____ ☐AmEx ☐Discover

Qty.	Author	Title	Price	Total

Use this order
form, or call
1-888-INDIGO-1

Total for books	_____
Shipping and handling:	
$5 first two books,	
$1 each additional book	_____
Total S & H	_____
Total amount enclosed	_____

Mississippi residents add 7% sales tax

WIN A
FREE
GENESIS PRESS BOOK

Please fill out this form with your email
address and send it to us at:

**Genesis Press,
Post Office Box 101,
Columbus, MS 39703**

or email it to
customerservice@genesis-press.com

and we will put your name into a
drawing for a free Genesis Press Book.

WRITE EMAIL ADDRESS HERE

Winners will be chosen on the first of
each month. ONE ENTRY PER CUSTOMER

GENESIS MOVIE NETWORK

The Indigo Collection

AUGUST/SEPTEMBER 2009

Starring: Usher, Forest Whitaker
When: August 22 - September 6
Time Period: Noon to 2AM

Taps meets The Breakfast Club in the inner city in this late 1990s answer to the Brat Pack flicks of the 1980s (with ex-Brat Packer Judd Nelson in attendance). When an incident with a high school security guard (Forest Whitaker) pushes a decent kid (Usher Raymond) past his breaking point, the boy unites a diverse and troubled student body to take the school hostage until they can make their voices heard.

Allied Media Partners
1629 K St., NW, Suite 300, Washington, DC 20006
202-349-5785

GENESIS MOVIE NETWORK

The Indigo Collection

S E P T E M B E R 2 0 0 9

"TERRIFICALLY ENTERTAINING"

Starring: Robert Townsend, Marla Gibbs, Eddie Griffin
When: September 5 - September 20
Time Period: Noon to 2AM

While being chased by neighborhood thugs, weak-kneed high school teacher Jefferson Reed (Robert Townsend) is struck by a meteor and suddenly develops superhuman strength and abilities: He can fly, talk to dogs and absorb knowledge from any book in 30 seconds! His mom creates a costume, and he begins practicing his newfound skills in secret. But his nightly community improvements soon draw the wrath of the bad guys who terrorize his block.

Allied Media Partners
1629 K St., NW, Suite 300, Washington, DC 20006
202-349-5785